I0762312

AMORY CANNON

This book is a work of fiction. References to real people, events, establishments, organizations, or locales are intended only to provide a sense of authenticity and are used to advance the fictional narrative. All other characters, and all incidents and dialogue, are drawn from the author's imagination and are not to be construed as real.

Printed in the United States of America

Library of Congress Cataloging-in-Publication data
Cannon, Amory.
The ancient heir /Amory Cannon.
p. cm.

Summary: Everything she thought she knew is ashes—her home, her crown, her future. Only one thing remains for Emilia. She must find the truth of the Narrow Gate and the Ancient One's power before the Emperor does. The future of the Insurgos depends on it.

ISBN
Paperback: 978-0-9973903-5-3
Hardcover: 978-0-9973903-8-4
1. Kings, queens, rulers, etc. —Fiction. 2. Christianity —Fiction. 3. Love —Fiction. 4. War —Fiction. I. Title.

First Edition, 2024

www.Amory-Cannon.com

To the girl who has walked through the fire and discovered the beauty in the ashes. May you experience the presence of the King as He stands in the flames with you.

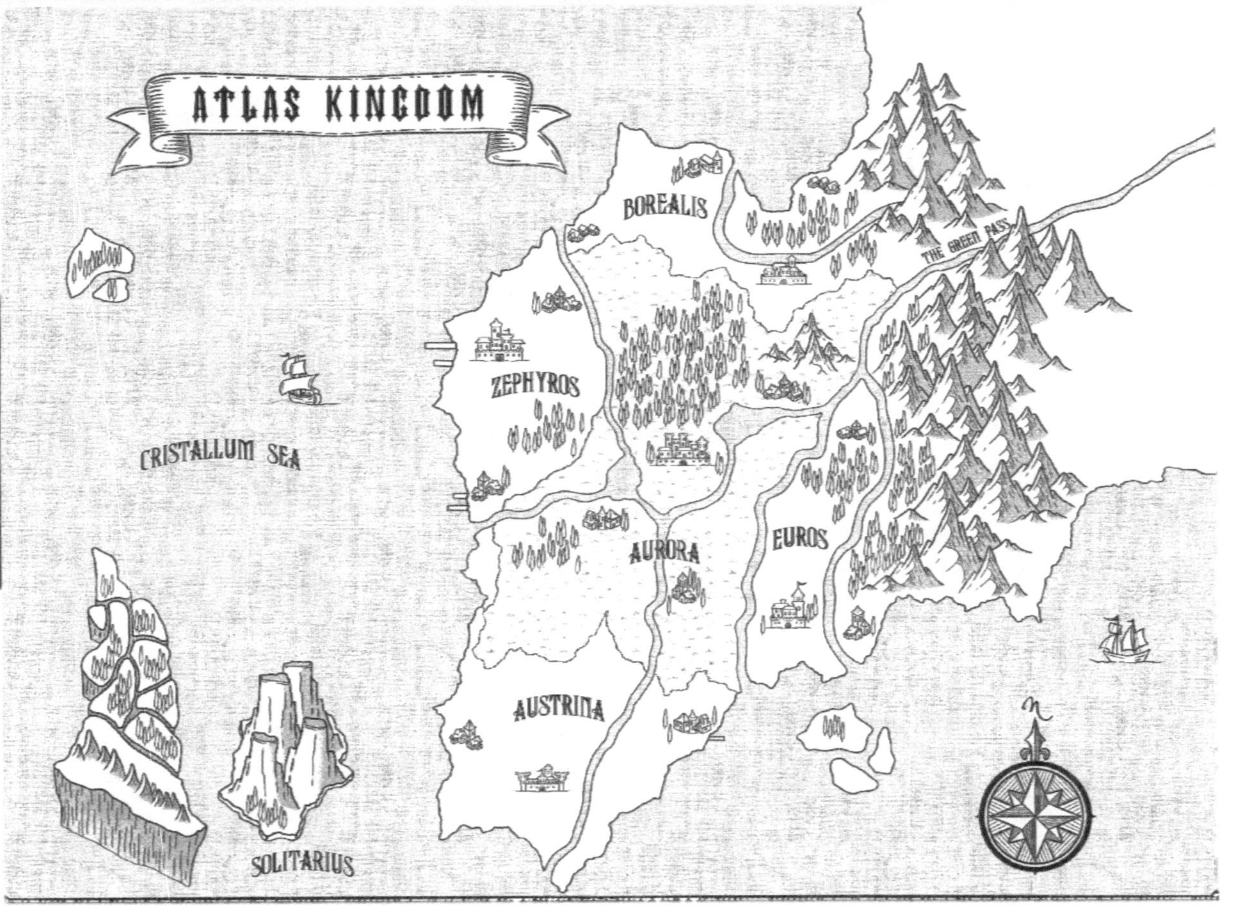

ATLAS KINGDOM
BOREALIS
THE GREEN PASS
ZEPHYROS
CRISTALLUM SEA
AURORA
EUROS
AUSTRINA
SOLITARIUS

When you pass through the waters, I will be with you; And through the rivers, they shall not overflow you. When you walk through the fire, you shall not be burned, nor shall the flame scorch you.

For I, says the Lord, will be a wall of fire all around her, and I will be the glory in her midst.

From the lost Aletheia

1

When I was a girl and dreamed of my wedding day, I never imagined it like this. Instead of standing at the end of an aisle in a gorgeous dress, looking into the eyes of a man I love, I am sitting astride a horse in a torn, ashen version of my wedding gown, no crown upon my head, and an unlikely entourage surrounding me.

In the last few hours, I have witnessed the annihilation of the Insurgo encampment around my city, called off my wedding, freed a dangerous prisoner, and set off on a quest with no destination. Oh, and I've also abdicated my throne. Although it remains to be seen if that will stick.

When I told my cousin Titus I was leaving Borealis in his hands I meant for good. I don't think he took it the same way. But I have no intention of returning this way again.

That thought causes my eyes to prick with the burn of tears again, but I hastily wipe them away. I don't have the luxury of them at the moment, and I shed far too many as I said goodbye to my few friends in Borealis—Titus, Hannah, Cecily, Antony... Hannah and Antony begged to accompany me, and though I considered it and the selfish part of me longed for it, our small group is conspicuous enough as it is. Adding to it would only slow us down.

I glance over my shoulder at the two riders behind me and shake my head at the unlikely coupling. Ronan, Crown Prince of the Atlas Empire and, until a few hours ago my fiancé, sits atop a dun stallion with all the bearing and confidence of years of training. Next to him, riding an equally impressive gray horse, is a stooped man cowled in a dark cloak and looking much older than his years. Antioch doesn't look at home on a horse the way Ronan does, but he hangs on valiantly despite the fast pace we've set. Having spent the last several years in a prison cell I'm impressed he's managed to hang on this long.

Straightening myself in my saddle, I let my eyes wander to the two figures ahead of me. Felix and Alara. Something in this pairing makes me uneasy, unsettled. Despite being separated as children, they seem to have easily reconnected in the last week. There's something unspoken between them that rouses the drowsing jealousy in my gut. She knows things about him that I do not. Things he is not inclined to share with me.

That none of my four companions have made a point to ride beside me is a testament to the bitterness and anger that must be roiling off me. But it fuels me in a way nothing else does, and it forces me to think of things other than that the last man I kissed was not my fiancé but the man riding in front of me.

It hardly seems important now, but I know it matters. How much is yet to be determined at some later time when the smells of ash and burning flesh don't still linger in my nose. When I can close my eyes and not see flames and bodies littering the ground outside my city.

A city I will never see again.

There is nothing for me there. I'm not sure if there's something for me anywhere, but I do know that I can't stand still any longer. I tried to follow God's leading when I ran from Emperor Cyrus—Ronan's father—and took refuge in Borealis, but the only thing I have to show for it is a broken engagement and a pile of burned bodies. Either I seriously misunderstood God, or He is not for me as everyone else keeps saying. That thought sends a chill through me despite the warmth of the night.

I embrace the solitude of this nighttime ride. Save for the pounding of hooves and the occasional snort from the horses there is silence. We'll have to stop soon. The horses need rest and so do we.

Having never been there, I'm not sure how far we are from the coast, but we've already ridden through most of the night, and no one has had any sleep in much too long.

Originally Felix and Alara had planned to ride for the coast with some of Alara's men the morning following my wedding. Though I haven't confirmed it with her, I suspect many of those men were killed in the torching of the Insurgo encampment as they waited for a peace that will never come. So, she got me, Ronan, and Antioch as companions instead, and though she hasn't voiced it, her displeasure rolls off of her in waves.

We have managed to avoid any small towns as we ride through the rural part of my country. Alara's doing, no doubt. Having spent who knows how many years as a clandestine Insurgo leader, she knows my country better than I do. She knows many things better than I do.

Finally, as the sky begins its transition from inky black to deepest blue, Felix circles his horse back to join me. Neither of us speaks immediately. Perhaps there is too much to say…or nothing at all.

"We're still half a day's ride from the coast, Alara says. And that's if we continue this pace, which we can't." Felix's voice is as steady and unemotional as ever. He glances over his shoulder to Ronan and Antioch bringing up the rear, and I know he's right. "You need to decide how you want to handle this."

"Why is it up to me to decide?"

He gives me a sidelong look but doesn't dignify my question with a response. We both know why. I'm being unfair by taking out my frustration on him. But the truth is, I don't even really know why I'm here. After the torching of the Insurgo camp, I knew I had to act, but with no plan of my own, I simply attached myself to Felix and Alara. What am I really hoping to accomplish by running away? Should I have stayed behind to fight?

"I don't want to show up as the Queen or Princess or whatever I'm supposed to be. I don't want to cause a big fuss. The quieter we keep this journey the better." That much I do know for sure. The decision to leave has already been made, so better to focus on making our path forward as smooth as possible.

Felix gives me a once-over, and I wish there was some light so I could see any emotion on his face. But there probably isn't any. He's much better about keeping his expressions under control than I am.

"You're going to need to get rid of that dress then. Even if the people this far from the capital don't know what the princess looks like, that dress would be a dead giveaway. Something that fine could have only come from the palace."

He's right, of course. Despite the tears and ash-covered hem, my dress is a work of art. Designed to be worn by both a woman fit to sit on her own throne and marry an Imperial Prince. As I am no longer either, I find I have no sentimental attachment to my wedding dress. It was ridiculous not to change out of it before I left the palace of Borealis anyway, but Felix was so insistent on getting me as far away from the city as possible that some basic things were neglected in favor of expediency.

"Tell Alara to hold up, and I'll use the trees ahead as cover to change." I hesitate because I don't want to stop, but I know it's the right thing. "And I suppose we should make camp. We can get a few hours' sleep before the sun's too high."

Felix rides ahead to do just that, and even at a distance, I can practically see the annoyance on Alara's face. It's more than clear I haven't measured up to her idea of what the Princess That Was Promised should be. I'd like to tell her to get in line behind all the other people I've disappointed, me included. Still, she acquiesces to my request and directs her mount toward the tree line.

I make quick work of the dress once I'm under cover of dense foliage. Rather than fool with all the tiny buttons Hannah so carefully fastened—could that really have only been hours ago?—I rip the fabric until the buttons go flying away from me, landing soundlessly somewhere in the dark. With a sigh I let the dress fall to the ground where its weight makes a soft rustle against the grass. I stand there for a moment in just my underclothes and let the slightest bit of a breeze prickle against my bare skin. It's soothing and cleansing in a way, and for a moment I can almost forget why I'm here and what I'm supposed to be doing.

But then Alara, who is standing guard while still atop her horse only a few yards away, clears her throat impatiently. Always the voice of pragmatism even without uttering a word. Still, I take the hint and reach into my hastily packed bag for a change of clothes. It's a wardrobe cobbled together from my time as a soldier in the Borealis army, some of Alara's extra clothes, and a few things from my handmaid Hannah. I brought no crown and no royal finery other than what I left the palace in. That is something I'm glad to leave behind.

Once dressed in a pair of pants and loose-fitting tunic, I wad my wedding dress up into the smallest package possible and attempt to shove it down in the bag. It's clearly not going to fit. Layers and layers of fabric and beads aren't really conducive to the small pack I brought with me. But I don't really need it anyway. Still, it seems unwise to just leave it here for anyone to find. If anyone is trailing us, this would be a dead giveaway that we had passed through.

"What's the hold-up?" Alara asks brusquely as I push my way back through the trees and rejoin her. She eyes the dress draped over my arm. "What are you going to do with that?"

"I don't know," I answer as I toss the dress over my horse's neck and then mount the mare. I miss Athena who I had to leave behind in Borealis. I planned to bring her with me, but Felix shot down the idea due to her wildness. But this horse is gentle and barely stirs as I settle myself into the saddle. "I didn't think it wise to leave the dress behind. Maybe I should just bury it?"

"We don't have time for that," she snaps as she brings her horse alongside mine and we rejoin the men. "We'll just burn it on the first fire we come to."

Ronan chooses that exact moment to look up and meet my eyes for possibly the first time since we left the city. The hurt is evident there, and I can't say I blame him. Given all that's happened, the suggestion of burning my wedding dress must feel like yet another slap in the face. But I don't think I imagine that his eyes linger a little longer than necessary as they take in my new outfit, particularly the trousers. Though they aren't tight fitting, they do show the shape of my legs, which is something I don't think Ronan has ever seen, given that I'm usually in gowns around him.

But he says nothing and neither do I. Is there any point in apologizing? Although I'm certain his feelings are hurt—to what degree, I'm unsure because I don't know how much he knows—but I don't think I'm ready to take responsibility for that. At least not now. Not now when people have died, and embers still burn around my city. Not now when his own father has likely issued a decree for me to be killed on sight. There is a deep, niggling fear in me that isn't sure how much I can trust Ronan despite my resolution to do so, and I realize that will always be between us. Given our positions, our history, I'll always wonder if there's a bit of his father driving his actions.

"Put that in your pack if you can." Felix eyes the bulk of the dress warily. Then his eyes drift down slightly to focus on the black jewel dangling from my necklace just below the hollow of my throat. I didn't realize it was visible with the neckline of my tunic. When I look up at him again, he's looking away into the distance. "We need to keep moving. There's a rock formation ahead that should provide enough concealment for us to get a few hours sleep. I don't want to be too close to the main road."

I somehow manage to stuff the dress in my pack after moving some of the items I brought with me to Alara's bag. My bag is straining at the seams and looks a bit suspicious, but not as conspicuous as using a white glittering dress as a saddle blanket. It will have to do.

We ride on, and I resume my sulky silence. I'm not sure who I'm most put out with—Felix and Alara for the ease that exists between them, Ronan for any part he might have played in all of this, or myself for dwelling on any of that rather than the real issue.

Expectations weigh heavily on me. It was impulsive of me to leave everything and agree to go with Felix and Alara to Solitarius. I'm still not sure if the driving force was my wish to run away from something or towards something. Either way I'm here now, and everyone is going to start looking to me for answers I don't have.

Soon enough we reach the rocky outcropping Felix spotted in the distance. It's not large, but it will serve well enough as concealment from any passersby. We all follow him to a relatively flat spot and begin to dismount our horses. I'm just about to swing my leg over my mount's back when I notice Ronan is beside my horse, waiting to help me down.

I haven't truly needed help mounting or dismounting a horse since I was a child, but I let him have this moment of chivalry. Maybe it's because I have so much to atone for, but it feels wrong to deny him this.

My hands rest on his shoulders as he places his hands at my waist and lifts me from the saddle. For just a moment, as I slide to the ground, my face is mere inches from his, and I feel his sharp inhale as he realizes it, too. It's hard to deny the chemistry that used to exist between us, at least back in Aurora when I believed him my only choice, but it's notably absent now. At least on my part. I'm not sure he feels the same.

Ronan doesn't immediately back away when I stand on my own two feet. It takes Felix clearing his throat for the prince to put some space between us. He ducks his head and rubs the back of his neck in a very uncharacteristic show of insecurity.

"Roll out your bedrolls here," Felix instructs as he pointedly looks away from me and busies himself with removing his own bedroll from his saddle. "No tents, no fire. Just sleep while you can."

I agree with him, but it would be nice to have a fire and something warm to eat. "And we should eat," I add. "Whatever we have between us. We can restock when we reach Salacia."

It's a meager spread we manage to put together as we all sit in a circle and lay out our supplies. Unlike when Felix planned my escape from Cyrus in Aurora, he didn't have days to prepare for this journey. We managed to scrape together some dried meat, a few apples, a lump of cheese, and... is that cake?

"Who wants wedding cake?" Alara asks proudly as she sets a mashed concoction of cake and icing right in the middle of the rest of the food. No one utters a word. "Oh, come on. We're supposed to be celebrating."

"You stole my wedding cake?" The question fights its way out through my gritted teeth.

"Gods above, Alara, have you no shame?" Ronan shakes his head as he looks at the mushed mess of what once was probably a beautiful creation. His cake, too, I remind myself.

"What?" Alara shrugs and reaches to tear off a piece of cake and icing. "Where I'm from, you don't snub your nose at any food you can get. Here, isn't this how the tradition goes?"

She stretches her hand toward Felix as if she's going to feed him the confection in her palm. Quick as lightning, he grabs her by the wrist and pushes the cake back toward her.

"Not now," he insists in a low growl.

Not now? It wouldn't surprise me if steam were coming from my ears. Not ever, if I have my say. That tradition belongs to husband and wife, and those parameters apply to exactly none of us.

"Suit yourself." She shrugs and takes a slow bite of the cake. "Mmm. It's delicious." Eyes locked on Ronan, she makes a great show of licking the icing from her fingers and then her lips. Is she just trying to get a rise out of him? Felix insisted she was integral to this trip, but I'd love nothing more than to bury her beneath these rocks before we continue on our way.

Antioch, who has been noticeably quiet since we sat down, reaches for a piece of cake as well. We all watch with wide eyes as he takes a small bite.

He closes his eyes to relish it as I imagine he hasn't had much cause to do in the years he's been imprisoned. "I haven't tasted something so fine in many years."

It's more than I can take, and I practically jump to my feet. "I'll take the first watch," I announce before I storm off. No one objects.

Half an hour or so passes before I hear someone approach from the direction of our camp. Ronan takes a seat on a rock beside me and lets the silence hang for a few moments more.

"Are you all right?" he finally asks.

"As well as can be expected," I reply. I dare to take a look at him. He's paler than usual, but that's nearly masked by the layer of dirt that covers all of us from our hasty travel. There are dark circles forming under his piercing eyes, and he carries none of the regal bearing typical of the Crown Prince. "How are you faring?"

"My mind is racing. I've had a lot to think about the last few hours."

I'll bet he has. Ronan has had his wedding canceled, learned the depths of his father's tyranny, watched a city burn, left everything he knows behind, and quite possibly realized his fiancée is in love with his best friend. This hasn't been easy for him either.

My mind is so busy trying to decide what's appropriate to say next that I miss all the signals he's giving me. By the time I register the shift between us, he's leaning in and angling his mouth over mine. Panic freezes me as his lips touch mine. How did I miss this? More importantly, what did I do to make him think I would welcome this?

With a cough, I turn my head away and rub the hem of my tunic between my fingers. Quick, think of something to say. Anything.

"There's still time for you to turn back," I try lamely. "We're almost to Salacia. You could rest there and then make your way back to Borealis or even Aurora."

"Emilia." Something in the way he speaks my name makes me look up. There is such a weariness in his face that reminds me I'm not the only one carrying a heavy weight. "You've made it pretty clear you don't want me here, but this is something I need to do. For me."

"No, it's not that," I rush to assure him. But isn't it? "There's just a lot to figure out, and I can't afford to be worried about anyone else—"

"I'm not asking you to worry about me. I know you think I'm one step above a child, but I can look out for myself. I have my own questions, and I need my own answers." Ronan stretches out his hand, hesitates, then squeezes my hand. "And despite everything that's happened, I still care about you even if that part of our relationship is over."

Which part? The part where his father tries to kill me? Or the part where I have to play a guessing game about how much of Ronan's feelings for me were his own and how much were dictated by his crown? Either way he's right. It's over.

I look down to where our hands are joined until the sound of footsteps draws my attention. Ronan drops my hand, and we both look up as Felix approaches. I know for a fact that Felix has a lighter tread than anyone I know, except maybe Alara, so he's made an effort to make noise to alert us to his presence. My stomach coils in knots at the thought that he might have seen Ronan's attempt at a kiss. Like he needs one more reason to be standoffish.

"Everything ok over here?" His tone is carefully neutral, but I note the concern with which he searches my face. There's so much that needs to be said, but I'm no longer sure I'm the one who needs to say it. I told him what I wanted before we left the palace, and he did not return the sentiment. Out of a sense of duty? Or because I have failed to live up to his expectations?

"Just checking up on Emilia," Ronan answers with a decided coolness to his voice. Is that for Felix or me? "Trying to make sure she's well."

"That's a full-time job," Felix quips, trying to add levity to the situation. It falls flat.

"One you're much better suited to. I'll leave you to it." Ronan nods to each of us then rises to return to the camp and Alara and Antioch, who are just visible in the distance.

Felix waits a beat then takes a seat on the rock Ronan just vacated. He holds out some dried meat to me, but I wave it off.

"You need to eat something," he insists. My skin tingles everywhere his gaze lingers.

"The cake turned my stomach," I begrudgingly admit, trying hard to avoid looking at him.

"I'm sorry. I'll talk to her about it."

"Don't." The word comes out with more frustration and anger than I intended. "Don't apologize for her." I can't stand the thought of him feeling responsible for her, or that he might make excuses for her.

"All right then."

His easy acquiescence does little to appease me. He's not being formal exactly, but there is a bit of coolness to our interaction. As if he's afraid he'll upset me or maybe Ronan. What I wouldn't give to get a reaction out of him, though. But that seems to only happen when I find myself in distress—either physical or emotional. Felix has a "saving people" complex, and I sometimes wonder if he would have even noticed me at all if I hadn't constantly been in danger. But maybe he would have, because his hopes, along with all the other Insurgos, seem to rest on me.

"What are we doing, Felix?" The words are so heavy because there are so many layers to them. Where do we begin to unpack all of this? "When we last spoke about it, we both agreed that the Gate was not a real place until Antioch told us differently. And now I can't help but think we're chasing some fantasy, and maybe we're just as crazy as Cyrus."

He considers my words for a long moment. "I didn't think it existed. But I've seen a lot of things since then, and I'm willing to keep an open mind. The storm at the temple...I would have never believed it was possible. I think it's likely that our God is much bigger and much more present than I ever realized."

I'll have to ponder on that, maybe speak to Antioch about it. He certainly believes the Gate is real. He told me so when I visited him in the prison tower. "So, in your original plan, why were you and Alara riding to the coast? Why were you going to Solitarius?"

He's silent so long that I think he won't answer. But then, his voice thick with emotion I don't understand, "To spread the message of peace. To tell the others they could come home."

"And so *you* could go home?" It's crossing some sort of line he's drawn between us. Just as I expect, the vulnerability in his face vanishes, quickly replaced by his usual stoic mask.

"If you're not going to eat anything you should at least sleep." He stands and shoves the piece of dried meat he offered me into his mouth. "I'll watch for a while."

"I'm fine," I try to say, but a yawn betrays me.

"It wasn't a request, Emilia."

I stare at him with wide eyes. The number of times he's commanded me could easily be counted on one hand. Arguing with him at this point will get me nowhere except frustrated. He's treating me like one of his soldiers, and some part of me is just thrilled he's no longer treating me like his queen.

But my tone still drips with sarcasm when I say, "yes, sir," and rise to leave.

"Emilia." Stern this time. The number of emotions he can put into that one word still astounds me. I simply raise an eyebrow in response. His eyes search my face for something, and when he doesn't find it, he groans in disgust. "Just go."

I do. And though I can feel his eyes on my back, I don't give him the satisfaction of looking over my shoulder.

I'm in the mood to pick a fight, but now that the bedrolls are laid out, even Alara seems too tired to fight with me. I drag my roll near hers because I can't bear the thought of being too close to Ronan right now.

"Spending your wedding night with me?" She asks through a yawn. "I can think of two boys who are going to be very disappointed."

The implication makes my cheeks flush with both embarrassment and anger. "If you mention my wedding again, I'll cut your throat while you sleep." I'm joking...mostly. Only because my dagger is buried somewhere deep in my pack.

She chuckles lightly, then rolls over so her back is to me. "Sleep well, princess."

2

My mother marches to her death. Her head low, wrists bound, she follows behind her guards and steps into the stone circle. I watch from the dais, overlooking the crowd of people who have gathered to celebrate her execution. I'm not a child anymore, but my feelings of helplessness are just as strong as they were when I was ten years old.

No. I can't watch this again.

I blink hard, and when I open my eyes, it isn't my mother but Levi tied to the pillar inside the stone circle. My mentor, with his bright green eyes and graying hair, looks over the crowd to lock gazes with me. The force of it slams into my gut, and I double over in actual physical pain.

And when I stand, I see the most horrifying sight of all. Not my mother, not Levi, but Felix now stands upon the altar. His head is bowed in defeat, a posture I have never seen from him.

"No!" I actually scream aloud this time, and all the faces below me turn to acknowledge my cry. All except Felix's. On either side of me, hands grasp my arms. I look between the two ghosts holding me up. My mother stands on my left, her hand black as coal where it grips my forearm. Levi is on my right, his hand stained red-black with old blood.

"You must let it happen," my mother tells me in the gentle voice she used to use when she told me bedtime stories.

"You must embrace what's coming. You are who you are, you've been placed here, for such a time as this." Levi repeats some of his last words to me.

"Felix!" I scream out into the night. This time he looks up. In the space of a breath, I remember what it was like to feel his lips on mine, I smell the leather of his armor, I feel his arms wrapped around me. Death, it seems, has become one of my senses. But those eyes. He doesn't even need to use his hands to touch every part of me.

His image is obscured by my tears, but still I strain toward him only to be pulled back by the ghosts that bind me. I hear the whoosh of the flames as they lick the oil anointing the altar.

By the time I clear my vision and fix my eyes on the altar, flames roar as high as the heavens. I can't stop the scream, the plea, that tears from my throat. Only those hands on my arms keep me from running toward the fire.

"Emilia. Emilia!"

Someone shouts my name with increasing urgency. I look to my mother and then to Levi, but they are gone. Everything fades to black. Still, I hear my name over and over, but I can't open my eyes to find who calls me.

"Be calm, my child."

It's the old man's voice that pulls me violently from my dream. My stomach contracts hard as I curl upward, roll to my side, and dry heave until spots dance in my vision. A gentle hand rests on my back, and the steadiness of the touch makes me aware that I'm shaking.

Slowly, after catching my breath and blinking the wetness from my eyes, I force myself into a sitting position. Three pairs of eyes look at me with shocked concern. One pair noticeably refuses to look at me at all. Naturally, I focus in on Felix's averted gaze and silently will him to turn it toward me.

He seems unsurprised by my condition but still visibly distraught. He saw the aftermath of these dreams when we traveled from Aurora to Borealis. I still remember how his fingers shook as he brushed my cheek and how his muscles tensed when I touched him back. How he said my name and managed to convey an entire tome's worth of sentiment in that one utterance.

"What was that?" Even Alara is shocked by this turn of events. Her dark eyes are wide, and her perfect mouth hangs open in a perfect little pout. "You were screaming, and…"

It must have been bad if she's not reprimanding me for all the noise I made. Maybe she does have some emotion other than anger under all those layers of sarcasm.

My eyes flit to Ronan who has yet to comment. Unlike Alara and Antioch, he looks terrified. How could I ever begin to explain this to him? I don't even understand it myself. But though I've never had this particular dream before, it feels like others I've had.

Those came from God, I had been sure of it. But I don't want that to be true of this one.

"Just a nightmare," I say as I swallow hard. Though there was nothing in my stomach to throw up, my throat still burns with the bile, and my abdomen aches from heaving.

"My child," Antioch whispers with a grim smile as he rubs my back. There's something uncanny in the way he's looking at me. As if he knows more than all the others. I don't like it. "You've seen a message from God."

"No." I don't leave room for argument as I try to stand. The world spins, and I grab onto whatever I can to keep from toppling over. It's Felix, who must have been lightning quick to reach me in the time it took me to stand. He steadies me with a hand on my back and finally makes eye contact. It nearly breaks my resolve. "Not everything is a message from God. It's just a bad dream."

And I will it to be so, because I won't have Felix be a casualty in this war. It's a war I never agreed to fight in the first place. But something deep within me screams that no one I love is safe. I only have to look as far as my mother and Levi for examples. When you're taught to see the world through fire, nothing is safe.

"Our God speaks in mysterious ways. When you hear His call, you should answer." The ethereal quality of Antioch's voice chills me. "You are His strong warrior, the Ruler Who Will Rise Up."

I'm sick to death of everyone telling me how strong I am, so I ignore him.

"Felix, are we safe to ride? We should reach Salacia soon, right?"

As if anticipating how I will respond, Felix doesn't hesitate with an answer. "We should leave soon. I want to be in the city by early afternoon, so we have time to finalize plans and gather more supplies."

I silently thank him for his practicality. It's just what I need to put this behind me. But from the expression on Antioch's face, I know he will not let this go.

The port city of Salacia can barely be called a city at all. More like a small village with a transient population of merchant sailors, traders, and the associated black markets. All of this I learned in my lessons as a child. Titus and I had to memorize all the major cities and villages in our country, and Salacia was notable only because it served as the official port for Imperial ships bringing goods to trade that were not easily transported over long distances by land. Most of the population was transient, though, as the port was also home to smugglers and their buyers, neither of whom wanted to be caught when Imperial ships made berth and usually made themselves scarce as soon as the Imperial flag was seen approaching.

Whether this is a good thing for us remains to be seen. It would be nice to get lost in a large mass of people, but we're also more likely to be recognized that way. As it is, we will certainly stand out among the sparse crowd that calls this place home.

But that doesn't seem to be the plan Alara and Felix have formed. Our group comes to a stop in front of a two-story stone building with a small sign identifying it as an inn. I can't see the sea or the ports from here, so I assume there is other housing for sailors closer to the docks. But for some reason, this is the place my companions have chosen to stop for rest. Lights shine in a few of the windows, and movement sways a few of the curtains. There's nothing ominous about it, but I don't feel safe here.

"Won't we be a bit conspicuous here?" I ask as Alara and Felix dismount their horses.

"Well, you weren't part of the original plan. We'll have to make the best of what we're dealing with," Alara answers as she tosses her reins to Felix and strides toward the inn as if she owns the place. She's right, of course, but that doesn't bring me any comfort. This trip was originally only supposed to be her and Felix, and I frown to think of the two of them cozying up at this quaint little inn.

By the time I shake this off, everyone else has dismounted and Ronan is standing beside my horse with his hands out in an offer to assist me to the ground. Once again, I don't need his help, but I let him anyway. His hands slide around my waist with familiarity as he lifts me from the saddle and sets me on the ground. He's careful to remove his hands as soon as I have my footing, and he's already turned to tie our horses to the post before I can say anything.

"Should we follow her?" Ronan asks, nodding toward the door Alara disappeared through. Felix shakes his head.

"Let her arrange things. She has a story that shouldn't cause too many questions, but I don't want many people to see you two until we're sure they're not waiting to slit your throats."

I look to my saddlebag where my dagger rests beneath layers and layers of my wedding dress. No way I could get to it without dumping the dress in the street for everyone to see.

"I want a weapon," I say to Felix. He wears a dagger on his waist, and I know he'll have more in his pack, possibly even more on his body. We couldn't really afford to bring the swords he and I favor, but there are plenty of other deadly weapons hiding among his things. "If there's a fight…"

"There isn't going to be a fight." Felix smiles grimly. "Either Alara gets us in, or we run. We're not making a last stand here."

He's right, of course. If news of Cyrus's wrath against me has reached this far already, then there is no way four of us—because Antioch is hardly a fighter—could hope to outmatch a mob intent on killing us for the price on our heads.

"Surely news of what happened in the capital can't have beat us here. We rode through the night, and we didn't see any other riders," Ronan says.

Felix nods. "I agree it's unlikely but not impossible. I won't gamble with either of your lives." He looks between me and Ronan with his characteristic intensity. His eyes linger on me just a moment longer. Then he sighs and reaches for the dagger at his waist.

He deftly unfastens the leather sheath with one hand and offers the weapon to me hilt first. "Hold on to this and stay with the horses. If something happens before I get back, you mount up and get out of here as fast as you can."

"Wait, where are you going?" I look from the dagger being offered to me to Felix's face, which is stormy but unreadable. He doesn't answer but looks past me to Ronan. Ronan steps forward and takes the dagger from Felix with a nod.

Felix nods back then heads down the street and around a corner, out of sight. I start after him, but Ronan stops me with a gentle hand on my shoulder.

"Let him go," he says softly. His eyes are distant, as if lost in some sort of memory.

"But where's he going?" I demand. "We need to stay together."

"He's going to the sea," Antioch speaks up. I had almost forgotten he was there. "He must make peace there."

I look to Ronan for an explanation, but he just shakes his head. How does Antioch know this? He doesn't even know Felix. As far as I know, they've never spoken. Why does everyone have answers except me?

"Well, I want to see the sea, too. I've never been on the shore," I say stubbornly.

"You're going to see plenty of it over the next several days," Ronan answers. "Felix needs to do this alone."

I don't know how he knows this, but I can sense it's not Ronan's story to tell. To appease me, he takes my hand and places the dagger in it. “Worry about your battles, Emilia. Felix can fight his own.”

3

Alara has somehow managed to charm the innkeeper and delude him into thinking that our party consists of a priestess and an augur of the god Caelus along with their guards. Antioch and I are supposedly making our rounds to conduct a ritual blessing at each of the cities in Borealis to consecrate the reign of our new monarch. I have to admit it's a clever lie and one they seem to swallow quickly. By introducing us as religious leaders, Alara has all but guaranteed we will not be bothered lest the citizens risk angering Caelus. I begrudgingly give her credit. When it comes to deception, Alara is the best of us.

In accordance with our feigned status, we are given the inn's best rooms. They're hardly anything to brag about, but there are two decent sized bedrooms and a common area with a fireplace. Most importantly, they're clean and the beds look comfortable. Of course, after riding through the night, a rock would look like a good place to lay my head. I don't like that there aren't any windows here. Not only does it make the room feel a bit like a prison, but there's only one entrance and exit. If someone were to come in on us, we'd be trapped. And Felix isn't here. I don't know if I could fight my way out of here without him.

I throw my things on a bed in the room designated for me and Alara and collapse on the mattress.

Thank you, God, for giving us safe travel this far. The prayer comes automatically and eases some of the tension in my gut. I haven't prayed as I usually do since we left Borealis. It's hard to find the words to say when I desperately need God's help, but I'm angry with Him as well.

"Don't get too comfortable," Ronan says as he leans against the doorway. I peer up at him as he steps into the room. "You need to eat."

"I just want to sleep," I groan as I throw my arm over my eyes and stretch my back, which aches from hours of riding hard and fast.

"Yes, but Felix will never forgive me if I don't make sure you eat first."

"Felix isn't here," I remind him with a bit of edge to my tone. He still hasn't returned from wherever he went, but no one except me seems the least bit concerned about it. I'd attempt to sneak away to find him if I could hold my eyes open for more than a few minutes. But now that we're in a relatively safe space with no urgency driving us, it's all I can do to think of anything but sleep.

"He is now." His voice comes from over Ronan's shoulder, and I bolt upright on the bed, eager to lay eyes on him. Felix stands in the doorway Ronan occupied seconds before, dripping wet from clothes that cling to him in ways that make heat rise in my cheeks. Fortunately, it's dark in the room so no one notices.

What they do notice though, is how I practically leap to my feet and start toward Felix before I catch myself. I slow myself under Ronan's watchful gaze and try to exude an attitude of nonchalant curiosity. I can feel both Ronan and Felix's eyes on me, and it's like being pulled apart by two opposing ropes.

"Why are you so wet?" I take a few more careful steps toward Felix and have to crush my hands into a fist to keep from reaching out to trace the lines of his chest visible through his soaked shirt. I see a muscle in his jaw flinch and wonder if he can read my mind. The idea makes me blush harder, so I duck my head a little so my long hair falls in my face.

"I went swimming," he answers evenly.

"On purpose?" Ronan asks. I chance a glance back at him to find he's looking at Felix with a quizzical expression. Evidently, he really had no idea what Felix was doing either. Do I imagine there's a bit of relief on his face to have his friend back? Maybe he was just as worried as I was but determined not to show it.

"Yes." Felix's answer isn't harsh, but it's definitive and leaves no room for more questions. I sometimes forget the imposing side of him now that I've been privileged to have glimpses of his more vulnerable side.

"Aren't any of you coming to eat?" Alara joins us, and suddenly the room feels too crowded. "I'm starving."

"What did you have them bring?" Ronan asks. He brushes past me to join her just outside the bedroom.

“Everything,” she replies with a sigh of delight. “They asked if the priestess and augur would require the religious restrictions to their diet, but I told them the rest of our party had no such restrictions.” She levels her eyes at me. “I’m not giving up bacon for you.”

I don’t blame her, especially when I move to follow her and Ronan, and the delicious aroma of savory meat and sweet bread fills my nostrils. I’m suddenly ravenous. But as I step past Felix who is still half in the doorway, his fingers brush mine. I freeze and look slightly over my shoulder at him. Though I’m not sure why, I feel like he’s asking for something from me. Comfort perhaps? More questions swirl around my head.

Conscious of Ronan’s presence mere feet away, I slide my hand into Felix’s quickly and give it a small squeeze. His shoulders relax ever so slightly, and he sighs softly. It’s such a quick and simple thing, but my heart swells to feel I’ve provided him with something instead of just taking like I always seem to do. It’s always him who comforts me, teaches me, protects me. I’ve always thought he doesn’t need me the way I need him. Maybe I was wrong.

We all join around a small table in the common room. Someone has started a fire and laid out several platters of food on the table. I’m grateful for it all, but I still don’t like how conspicuous we must be. I can’t imagine this area often has occasion to serve guests who can afford such a spread. Hopefully, we won’t be here long enough to arouse too much suspicion.

Felix bypasses the table and stops in front of the fireplace. No one else seems to be paying him any attention, and I try to look away as he strips his shirt off and lays it on the hearth to dry. It's hardly the first time I've seen him shirtless, but something about the water glistening on his skin and the lines of scars across his back make me ache to be near him. What I wouldn't give for just a few minutes alone with him. The last time we had that luxury I couldn't keep myself from kissing him even though I was wearing my wedding dress and about to walk down an aisle to Ronan. Given all that's happened since then, I'm not sure when we'll have the chance to be alone again.

He disappears into the room where Ronan placed the men's belongings earlier, and I turn my focus to the food in front of me. Felix rejoins us moments later, now dressed in dry clothes, and his hair no longer dripping. His dark waves are extra curly at the nape of his neck. He catches me staring, and I quickly look away.

"So, is everything all set for tomorrow?" Alara asks as she shovels a fork full of eggs into her mouth. There's certainly no posturing from her. Though I suppose when you've lived on the streets and had to make your movements in secret, you don't think too much about table manners.

"It's all arranged," Felix says around a mouthful of bread. He must be ravenous as well because he took no time to fill up his plate and already half of the food is missing.

Me? Despite feeling my stomach rumble with hunger, I can hardly stop my mind from racing long enough to focus on the food in front of me.

"Are either of you going to share any details of this plan? You may have failed to notice you have three other people who need to have some idea of what's going on." There's more of an edge to my voice than I intended, but I'm tired of being the one in the dark on everything when I'm supposed to be so vital to our journey.

"Well, we could hardly fail to notice," Alara snorts as she looks between me, Felix, and Ronan. "You could cut the tension with that dagger of yours."

Heat flushes my cheeks once again. *Don't get distracted.* But Felix saves me from crafting a response.

"Alara and I had planned to sail with a merchant ship bound for Solitarius. His voyages to the island are not exactly legal, so he does everything he can to keep a low profile. He is willing to take additional passengers for appropriate compensation."

I don't ask what Felix paid, but I vow I will return it to him one hundred-fold as soon as I am able.

"The ship sails at first light," Alara continues for him. "That means we need to be on board well before then to avoid being seen boarding the ship. And we need to be out of here before anyone comes to check on us in the morning. Felix and I will go out into the city this afternoon and secure clothing and a few supplies for us to take with us."

"And what happens when we reach Solitarius?"

All eyes turn to Antioch. This is the first time he's spoken to our group as a whole. He was more than willing to come with us when I told him of our plan to find the Gate, but he's been oddly mum about what he does or doesn't know about it.

"Solitarius is the only place I know of that might have a complete copy of the Aletheia," Felix says. "It's also the last known place where the Palanquin was seen."

He says this as if it means something to us, but I'm not the only one who looks lost. Ronan furrows his dark brows and clears his throat.

"Someone needs to explain this to me. I want to understand what we're doing. What all this is about."

"Before the empire began," Antioch begins in a soft but steady voice, "the people you call Insurgos lived peacefully in villages scattered across Borealis. They had no king but were ruled by judges and eventually lords. When the King of Aurora decided to expand his horizons, he conquered Borealis and the surrounding countries by force. The Insurgos were taken as slaves to help build the dazzling cities we have today. Over time they grew so numerous that the Emperor began to worry they would overthrow his army in Borealis. And, of course, by that time they were scattered throughout his empire and posed a very real threat to the sanctity of his rule. So, he decided they should be eradicated."

When he pauses to catch his breath, no one speaks or even moves. Even Alara and Felix, who I imagine have heard some version of this story before, seem transfixed by the old man's words.

"With the annihilation of their kind looming, the high lords from the seven tribes gathered and prayed to God that He would go before them into battle to save His people. And God answered and told them to build a Palanquin where His presence would sit as they carried it into battle. The stories differ on what happened after that, but some say that as the Emperor's army marched toward the Insurgos, the Insurgo army placed the Palanquin on the ground before them, and a great earthquake occurred and swallowed up many of the Imperial soldiers. It is said to have created the steep mountains and valleys in northern Borealis which have allowed the Insurgos to hide so successfully for generations from anyone seeking to destroy them. Afterward, many of them remained on the mainland, but the High Lord Caspian and many others believed that God had promised them a land of their own, not merely safety within the borders of the Atlas Empire. So, they took the Palanquin and went in search of this new land. Many years later, six lords from the original villages returned to the mainland with some of their people saying that they had taken the Palanquin to return it as God's throne to the Gate of Life. Caspian was not among the returning lords, and none of them ever spoke of his whereabouts. Some of the Insurgos remained behind on Solitarius where they have been allowed to worship and live as they please without interference from the Empire."

"But why have they?" I ask. Because if Cyrus or any of the rulers before him was aware that Solitarius was not uninhabited as they wanted us to believe, why would they not have mounted an attack long ago?

Felix picks up the story here. "There was a period of famine in the empire, and the Insurgos of Solitarius offered to supply food to the empire in exchange for peace and some materials. The rulers of that age were more concerned about feeding their people to avoid an uprising than they were about a people on a remote island who seemed incapable or unwilling to cause them any harm. The threat of revolution seemed over, so the treaty was made."

"But then my grandfather was given the vision from the Oracle," Ronan supplies softly. His eyes are unfocused, as if he's in another place altogether. Perhaps revisiting his history lessons in the palace and trying to reconcile all this as I am.

"Yes," Antioch confirms. "I traveled with the Oracle from Borealis to Aurora to give your grandfather the message and confirm the signs. The priestess told the Emperor that she'd had a vision from Caelus in which an Insurgo would rise up to overthrow the entire empire. Not the group as a whole, but one who had power from the Gate of Life. One that was imbued with the might of The Ancient One. This Ruler Who Will Rise Up was spoken of in the Insurgo scriptures as one who would be ushered into the presence of the Ancient One—the permanent presence, not just the Palanquin—and given authority, glory, and sovereign power. All nations would worship this Ruler, and their dominion would be an everlasting kingdom that would never be destroyed. This person would rule forever. And as the scriptures said 'narrow is the gate that leads to life.' And from that moment, the Emperor believed if he could destroy this gate, the threat of the Insurgos would be quashed forever."

“Careful,” Alara warns. “The last person who mentioned the prophecy around this one ended up dead.” She narrows her eyes at me, and I know she knows about Levi.

“And the person who dares to bring that up may be next on the list,” I growl, unwilling to back down. That’s my private grief, and I certainly don’t want to go into the details of it with everyone here. Ronan, at least, seems willing to let it pass.

“And then my father decided it wasn’t enough to simply destroy the Gate to diminish the threat. He wanted to be the one who was ushered into the presence of the Ancient One so that his kingdom could endure forever.” The bitterness in Ronan’s voice is biting, and I can’t resist putting my hand on top of his in a feeble attempt to comfort him. He doesn’t pull away, but he doesn’t reach for me either. “So, for these last few years he’s burned Insurgos to the ground while looking for any scrap of information he can get on this Gate and The Ancient One. And I just stood by and watched.”

“Better than being the hand of that destruction.” Felix’s tone is as dark as I’ve ever heard it. My instinct is not to reach out to him in comfort, but to give him space. “The things I did for that man... and just to spare my own life...”

“Yes, but none of us would be here now if you hadn’t played along.” It’s an uncharacteristic bit of sympathy from Alara, though she delivers it with an edge that suggests Felix is being ridiculous for dwelling on such a thing. But it’s a grief I understand all too well. “I dare say Emilia wouldn’t have survived the Imperial court without you, and she certainly never would have escaped the palace with her head intact. You saved the Princess Who Was Promised. That has to count for something."

I can tell by the way Felix refuses to look at any of us that it doesn't begin to calm the storm raging inside him. I don't know the extent of what he did in Cyrus's name—apparently nothing as bad as burning the village we encountered in our escape from Aurora—but it's enough to weigh on him. And as bad as he feels for what he did, he most certainly gave the orders to do much worse. It's a guilt I feel a kinship with, and just like that I see Levi's bloodied face before me. I blink rapidly to chase it away.

"So, we go to Solitarius, and we find everything we can about the Gate, the Ancient, and how to stop Cyrus from getting there first. Between all of us we must know more than him. You especially, Antioch. Can you make notes of the things you've told us and any scriptures that might pertain to it? I have Felix's notes from the Aletheia. Maybe together we can narrow down where we need to begin the search." Even though I feel like I'm playing catchup, it feels good to take charge for a moment.

Antioch agrees to begin writing down everything he knows, and I promise to loan him the precious book that's hidden in my saddle bag. Because my mind is racing and I can't imagine sleep at the moment, even though I was ready to fall asleep just hours before, I volunteer to sit up on a sort of watch while everyone else gets some rest. Felix protests at first, but I insist he and Alara rest if they are going to go into the city this evening to procure supplies. Neither of them argues further, and everyone else disappears into their rooms, leaving me alone with my racing thoughts.

Prayer is the only thing that comforts me while I sit alone in front of the fireplace. I begin with words of thanksgiving—for our safety, for our health, and for my company. At the very least, this is not a journey I have to take alone. Then I ask God to show me the way, both literally and figuratively. Alara's mention of "The Princess That Was Promised" has renewed the worries in my mind and heart. There must be more to this prophecy, but I don't know how to ask.

Is this really my destiny, God?

But I receive no answer.

4

By the time Felix stumbles sleepily from his room, yawning and stretching, I've worked myself into an anxious knot. He stops in his tracks when he sees me and frowns. I must look terrible. On top of having no sleep, I've tugged my hands through my hair until it must be a tangled mess, and I'm still covered in so much dust from our travels. Definitely not the princess he's used to seeing me as.

"You need rest," he insists as he walks to the table to pour himself a drink from the pitcher still sitting there from breakfast. "You should have woken me sooner."

"You need rest, too. I can't have you at less than your best."

"The same goes for you." He peers at me over the rim of his cup. "We're not out of the woods yet, and I need you sharp for what's to come. It's going to take all of us to do this, so we can't afford to have a weak link."

He knows exactly what to say to me to ensure I will comply. I have to think about the greater good and not my own selfishness. That part of my personality has always been both a blessing and a curse. I duck my head in submission, not to Felix, but to the greater purpose. Honestly though, I'm terrified of more nightmares when I close my eyes.

"And," he says softly in a tone that draws my eyes back to him. "I can't focus on anything else when I'm worried about you."

An ache for his touch settles deep within me. Other than that quick brush of hands earlier, we haven't shared a meaningful touch at all since we left Borealis. I want to know where we stand, where his heart is. Since he is a man of few words, I know he could communicate all that to me with a simple touch. But Felix is also a man of great restraint, and I know he won't risk taking me in his arms with Ronan in the other room.

Nothing else is said between us as the rest of our party joins in the common room over the next few minutes. I have no idea what time it is, but Felix guesses it's late afternoon, and he and Alara need to leave soon if they are to gather all we need.

Alara rings down for dinner to be brought to our quarters. When the servants arrive with the food, Ronan and I hide out of sight at Felix's insistence. I suppose he's right. We can't be too careful and take a chance that someone will recognize either of us. We emerge to eat a bit and then bid farewell to Felix and Alara as they venture out into the city.

Ronan offers to stay awake and stand watch while they're gone, and Antioch agrees to sit up with him. Mindful of Felix's instructions, I retreat to my room and wash the grime from my body with the cold water in the wash basin. By the time I'm finished and have sort of managed to wash my hair, I dress in another pair of pants and a tunic and, instead of lying on my bed, venture back into the common area to warm myself by the fire.

Ronan looks up as I walk in, once again looking me up and down as he takes in my unbound hair and choice of attire. There's a flicker of something in his eyes, but it's not the spark I've seen from him before.

"Shouldn't you be sleeping?" he asks as I stretch out in front of the fireplace.

Immediately my eyes feel heavy as the warmth washes over me. "Working on it," I mumble.

I know I should rest. We have a long journey ahead of us, and I haven't slept well in who knows how long—much before our trek across my country. But now I lay myself on this hard floor, still grateful to have the opportunity to lay down at all while Felix and Alara are out making arrangements.

Ronan and Antioch sit at the table behind me. Neither seem willing to leave me alone, but also not willing to be silent.

I close my eyes and lie still for as long as I can, hoping they'll think I'm asleep. It seems to work because after a while they begin speaking softly to each other, and based on the vulnerable nature of Ronan's words, I think he thinks I'm asleep.

"I'm worried for her." Ronan's tone is somber with no levity that I'm used to hearing from him. It's also weary in a way I hadn't expected. To be honest, I've barely considered him in the whirlwind of the last few hours. My mind has been elsewhere, and I simply don't have the capacity to coddle his feelings or explain everything at the moment.

"She is well," says Antioch in a hushed voice.

"How can she possibly be well? You saw her earlier. She was pale as death when she woke from that dream. How can you say she's well?" Ronan laughs bitterly. "How can any of us be well? I still can't fathom what happened outside the city. I still can't believe my father would… Well, maybe I can. After all, he did try to kill me."

Antioch says nothing in reply, and there is silence for a long moment. So long that I think maybe they will speak no more. But just as I'm ready to open my eyes, Ronan speaks up again.

"What is she going to do? These Insurgos, these people you both serve—"

"We do not serve a people," Antioch interrupts. "We serve the one true God, and it is His people that we hope to help. But we are not at their beck and call. Nor do we act in ways that they may see fit. You need look no further than Alara for confirmation of that."

Ronan chuckles again. "Yes. Well, Alara has her own mold, doesn't she? She is everything my father fears and everything that Emilia has proven herself not to be."

I don't think he intends for his words to sting, but they hurt because there's so much truth in them. Alara is everything that I am not. Isn't that my biggest fear when it comes to her and Felix? Because he will see that she is the one who should have been queen, or she is at least the one who should have led the Insurgos. What have I done except cause more chaos and mess? What have I done except make sure that people die because of my poor choices or lack of decision making? And yet Alara managed to lead a band of Insurgo rebels and make a statement to the entire city of Borealis.

But it was my prayers that God answered when He sent that storm to ravage the temple. Or was it? It was at the same time that Alara sent a message with her burning arrow that our God was a consuming fire. Perhaps His show of strength and power was in response to her and not me. Perhaps my one claim to greatness is not really mine to claim at all, but hers.

"Our God has a plan for our princess," Antioch says quietly. "And no one knows the details of that plan. But there is a prophecy, and many believe she is the answer."

"She does seem to have the hopes of many riding on her shoulders," Ronan agrees. "Or at least she carries herself that way, but she is a queen after all. And that comes with the responsibility of royalty."

"Yes," Antioch hedges. "However, there is something more here. The Ruler Who Will Rise Up, the one the prophecy speaks of, has much more involvement and much more on their shoulders and their head than a simple crown."

"There is nothing simple about the crown." Ronan laughs bitterly. "Again, trust me when I say that, even having worn but a prince's crown to this point, I can tell you there is nothing easy or simple about it. Wearing the crown is in fact likely the most complicated position to be in at all. If you need evidence of that, you simply have to look at the relationship between Emilia and me."

I cringe inwardly because I know this is a sore spot with him, and it's going to be a very awkward conversation when we finally have to have it. Because whether Felix was in the mix or not, I'm not sure I could have married Ronan. But since Felix *is* a factor in all this, it makes the situation ten times worse. So many conversations need to be had, but I don't know where to begin any of them. So, for the time being, I'm grateful for the silence that falls between Ronan and Antioch and the heaviness that keeps my eyes shut.

After what feels like no time at all, I fall asleep.

I sleep until Felix and Alara return, thankfully without the interruption of dreams. I start when the door swings open but relax a bit when Felix pushes through the door with large bundles in his arms. Alara follows, similarly weighed down. We all gather around the table to sort through the clothing and supplies they've brought back.

"Where are the weapons?" A cursory glance at everything laid out on the table reveals several sets of clothes, some dried meat, a couple flasks, and a few other miscellaneous supplies. Notably absent are any swords or extra daggers. I look to Felix for the answer, but Alara speaks up instead.

"Someone insisted on no weapons," Alara huffs.

"It's not a good idea." Felix sighs as if they've had this conversation many times already. "We have a couple daggers, but anything larger would attract too much attention."

"You don't expect us to fend off Cyrus with a couple of daggers, do you?"

"Cyrus is not going to be on this ship. Any weapons we need we can pick up in Solitarius. What I don't want is to give this crew any reason to feel threatened by us or to suspect we are anything other than a few travelers returning to our home on Solitarius. The lower profile we keep, the better."

"That may be fine for the three of you." Ronan looks between Felix, Alara, and I. He's referencing our darker skin, our dark brown hair, and our dark eyes that mark us as descendants of outsiders on the mainland. "What are Antioch and I supposed to be?"

"A fiancé and his grandfather." Felix pointedly looks away from me when he answers. "We're all returning to Solitarius for a wedding."

"What a happy occasion," Alara grumbles as Ronan harrumphs.

"It makes the most sense. It's the best cover we could hope for." But Felix sounds miserable. Great. We're all unhappy. "And the hope is that if the crew thinks one of you is spoken for," his eyes dart between me and Alara, "they might leave you alone."

If I could be objective, it's a decent plan. But perhaps because this wound is so fresh, I balk at the idea of going along with it.

Now it seems foolish that I ever hoped Ronan and I could make a clean break as a betrothed couple.

No one seems to have any arguments against the plan, at least none they're willing to voice, so we all return to sorting through the haul.

Alara retrieves our bags from our rooms so we can repack them with our new additions. As I open mine to begin stuffing it full, I catch sight of my wedding dress and pause.

I hastily tie the bag closed, but not before Felix catches my movements. He approaches me with the pretense of handing me a plain blue dress. His hands brush mine underneath the fabric, and our eyes meet.

"Get rid of that dress," he mutters, low enough so no one else hears. I know he doesn't mean the one in my hands. I acknowledge the instruction with a slight nod. It will have to wait until everyone has gone to bed. I don't want to make a scene of it.

The blue dress he hands me is simple enough, but it's not as practical as the trousers I'm wearing now. He must know this. "Why did I get a dress?"

Felix studies my face for a moment as if deciding how much to say. "Once we board the ship, there's no hiding that you are a woman. But I'd like to not draw any more attention to your...shape...than necessary." His eyes flick down the length of my body and then right back to my eyes. Rather than make me feel uncomfortable, his gaze leaves a trail of heat in its wake.

He has seen me in trousers before, namely when he first arrived in my military camp to escort me to Aurora. But we didn't know each other then, hadn't known what it felt like to have him pressed against me as he held me or kissed me. Now that we both know, there's something quite different in the way he looks at my legs. Or maybe it's just that I'm noticing him noticing me for the first time. It makes me feel strangely powerful.

"I won't let anyone hurt you," he promises, "but don't expect these sailors to be kind. They aren't used to having women on board, and many of them will view it as bad luck."

If only they knew how much bad luck I tend to bring with me. "I'm not trying to make friends."

"Just try to keep a low profile. Both you and Alara. Don't draw any more attention to yourself than you have to."

I look over at Alara who has her finger in Ronan's chest and seems to be giving him a piece of her mind over something. "I think you might be having this conversation with the wrong woman," I say with a smirk.

Felix chuckles. "Probably so. With her, I just hope for the best. But with you, well, I thought you could be reasoned with."

Ugh. I want so badly to kiss him in this moment. When he looks at me like that, I would do practically anything he asks.

"I'll try to be on my best behavior."

"Try a little harder than usual, please?" He winks at me and then leaves me holding the dress while he returns to unpacking supplies.

Instead of packing my bag in the common area like everyone else, I gather the clothing and supplies assigned to me and return them all to my room. Once alone inside, I wrestle the wedding dress from the pack and lay the ruined mess across the bed. Then I fill the pack with my new acquisitions and arrange things the best I can. I remove my dagger from the pack and tell myself I'll find a way to strap it to my body underneath the dress before we board the ship in the morning.

Once everything is arranged, I leave the bedroom and rejoin the others. They are all packed as well, and we stand there for a minute, looking at each other as if waiting for someone to decide. Finally, I do.

"We all need to get as much rest as we can," I say. "I've slept most recently, so I'll watch for a while so the rest of you can sleep. Alara, I'll wake you in a couple hours to take over watch so I can try to sleep a bit more. You can rouse us all when it's time to leave for the docks."

I look around, but no one seems to disagree. So, we all say goodnight and retreat to our respective rooms.

I wait half an hour or so, until I believe Alara to be asleep, before I sneak back into our room to retrieve my wedding dress. It's no secret that this has to be done, but I didn't feel right about destroying it while Ronan was still awake. I don't really want anyone to witness this.

Though dingy with dirt and ash, torn and ripped from travel and my hasty undress earlier, the fabric of the dress is still smooth and supple as it slides through my fingers. I kneel at the hearth in front of the fire, letting the flames warm my face as I work up the courage to rip this to shreds.

"It truly was beautiful."

I whip around at Ronan's voice, guilt rising like the tide inside me. It's too late to stop the motion of my hand, which rips a piece of fabric, sending beads and pearls rolling across the floor. He kicks a few toward the hearth as he pulls up a chair next to me. He leans forward with his elbows on his knees which makes us eye level even though I'm kneeling on the hard stone. It's a thoughtful gesture, but try as he might, Ronan will always be above me.

"I hate to get rid of it," I admit. "It was lovely. But we can't arouse suspicion by being found with anything so nice."

"Of course," he agrees with a solemn nod. But I can tell he knows there's more to it. "I never got to tell you, but you were a breathtaking bride."

I duck my chin to avoid meeting his penetrating gaze. He deserves the truth, but I'm not sure what that looks like just now.

"Thank you," I whisper as I watch the next piece of fabric burn. The edges turn the same deep red-orange as the flames before blackness overtakes them. It's the same every time, and yet I still find it mesmerizing.

"I suppose this was a fitting ending for the dress—for us—given all that's happened."

"You mean your father's weapon of choice?" I try to keep the edge out of my voice, but I can tell I haven't succeeded when Ronan sighs.

"Yes, but not only his. The Insurgos as well."

My head snaps up, and I find myself staring into those cool, piercing eyes. "What? What do you mean? Your father has repeatedly used fire against the Insurgos."

"Yes, but I heard what happened at the temple in Borealis. When you were supposed to be making the sacrifice? We've never talked about it, but I know what you—"

"That was Alara," I snap a little too quickly.

"With the flaming arrow, yes, but are you forgetting how you prayed down a storm that set the whole place ablaze?"

"I-I never intended…" Ronan wasn't present for any of that. He doesn't know what was being asked of me and wouldn't understand even if he did.

"Intent matters very little when the result is death and destruction."

That's it. He's said the very thing I've feared since Levi died because of me. Because I killed him. No matter what the intent was, no matter if it was God's plan, I still killed him, and I'm not sure I can ever be forgiven for that. Not according to Ronan anyway.

I'm unaware of when I began to cry, but now I feel the tears dripping off my chin and onto the remnants of the dress I clutch in my lap. The fabric soaks up the tears as if it's a desert waiting for rain, so I let myself keep crying.

When I look up, Ronan is gone.

5

I fall into a fitful sleep after I rouse Alara to take over the watch. My dreams are filled with images of Levi and burning villages, and when I wake, I nearly gag on the imagined taste of ash. My throat burns with rising bile, and I roll on my side and heave my dinner into a chamber pot beside my bed. Tears sting my eyes as I rub the back of my hand across my mouth, wiping away the residual wetness. Breath coming in pants, I close my eyes and take a quick inventory of my body. My hands shake a bit, but I don't feel feverish or achy. Other than a roiling stomach, I seem to be fine.

"What's wrong with you?" Alara asks from the bed across from me. I didn't expect her to be here. She's supposed to be standing watch. But I take a moment to listen and realize everyone is awake and milling around the common area except me.

"No idea," I mumble as I flip onto my back and stare up at the ceiling. The skin on my arms is dimpled, making the fine hairs stick almost straight up. A churning inside me starts in my stomach and goes all the way up my chest. "Not a word about it though."

The last thing I need is to have Felix, or anyone really, fussing over me. Especially not before I've had a chance to figure out what this is. Why are these dreams back with such force? The battle on a beach, Felix dying before me, running through a forest with a strong tug in my gut. And something new this time. Just a single word: Zephyros.

"I won't mention it, but you better pull it together or he's going to see right through you."

I don't have to ask who "he" is.

I drown the taste of ash with a glass of water before changing into the dress Felix procured for me.

We all gather our things in silence. Once or twice, I catch Ronan looking at me as if he wants to say something, but I look away, and he never approaches. Everyone else seems too preoccupied with their own thoughts to notice. Even Felix is noticeably distracted.

I take the opportunity to step away from the group and rest against the wall so I can regroup. My arms wrap around my midsection as if this will somehow soothe the ache inside me. This has to be a misunderstanding. My dreams are crazy, and I can hardly use them to make decisions, especially about something this dangerous.

Zephyros. Nowhere on the mainland is safe for me anymore, least of all the land of my country's biggest adversary. Most of my combat experience comes from fighting the Zephyros army intent on expanding their borders. And I can hardly forget the two Zephyros princesses I met in Ronan's court who killed at least one of our competitors and my only friend at the time. Why would I possibly feel any pull to go there?

"How are you feeling, my child?" Antioch joins me against the wall as Felix, Alara, and Ronan engage in a heated discussion about the distribution of weapons. "Are you ill?"

I press my palm more firmly against my stomach as if it can calm the butterflies inside. "No, not ill exactly." I hesitate, but what's the point in keeping this from him? If anyone can help me understand this, it's him. "It's these dreams."

"Tell me about them."

"I see Levi and my mother...and Felix."

Do I imagine that he perks up at this last bit of information? Earlier he seemed to know more about Felix and his need for the sea than I did. What else does he know, and why?

"All people who have sought to protect you. Those who love you."

"Felix doesn't—"

"Do not mistake his restraint for apathy. It would be a shame to underestimate him." There are more layers to these words than I can unpack right now.

"But why am I seeing this at all? And then, just now, I had another dream. Mostly more of the same, but there was something else." I'm about to tell him when Felix joins us. He's shaved his beard down to stubble, and while that usually makes him look younger, the circles under his eyes counteract the effect.

“Are you well?” His tone is carefully measured, and I think about what Antioch has just told me about underestimating him. I could lie, but Alara is also right—he sees right through me.

“I had another dream,” I admit.

Felix frowns. “I didn’t hear you call out.”

“I don’t think I did. It wasn’t as clear this time, but there was something new.” I look from Felix to Antioch and back again. “I need to go to Zephyros,” I say quickly.

“To Zephyros?” he clarifies in a hushed voice. He glances over his shoulder to make sure the others are distracted. Clearly, he doesn’t want anyone else to hear how crazy I sound. To his credit, he doesn’t immediately discount me but simply asks “Why?”

“Why indeed?” Antioch echoes with a frown. “There is nothing for you there, princess, except more death and destruction.”

Something about this pronouncement rubs me the wrong way. It’s not that I disagree exactly, but I automatically bristle when someone tries to presume what’s best for me. It’s something Felix knows well, which is probably why he didn’t immediately offer his opinion.

“Most of my life has been death and destruction. I’m not new to those feelings. But something inside me is pulling in that direction. I can’t explain it.”

“The prophecy says nothing about the chosen walking into the lion’s den.”

This doesn't sit right with me. "When I first met you, you didn't seem convinced I was the fulfillment of this prophecy. You said that it wasn't about a person and that God's work would be accomplished regardless."

"And so it will be, but I have more information now. When you shared with me the scriptures you possessed, I learned much about the timing of the Insurgo rescue, and I believe it is at hand. You are to lead these people, and you can't do it if you walk straight into the enemy's camp."

So, he's changed his mind in these last few hours. Should I believe him? It's not that I want to go to Zephyros, but the feeling was so strong when I woke from the dream. But the more distance I put there, the more I second guess my decision.

"Thank you for your counsel, Antioch." I place my hand on his forearm in what I hope is a reassuring gesture. "I'd like to speak to the Commander alone, please."

"As you wish." The old man dips his head at me, gives Felix a long look, then excuses himself.

We wait until he has engaged himself in conversation with Ronan before either of us speaks.

"You didn't like what he had to say," I observe. Felix's silence was notable while Antioch expressed his views, and I'm anxious to find out what's going on behind those dark eyes. "I thought you would agree with him."

"I don't disagree with him, but I don't like how he presumes to know what's best for you."

“Why? Because that’s your job?” I say it without heat. Though he’s been gentler about it than most, there have been times when Felix has voiced his belief on God’s will for my life. I’ve tried to make it clear that this is not an observation I welcome.

“I thought so for a while. But while I don’t always appreciate your methods, your instincts are usually right. My job is to keep you as safe as possible while you plunge recklessly into the madness.”

“So, if I insisted we go to Zephyros?”

He sighs heavily, and I think I have underestimated the weight he carries.

“I have to go to Solitarius, Emilia. Please don’t make me choose.”

He’s rarely asked me for anything. Why does he feel so strongly about this? There must be something more to it, but I know I won’t get those answers at the moment. And I can’t bear the thought of being separated from him.

“No, you’re right,” I finally concede. “Of course, it would be stupid to go to Zephyros. Everything we’re chasing is in Solitarius.”

The relief that sweeps over him is dramatic. Exactly how much has it cost him to go along with my plans in the past? I think about how I asked him to chase down my father, to prevent his murder only for him to fail. We’ve never really discussed that and how it affected him. I suppose in many ways I’ve taken his strength for granted. But I need it now more than ever.

"Thank you," he says under his breath. "Now gather your things. It's almost time to leave."

Alara and Felix bookend our quiet procession from the inn. Alara walks past the stables, and I frown at her direction.

"We don't need the horses?" I ask softly to Felix who is right behind me.

"It's not far to the harbor. We don't need to ride."

He's right. Within minutes we reach the edge of the village. A few stone buildings and a rocky beach are all that stand between us and an infinitely dark sea. I can't exactly see it in the waning moonlight, but I can hear the soft roar of the waves as they break and race toward the shore. Behind me, Felix gasps softly, but when I turn around to check on him, he just gives me a nod to indicate I should keep moving forward. What is it with him and the sea exactly?

There's no time to ponder this question for too long because Alara has directed us down a narrow path to a wooden walkway that stretches out into the sea. A pier, I think. At the end of it rests a ship. Having never seen a ship in person, I can't say if it's large or small by comparison, but it seems huge to me. A great, big, wooden thing with three masts stretching toward the sky. I pause to stare up at them, but Felix collides with me and nudges me forward none too gently.

"Keep moving," he mutters. I can sense his unease and find the cause of it when I see a few men cleaning fish on the side of the pier and eyeing me hungrily. I've been ogled before, after all I came into my womanhood while I was in a military camp, but this does send a shiver through me.

I quicken my pace to catch up to the others. Alara stops at the base of a gangplank where two men have stepped in front to bar her entrance. Behind me, Felix groans.

"Ro," he calls ahead. Ronan turns around and gives him a questioning look. "Stay with her please."

Ronan's eyes catch mine as he comes to take Felix's place by my side. Without further discussion, Felix approaches Alara and the two men and begins some sort of explanation I can't hear.

"I owe you an apology," Ronan whispers to me. I look up in response, but his eyes are still focused straight ahead, keeping an eye out for dangers as Felix silently asked him to do.

"I'm not sure you do." He really only voiced what I'd been thinking.

"No, Emilia, I really do. I've seen people do horrible things in the name of something good, but you're not like that. You're not malicious and you're not conniving. I spoke with Felix, and he told me how all that affected you. He was pretty angry with me for suggesting your motives didn't matter."

Oh, I can only imagine. Felix is my fiercest defender... even when he's defending me from myself.

"I don't want to hurt people. But that seems like all I've done lately. Every time I think I understand God's plan, something horrible happens and people die."

"Because you misunderstood?" He sounds genuinely curious, and I wish I had a better answer for him.

"Maybe. Or maybe it would have happened anyway. But I don't want to be part of that death and destruction. I want healing and peace from both sides. I've seen hatred from your father and from Insurgos." I have to think no further than the anger that burns inside Alara.

A sharp whistle pulls our attention to Felix who is motioning us forward to join Alara and Antioch on the gangplank. Ronan and I approach cautiously, and I eye the two men Felix convinced to move out of the way with uncertainty. They stare back at me with equal wariness.

"Captain's waiting," one of them spits out, and then quite literally spits at my feet. Ronan tenses, but Felix just steps between me and the man and ushers us up the gangplank. I admire his control, because I'm sure he'd like to hit the man just as much as I would. Ronan grabs my forearm and marches me forward. I know it's his way of protecting me, but I have to work not to recoil from him. I don't need to be man-handled.

Still, I accompany him the rest of the way until we finally set foot on the ship. Alara and Antioch are waiting for us, though not by choice judging from the unfriendly faces of the men forming a small circle around our group. Felix and Alara both step to the front of the group, and Ronan positions himself in front of me. Through the gap between their shoulders, I watch a tall man, dressed all in black with a ridiculous hat step through the ring of sailors until he's nearly nose to nose with Felix.

“Captain,” Felix greets cooly. I can tell he’s not completely comfortable with this arrangement, but it’s necessary. “We appreciate you granting us passage.”

“You paid well enough,” the man responds. “And the work we’ll get out of you,” he looks between Ronan and Felix, “will make up the difference.”

I don’t like that at all. Not only have we apparently paid this man a substantial amount of money, but he also expects at least Felix and Ronan to work? I suppose Antioch looks too frail to be of much use, and Alara and I... well, I shudder to think about what work he would have in mind for us.

“A fair bargain,” Felix says, though I can tell he doesn’t believe it.

“There are two cabins for you lot,” the Captain growls. “Sorry to say there’s only four beds. One of you will have to sleep on deck or with the crew. Keep to yourself, and they’ll leave you well enough alone. As for you...” His gaze lingers first on Alara, then turns to me. He nods slightly, and I feel a rush of movement behind me.

Arms wrap right around my waist, nearly lifting me off the ground as the foul-smelling man behind me restrains me. I look around to find Alara is in a similar position. Ronan shouts and starts toward me until two other men grab him by the arms.

“Felix, do something!” he insists as he looks wildly at his friend. So much for posing as my protective fiancé, but I shouldn’t be surprised. Ronan has never been a man of action.

If I didn't know Felix so well, I would think him perfectly calm. But I see the way his hand drifts toward his dagger and the tight clench of his jaw. Our eyes meet, and I try to ask his permission. I'm being restrained, yes, but not hurt. He asked me not to cause a stir while we were onboard, and I'm sure this is exactly what he was talking about. He holds up a single finger on the hand that hovers above his dagger, and I nod slightly even though I'm dying to break free.

The Captain swaggers toward me, and I cease struggling. The man behind me doesn't relax his grip though.

"And what a pretty little thing we have here." He tips my chin up with his finger until I'm forced to meet his eyes. I find no kindness there, and I give him none in return. It takes everything I have not to bite that finger that lingers on my face a little too long. His eyes trail down my face to the neckline of my dress. It's hardly low cut, but I feel exposed anyway. "And what's this?"

Before I can protest, he drops his hand to finger the chain around my neck. He pulls it up to reveal the black opal that had dipped below my dress. Felix's gift to me on my birthday.

"Drop it," I hiss. He raises an eyebrow at me.

"Unwise to bring such a valuable trinket aboard a vessel with all these disreputable men," he chuckles. "Perhaps I'll just hold onto it for you until we reach our destination. Wouldn't want something to happen to it."

With a quick tug, he yanks it from my neck, snapping the clasp and letting the chain dangle from his palm.

Red haze clouds my vision as I try to hold my composure. Ronan is pulling hard against his captors now, though I can see it's useless. Just remember what Felix said. This isn't unexpected...

"I'll keep it safe in my chambers until we reach port. Then you'll have it back. You have my word." He looks over my shoulder to address the men behind me. "Put the girls up in the officer's quarters. And see to it that they are not harmed on penalty of death. We don't need to bring the wrath of the gods on us." With that, he turns and pushes his way back through the circle of onlookers.

Felix waits a beat and then addresses my captor. "You heard Captain Meridan. You can let her go now."

The man laughs, and his rank breath nearly makes me vomit. "Oh, I don't think so. I might need to search her myself to see if she's hiding any more valuables."

"Aren't you going to do anything?" Ronan demands of Felix.

I'm tired of waiting for permission. So, before Felix can say anything, I slam my heel into the man's instep, and he doubles over in pain. The bones crunch in a satisfying way under my foot as I twist out of his arms and pull the dagger I had hidden inside my dress. When I look up, Ronan is stunned, but I think I see a small smile on Alara's face. The rest of the men circling us have taken a step back and released both Ronan and Alara. No one moves for a moment until Ronan steps toward me and slides an arm around my waist.

The last thing I want is to be supported by someone after my show of strength, but there isn't a good way to throw off Ronan's arm without causing a bigger scene. And he is supposed to be my fiancé if we're to keep up this charade.

"You're not hurt, are you?" he asks in a low voice.

"I'm fine," I insist, a little surprised to find that it's true. My eyes flit to Felix who has come to check on me, but he keeps his distance.

"Well done," he says with a small smirk that draws a scoff from Ronan. Behind that smirk is something darker. A warning. I've already broken the one promise he asked me to make for this voyage.

"'Well done'?" Ronan almost snarls. "That's all you have to say? Were you going to step in?"

"I didn't need to. Emilia had it under control. She's stronger than you realize."

It might be the most empowering thing he's ever said to me. While I can appreciate Ronan's instinct to run in and save me, I revel in knowing Felix has so much confidence in my abilities. I'm not just a good fighter for a girl. I'm a good fighter in any situation, and that assessment means the world coming from him.

"I tried to behave," I remind Felix. It's as close to our old banter as we've come in a while, and I relish it.

"Yes, I was impressed by your restraint. But," he raises his voice so everyone around us can hear him, "if they ever touch you again, you have my permission to use every move in your arsenal."

Despite the awfulness of it all, I can't completely suppress a smile as we're shown the way to our quarters.

⁂

The officer's quarters turn out to be just a tiny room with two beds and a small table between them. Apparently, there are no officers on this ship, which makes me think it might not have originally been Meridan's ship. Perhaps he commandeered it. Either way, I'm still grateful to have a separate room from the crew.

Other than the ones that greeted us when we first boarded, the rest of the sailors seemed mostly indifferent to our presence. They do a double take as Alara and I walk by but quickly return to their tasks. I sense this is a place where questions are not welcome, which is just as well. The less they know about us, the better.

The men who led us to our quarters dump our bags onto one of the two beds, light two lamps that don't give off much light, then slam the door as they leave Alara and me alone in our room.

Alara sighs and then grabs her things to claim the other bed. I just wring my hands in indecision. Where did they take Felix and the others? Are we locked in this room? What if this is some sort of trap and they're holding us here until Imperial soldiers can arrive to arrest or kill us?

"You might as well get comfortable," Alara suggests with a sigh as she rifles through her pack in search of something. "This is all you're going to see for a while."

"Surely we can go on deck once we set sail."

"Oh, I'm not saying you can't, but you're not going to feel like it." She tosses me a small flask that sloshes with liquid as I catch it. "Drink that, and it should help."

I open the flask and sniff. It smells faintly of ginger and mint. "What is this?"

"Herbal tea. Felix said you'd never sailed before, and it can be rough until you get used to it. The tea should help with some of the symptoms, but I'd also suggest you just get really comfortable in your bed and keep your eyes closed. It will help you sleep, too."

"Thank you," I say before taking a small sip. It's a very thoughtful gesture from the girl who seems like she wants to strangle me most of the time. I hold it out to offer it back to her, but she waves it away.

"I grew up on the sea. I'll be fine. Besides, I don't think it's a good idea for both of us to be out of it at the same time. Felix and Ronan will be busy helping the crew, and Antioch could hardly fend off any sailors with mischief on their minds. Well done handling that one from earlier, by the way."

I just stare at her. What exactly was in that tea? She's being far too kind for the usual tension between us.

"Th-thanks," I slur as my knees give out and I fall onto the bed.

Great. She's managed to drug me again.

It's the last thing I remember thinking before I black out.

6

I must sleep for at least a day because my body hurts from lying still so long. I sit up slowly, but the room still sways a little. Alara's bed is empty and made up as if she hasn't been in it for a while.

My mouth is parched, and my lips cracked, but I don't dare drink anything I might find in this room. That's how I ended up in this predicament. Very slowly, I push myself from the bed to my feet. The room spins, and I nearly fall back, but I'm not sure if that's the aftereffects of Alara's tea or because the ship itself is gently rocking back and forth. We must be well out to sea now.

The sea. A childlike anticipation grows within me as I realize I'm going to get my first real look at it. It was much too dark when we boarded the ship to see anything other than a vast darkness stretching out before us, but now I'm free to roam and discover what it is about the ocean that holds such sway over Felix.

It takes a bit for me to feel steady enough on my feet that I can leave the room and make my way onto the main deck. After a few steps I find I'm comfortable enough on my feet. And other than the gnawing of hunger in my belly, I don't feel ill at all. Either Alara's tea was helpful after all, or the sea just comes naturally to me.

When I step out of the shadow of the quarterdeck onto the main deck, the sunlight nearly blinds me. I immediately take a seat on a wooden barrel as I blink until my eyes adjust.

"There you are!"

Ronan's exclamation startles me, and I clumsily rise to my feet to greet him. He's right there, steadying me as I try to gather my balance. "Take your time," he says. "You haven't developed your sea legs yet."

"I haven't had a chance," I retort. "Alara drugged me...again."

"Again?"

"It's a long story." I wave him off because I don't feel like going into it. With my eyes adjusting to the light, I get my first good look at him.

Ronan looks just like the roguish pirates in the romance novels my mother's friends from court used to read. I would always hear them talking about the hero of their books as a devilishly handsome man with a shirt that just accidentally happened to be unbuttoned halfway down his chest. The prince certainly has that look down. I can't think that I've ever seen him shirtless before, but the glimpse I get makes less of an impression on me than I expect it to. After all, despite any romantic feelings or lack thereof, Ronan is an objectively handsome prince, and I am certainly a woman who can appreciate such beauty.

"What have I missed?" I take his arm to continue to steady myself.

"You've been out for roughly a day. We set sail, obviously, and Felix and I have been helping crew the ship." He straightens a little, and I realize he's proud of his contribution. It's probably very rare he can work alongside commoners without causing a stir. "Felix is still remarkably good at all this. It's like he never forgot it."

He's inadvertently opened up a whole lot of questions, but he's not the one I want answers from so I remain silent and let him keep filling me in.

"Once they put you and Alara in your quarters, they took me, and Antioch to the other officer's room. Felix insisted he'd sleep on the deck, and you know there's no arguing with him." He frowns, but once again I get the sense he likes playing the pirate instead of the prince. "They searched our bags, too. Took a couple daggers they found and that book you gave Antioch."

"The Aletheia?" I look up so quickly I nearly bump the top of my head on his chin. Now the captain has my two most precious possessions—Felix's necklace and the book that holds our only clues to information about the Gate and the Ancient.

"Yes. I wanted to go after it, but Felix said to let it go."

That doesn't seem right. It was Felix's book to begin with, and he certainly understands its importance. "Where is everyone else?"

"Antioch pretty much stays in his bed. He's always praying or writing." Ronan shrugs. "Alara is wherever she wants to be.

Nothing seems to be off limits to her, but she's usually just wandering around, occasionally heckling me and Felix."

"And where is he?" I try to keep the eagerness out of my voice, but I'm not sure I succeed.

"He's made himself right at home," Ronan chuckles. "I think he's trimming the sails or something. Our shift is over for now, but he rarely comes down when he's supposed to."

Neither of us speaks for a bit as we look out over the side of the ship and continue to watch the endless miles of ocean pass beneath us.

"I've been talking to Antioch a lot." Ronan finally breaks the silence. "And I don't really know what to make of everything. What he's told me, it fits with what my father thinks. So, on some levels, I suppose it must be true."

"It" seems too small a word to encompass everything Ronan or any of the rest of us is trying to understand. And how can it line up with what his father thinks? Because anything Cyrus thinks or says is automatically assumed to be a lie in my book. But then again, Ronan is his son, and despite whatever he may have done to Ronan, despite however he's treated him, that is his father. And I assume there is some innate loyalty there. I don't like it. I don't know how much I can trust him.

And I realize that's been the problem with Ronan all along. I've never known where his allegiance truly lies. I'm not sure he does either, but this seems the moment to delve a little deeper into that.

"Why is your father so afraid of the Insurgos? Does he actually believe in this prophecy?" I ask because it doesn't really make sense to me. "At least in Borealis, Alara was leading some attacks on the temple or on the priestesses. And they had a reason to be legitimately concerned. From my time in Aurora, it doesn't seem as if the Insurgos were bothering anyone. Your father simply used them as a scapegoat for his own plans and tricks to gain what he wanted."

Ronan looks at me sideways and frowns. "It all comes down to the prophecy. Surely you must know that. It's all Antioch can talk about. And I'm sure he's spoken of it with you." There's something behind his eyes that tells me he knows more than he's letting on. He knows more about my role than he should. At this point, if he's been speaking with Antioch, he maybe even knows more than I do.

"I know what he told us back at the inn—there's a prophecy in the Insurgo camp that says there is a Princess That Was Promised that will deliver the people from the empire and let them worship in freedom. But there's nothing in there about any sort of violence necessarily. There could be a peaceful resolution to all this."

It seems highly unlikely, but it is ultimately my hope there could be some sort of peaceful talks. Then again, the last time that was proposed, Cyrus burned the Insurgo encampments around my city to the ground, leaving nothing but ash, death, devastation, and desolation in his wake. Maybe the time for peace has passed.

"Remember it also indicates that this princess or ruler will overthrow the empire. Not simply liberate these Insurgo rebels. You have to agree that if you were emperor of said empire, that would concern you just a little bit."

Yes, it would. But as queen, no matter how temporarily, of my own country, I'm not sure how much store I would've put in prophecies when I had the most elite fighting forces around me. So, I'm not sure why Cyrus has chosen to latch onto this. Perhaps it wasn't even him. It seems as though this goes back generations—at least one—to his father as well, because Cyrus didn't start this vendetta against the Insurgos. He simply escalated it.

"Antioch seems to think you are this princess," Ronan says after a pause, "but he's also sort of vague about the whole thing."

"Yes," I agree. "He tends to be that way. It's what makes the whole thing even more frustrating and infuriating, but then again, it is a prophecy, and who knows if it's even true. Who can say?"

"Well, the priestesses of Caelus have even seen this vision of the empire being overthrown," says Ronan. "So, if it's coming from both sides, perhaps it is true. Perhaps it means you?" The lilt of his voice makes it more of a question than a statement. And I don't know how to answer it.

"Antioch told me the Insurgos believed it was my mother, and we both know how that ended."

"You are not your mother."

"No." I'm not sure I could be even half as noble as she was.

"And you have support. Felix is dedicated—"

"Felix is not up for discussion." Because it's too dangerously close to a conversation I'm not ready to have with Ronan. "We just have to get to Solitarius, that's all. And then we'll figure out what we're actually dealing with."

I'm trying so hard to wrap all this up in a neat little box, but it just won't fit. The frown on Ronan's handsome face tells me he knows it's a fool's errand as well, but he's willing to let me have my folly a bit longer.

Ronan stretches his arms overhead and then tries to stifle a yawn with his fist. "If you'll be all right, I'm going to take advantage of the break and sleep a little."

"I'll be fine," I assure him. I'm not exactly confident of this, but my wish to explore on my own outweighs the want of company...except maybe for a certain person. "Get rest while you can."

Ronan squeezes my arm and then heads back to the cabin he shares with Antioch. Finally, I take my first deep breath of salty air, and tilt my face to the sky while the wind whips my hair around me. It will most certainly be a tangled mess in no time, but I don't care.

In the daylight, the unfamiliarity of it all seems less intimidating. Everyone seems too busy to pay me any attention. This time when I walk by, I barely even draw a second glance. Which is just as well, because I am entirely focused on what lies before me.

As far as I can see, water shines and glistens under the sun's rays. My hands tighten on the wooden railing as I lean over the side just a bit to watch as it passes beneath us. The ship cuts through the waves like a knife, and I am both intrigued and terrified of the dark depths of the water below.

Eventually, I make my way to the front of the ship. Water stretches before me along with endless possibilities. Tentatively, I stretch my arms out and once again tilt my face to the sun. It's what I imagine flying must feel like.

With my eyes closed I offer a prayer to God. A prayer for wisdom and guidance and clarity. If there really is some prophecy and I'm the fulfillment of it, what exactly have I been called to do? Every time I've thought I've understood God's will in the past, things have gone from bad to worse. I can't afford to make those kinds of mistakes again. Not now and not ever.

"Good weather we're having so far." Captain Meridan appears beside me, and I instantly shrink in on myself, lowering my hands to my sides and straightening my spine. He seems less imposing in the light of day, but I'm still wary of him and what his presence means.

"It's beautiful," I concede carefully. There's no denying that.

"I wasn't sure you would be able to leave your cabin long enough to enjoy it."

I can feel his eyes on me, but I don't dare look at him. "Well, you and your men didn't exactly make me feel welcome, so I thought it best to remain in my cabin for a while." Not that I had much choice.

"I'll wager you had a touch of the sickness, too. Your companions tell me you've never sailed before."

When I do chance a glance at him, I find the Captain is no longer looking at me, but he's studying two figures positioned high on one of the masts. It's difficult to make out details from this distance, but I see the movement of a skirt in the wind. The possibilities narrow to exactly one. Felix and Alara.

"Just because I haven't doesn't mean I can't." I'm feeling sulky now. What are they talking about up there? And why hasn't Felix come to check on me?

"True enough," the Captain agrees. "You seem to be doing well for yourself. Still, I would advise you to stay in your cabin as much as possible. Most of my crew will be afraid to touch you, but there are a few who might chance it."

"Did you give the same advice to her?" I nod toward Alara's figure on the mast. Meridan just laughs.

"She seems spoken for. He's quite formidable. The men's fear of the soldier outweighs their need for female companionship."

The idea that Alara is spoken for by Felix and therefore safe from unwanted attention makes my blood boil. Was I not the one who injured one of his crew when we arrived? Apparently, no one is threatened by Ronan or me.

"I can hold my own. Perhaps you heard?"

"Against one man and only after I instructed them to leave you alone."

"They don't listen well." I consider telling him I can do more than stomp on toes and swing my elbows, but something holds me back from sharing. Felix would want me to keep the extent of my skills quiet. On this voyage I'm not a queen and not a warrior.

To be either would put me in more danger. I'm just a woman, and on this ship that's less than nothing.

"They listen well enough. You're unharmed, aren't you?" He looks me up and down, and though I don't detect any desire in his gaze it still makes me uncomfortable the way he studies me. "What is it you seek in Solitarius? The soldier won't say, but you're clearly running from something. I don't believe you're sailing to your wedding."

"What does it matter to you? We paid well enough, and we're not causing any trouble."

He narrows his eyes and studies my face for a long moment. "Because whatever you're running from will follow you. And that means it follows me, too."

Despite the heat of the midday sun, his words send a chill through me. Does he know more than he's letting on?

When Meridan walks away, I resist the impulse to return to my room. It might be the safest thing to do, but I won't let him scare me into hiding this whole journey. There's been too much hiding on my part since I found out who I'm destined to be. Like it or not, I have to stop running away from that.

7

The gentle sway of the ship, the warm sun, and the creaking of the wood and ropes lull me into the first semblance of relaxation I've felt in too long. No one pays me much mind as I walk back and forth on the decks, marveling at all the work it takes from the crew to keep us moving forward. It feels good to stretch my legs and let my lungs breathe the salty air.

"What do you think?"

And just like that, all the tension in my muscles returns. Alara has managed to sneak up on me, and she's smiling in that way she does that sets my teeth on edge. Despite my best efforts, my eyes flit up the mast to see Felix is still up there by himself.

"It's beautiful," I admit. I know she and Felix have this in common. "And a bit terrifying, if I'm honest."

"You're smart to be a bit afraid of it. The sea is changeable. Don't get too comfortable with it."

"So, it's a bit like you then?" I arch my brow at her in an accusing fashion. "I thought we were moving past all this nastiness, and then you drug me...again."

"It's not my fault you're entirely too trusting. Maybe one day you'll learn your lesson."

"Felix trusts you."

"Well, he can't be perfect in every way," she answers with a shrug. "And I was helping him out. He asked me to look out for you while we were on the ship. It's not my fault he failed to be specific on how I should go about it. Trust me, he's since made it more than clear he's not fond of my methods."

That's interesting. Once again, I have more questions than answers. "And why does he think I need someone to look out for me?" More importantly, why didn't he designate himself as that person?

"Because he's in love with you, you idiot. And he's too kind to show it in front of Ronan, but it's painfully obvious to anyone who has eyes. Felix is entirely too noble to step over the ashes of your wedding dress to claim you as his."

She says all this with no hesitation, no whisper of decorum. It's all out there for anyone to hear. But I can hardly believe I'm hearing it. And I consider the source. My relationship with Felix is between the two of us, and I won't bring Alara into it no matter how badly I want to ask her how she knows this, what she's seen, and what she's heard. If he's avoiding me for whatever reason, I want to hear it from him.

Alara catches me eyeing him in the crow's nest and smiles knowingly. "He's alone up there now. You should join him."

If she's suggesting it, it probably means my company would not be welcome. The ache to see him, to finally be alone with him, is so strong that I just don't care.

"Just climb the ropes then?" Attached to the mast are countless lines of rope, some nearly as thick as my forearm, and a net woven with rope. I'm sure it serves some purpose, but right now all I see it as is my stairway to Felix.

"Just climb the ropes," she affirms.

It's a bad idea. And not only because Alara suggested it. If Felix has not sought me out, it's because he needs space. There have been very few times when I've had to find him rather than him come to me. That period of time in Borealis when Ronan first arrived comes to mind. The ache of going without him for days only to end up arguing and quite literally fighting him in the training arena is seared on my memory. But maybe that's the only way to get him to admit to me how he truly feels. Only when I'm in danger or there's been some supercharged emotion between us has he been pushed to react.

Despite its thickness, the rope sways when I put my foot on the first rung of the net. With a few shaky breaths and my eyes closed, I take the next step. Though my grip strength is excellent from years of handling swords and other weapons, my hands still shake as I climb higher and higher, leaving Alara behind on the deck.

I make the mistake of looking down only once and quickly shut my eyes tight. Everything spins, and it takes several steadying breaths before I have the courage to continue climbing. From that point forward, I keep my eyes lifted and focus on my end goal.

Finally, my fingers find purchase on the wooden floor of the small platform. I'm still working out how to hoist myself up onto the actual lookout basket when large hands encircle my wrists and pull me up. For the breadth of a second, I'm suspended in the air until my feet land solidly on the floor of a small, circular platform with a very skimpy-looking excuse for railing. Immediately I press my back against the giant width of the main mast to gain my bearings, and then I allow myself to take in Felix.

He stands before me, hands at his sides and a poor attempt at a nonchalant stance. If Ronan looked like he was playing dress-up, Felix truly looks the part of the roguish pirate hero.

His plain linen shirt is slightly open at the neck, and his trousers are rolled up nearly to his knees. The exposed skin on his forearms and calves is already a darker shade than when I last saw him. The scar on his calf where he was shot with an arrow escaping the collapsing temple is a pale line across his otherwise tanned skin. The wind and moisture have whipped his usually tamed curls into a dark lion's mane dancing around his scruffy face. But there's something even more remarkable about his appearance. His eyes dance with something I haven't seen before. Though I don't yet understand it, I can clearly see the love of the sea in his eyes.

"What in the world are you doing up here?" I can't tell if he's angry or impressed. Probably some of both. The width of the platform leaves little room between us, but still I have to lean in to hear his words over the roar of the wind.

I try to think of what to say, but suddenly "I just wanted to see you" sounds embarrassingly weak, and I am not that girl. But he's waiting expectantly for an answer. Though he's trying hard to appear somewhat casual about the whole thing, I can see the tension in his shoulders beneath the thin shirt and the way his knuckles whiten as they grip the rail.

"Meridan told me I should really spend the rest of the voyage in my cabin." That should be explanation enough. I was told to do something by someone I don't like, and I have therefore done the opposite of it.

Felix makes a noncommittal noise of consideration. "I might not disagree with him on that." He seems to be trying very hard not to touch me even though there's no room for him to escape up here.

"Well, Alara certainly tried hard enough to make that happen. I don't know whether to strangle her for that or thank her."

His shoulders slump just a bit, and I know he's taking this as a personal failure. "For what it's worth, she and I had a shouting match after I found out what she'd done. I told her I... Well, she won't do it again."

What exactly did he tell her? Her insistence that he loves me springs to mind, but I shove it back down. I want to hear it from him. "You could have just asked me to stay out of the way."

Felix laughs darkly. "We both know that would never have happened. Look at where you're at now. Look at what you did to that sailor when we boarded. Even when you try to restrain yourself, you can't help but charge right into the middle of everything."

"And usually you're right there with me." My voice raises without intent. I don't mean to yell at him, but it definitely comes out more forcefully than I meant. I can't help but think if I had insisted on going to Zephyros, he wouldn't have been by my side. Is he trying to pull away from me? "Why ask Alara to look after me?"

"Someone needs to, and it can't be me."

"Why not?" I do yell this time, and I mean it. His dark eyes widen.

"I'm trying, Emilia. I don't know how to be," he pauses and gestures between us, "whatever this is. I promised myself I wouldn't let it affect my duty, but when you're there I can't think of anything else except... When you had that last dream and you woke up screaming my name, it nearly killed me. Look, it's one thing to try to keep you safe from outside threats, but I'm struggling to keep you safe from yourself. Every time I think I've reasoned with you, you go and do something crazy like this. What on earth possessed you to make that climb?"

"I'm more than capable—"

"Yes, I know you're capable. But you don't have to prove that to me or anyone else. It kills me when you put yourself in harm's way, and sometimes I think you do it just to torture me. Like wanting to go to Zephyros. Where did that come from?"

I consider his words for a bit. There's never really been a doubt that he would step in front of a sword for me. In fact, he's done just that. But the times we've butted heads, it's usually been about him nearly smothering me to keep me safe, failing to let me act. Because he's been doing his *job*. But it's not a job now. I'm no longer a queen and he's no longer my soldier. It's a new balance of power we're both trying to figure out while staying true to who we really are.

"I know." My words are so soft I'm not sure if he hears them before they're carried away on the winds. "What if I don't want the space you're offering? What if I don't want you to back off?" I take a step toward him to illustrate my point. There's barely room for the wind to slip between us.

"Emilia." He sighs and places a hand on my cheek, and I lean into it.

"That's the first time you've really touched me since we left Borealis." It's such a stupid thing to say, but I've been so starved for his touch, for any sign of affection really, that I latch on to even the smallest thing.

"I couldn't," he admits, looking truly apologetic. "I knew that if I touched you, if I even looked at you too long, I wouldn't be able to hide it from Ronan. And I didn't want to cause you trouble with him. There's a lot to figure out…"

Except there isn't, not for me. I know exactly what I want, what I've always wanted. It just took me a while to realize it. But I need him to realize it for himself. Memories of that last kiss—me in my wedding dress and him in that absurdly fine uniform—flood back to me. Heat and so much sadness wrapped up in a desperate gesture. I want a do-over. That can't be the last time I kiss him. I don't want to remember the taste of him mingled with tears. I told him I wanted him. What else is there to say?

"Felix, I—"

"The truth is, I can't focus on anything but you when I'm this close. We can't afford the distraction right now. I have to focus on keeping you safe. On keeping us all safe," he corrects quickly as he drops his hand from my face and gives my hand a quick squeeze. "You have a job to do. When I think about you like... like the last time we... well, I can't focus on protecting you." He pounds the railing with a fist, angry at himself and maybe the world. "Do you know what I was doing while Alara was buying the concoction she used to knock you out? I was picking out this dress for you because I love how this shade of blue looks with the flush on your cheeks."

My cheeks do flush in response to his words, and I duck my head a bit so my hair falls in my face. But he brushes it from my cheek and tucks it behind my ear.

"I'm not trying to be vain, but you need me right now. Maybe more than you ever have." He pauses to let those words sink in. "But I don't want to be *needed.* I don't want to be just a necessity to you."

"Necessity? Felix, I told you I wanted you." Tears sting my eyes, but I'm determined not to let them fall. Something else bubbles up inside me too. Anger. Because how many times do we need to discuss this before he believes me? "What else could you want me to say? I told you I wanted you while I sat on the floor in my wedding dress, about to marry another man."

"Exactly. You needed that escape, a reason not to marry."

I try not to roll my eyes. He's so predictable. There's no way to prove to him that he's more than just a necessity to some mission. He is my choice no matter our circumstances. How foolish I was for thinking now that political obstacles had been removed, we were free to be together. As long as he makes these excuses, we can never be what I hope for. Despite my words, he can't see my need for him is not a physical one but something much deeper. And for my part, I have too much pride to beg him to love me.

"You're right," I finally say. Not because I agree, but because I simply don't have it in me to argue with him. Let him think what he will of that. "But know this, I don't want to be just a job to you either."

He recoils a bit at my response. Well, he can't have it both ways. "It's God's will that you make this journey, Emilia. And I believe it's His will that I protect you."

"I'm so sick of everyone presuming to know what God's will is for my life." The conversation with Ronan opened old scars, and the wounds are still fresh. And just yesterday Felix seemed upset that Antioch would assume to know God's plan for me. What makes him any different? "Maybe I'm not supposed to survive this. Did you ever think about that? You can protect me from a lot of things—sailors, assassins, and Cyrus himself—but you can't protect me from God's plan."

In my attempt to make a dramatic exit, I forget just how high up we are. When I take a step back toward the rope ladder, the ship lists a bit, and I crash into Felix. My hands fly to his chest, and his arms wrap around me as a reflex. I hold on for a moment too long to be convincing as angry.

"You are so infuriating," he growls into my ear, but I don't fully believe his anger either. Breath catches in my chest at the intensity of those dark eyes. In that moment, I wish he was the only thing I had to think about, and I could claim him as mine.

Without another word, he tosses me over his shoulder as if I weigh nothing at all. I slam my eyes shut as he spins around to climb down the rope.

"Wait, wait," I plead. "I-I think I can climb down on my own. I just need a minute."

"Not a chance. Just don't move and keep your eyes closed."

I'm too scared to argue with him. It turns out I'm not a fan of heights. At all. But instead of focusing on how hard the wind blows and how much the ladder moves, I keep my eyes closed and focus on the feel of his muscles under my palms. His back twists and moves with fluid grace as we descend the ladder. It's the most I've ever been allowed to touch him.

But it's over as soon as we reach the main deck. Felix slides me from my position on his shoulder until I stand on my own. I don't even have a chance to thank him before he spins on his heels and begins to walk away.

"Felix!" I shout after him. He keeps walking. "Don't you walk away from me!"

That makes him pause, and then he's striding back toward me with such fire in his eyes that I'm sure I'm about to erupt into flames. He leans into me, pinning me to the mast with his proximity while one of his hands rests against it beside my head.

His mouth is close, and he's panting so hard that his warm breath cuts through the sea breeze and fans my face. I close my eyes, anticipating the hardest of kisses, but it doesn't come.

"Why?" he whispers, and he's so close I almost swallow the word rather than hear it. "Don't torment me, Emilia. When you look at me like this..."

Say it. Just say it.

But he doesn't. Instead, he pushes himself away from the mast and walks away. I don't follow him. Maybe it isn't fair. I don't mean to torture him, but I'm also not willing to give up on this just because it's difficult. My safety is not more important than what I feel for him. I just don't know how to convince him of that.

Slowly I peel myself away from the mast and straighten my skirt the best I can before I march back toward my quarters. Hopefully there's some of Alara's tea left, and I can just knock myself out until this is all over.

8

I don't drink the tea, and I don't stay in my room.

Against my better judgment, I find Alara and accompany her on a clandestine mission to assess the weapons situation on the ship. It's a fruitless excursion because, aside from the cannons on deck, we find very little in the way of weaponry.

When she saunters off to annoy Felix and Ronan, I make a point to visit Antioch. He is predictably in the cabin he shares with Ronan, diligently writing notes by the light of a lamp. This room is laid out the same as the one Alara and I share, and I think maybe Felix got the better end of the deal by volunteering to sleep on the deck.

"Don't you want to come out and see the sun?" I ask once he lets me into the tiny room.

"After so many years without it, it hurts my eyes," he admits as he reseats himself on a bed. I take the other one without asking.

"When I visited you in the tower, you told me I was part of God's plan. And now we know there's a prophecy. How do I fit into that?"

"If I had the answers you seek then I would be God." Antioch smiles weakly, but I'm not amused.

"I brought you with us so you could give us direction. So you could tell us what you know of the Ancient and the Gate and guide us in the right path. Don't make me regret your company." My words are harsh, and it's unfair that he's bearing the brunt of my anger with Felix. But I didn't say anything I didn't mean. I would not have brought along such a frail old man on a rigorous journey where time is of the essence if I didn't expect him to contribute something.

"I have told you what I knew of the Gate and the Ancient. It is a real place where the veil between Heaven and Earth is thin. Not all men are fit to set foot there."

"And what about a woman?"

"I suppose we will see."

That's not the bit of reassurance I'm looking for.

"So, this Princess That Was Promised—"

"I now believe it is more accurately translated as the Ruler Who Will Rise up," he interrupts.

"Fine," I snap. "This Ruler then. What is she supposed to do?"

"The Ancient will give the Ruler power to reign over all nations."

"Actual military power? Because without that I don't see how we can possibly hope to defeat Cyrus. He has an entire army at his disposal." I've begun to let myself consider what this confrontation might look like, but no matter what ideas I chase, it comes down to his army against me. What kind of odds are those?

"I cannot speak to the specifics of the power. It's something I will never know. But, as you say, this power may be the only thing that will allow you to overcome the might of the Empire. I fear you and many others will be dead without it."

I refuse to let that happen. Cyrus intends to take the power of the Gate for himself, but I'm not sure it's that simple. It's not just a matter of getting there first but of being able to approach the Ancient to let His power flow through you. Surely God won't allow Cyrus to approach. But that hardly means I've won. If Cyrus can't access the Gate to ensure his own immortality, he'll at least slaughter every Insurgo he can find in order to stamp out the threat that the prophecy will be fulfilled and his kingdom overthrown.

"Even if we can find the Gate, how do I approach the Ancient? How do I access that power?"

"In order for the power of the Ancient to flow through them, the Ruler will be required to make the greatest sacrifice."

My blood runs cold, and my stomach turns over as it often does when I wake from my nightmares. "What?"

"I did not realize until I was able to study the scriptures you shared with me. There are many passages that mention a sacrifice. The Ruler will be shown by signs and wonders to be chosen of God. The scriptures say that God will provide Himself a sacrifice. I believe the meaning is plain."

I'm grateful to be sitting down because the room is swimming, and I think it has little to do with the waves that knock against the ship. This can't be right, can it? When I mentioned to Felix that perhaps I wasn't supposed to survive this, I didn't mean it. I have feared for my life many times—have even resigned myself to losing it—but not because I thought God would require it of me.

Do I take Antioch's word for it? Is it enough that I die, or must I die at the proper time?

For such a time as this.

Levi's words which set this whole thing in motion come roaring back to me until the blood pounding in my ears drowns them out. I desperately want to search the Aletheia for answers myself, but Meridan has confiscated the only bit of it available to me. And do I really think I'm more qualified to interpret it than Antioch who has studied the scriptures of both Caelus and my God for decades?

I clear my throat and try to pull myself together. "H-how am I supposed to set people free if I die?"

"Our God works in mysterious ways." Antioch sounds almost pleased by this, and I wonder if he's so enthralled with the fulfillment of God's promise that it hasn't occurred to him that this is my actual life. Or maybe it has. Maybe he expects me to go selflessly to my death so that others can live. If that's the case, I'm going to disappoint him. Because, ironically, by embarking on this journey, I have just realized I have so much to live for…even if the object of that is upset with me right now. "No greater love exists than that of a man who lays down his life for his friends."

Oh God, what will Felix say? Can You possibly prepare him for this?

I have no doubt he will view this as the ultimate failure, not on my part but his. When I told him he couldn't protect me from God's plan, this was not what I had in mind.

And Ronan. How will he ever come to believe in the goodness of God if he has to watch me die?

Standing abruptly, I excuse myself from Antioch and return to the confines of my quarters just as everyone has been telling me to. Once inside, I'm relieved to see Alara isn't here. But maybe she can still help me out.

I flip open her pack, pull out the flask containing the tainted tea and toss my head back to drain it. Then I throw the flask back on her bed and lie down on my own to pass out.

I have no idea how much time has passed, nor do I care. Something slowly pulls me from the depths of a dreamless sleep, and I go reluctantly. Though the nightmares did not haunt me while I slept, I still wake with one word in the front of my mind.

Zephyros.

Once again, I shake my head in an attempt to clear it. There is no reason to even entertain the thought of that place. I've never been, but I've had more than enough interaction with people from there to know that it's not a place I want to visit. In addition to the skirmishes I fought against them while in the Borealis army, there's a bitter, vengeful place in my heart for their two princesses—Cassia and Gloriana.

Alara is in her bed now, sleeping soundly from the looks of things. She is much less ferocious when she's sleeping. I wouldn't call it peaceful exactly, but it definitely dulls her sharp edges.

After digging in my pack, I choke down some dried meat and stale, crumbly bread. It's not much, but it's more than I've been able to keep down in a couple days, so I make sure not to overdo it. If this stays down, I can have more later.

Once fed, I stand and smooth the fabric of the blue dress I'm still wearing. What I wouldn't give for a bath. Maybe when we get to Solitarius I'll be able to indulge a bit. Of course, I have no idea what to expect there. For so long I've believed, as has most everyone in the Atlas Empire, that the island was uninhabited and merely used as a source of imported delicacies. Not until Felix told me Solitarius was his home did I realize there was more to it. Still, I didn't have a chance to ask him any of the questions swirling around in my head about the place.

My fingers make deft work of twisting my hair into a long braid before I quietly sneak out the door. A gust of wind hits me full in the face, bringing with it the briny scent of salt water and old wood. I blink my eyes to get them used to the light, then inhale sharply.

The colors of the sky are magnificent—from black to blue to purple to red. The rising sun reflects off the clouds and the water, turning them various shades of red and gold so it looks like they are on fire. As far as I can see, sky melts into sea seamlessly. We could be sailing off the edge of the world and I'd never be able to tell.

I lean against the ship's railing to take it all in. On the deck below me, sailors mill about in what seems to be a carefully choreographed routine. Sails checked, ropes tied, inventory being taken. Nothing seems rushed or urgent as we glide peacefully through the open sea.

After some time, I feel the air shift around me and realize I'm not alone. I brace for Meridan or one of his sailors, but it's Felix who joins me at the rail.

"There's a storm coming," he says as he places his hands on the rail beside me. His tone is completely neutral as if what happened yesterday never happened at all. Except it did. And though he may be pretending he's forgotten about it, I never will. It seems the only way to get a response from him is to do something irrational.

I look up slowly, but he's not looking at me. He's all business, and his eyes are fixed on the gorgeous horizon in front of us. The purple, red, and orange hues create a dramatic backdrop for the rising sun. Sure, there are clouds in the sky, but they hardly look menacing.

"Storm?" I ask, straightening up so I am shoulder to shoulder with him. But I leave the smallest bit of space between us so I can leave it up to him if we actually touch. He doesn't take my hint.

"Red sky at morning, sailor take warning," he says, eyes still fixed in front of him.

"Well, those sailors don't seem too worried about it." I gesture toward the men below us, calmly going about their business.

"Worried? Maybe not, but they're preparing for it." Felix glances at me and just as quickly looks away. "Look there. They're stowing the sails in the rear. Might even put up storm sails if they have them. Regardless, things could get bad."

Oh, he has no idea. I feel guilty for not spilling the news to him about the prophecy, but there's not exactly a good way to bring that up. Especially since there's still unresolved tension from yesterday. Letting him know I plan to die on this journey seems a poor way to make up.

"Emilia, I owe you an apology." He finally turns to look at me. "I promised myself after that night on the rooftop that I wouldn't act like that around you."

I don't have to ask which night he means. It's seared into my memory as the moment he came so close to telling me what he felt for me. The moment he was actually angry at me for the way everything was playing out, and I chose to walk away because I was a slave to the crown. The very argument that led to him turning in his resignation and deciding to leave me behind.

"You're allowed to feel something," I say softly. "It reminds me that you're human."

"If you only knew," he scoffs.

"Then tell me." I don't mean to plead, but I would give almost anything just to hear those words from him. Just to know that everything that's happened in the last few days hasn't changed how he feels about me.

"It's not my place. Especially not here and now. Too many things are changing, and I need to be—"

"Yes, I know you need to be focused on protecting me." This time I do roll my eyes. It's such a circular argument that I could have it in my sleep. But if Antioch's right, Felix has already failed.

"Yes. And with that in mind, I'd like for you to stay in your cabin today. Please."

There's a deeper layer to his tone that keeps me from outright dismissing him. I study his face, a face I know so well and yet not at all. I just can't bring myself to hurt him. Besides, what else am I going to do?

"Because of the storm?"

"It could come up with little warning. Maybe it will be nothing, but I don't think so. I'd like to know you're in the safest place. If something happens, I'll come get you."

And go where? It's not like we could escape the ship, especially in the middle of a storm. I hope I don't have to find out.

With a sigh, I turn to go back to my room. I've almost reached the door when he calls out to me. I whip around so fast that my braid almost smacks me in the face. He's leaning against the railing, much like he was on that rooftop in Borealis, but he says nothing. We lock eyes, and I try to will him to say what I so desperately want to hear.

Instead, a sailor calls his name, and he looks away to receive his instructions. I watch him as he acknowledges with a nod then looks back to me. But the spell has broken, and all he offers me now is a nod while mouthing the words "be safe".

Alara looks up as I enter the cabin then collapses back on her bed with a roll of her eyes.

"Oh, it's you." She sighs dramatically.

"Who were you expecting?" I'm genuinely curious because her options are limited unless she's somehow managed to make friends with the crew.

"Doesn't matter," she mutters as she covers her eyes with the back of her hand as if she were a swooning maiden.

"Well, sorry to disappoint you, but you're stuck with me. I got sent to my room." I collapse on my bed in equally dramatic measure and attempt to kick off my shoes. They're tied too tightly, and I quickly give up.

"By who?" Alara rolls onto her side, props her cheek on her hand, and surveys me.

"Felix," I answer flatly. "Something about a storm coming."

"Hmm..."

I wait for her to say more, but she doesn't. So, I roll to my side and mirror her position with my cheek on my hand. "What?"

"Nothing," she replies with a smirk.

"No, what is it," I demand.

"Do you do everything Felix tells you?" She's grinning at me now, a mocking sort of smile as if I'm a child and she's the knowing adult.

"He's just trying to keep me safe," I shoot back, unsure why I'm angry. Okay, maybe I'm just frustrated at everything.

"And is 'safe' what you want to be?"

I open my mouth to answer, then pause. Because I think maybe she's onto something. If I wanted to be safe I wouldn't be on this ship at all. Come to think of it, I'm not sure it's possible for me to be safe while Cyrus is alive. And if that's the case, shouldn't I at least live while I can? Besides, I can only manage to draw some sort of emotion from Felix when I'm in distress, and I desperately want to poke the bear until he's forced to react.

"What did you have in mind?"

"Well, if there really is a storm coming—and Felix would know about that—then the crew is going to be otherwise distracted, aren't they?"

I nod and wait for her to continue.

"And the captain will be on deck giving orders and making sure we make it through the storm, so his cabin will be empty."

"You're not suggesting—"

"Well, why not?" She sits up and crosses her legs on the bed. "Don't you want your things back? Your book...your necklace?"

Reflexively I reach for my neck where the opal Felix gave me should be. Despite owning it for such a short time, I feel naked without it. And the Aletheia, or what we have of it... It's precious not only because it belonged to Felix, but because it is all we have written down of God's words. And it might hold the key to the answers around my death.

Still, I'm cautious about her suggestion.

“Don't you trust Meridan to give us our things back when we arrive?”

“Meridan is a pirate. Sure, he masquerades as a merchant, but you have to be a little ruthless to illegally trade goods that belong to the Emperor. Solitarius is ripe for the picking, but Cyrus dictates who can gather the harvest. All others are traitors and pirates by definition. So do you really think Meridan's going to give you back a precious gem and a book that may be the only one of its kind on the mainland?”

Of course, he isn't. And some part of me has known that since he confiscated the items for “safekeeping”. Still... “Felix says the storm is going be really bad. Maybe we should just stay here and wait for another opportunity.”

“Felix hasn't been on the water in years, and you haven't been on it at all. Of course, he's going to overreact, especially where you're concerned.”

I don't ask what she means by this, but her words give me a funny feeling in my stomach. He would never be okay with this, but he doesn't know what's at stake. And shouldn't we know as much about this prophecy as we can? Even if I can't understand it, it would be beneficial if Antioch had more time to study the scripture. And as foolish as it may be, I desperately want that necklace back so I can hang on to a small part of Felix no matter what.

"Okay fine," I agree with a huff. "*If* a storm comes up, and only if, then we'll try to sneak into the captain's quarters and retrieve our things."

"And a few weapons," she adds.

"Alara," I warn.

"Emilia," she mocks. "Don't pretend you don't want a sword in your hand."

I swallow hard. She's right, of course. Daggers are fine and more practical, but what I wouldn't give to hear the fine sing of a blade in my hand.

"Fine. But only if we find them quickly. I don't want to risk getting caught."

She seems satisfied with my conditions, but then a strange look comes over her as she studies me. "I noticed the flask was empty when I came in last night."

No judgment. Just a statement, but still, I feel defensive.

"I was thirsty."

No response for a moment and then, "I know what it's like to want to sleep until you can forget everything. But the nightmares are always still there when you wake up."

For the first time, I really let myself wonder about Alara. I know very little about her and honestly haven't cared to learn. She grew up on Solitarius with Felix yet somehow ended up leading an Insurgo rebellion on the mainland. She's never mentioned any family, and it doesn't seem like she had a difficult time leaving anyone behind to come on this journey with us.

I'm really bad at this. Should I ask her to elaborate? I don't for one minute think she's about to tell me the story of her past, but it seems insensitive not to show an interest. And I am interested, but I know what it feels like to not want to talk about nightmares. My conflicting emotions must show on my face because Alara laughs darkly.

"Relax, princess. I'm not planning to unload my troubles on you today. Let it suffice to say that you're not the only one with a dragon to slay."

Then she rolls over to go back to sleep.

9

Felix is right.

It must be early afternoon when the storm begins to roll in. There are no windows in my room, so I can only imagine how dark the sky must be, but the gusts of wind that slam into the side of the ship are enough to toss me from my bed. The ship lists back the other direction and Alara pitches out of her bed and lands on top of me.

"Ouch!" She's elbowing me in the side, and I think it might be on purpose. But she ignores me and crawls a few feet toward the door. She pushes and nothing happens.

"Come help me," she grunts as she twists the knob and puts all her weight against the door. "The wind's pushing it closed."

I try to stand and immediately fall to my knees. So, I crawl as well until I can press my shoulder against the door beside her. We count to three, then both shove until the door flies open, and we spill out onto the covered portion of the quarterdeck.

It takes a moment for the chaos playing out in front of me to register. Rain pounds the deck, falling in such a thick curtain that it's difficult to see more than a few feet in front of us. Everything is soaked and flooded, and I can just make out waves tall enough to crest the side of the ship. I don't know where the sky ends and the sea begins. The few sailors I can make out run back and forth across the deck, securing lines and cannons that threaten to break free and crush anyone in their path. The wind roars so loudly that I can't make out anything they are shouting to one another. Their mouths move, but from here there is no sound above the storm. Barrells roll around the main deck, crashing into the side of the ship and spilling rum which is quickly washed away by the downpour.

My eyes dart to each man until I realize I'm searching for Felix. Certainly, Ronan and Antioch are safely inside their quarters, but Felix has no room, and even if he did, he wouldn't stay in it if there were lives in danger. I bet he's right in the middle of the rest of these sailors.

"C'mon," Alara yells into my ear. She grabs my arm and half drags me backward until we're standing in front of Captain Meridan's door. Still, neither of us can make it to our feet for more than a few seconds, but from our knees, we lock eyes and nod a silent agreement. It's now or never. And if I am to have any idea about this prophecy that might lead to my death, I need that book back.

Alara wraps a hand around the door knob and pulls until her shoulders strain, and her hand slips from the slippery metal. Once again, the wind is working against us.

"I can't hold on," she admits.

I push her aside and plant myself on my knees in front of the door. My grip strength is exceptional from years of wielding swords and daggers, and while Alara is eager for weapons, I don't think she's had that much practice with them. Hopefully, I will be enough.

I wrap my fingers around the knob and focus to concentrate all my strength there. Muscles strain, and I let out a frustrated scream before the door flies open, caught by the wind. We scramble inside with no care to shut the door behind us.

There is no time to take in the details of Captain Meridan's quarters. I'm aware that it's large, with a few more pieces of furniture than just a bed, huge windows banking the back wall, and it's relatively dry compared to the deck we just crawled in from. But that's changing rapidly since we left the door open and there's nothing to impede the flow of rain and sea from rushing in the door every time the ship rolls from one side to the other.

Alara and I fling open every drawer and cabinet we can find. We toss clothing, papers, maps, and charts to the floor in our haste. I can't think about the ramifications of that, but we don't have the luxury of stealth here. Finally, while blindly searching the bottom drawer of a small dresser, my fingers wrap around something thin and metallic.

I pull it out and am relieved to see my necklace. The black opal still dangles from the dainty chain with the broken clasp. Since there is no way for me to wear it in its broken state, I shove it down the front of my dress and continue rifling through the captain's things.

"Find anything?" I call out to Alara.

"Just this," she yells back as the wind gives an inhuman howl. She's holding up a cutlass as if she has no idea how to use it. I've never swung one myself, but it can't be that different than the double-edged short swords that I favor.

"Give it to me." I hold out a hand to take it from her just as the ship lists violently, and from the deck outside, I hear the splintering of wood. My eyes widen as Alara drops the weapon and we both go skidding across the soaked floor until we slam into a wall.

Just as suddenly, two pairs of hands grab each of my arms and jerk me violently to my feet. I can't see, but judging by the scream Alara lets out, she's in a similar predicament. Four of Meridan's men, with hair and clothing plastered to their bodies, drag us from the captain's quarters and out into the storm.

Out on the deck, everyone is oddly still given that we're in the midst of a storm that's threatening to break apart the ship. No more running about to tend to sails or cargo. As if they've given up. They all stand in a circle but part to allow our captors room to drag us through. And when I see what's in the middle of that circle, my blood runs cold.

Ronan and Antioch are held by one sailor each, neither struggling. Antioch in fact, almost looks at peace. As if he's unbothered that this might not end well.

And then there's Felix. Two men restrain him as well, and even through the torrential downpour, I can see the cut on his head that indicates they had to ambush him to even get this far.

When he sees me, he strains toward me and causes such a fuss that one of Alara's captors leaves her to help restrain Felix.

Is all this for being found in Meridan's quarters? How did they even know to look for us there, and why were they looking for us at all when there are clearly much bigger problems at hand?

But when one sailor steps forward, eyes boring into me as he shakes something in his hand, I know this is about something much more.

"All right, dearie," he yells over the storm. "We've cast lots for everyone except you two to see who's responsible for this. Now it's your turn."

I don't understand his meaning, but he turns to Alara and tosses two dice at her feet. They must be carved from some heavy stone because they remain still long enough for us all to see that they come up with white paint on top. A low mumble passes through the crowd as the man turns his attention to me. I hold his gaze with my chin tilted as high as I dare. What do I have to fear from a pair of dice?

A lot, as it turns out. I imagine I hear them hit the deck, but I definitely hear the collective gasp that rises up around me as all eyes turn to the two stones. I meet Felix's eyes from across the circle for just the briefest of moments and then look down at my fate.

Two black die.

"It's her!" A shout comes from somewhere in the back of the crowd, someone so far back they couldn't have possibly seen the dice. But maybe they didn't need to. They've known it was me all along. "Emilia Stormbringer. I knew it!"

And several more sailors join in the shouts, some with my name, some with yells of anger and terror. I'm right there with them. I want to shout my highest hopes to the heavens and release the fear swelling so fast inside me it threatens to drown me. But I remain silent because words won't come. Not that they would hear me over the roar of the waves and wind anyway. The sound is unlike anything I've heard before, and with every crashing wave I'm sure the ship is going to break into pieces.

"It's because of her we're going to die!" One voice cuts clearly through the downpour and pierces my heart. If only that were the first time it had been said about me. But this isn't my fault. I can't control the weather, no matter what happened at the temple in Borealis.

"Throw her overboard!"

I can't pick out which one starts it, but soon a chant erupts amidst the sailors of "Overboard, overboard!"

"No!" Felix strains against his captors as the word tears out of him. I glance over and see it seems to take everything all three men have to keep him restrained.

Felix's face is wild with terror and desperation. When I look to his right to see Ronan's reaction, it's one of solemn resignation, as if he has already accepted my fate. As if he is powerless to change it. That, more than anything else, sparks a fire within me. He may be powerless, but I am not.

"I am no Stormbringer," I scream into the rain and nearly choke on it. "This is not my doing."

A few of the sailors' lips still to hear my words, but most keep chanting. Captain Meridan pushes his way through the knot of men until he stands directly before me and my companions. He raises a hand, and the chant dies away. For a few seconds, only the sound of the raging storm echoes around us.

"I knew it was bad luck to have women on board." His eyes fix on me, not even sparing Alara a glance. "But I was willing to risk it for the price you paid. Now the toll is higher. You will kill us all."

"I won't," I say, but I'm sure he doesn't hear me because my voice is so hoarse.

"Do you deny you are Emilia Stormbringer. The one who brought down the temple and caused so much devastation?"

Is there any point in denying it? In trying to explain? I've seen that sort of fear in a man's eyes before and know instinctively he will try to kill me no matter what I say. There is no reason to be had in this conversation even if I had some to impart…which I don't. I still can't make sense of what happened at the temple. How could I begin to explain that it wasn't me to a ship full of panicked men in the middle of this raging storm?

I raise my chin, hoping to exude a courage I don't feel, and reply as calmly as I can, "I am she."

Though it must come as a surprise to none of them, the confirmation sends another wave of shouts throughout the crowd of men. In the periphery of my vision, I see Felix lash out at one of the men holding him, almost succeeding in breaking free, but not quite. This earns him a hard blow across the face and a kick in the back until he buckles to his knees. I want to scream at him to stop fighting. It's useless. Even if he could break free, what then? What could he possibly hope to do against all these men?

"Forgive me, Captain." Several heads whip around as Alara's voice somehow rings out over the wind and waves. "Wouldn't it be worse luck to kill a person than to let women remain onboard?"

"She brought this storm upon us," Captain Meridan insists.

"I thought you said it was bad luck?"

I can't believe she's actually going to argue semantics in this situation. She's got even more guts than I gave her credit for.

"I-it is." But he doesn't sound as certain now.

"Well then, if it's simply bad luck, then she can't be the one controlling the storm, now can she? And in that case, will it really do much good to throw her overboard to certain death and bring more bad luck upon the vessel?"

An eerie quiet falls despite the chaos around us, and for just a moment I have a glimmer of hope. I'm actually going to owe Alara for saving my life, or so I think. Because just when I think we might somehow make it out of this, the expression on Captain Meridan's face hardens, and he lunges toward me, pulling me from the arms of the sailors who held me back. With three quick steps, he drags me to the railing, hoists me in his arms, and hurls me into the sea.

10

The first thing I'm conscious of is the darkness surrounding me. I can't see anything, and it takes interminable moments to realize it's because my eyes are clamped shut. I force them open, and my body immediately seizes into a panic as all my other senses return to me. Or most of them do. But the iciness of the water has left my limbs numb, and for that, I'm a bit grateful. Because I'm already overloaded.

My lungs heave for air that does not come. Wave after wave slams into me, turning me head over heels until I'm not sure which way is up. It's still so dark.

Oh God, this is it. This is how I die. Before I've even had a chance to fulfill Your plan.

"You are my plan," a voice whispers back to me. Or maybe it's all in my head.

"Be still," the same voice says. But that doesn't make sense. Shouldn't I fight? It's too difficult to think right now. It's too difficult to do anything.

So, I close my eyes again and let the darkness take me.

11

"She's awake!"

A voice, distant and muffled, makes a tiny crack in the darkness. Am I awake? Or is this just another dream, another hallucination my mind has concocted to cope with the uncopable?

Rough hands pull me toward something solid, and some extra sense I didn't know I possessed registers that it's Felix. Felix who is holding me. Felix who is shaking slightly with what might be tears. I can only open my eyes a sliver so I can't be sure about the tears, but my face is pressed against his chest as he holds onto me as if I'm the only thing keeping him from slipping off the edge of the world.

"Emilia!" It's Ronan this time. His voice seems somehow closer, though I know he can't be closer than Felix. "I thought we'd lost you."

Then he's right there, too. He doesn't pull me from Felix's arms, but his much smoother hand cups my cheek, and I manage to open my eyes a bit more to take in the worried expression on his handsome face. Just beyond him, I can make out the blurry silhouettes of Alara and Antioch sitting toward the back of whatever vessel we're in. Because we are definitely still in a boat and not on dry land. I can feel the gentle rocking of the waves.

And they are gentle. The storm no longer rages, and the wind no longer howls. It's as if the lion has transformed to a lamb. I guess Captain Meridan was right, but I have no idea what that means. Did I really do that?

"Wh-what happened?" My voice is hoarse and barely above a whisper. I'm not sure anyone can hear me since my face is still crushed against Felix's chest. He seems unwilling or unable to let me go, and I am not about to protest. It's warm here. But with that realization comes the revelation that I am absolutely freezing, and Felix and I are both shaking.

"Shhh, don't try to talk," Ronan insists as he removes his hand from my face and sits back to take me in. "There will be plenty of time for explanations later. Felix," he turns his gaze on his friend, "we should get back to rowing."

Slowly, reluctantly, the hands that hold me so tightly relax their grip, and I am able to recline back and take in the face of the man who has still yet to speak. Felix looks wrecked. Even beneath his tan complexion, his skin is pale and drawn. As if he's aged years since I last saw him. He mouths wordlessly as if he's trying to decide what, if anything, to say. But nothing comes out, and he hangs his head for a moment then moves to take his place at an oar without another look my way.

I'm not offended. I understand. Even if I could get the words out, the things I want to say to him are best left until we are alone and not said in front of Alara, Antioch, and especially Ronan. Who knows when we will be alone again, but I'll hold my words in my heart until then, and I pray he will do the same.

Pray. I remember now praying just before I slipped under the waves for the last time. Feeling some unnamed emotion as I realized I would not fulfill the quest I set out on. But then that voice—God I suppose—answered me. Clearly. I'm certain of it now. *You are my plan.*

I still don't know what it means, and I'm not sure why it should make me feel better, more assured, when the weight of this ambiguous prophecy has filled me with almost nothing but dread. But these words feel more personal, a bit comforting even. As if who I am has not been forgotten in the bigger plan. Apparently, I am necessary, at least for a while longer, or I wouldn't still be here. Right?

It's just too much for right now. My body aches, I'm still shivering with cold, and my voice is completely useless. My eyes are heavy, but just as they are drifting closed, Alara positions herself next to me in the bottom of the boat and shakes me none too gently.

I moan because every inch of my body hurts, and she actually gives me an apologetic look.

"You need to stay awake," she insists. "At least for a few more hours until we know you're not going to die on us."

Well, that's comforting. "I'm not dead?" I mumble. "Because it really feels like it."

"You did give it a valiant effort," she answers with a shrug. "If Felix hadn't…"

Hadn't what? "He's going to be furious with me."

Alara gives me a sidelong look. "I don't think furious is the word you're looking for."

"How are you, my child?" Antioch joins us, preventing me from asking Alara to expound upon her statement. But I don't like discussing Felix with her anyway. I always end up feeling inadequate.

"Like I've been stampeded by a thousand horses and then drug behind a carriage." I try to sit up, but the pain in my abdomen is sharp and takes my breath away. I gasp and immediately lie back down. My chest and throat burn, and even the smallest movement requires the maximum effort.

"But you're alive." He smiles, but I wonder if he's somewhat disappointed. I was supposed to be a sacrifice, and I can't even manage to die properly. "It wasn't your time," he continues as if he guessed my thoughts.

No one has any pithy response to that, so the three of us sit in silence while Felix and Ronan row the boat. I'm shivering, but there's nothing dry to add warmth, so I just curl in on myself. Alara shakes me periodically to make sure I'm still breathing but mostly leaves me alone.

It must be hours before anyone speaks again. It's Ronan who makes the announcement.

"There's land ahead."

Forgetting my condition, I sit up suddenly, eager to get a glimpse of what he's seeing, and immediately gasp as white, hot pain shoots through me. Felix is there, supporting me as I try to remain seated and not collapse back into the fetal position. But he says nothing.

Alara joins Ronan at the oar Felix abandoned and peers ahead at the solid mass in front of us. Once my vision clears from the pain, I take it in as well. There is coastline as far as I can see, most of which is built up with towering structures and several piers. This is no obscure coastal town like the one we set sail from.

"Zephyros," Ronan says flatly. Something inside me flutters in response to his pronouncement, but I say nothing. Beside me, Felix sighs heavily. "Not my first choice of port."

"Are you insane?" Alara's voice knifes through my haze. "It's suicide to go ashore here."

"I don't see what other choice we have. We need a place to rest and regroup." Ronan rakes his hands through his hair before pinching the bridge of his nose.

"Felix," Alara glares pointedly at him. "Talk some sense into your friend."

Ronan flares up. "I am the prince, and—"

"I don't care who you are. You're going to be just as dead as the rest of us if we get caught."

Felix looks down at me, and his eyebrows lift slightly in question. He's asking if this is what I want. And it's not, but I still think it needs to happen, and I don't have the strength to voice my opinion on the matter. I'm so tired. So very tired. So, I nod slightly.

His jaw tightens, and I know he's going to have to make a decision he very much doesn't want to. "I think we have to go ashore. Emilia needs to get some place safe and—"

"There is no place safe. Especially here." Alara is clearly exasperated with both men. I understand her more in this moment than maybe I ever have. She's right about no safe place, and it does seem foolish to go ashore at the one place that might be more dangerous to me than anywhere besides Aurora itself.

"Look." Ronan sighs and reaches for his oar again. "We need to buy some time and make new plans. I have an idea that will give us that time and maybe a few resources."

"Ro, are you sure?" Felix addresses the prince but glances down at me. He's really asking me.

"No," Ronan admits. "I have no idea what information my father is sharing with the other kings or how fast it will reach them. We have to hope that the last news they received was that Emilia and I were to be wed in order to broker peace with the Insurgos."

"And if they know more?" Alara challenges with narrowed eyes.

"Then we're dead."

No one has a response to that. Felix removes his hand from my back and resumes his spot at the oar opposite Ronan. Alara comes back to join Antioch and me.

"This is madness," she mutters. "And you didn't even try to stop them. You outrank them all, and you just let them…"

Just a few days ago her statement would have been entirely accurate. I was to be Queen of Borealis with Felix as my

Commander of the Queensguard and Ronan as my Prince Consort. But now I am none of those things and neither are they. We are just five people in a rowboat who have impossibly survived a storm at sea.

"Where else could we go?" I finally speak up. My voice is still weak and my throat aches as well. Every syllable requires effort. I am in no shape to fight or protest even if I wanted to.

"Can't you pray and have God blow us to Solitarius?" It's a halfhearted ask, but Alara looks hopeful all the same.

"Doesn't work like that," I mutter. How it does work is a mystery to me as well, but I don't presume to think I can ask God for my every whim, and He'll grant me my wish. My prayers may be heard, but I don't control which way the wind blows.

Alara, Antioch, and I remain silent as the shoreline of Zephyros grows larger and the danger grows closer. Felix and Ronan speak softly to each other, but I can't make out anything they're saying. Formulating some sort of plan, no doubt. After all the years they've spent together, they have a sort of shorthand language between them that no one else is privy to. I wonder if they've ever had to use it in a situation like this.

After some time, our boat runs ashore on a small section of barren beach hemmed in by rock formations on one side and what looks to be a guard post in the distance on the other side. Ronan and Felix hop out of the boat and pull it further onto the sand so it won't float away as Alara and Antioch disembark.

Then it's just me left in the boat, and I'm puzzling how I'm going to manage to stand when Felix puts one foot back in the boat and stoops as if to lift me.

And then Ronan is right there as well. "I'll carry her," he insists. Felix frowns.

"No, I really—"

"Felix, if they attack us, it's better that your hands are free than mine. I promise I'll do everything in my power to keep her safe."

The three of us look between one another as if trying to gauge everyone else's reaction.

"Besides," Ronan continues. "How will it look if I have someone else carry my wife? If we don't sell this, we're done for."

Ah. So, the deception they've agreed upon involves me being Ronan's wife. A step up from the fiancé I was on Meridan's ship. Necessary to whatever plot they've concocted, but I cannot wait for the day when I don't have to pretend to belong to anyone.

Felix shakes his head slightly and steps out of the boat to give Ronan space to pick me up. "If anything happens, take her and run."

"No. We're not leaving anyone behind." I put as much authority in my voice as I can manage, but it's not much.

"We won't leave him," Ronan agrees. "Now, for this to have a hope of working, I need you to just stay quiet. I'm going to tell them that we were shipwrecked while on our honeymoon tour of the empire, and you need immediate shelter to recover. The hope is they will see that you're in dire condition and not ask too many questions."

"Or they might just celebrate that she's on the brink of death," Alara points out.

"You underestimate just how much power the Imperial Crown holds," Ronan replies. His tone holds the first bit of authority I've heard from him in a while. With the way his world has been turned upside down as of late, it's easy to forget that this authoritative, commanding nature has been bred into him.

Alara doesn't argue further, and we begin the trek toward the guard post in the distance. I burrow my face into Ronan and try not to think of how different he feels than Felix.

After a while his pace slows, and I know we must be getting close now.

Please, God, let us live.

The prayer rises up in me, unbidden, until I remember that maybe I'm not supposed to live. But surely my companions are. So, I amend my prayer.

Keep them safe.

"You there!" Ronan's shout jostles me from my prayers. "We need help here."

Seconds later two guards stand before us, hands on the pommels of their swords and giving us a wide berth. A smart move even though we appear unarmed. I'm not sure if anyone made it off Meridan's ship with a dagger, but we outnumber them and could easily disarm them if we wanted to.

"Who are you? Where did you come from?" One guard demands. I turn my head a little to get a look at him.

Both of them are young and seem nervous. No doubt they've been given this stretch of beach to guard because nothing ever happens here. They are definitely in for a surprise.

"I am Ronan Dominus, Prince of Aurora and Prince Consort to Queen Emilia Aurelius of Borealis."

The guards exchange wary looks. It's not every day a queen and a prince wash up on the shore, but Ronan says it with enough authority that they can't outright dismiss it.

"What would a prince and a queen be doing in Zephyros?" The other guard asks skeptically. "No one here is expecting you. Do you expect us to believe that you planned to walk into our country with no preparation and no planning?"

Good point. If we had been heading to Zephyros intentionally and on an official visit, there would have been weeks of planning leading up to our arrival. Extra security, celebrations, all sorts of kinks to work out. But we have none of that.

"It was a surprise wedding gift for my bride," Ronan insists as he reflexively pulls me tighter against him. "I wanted to take her on a tour of the empire for our honeymoon. No fanfare, I just wanted her to see the beauty each country had to offer. But while we were at sea, a storm came up. Surely you must have seen it."

The men exchange looks, and I know they witnessed the storm, too. I don't know how far out to sea we were when it hit, but I imagine it could be seen if not felt for miles.

"I don't know..." One guard hedges.

"Look." Ronan shifts my weight until he can hold out his right hand just a bit, and I hear the guards gasp. The signet ring. Somehow through all this, Ronan has managed to hold on to his ring, his symbol of power. He is no longer holding back.

"I'm asking you to escort us to the palace so my wife can rest and recover." Though he says he's asking, he gives the request like a command. "She's ill and freezing, and you don't want the death of a queen on your hands, do you?"

"N-no, sir. Apologies, Your Highness. Majesty," he corrects quickly. Both guards drop to their knees and bow their heads. Ronan adjusts his grip on me, and I feel a bit of tension seep from him. He's just as relieved as I am that we appear to be over this first hurdle.

"Enough of that." Felix steps in, brushing past us and standing between all of us and the guards now. "Just get us to the palace as quick as you can."

"Yes, of course." They stumble to their feet. "Follow us. We'll arrange for a carriage to take you straight there."

Good. Because I don't think I could sit upright on a horse right now.

"Do you think they believe you?" I whisper to Ronan as we follow the guards up a trail on the beach to a stable.

"I hope so," he whispers back. "I'm sorry I had to lie to them. But hopefully it won't be for long. We just need to buy enough time for you to heal and for us to gather supplies, and then we'll be off again."

It takes longer than I'd like for the carriage to be prepared for us. Though the wind has dried my clothes for the most part, I'm shivering. What I wouldn't give for a warm bed and some hot food.

Ronan passes me off to Felix in order to finalize the arrangements with the carriage driver, and I snuggle into the Commander unabashedly. Felix sighs and lowers his mouth to my ear. His breath fans my face and sends a desperately needed warmth through me.

"You know," he whispers, "you really don't need to go to such lengths to be right."

"What do you mean?" I whisper back.

"You wanted to go to Zephyros, and here we are. You didn't need to call for a storm to do it." He shifts slightly until his forehead rests against mine and mutters softly, with an almost incredulous chuckle. "You were right. I can't protect you from God's plan."

But he doesn't sound defeated. In fact, he sounds almost relieved. Something changed when I went into that water, and I desperately want to explore it. But I also desperately want to sleep.

"Can I rest now?" I ask. "Because I'm not dead." No, that didn't come out right. Alara said I couldn't sleep until they knew I wasn't going to die. But Felix doesn't seem to need me to explain it to him. He laughs again and tightens his hold on me.

"Yes, you can rest."

12

But rest doesn't come. It's a somewhat short ride from the stables to the palace, but every bump in the road jars my body. All five of us are crammed into this small carriage, and I'm positioned between Felix and Ronan, both of whom are wound as tight as I've ever seen them.

After we pull through the gates of the palace, Felix exits the carriage first, followed by Alara and Antioch. Despite the hasty arrangements Ronan made with the guards at the stable, several wary soldiers gather around our transport, hemming us in in case we wanted to make an escape. We are well and truly trapped.

I feel the weight of a thousand gazes upon us as Ronan lifts me from the carriage and places me into Felix's waiting arms. No argument over who will carry me now, except from me.

"Can't I walk?" I look between the two men, hoping one of them will be persuaded. I might not be able to manage it, but I want to try.

"It's important we keep up the story that you're ill or injured," Ronan answers apologetically. "I know you don't want to appear weak, but our charade sort of depends on it."

He understands me better than I realized. But this is about keeping us all alive and not my pride. After a weak nod, I duck my head against Felix, and Ronan leads us toward the palace.

In my attempt to look as weak and pitiful as possible, admittedly not a difficult feat, I don't get a good look at the palace as we approach the front entrance, but my impression is that it's huge. Much bigger than my home in Borealis, and possibly bigger than the Emperor's palace in Aurora. The courtyard where we stood is as large as the marketplace in my city and is hemmed in with golden gates. The palace itself is a wonder of soaring marble columns and arches.

"We could get lost here," I whisper to Felix as we step into a great hall with black and white checkered floors that disorient me with just a glimpse.

"I won't let them separate us," he promises. "Whatever happens, we stay together."

But we follow the guards through so many turns and passageways that I quickly lose track. If I had to find my way back out of here, I would be completely lost. Finally, our party comes to a halt outside an intricately carved door, and the guard leading us turns to address Ronan.

"The royal family is having their meal, but the king has asked that you be brought in so he can hear your petition and your identity can be verified by the princesses."

Oh no. Cassia and Gloriana. They've hated me since we met in Aurora. Would have no doubt killed me then if they'd had the chance. But they loved Ronan or at least the power he symbolized. Hopefully, that's enough to keep us safe. Then I remember something else. They are the ones who started the rumors about Felix and I having some sort of secret tryst behind Ronan's back.

"Put me down," I hiss to Felix as I press my hands against his chest. They cannot see me cradled in Felix's arms if this deception is to work.

Surprised by my resistance, he nearly drops me before relaxing his hold so I can land on my feet.

"What are you doing?" he whispers as he places a steadying hand on my back. All eyes have turned to us, so I do my best to give a weak smile.

"I'll explain later. Just don't let me fall," I mutter. To everyone else I say, "I'm ready."

Ronan gives me a questioning look, and I know he thinks I'm undermining everything he's done thus far, but he'll have to trust me on this. Finally, he nods to the guard who pushes open the door and announces us.

"His Imperial Highness Prince Ronan, Queen of Borealis Emilia Aurelius, and Lord Commander Felix Fidelis of the Royal Guard." His voice booms into the silence of the room at large, and Felix nudges me forward to follow Ronan inside.

My steps are shaky, but Felix walks close beside me, careful not to touch. He must have some idea of the reason for my insistence that he does not carry me inside.

Ronan notes my slowness, and returns to my side, offering his arm. I take it with a grateful look as we slowly approach the table where six people sit. Two are Cassia and Gloriana—just as icily beautiful as I remember. Even in the absence of a court audience, they look like perfection. Their light brown hair swept up into elegant chignons, pale skin perfectly powdered, blue eyes accentuated by just a bit of kohl strategically smudged. I don't have to look down to know I pale in comparison.

Across from them sit a small boy and girl, maybe as old as six or seven. Twins perhaps? Certainly, very close in age with striking dark hair and pale green eyes. Eyes that look strangely familiar to me, but I can't quite place them.

Next to the children, at the head of the table sits a man who is unmistakably the king. Not because he is wearing any official regalia, but because his bearing exudes confidence and certainty. I'm shocked to find he's much younger than I anticipated—probably only a few years older than Felix. I expected someone my father's age.

Then the grief hits me like a punch to the gut. Of course. This is a new king, put into place after Cyrus murdered the reigning monarchs of each nation as they departed the King's Council in Aurora, my father included. This must be the princesses' older brother then.

A tense standoff occurs as the king rises and faces Ronan, both waiting to see who will bow first. I'm not sure what the proper protocol is. Normally Ronan would outrank any of the vassal kings of the Atlas Empire, but he has supposedly renounced his position as Crown Prince to marry me. Still, the fair-haired king inclines his head slightly to us and stretches out an arm to gesture for us to approach.

Ronan leads me closer to the table, and I feel Felix right behind me. I'm hemmed in by the strength of these two men, and I'm grateful for it. Because the daggers Cassia and Gloriana glare at me make my hands shake. I tighten my grip on Ronan's arm and crush the other hand into a fist to hide this.

"Welcome, Your Majesties. Please excuse our less than warm welcome, but we were not expecting you." The king's tone is calm and deliberate but not suspicious. "As I'm sure you understand, there has been a lot of unrest around the empire of late, and we cannot be too careful with security. Since I've not previously had the pleasure of meeting either of you, my sisters will need to verify that you are who you say."

Cassia and Gloriana are already clambering to their feet, almost tripping over one another to perform deep curtsies in front of Ronan and me. If I had the energy, I'd roll my eyes at the display. Even after everything that's happened, even after being told that he's *married*, they are still competing for Ronan's affection.

"Oh Ronan, Emilia, it's so good to see you," Cassia gushes as she rises and envelops me in a hug that has Felix stepping even closer to me. She releases after a moment and holds me at arm's length. "But oh, you look dreadful."

"Poor thing," Gloriana agrees as she pats my hair as if I'm some sort of pet. But she's not fooling me. I see the deception in both their eyes.

Ronan clears his throat, and both girls take a respectful step back. "As you can see, we are all very lucky to have survived the storm that blew us so near your port. But I'm afraid my dear wife received the worst of it. She isn't well. Would it be possible for us to stay a day or two in the palace while she recovers? We don't require any fanfare or special services."

"Well, of course, you shall have anything you need." The last person at the table, a woman who I hadn't gotten a good look at until now, approaches us with a tender smile on her pretty face. I take her in—dark hair, olive-toned skin, and pale green eyes—and fail to stifle a gasp as my knees buckle.

Ronan reaches for me, but it's Felix who scoops me up in his arms before I can fall to the ground.

"Perhaps the infirmary first?" Felix suggests as he tries his best to shield me from prying eyes.

"Of course not," the woman—the queen—insists. "You will take rooms in my apartments. There is plenty of space, and I will have my personal attendants see to you."

"Verity, my dear, it's not proper—"

"She's been through enough," the woman pleads with her husband. "Wouldn't you want me treated the same if I washed up on the shore somewhere?"

"Yes, of course, my dove, but those are your private chambers."

"I've been lost in all that space since I moved in there." Her tone is kind but firm, and for all my shock, I'm intrigued by the way they interact. I've never heard a queen speak to her king this way and not be reprimanded for it. "I might as well fill it with our friends who need our help."

"Very well," the king acquiesces. "Guards, take them—"

"Oh, no I'll take them," the queen—Verity—interjects. There's a moment of silence where I imagine her husband must look at her in exasperation, but I don't witness it, because I'm too afraid to look at her. At least in front of this audience. Because I know what I saw in those green eyes. I've seen them several nights in my nightmares.

Levi.

13

We spill into the queen's apartments, and the rest of my group breathes a collective sigh. I don't join in until the queen shuts the door behind us, leaving the guards outside the door. She must be very sure of herself if she's willing to lock herself in a room with the five of us.

"Please, sit," she instructs. Gone is even the hint of formality she displayed in the dining room. Her tone is quick and fervent as if we all share a secret. "I'll be right back with my maids and some things to fix you all up."

We all just stare at her, waiting on the ambush or whatever dreadful thing is to befall us next. No one expected this welcome. When we don't follow her instructions, she redoubles her efforts.

"Please. You can trust me." She lifts the hem of her dress just enough to show the edge of the shift underneath. In stark contrast to the crisp, white linen is a tiny cross embroidered in red thread.

Alara gasps, but she seems to be the only one other than me to understand the significance. It's the symbol Insurgos rebels in Borealis—and maybe elsewhere—wove into their clothes in inconspicuous places to identify themselves to others. And the new queen of Zephyros has just outed herself as one of those rebels.

Ronan and Felix exchange puzzled glances, and Antioch remains silent as usual. The queen's eyes focus on me, waiting for me to acknowledge her allegiance. It's unsettling the way those eyes search me. As if I'm transported back to that military camp where all this started. As if I'm looking into Levi's face before I swung the death blow.

"It's all right," I say with a resigned sigh. "She's safe."

Relieved that I have not dismissed her offering, she excuses herself from the room as Felix sets me on a divan, and the others take seats in various chairs and cushions around the room. All except Felix that is. He stands beside me, refusing to sit as if he needs to be near me but doesn't want to seem improper.

"What was that all about?" Ronan asks.

So, I explain to him about the cross and what it means to mark yourself as Insurgo. His eyes grow wider as Alara adds in details she knows from her time in various Insurgo camps.

Finally, he says, "the Queen of Zephyros is an Insurgo?"

"Did you know this?" Felix asks me. Perhaps he suspects I had some inkling of it, had heard some rumor, since I wanted to come here.

"No," I answer truthfully. "I couldn't have anticipated this."

"We should still be careful," he warns. "Even if she's willing to help us, she is surrounded by people who would just as soon see us dead." I know he's thinking of the princesses. "We should still take turns with a watch. I can—"

"No." My tone leaves no room for argument. Four pairs of eyes turn to me. "No. We're all going to rest. We're going to patch ourselves up, hopefully have something to eat, and then we're all going to sleep."

"Emilia, I—"

I cut Felix off with a level gaze and silently dare him to challenge me.

"I'll be fine," he insists weakly, but it's unconvincing because he's literally swaying on his feet.

"It wasn't a request." I feed his words back to him, and his lips twitch as if he considered a smile. Then he retreats to a cushion on the opposite side of the room as Alara joins me on the divan.

"You two really need to work on how you say 'I love you'," she says under her breath but with a roll of her eyes.

I'm saved having to respond when the door opens, and Queen Verity reenters followed by three maids whose arms are laden with small jars, bandages, and blankets. Alara is directed to a chair to make room for the work they need to do. The women make quick work of Antioch and Alara, who are relatively unharmed save for a few blisters on Alara's hands from rowing. Still, they spread a salve on her hands, wrap them in bandages, then place plush blankets around both their shoulders.

Then the maids turn their attention to Felix, Ronan, and I. I try to see what they're doing to them, but Verity and my nurse block my view.

"Tell me what happened," Verity insists gently as she takes my hand while the nursemaid drapes a blanket around me. Both the weight and the warmth of it pull a soft groan of comfort from me. "We could see the storm from here, but I had no idea you were in it. I have prayed for you, and I sensed you would be coming, but I didn't expect it to be like this."

"You sensed I would be coming?" Tension tightens my shoulders as apprehension builds in my chest. Is this all a trap?

"Yes, I've been preparing things for you. It was just a feeling, something God kept nudging me toward. I felt a bit foolish for gathering things, but here you are."

"Here I am." There must be a reason for this then. My dreams pulling me toward Zephyros and Verity preparing for my arrival. What are the chances those things aren't connected?

"But the storm," she reminds me. "How did you survive in that tiny boat?"

"I don't know exactly what happened," I confess. "The storm came up from nowhere, and I thought the ship might break apart. The crew cast lots and said I was responsible for the storm. They threw me into the sea."

Both Verity and the nurse gasp and exchange alarmed looks.

"B-but how did you survive?" she prompts.

How *did* I survive? I have no idea what happened after the dark sea swallowed me. So, I just regurgitate Antioch's words back to her. "It wasn't my time."

"Of course." She nods gravely. "It was all part of God's plan. But we'll discuss that later. For now, where are you hurt? What do you need?"

What I need is to make sure Ronan and Felix are okay. I try to look around the nurse to make eye contact with one of them, but Verity squeezes my hand gently and draws my attention back to her.

"They are in good hands, I promise." Her smile is tender and genuine, and some of the anxiety in me begins to ebb away. In its wake is a wave of exhaustion that nearly bowls me over.

"I'm just so tired," I admit. "And there's a pain here." My fingers hover over the spot just below my breasts in the center of my abdomen. It's not as bad as it was in the boat, but every twist and turn still sends a stab of pain through me that nearly takes my breath.

"May I look?" the nursemaid asks as she places her fingers atop my own to verify the source of the pain. "You will need to remove this dress."

Remove the dress? It's torn and well beyond repair, but I'm not keen on undressing in front of everyone. And I'm not sure I can move well enough to take it off anyway.

"Perhaps more privacy?" Verity suggests. "Can you walk? My bedchamber is just through those doors."

It's not very far away, and I tell her I think I can manage. Slowly I stand with the two women supporting me. I hold the blanket around me as we shuffle toward the bedroom.

"Emilia?" Felix calls my name, but I don't turn around. I'm afraid if I do, I'll fall.

"It's all right, Lord Commander," Verity tries to assure him. "I'm going to give her some fresh clothes and have her examined further." Then she ushers me into her room before he has time to object.

When I collapse onto her bed, I sink into the down of the mattress and close my eyes. I could just lay here forever. Forget everything. Inside these walls there is no prophecy, there is no sacrifice, and there will be no nightmares because I am too tired to dream them. But my eyes flutter open again and meet Verity's green ones, and I know I'm wrong about that. It's as if Levi stands right here in front of me.

Before I can ask the question on the tip of my tongue, Verity leans in conspiratorially. "Can you tell me what's really going on? We received word you were to marry the prince and there was to be a summit for peace, but I received word from my spies just this morning that none of that happened."

My blood runs cold despite the blanket wrapped around me. If she has already heard word from Borealis, information from Cyrus cannot be far behind. We're running out of time before we are trapped.

"It didn't," I confirm. "The prince and I did not marry, and Cyrus had no interest in peace talks. He had the Insurgo camps right outside my city walls burned to the ground. Hundreds dead because of me."

"No, no, my dear." She takes my hands in an attempt to calm me. "Not because of you. You didn't light the match."

"But they were there for me. Because everyone seems to believe I'm the fulfillment of some prophecy that will grant them freedom." I have no idea why I'm telling her any of this. I don't know her, and I shouldn't trust her, but the words come spilling out anyway.

"Hmmm..." she considers. "That seems too big a job for one person.

The response surprises me. I expect her to pin her hopes on me as well, but she doesn't. "I have failed every Insurgo I have tried to help." I left Hannah behind in Borealis, I gave Felix a false hope, I failed to act as decisively as Alara, and I actually killed Levi. That's not counting the hundreds of others who have suffered and died just because Cyrus knows it will hurt me.

"Emilia, you are not responsible if people put their faith in the wrong thing. It is God they should trust to save them, not you."

"So, you haven't heard of a prophecy, then?" I can't quash the hope that kindles in me. Maybe it's not true.

"I have heard of a promise," she says thoughtfully. "I'm not sure that's the same thing. God has promised to rescue His people, but I'm not sure anyone knows what that rescue is supposed to look like. I have heard it said that some believe this rescue will come through Caspian's line, but as far as I know, it's died out along with the hopes of a people."

"What about the Gate? The Gate of Life? Have you heard of it?"

"Of course. It is God's seat of power, and it leads to eternal life. But we already have the promise of eternal life if we accept the sacrifice of His Son. The Gate needn't be a concern for us."

But it is. "Cyrus seems to think the Gate will give power to an Insurgo leader who will overthrow the empire. I believe he thinks if he can reach it first then he'll be able to claim that power and immortality for himself."

"Admittedly I am not well studied in these things. But I don't believe it works that way. Cyrus, an unbeliever, could not simply plant a flag at the Gate's location and harness the power there."

I don't know if that's true or not. If it's not as simple as reaching the Gate first, then what hope do I have? Are Antioch's words true? Does the Gate require a sacrifice to receive the power of the Ancient One? "I don't know either. But if Cyrus believes it to be so, he will slaughter anyone that stands in his way."

"Which is why you are here." She shakes her head as if she has realized some of the burden I'm bearing. "You are in a very unique position to use both physical and spiritual might against the Emperor. You could use your position to save countless lives and point nations to the truth of our God."

"You sound like someone I used to know."

She smiles, but there's sadness behind it this time. "I first heard about you from Levi. He was my grandfather's younger brother. I grew up around him until my parents moved us to this country. Then we only exchanged the occasional letter. He wrote about you in his last few letters. I saved them for you. When I felt you would be coming, I compiled all the documents I could that I thought you might be interested in."

"Oh," I say because I don't know how to respond. The nurse has finished unlacing my dress with her deft fingers and slides it forward so I can slip it off. It's still a chore, but it finally falls to the ground with a heavy thud. Something goes skittering across the floor from the pile of fabric, and the nurse retrieves it with a curious frown.

"Your necklace came off with the dress, Majesty." She hands me the thin chain with the black opal still dangling from it, and my heart soars. I had forgotten I shoved this into the bodice of my dress just before I was dragged back into the storm. How did it survive?

"Here," Verity says as she rises and crosses the room to a wardrobe. "Let me get you some undergarments to change into. Perhaps a bath first?"

I would love one, but the thought of submerging even a little part of myself in the water sends a panic creeping up my throat until I'm afraid I'll choke on it. "N-no bath please."

She nods as if she understands and moves toward a basin near the fireplace instead. "At least let me wash the salt from you."

And I do. They strip off the rest of my clothes and wash my body with soft rags. The water is warm and soothing, and by the time they bring the basin nearer to rinse the sea from my hair, I'm just barely holding my eyes open.

I rouse enough to help them dress me in the underclothes Verity picked for me. The soft silk is delicious against my skin until it reminds me of my wedding dress. Still, I swallow my pride and say thank you as they begin the examination of my body.

It turns out, I'm relatively unscathed from my ordeal. There are a few scratches here and there, but nothing that requires extra attention. Then they turn their attention to the pain in my abdomen. I bite back curses as the nurse presses and prods all around my ribs and up to my breasts before sitting back and pronouncing that none of my ribs are broken.

"You are starting to bruise," she tells me as she sets a jar on the bedside table and opens it to reveal a yellowish green cream. "I suspect someone applied pressure here to make you cough up any water in your lungs. It's dangerous, but lifesaving."

Felix. There is only one person who would have known to do that and have the courage to act on it.

"Your Lord Commander is a very brave man." Verity smiles knowingly at me. But how can she know? Is it that obvious to everyone? Has everyone discussed this except Felix and me? "We've heard great things about him. Word travels fast in our circles."

"You've heard about Felix?" My question comes out as a near yelp as the nurse gently rubs some of the salve onto my skin where the pain is the worst.

"He's nearly as famous as you. The way he warned the encampments before the Emperor could burn them. The way he left everything behind to follow you to Borealis..." She sighs dreamily but sobers when she sees the look on my face. "Oh, that's not common knowledge. Just within the Insurgo circles. The Emperor would never openly admit that his best soldier defected in favor of you. Of course, I can't imagine he's too thrilled that his son seems to be on your side as well."

"I think it's safe to say there's not much about this situation that Cyrus would be happy with," I hiss through gritted teeth as the nurse winds bandages around the area where she placed the salve.

"There you are, Majesty. The salve will help the bruising and soreness."

"Thank you." It's inadequate, but it's all I can manage right now. I grab Verity's hand as she stands to leave. "Truly, thank you. I didn't expect… Well, we thought just walking into the palace might be a death sentence. I was unprepared to meet a fellow…" I hesitate. Because even though I trust Verity, it seems dangerous to say the word 'Insurgo' aloud in the palace. "Another Daughter of the King."

She releases my hand and gives me a small curtsy. "It is my pleasure to help you in any way I can. Our God has great plans for you. Perhaps we have both been placed here for such a time as this."

Her words reverberate in my head. Levi's words. I want to ask more, to talk more, but I'm not sure I would be able to process her answers at the moment. Sleep still threatens to drag me under. Verity seems to understand my quandary because she just smiles gently and squeezes my hand once more.

"We'll have time to talk more after you rest."

"Wait, I can't take your chambers," I say hastily. "Where will you sleep?"

Her eyes brighten a bit. "Oh, I usually share a room with my husband. I keep these chambers as a matter of tradition from previous queens, and I occasionally sleep here if he is away, but I prefer to share a bed with him."

Of course. Because that's what normal couples do. Or so I've been told. But my experience with relationships and love has been anything but normal. Still, it makes me smile to think that she's so in love with her husband that she doesn't want to be separated from him.

"I'll see to it that the rest of your party is fed and given plenty of comforts to rest. Would you like me to send your handmaid in to you?"

It takes a moment to realize she means Alara, and I have to bite back a laugh at that assumption. I can only imagine what my reluctant friend would have to say about that.

"No, let her rest." Because I don't want to poke a sleeping bear. I would never hear the end of it, and right now I desperately want sleep. "And make sure Felix rests as well?"

She smiles knowingly. "I will do my best."

Then she and the nursemaid are gone, and I am left alone to fall into a blissfully dreamless sleep.

14

My morning is filled with the hovering of Verity's maids who give a valiant effort to make me presentable. For what, I'm not sure. Because there's no one here but Antioch and Alara to impress. Ronan and Felix have both disappeared with their own missions.

They dress me in one of the queen's dresses—a sleeveless deep red gown that fastens over one shoulder with a gold brooch and ties around my waist with some sort of gold tasseled rope. The fashion here is much different than I'm used to. Lighter fabrics and more skin showing, but I find I can move well in it. I'm informed that later this morning I will meet with the queen's tailors who will fit me for some clothes of my own.

I join Alara and Antioch in the antechamber where a breakfast of warm pastries and various meats awaits us. Though it's probably unwise given how little food I've been able to keep down the last few days, I stuff myself with the rich delicacies. Alara follows suit, and I almost laugh about the pair we must make. Neither of us displays the manners expected of highborn ladies, but if the queen's ladies notice, they have no reaction.

Full to bursting, I sit back in my chair and finally take a good look at my company. Antioch looks no worse for wear, and Alara is as disgustingly perfect as ever. And she's looking at me with those eyes that suggest I've already disappointed her in some way.

"I would have thought you'd have a million questions." She reclines back in her chair with her arms crossed. Of course I do, but there are so many that I'm not sure where to begin. So, I start with the most basic one.

"What happened?"

She doesn't need to ask what I'm referring to. "You did a spectacular impression of an anchor, and Felix came to your rescue," she snaps back.

I wait. Because I know she needs to get out whatever indignation at my inadequacies before we can get to the details.

"Can you really not swim? I mean, your country isn't landlocked. Surely, you've spent some time near the water."

"Only small lakes and pools." I groan again as I adjust myself in the chair. "Not much chance to see the ocean when you've been exiled to the mountains and sent into combat before you were ten. Besides, it's not so easy when waves that could sink a ship are smashing into you."

She's silent for a moment as if considering my conditions. "Fair enough. Felix managed it though."

"Yes, well, Felix is... Felix." I wish I could have seen him this morning before he left. There's much I need to say to him.

"It is remarkable what a man in love is capable of." Antioch chooses that moment to speak up, and I really wish he hadn't. I don't want to discuss my feelings for Felix with him or anyone else. They are mine alone.

"What exactly happened?" I ask again, choosing to ignore his words. "The last thing I remember is being thrown overboard and then going under."

Despite the warmth of the room, I shudder. So dark and so cold. I had resigned myself to death, not for the first time in my life, but with a surety that there was no possibility of saving myself. I could not fight my way out of this one.

"As soon as you went overboard, Felix lost it. I mean... I've never seen anything like it. He somehow threw off his guards, and I thought he was going straight for Meridan, to kill him, but he ran to the edge of the ship and dove in after you without even a glance at anyone else. It stunned everyone. And while everyone was trying to wrap their minds around what had just happened, Ronan and I were able to break free. Ronan told them who he was, showed them his signet ring, and demanded the captain give us a longboat. They, of course, thought we were crazy because who could possibly sail a longboat in that storm? But as soon as they agreed, the wind began to die down, and we were able to launch the boat. How we actually found you and Felix..." She stops then shrugs. "I didn't think it was possible, but as soon as we were a short distance away from the ship, we saw you both bobbing on the waves. Ronan and I managed to row in that direction, and Felix swam to meet us, dragging you under his arm."

Alara pauses again, and I see what happened in the words she doesn't say. Felix frantically trying to revive me. Ronan pacing the boat without the slightest clue how to help. Antioch praying. Alara... Alara actually thinking I might die and maybe even helping Felix in his attempts to bring me back from the darkness. I see it all as if I had been hovering over the scene. The ache in my chest to lay eyes on him increases.

"The storm was a sign. Pointing to God's chosen one," Antioch affirms gravely. I meet his eyes and remember the conversation we had aboard the ship where he informed me I am to be a sacrifice. How I would be marked as the chosen one by the signs and wonders of God. It's hard to argue with what happened after, but I try anyway.

"Or maybe it was just a storm." I cross my arms, mirroring Alara's posture. Though everyone else seems beyond convinced, I struggle to believe I have been chosen for this when there are so many better candidates for this Princess That Was Promised. Alara for one. Maybe even Verity. Who knew there was another Insurgo queen? One that is certainly much nobler, probably much wiser, and who doesn't have blood on her hands.

"Emilia." Something in the way Alara says my name gets my attention in a way nothing else in this conversation has. "Until you prayed down that storm on the temple, God had not shown Himself like that in at least three hundred years. These storms are not a coincidence."

"So why me? Why now?" My words are barely a whisper.

"Who knows?" Alara stands from the chair with a nimble grace and stretches her back. "You certainly wouldn't have been my pick."

At least we agree on something. I'm not sure what it is that causes her to throw up defenses any time our conversations threaten to get too vulnerable. Maybe it's just that she dislikes me that much or is angry that I seem to have been chosen instead of her. Either way, there's no way I'm getting more information out of her right now.

"Where are you going?" I call after her as she moves toward the door. I'm unsurprised when she walks out of the room without an answer. With a sigh, I turn back to Antioch. "It should have been her."

"God will have His own plan for her, but this is your story. God has called you to a purpose. How exactly that is to play out remains to be seen."

I shove my chair back and stand, pacing away from the table in frustration. "Why all the uncertainty? One minute you seem so sure I'm this Ruler Who Will Rise Up and lead the Insurgos in a war for freedom, and the next you're saying you have no idea how this ends."

"God has called you, Emilia. The specifics of that calling are between you and Him. Even I cannot answer with surety."

"So, you're telling me this prophecy might not refer to me at all?" I'm not sure whether to be hopeful or disappointed. Just as I'm ready to accept my destiny, my purpose, I'm learning that it might not be mine at all.

"Prophecies are...difficult," Antioch says cautiously. "Many thought your mother was the fulfillment when she left Solitarius to marry a king. But a prophecy's fulfillment is often not seen except in hindsight. In the moment, well, they are rife with confusion and ambiguity. But does any of it really matter?"

Does it matter? I don't even think before I respond.

"The greatest sacrifice will be required of the Ruler Who Will Rise Up." I quote his words back to him. "Don't you think that matters? If it's me..."

"If it's you, what then? Would knowing give you some comfort? Dread? Courage? Fear? None of those will help you when the moment comes. Either a sacrifice will be required of you, or it will not. The most important thing is that you hear the voice of God and follow it. Follow it to the ends of the earth, and you will have fulfilled your destiny whether it relates to the prophecy or not."

The words sink in. He makes it sound so simple, but there is nothing simple about pondering death even for a cause as great as this. Yet, I don't disagree with Antioch. I will do what needs to be done. I've known this from the beginning when Levi set this whole thing in motion. Maybe even before then.

We don't pursue the conversation further because Verity enters the room. She smiles warmly at the two of us and greets her maids as well. She reminds me of Hannah, my lady-in-waiting I was forced to leave behind in Borealis. One of my only true friends and such a gentle presence in my life. What I wouldn't give to have her here with me now.

"Emilia," Verity says gently as if she can sense the turmoil inside me. "Could I borrow your friend? I have some documents I'd like to show him." She dips her head in a quick nod to Antioch.

“I can come along,” I offer. I look to Antioch, wondering if it would be wise to leave him alone in this unfamiliar place. He’s not a fighter, and while I don’t sense danger from Verity and her staff, that’s not to say there aren’t threats within the palace.

“I'm afraid the Lord Commander has asked that you stay in bed this morning. He asked me to emphasize that it *is* a request, but he hopes you'll honor it anyway.”

A smile tugs at my mouth. I wish he was the one in front of me asking, though. Aches and exhaustion weigh me down almost as much as the thoughts running through my head. Perhaps this is a request I should honor.

“Will you be fine with the queen?” I ask Antioch.

“Of course, my child. You should stay here and pray.”

Good point. I should do exactly that, but I'm still not sure what to say or what to ask. I'm afraid of the answer to the question at the forefront of my mind.

Once I'm alone in the room, I treat myself to a few more bites of breakfast then withdraw to the bedroom. It's nice to be alone for a change. Without people hovering over me or asking for my thoughts and opinions. It's a rare chance to just be me without an audience.

Carefully I remove the dress the maids put me in and drape it across the back of a chair. I don't want to wrinkle it by wearing it back to bed. While I'm undressed, I unwrap the bandage around my midsection and examine the damage. A bruise colors my skin where Felix must have applied pressure to expel water from my lungs. Even the lightest press of my fingers confirms it's still tender, but at least I'm alive.

I slide the nightdress I discarded earlier over my head and tug at my braid to loosen it a bit. Before I pull the covers back to lie down, I retrieve my dagger from my pack near the wardrobe and slide it under my pillow. Can't afford to be too careful given that there is no shortage of people who would like to see me dead...including some I think of as allies.

I curl in on myself and roll to my side, tucking my arm underneath the pillow and feeling the reassuring brush of the dagger's handle. Though I don't think it's malicious, Antioch seems almost eager for me to die. Now that he's discovered this bit about the prophecy, there's an excitement in his eyes when he mentions it. His curiosity to see it fulfilled seems to outweigh any regard for my feelings on the matter. Then there's Alara.

Where to even begin to understand our relationship? She's all sharp edges and cutting remarks, but I want to believe there's something more underneath that. But she has drugged me twice. She could do much harm if she truly wanted to and perhaps if she didn't fear Felix's wrath. I shake my head because I don't like thinking of the two of them in the same thought, no matter the reason.

Show me Your will, God. Everyone seems to think they know it, but I need to hear it from You. I know You have been preparing me for this moment, but I'm scared for what it will bring.

Silent words rush from me like a geyser spewing to heaven. All my fear, indecision, and hopes pour out of me as I attempt to empty myself of all secrets and shadows. I confess my selfishness for wanting to live and stop just short of promising to die. I'm not there yet. So, I ask for strength, because I know I'll need His to get there.

It's not sleep exactly, but I'm in a peaceful place of communication when a stab of fear turns my blood to ice. Though I haven't been moving, I still completely and hold my breath, listening to any sound. There. Just the soft pad of footsteps against the stone floor. Did the door open? Was I so lost in my prayers that I didn't hear it?

"It's definitely her." A breathy whisper, a man's voice at my back. Tension coils in my gut as I prepare to spring up. It's torture to wait, but I strain my ears to gather any information I can about the number and position of my would-be assailants before I jump into action.

The air shifts, and my body goes into motion, relying on years of training and muscle memory. I roll toward the opposite side of my bed, but not fast enough, and a hand fists in the fabric of my nightdress, yanking me backward and choking me as he pulls tight. Adrenaline pulls me forward, the neck of the fabric digging a furrow into my skin. Finally, it rips, and my knees slam against the floor as I fall from the bed. I blindly reach for the dagger I shoved under my pillow and almost cry with relief as my fingers find the hilt.

When I get my first deep breath, my eyes finally register the situation in front of me. Two men stand between me and the door, daggers of their own raised in my direction. My brain screams to run, but there's nowhere to go. I catch myself taking a step backward and force my feet to still. I can't let them trap me against a wall. At this distance, I'm confident I could hit them with my dagger, but I only have the one. Taking one down would still leave me with one opponent and no weapons.

The last time I was cornered by more than one attacker, I had Felix here to boost me over their heads. As long as they remain on the other side of the bed, I might be able to use it as leverage to jump over them and hope I make it to the door. But it has to be done before they realize what I'm doing.

I sprint toward the bed, leap onto it, and push off the headboard as I pray my momentum carries me far enough.

It's so close. But just as I think I've cleared them both, a hand wraps around my ankle, and I crash to the ground. The pain licks through me like lightning, but I have no time to feel it. No time to do anything except kick out and fight.

Immediately and with absurd ease, I dislodge the dagger from the hand of one of my attackers with a kick to his wrist. Rather than retrieve it, he pounces on me. On instinct, I drive the heel of my hand upward into his nose and feel a crunch on the impact. He rolls off me, blood gushing from his nose as he rolls around in agony.

His partner is on top of me before I have time to recover. I swing my knife, but he pins my hand above my head and holds his own dagger to my throat. I buck my hips, kick my legs, anything I can think of to try to dislodge his weight. But he's stout and determined. He slams my wrist to the ground, and the impact jars the dagger from my grip. It goes sliding across the floor along with my hope of surviving.

Then, with a sick smile, he drops his own dagger that he's been pressing against the skin of my neck and releases my wrist. Quickly, both of his hands find my neck and he begins to squeeze. My fingernails dig into his forearms as I claw at him with everything left in me.

No. No. No. Not like this.

He doesn't seem to register the blood I draw from my scratching. He leans down, mouth hovering right above mine. I'm gasping for air, so I taste his hot breath and suffocate even more.

"I'm going to do this with my bare hands. You're too pretty not to enjoy all of you before you die." One hand moves from my throat to rip the skirt of my dress, exposing more of my legs than anyone except myself and my ladies have ever seen.

God, please no! This can't be happening. I'd rather die than let him take me like he's insinuating. There's no air in my lungs to scream for help. I wish I had drowned. That death was easy. This burns my whole body as if I've been lit on fire. Panic and anger and fear war within me, but I can't seem to muster up much of a fight.

With one hand still around my throat, he trails the other down my neck, over my collarbones and toward my chest. My vision tunnels, and I hope I go unconscious before he gets much further. But just as everything is fading to black, his grip relaxes a fraction, and a slim stream of air rushes into my lungs.

My back arches with a gasp as my chest heaves in an effort to pull in everything I can. Then even that short-lived relief is cut off as he covers my mouth with his. I clamp my lips firmly closed, but he tightens his grip on my throat again, and my mouth flies open involuntarily, futility searching for air.

I have seconds left if that. Just let me die.

"Not yet. It is not finished."

"It" might not be finished, but I am. My attacker leans forward so his chest is pressed against mine, his full weight pressing into me, constricting any hope I had of catching one more breath. The edges of his leather armor cut into me, and my hands claw helplessly at his sides.

My vision tunnels as my fingers curl around something strapped to the man's armor. I'm incapable of coherent thought as I pull a dagger from a sheath at his side and stab. My arms are weak, and I can't put much force behind the motion, but my aim is true. Over and over, I stab him in the back right where his armor ends. From this position, the leather has ridden up, exposing his back just where his kidneys are.

His hands fly away from my throat and try to reach back to grab the dagger, but it's useless. Air rushes back into my lungs, and I manage enough strength to raise the knife and plunge it into the back of his neck. He stills, a gurgling sound rising in his throat. Hot, wet blood spews from his mouth all over my face as he sags against me.

Pure adrenaline allows me to push him off to the side as I roll out from under him.

It all happens so fast that my first attacker still lies on the floor near us, writhing in pain and holding his bloody nose. I don't wait for him to regain his composure. I'm trembling all over as I crawl out the door and slam it behind me.

15

Keep going.

I repeat this to myself several times before I can manage to get my feet under me and stand. The empty drawing room spins before me as I look for something, anything, to place in front of the door. There's only one left who could come after me, and he's wounded, but I'm still not sure I could muster enough strength to fight him if he manages to get out of that room.

The divan I sat on last night as the nurse looked me over catches my eye. Somehow, I managed to slide it from its position so it rests in front of the door. If I can move it, it wouldn't stop him for long if he managed to put all his weight against the door, but I don't think he's going to be moving any time soon.

Still, I stand facing the bedroom door, eyes fixed on the handle and alert for any movement. I mentally check in with my body. My lungs burn, my throat is on fire, and the pain in my abdomen is sharp but manageable. My knees ache from crashing to the floor, but otherwise I seem to be physically intact.

Somehow, I managed to avoid any cuts from their daggers or my own.

Minutes tick by as I focus on evening out my breathing while still keeping an eye on the door. I've been in battle before, but it's never felt so personal. Still, I resort to my tried and true techniques to calm myself. Eyes closed, I clench my fists until my nails dig into my palms. The sharpness of the pain allows me to focus, drawing all my attention to a single point rather than the fractured thoughts that otherwise occupy my mind.

A hand grasps my shoulder. Adrenaline that I've just tamped down roars to life again. I duck as I spin around, driving my fist upward toward my opponent's diaphragm. A hand catches my fist as I swing the other toward the jaw. He catches that one too and spins me around, crushing me against him with arms wrapped around my midsection.

Pain flares within me as I raise my foot to stomp on my attacker's foot, but before I can bring it all the way down, he hooks his leg behind mine, twisting until we crash to the ground, him on top of me.

Blind rage surges through me, barely dulling the pain as I force what's left of my strength into my limbs to kick, to flail, to do whatever I can to keep from being pinned down. It's useless though. A sob tears from me as my hands are pinned to the floor above my head. I can't see through the tears anyway, so I squeeze my eyes shut and wait for the worst to come.

One heartbeat. Two. If this is what being a sacrifice means, I'm terrible at it. Twice I've failed to die when I surely should have. Maybe third time's the charm.

"Emilia?"

There's no mistaking the way he says my name. Am I imagining him? Did my traumatized brain just conjure him out of longing to see him one last time? I blink once, twice, and force my eyes open.

Felix hovers over me, chest heaving, eyes roving frantically over my face to the torn neckline of my gown. Then he focuses on the blood I know must be splattered all over me. Every muscle in his body tenses as he releases my hands from above my head. He places his hands on either side of my shoulders and shifts so I'm not bearing all of his weight. He doesn't move away though.

"I don't want to fight." It's all I can think of to say. Because I can't stand it if he somehow turns this around to me being reckless or weak. I don't have the energy. I can't stand the thought of arguing with him about how I've gotten myself into another dangerous situation.

"If that was you not wanting to fight, I'd hate to see you when you do." Taking my chin between his thumb and forefinger, he tilts my head up and then side to side, assessing me for injuries.

He's entered soldier mode, triaging the situation and putting emotions aside. His ability to compartmentalize is infuriating, but right now it's exactly what I need. "What happened?"

"I don't know. I was praying, and I didn't hear them come in. They were just…there."

"Anyone you recognize?"

"No," I sigh, and he finally pushes back until he's sitting on his heels though still straddling my shins. I take his hand, and he pulls me to a sitting position. Debriefing is protocol, but I don't want protocol from him. This isn't how I pictured my first moments alone with him after almost drowning going.

"Anything I need to take care of in there?" He nods to the bedroom door behind us.

"One dead, one incapacitated," I recite as if there are not faces and feelings attached to each of those. It's been a while since I've drawn on my military training, but I grasp for it now.

"Two?" His eyes flash for just a second before he blinks hard and resets himself. That self-control is epic. He stands and motions for me to sit on the divan. "Let's get you cleaned up."

"I can't get blood all over the queen's furniture."

"You left two bodies in her bedroom. I hardly think she's going to mind a little blood on the cushions." But he doesn't push it, and I remain seated on the floor.

My eyes follow him as he retrieves the wash basin from near the fireplace and sets it on the floor beside us. Every movement is deliberate and precise as if this is one thing he can control, and he's not about to let it slip away.

I watch as he dips a cloth into the water. None of this feels real. If it weren't for the aching in my lungs and the burning in my throat, I might think it was all a nightmare. I've had enough of those for a lifetime.

Large, strong hands ring the cloth over the basin to expel the excess water before he raises it to my face. Rivulets of red-tinged water run from my face, down my neck, and disappear below the torn neckline of my gown as he gently presses the cloth to my face. With gentle swipes and incredible concentration, he removes the blood.

He is a study in contrasts. His face is all strong lines, and the beard lends him a rugged appearance. But his eyes are soft even though they refuse to meet mine. I've never had a chance to study him this closely. Dark lashes frame those deep brown eyes, not delicate exactly, but definitely noticeable. A faint line of a scar is just visible on his cheek through the stubble of his beard. My eyes drift down to his lips. Was it really only days ago that they were on mine? Muscles twitch in his jaw as he takes care to focus on the movement of the cloth over my skin and avoid my eyes.

"You are remarkably calm considering I'm covered in blood."

"Not your blood," he mutters, pausing to ring out the bloody rag in the basin. A sigh parts his lips as he finally looks at me. Little by little, I can see his defenses crumbling. "You're always going to attract trouble, aren't you?"

"You're just now figuring that out?" I try for a laugh, but it dies in my throat as his fingers just barely brush the strands of my hair that have fallen from my braid into my face, heavy with dried blood.

"No, I'm well aware. We need to rinse this out of your hair."

As he turns back to the basin, I pull the pins from my hair and let it tumble down in waves. His eyes widen and he swallows hard as he takes me in.

"That hair." He shakes his head. "You really are incredible, you know that?"

"Well aware." I smile back.

"You're also going to be the death of me."

I frown. *God, why can't we get past this?* "It doesn't fall to you to protect me."

"I'm still recovering from nearly watching you die at sea." His voice breaks a little despite the teasing tone he tries to give it. "There's only so much my heart can take."

"Mine, too," I whisper, and I practically launch myself into his arms. As if my life depends on it. As if there is nothing else except us.

"Thank God you're okay," he murmurs against my temple as one hand presses into my back, pulling me closer, and the other strokes my hair. Gone is the business-like demeanor of the soldier. Here is the Felix I adore, who makes my knees weak and my heart race.

"I'm okay," I assure him because I can feel his heart pounding against my cheek resting on his chest. "I really am okay."

It's the first time we've been alone since I almost drowned. Practically the first time we've been alone since that hallway in Borealis where I kissed him last. And all I want is for him to hold me like this. For all my bravado and strength, I want him to make me feel safe. And he does just that.

There's no concept of time as we sit there wrapped in each other. It could be hours or maybe just minutes. All I can think is that it will never be long enough. It will never be enough to only have him in these stolen moments in the aftermath of whatever tragedy has occurred. There have been enough of those moments.

What I want are the mundane things—the sleepy smiles in the mornings, the laughter in the afternoons, and the deep, even breaths of night. And I don't want to share them with anyone else.

He leans back a bit to look me over again and seems to notice my state of undress for the first time. With deft fingers, he unfastens the cloak at his shoulders and drapes it around me. The fabric is thick and warm, much too hot for this climate. But it's the one I had made for him to wear to my wedding as part of that dress uniform.

"I'm sure you must have questions."

Too many to even know what he's referring to. "I have a million questions, but I'm not sure you can answer even half of them," I say, thinking about the prophecy and the Insurgos and why we're in Zephyros in the first place.

"All that matters at the moment is that you're okay. There will be time for figuring the rest out."

"We can't have much time," I remind him. "Obviously news from the wedding hasn't reached here yet, but it can't be more than a day behind. Verity received news yesterday about the Insurgo camp outside the city. If the news traveled that fast, then whatever official information Cyrus is spreading could be here by tomorrow."

"If we're fortunate," he agrees with a nod. "But we've got a plan. I gave everyone their assignments last night, but I thought they had more sense than to leave you alone. None of this matters if something happens to you."

"To be fair, Antioch was with me until Verity asked him to come with her to look over some documents she thought might interest him. Ronan wasn't here when I woke, and Alara left just after breakfast. She didn't say where she was going."

Felix pinches the bridge of his nose. "Ronan is meeting with the king to request supplies. Alara is working with the queen's spies to make the necessary arrangements…"

"And you trust her?" The question comes out with a bit more bite than I intended, and Felix drops his hands from my sides. In an uncharacteristic gesture, he runs his hand through his hair and then scrubs his face. I get the sense that he's heard his fair share of snide remarks from her side as well.

"Look, I don't know what there is between the two of you, but we have to work together. This is bigger than all of us, so can you two just put aside the pettiness until we get where we need to be?"

Stunned, I recoil. Though I'm sure he chose his words carefully, it feels an awful lot like he's taking her side. I guess the time for blind faith in me has passed. Maybe the shine's worn off me now. I hate I'm second guessing myself after I just held off two attackers and saved my own life. Nothing he has said or done has fed this growing feeling in me. Except maybe withholding the one thing I long to hear from him.

“Are we really going to pretend we don’t know what she’s doing?” I wait for his response, but he just stares at me quizzically. “Someone had to tell Meridan’s crew who I was. And in case you've forgotten, two men just tried to kill me.”

I don’t exactly know where the accusation comes from, but I’ve been harboring suspicions of Alara’s intent for a while now. My emotions are raw, and I want to cry because this is not at all how I imagined my meeting with him going.

“Emilia, you don’t mean that.”

I don’t know why, but his words sting. Why is he defending her? Tears burn my eyes, but I blink them back. I will not cry in front of him. Not over this.

“She thinks she can do this better than me.” I gesture wildly, but my voice is childlike, and I hate it. It all breaks loose. The weight of the crown, the prophecy, unrequited love… “Maybe you’d be better off if I let her try.”

Felix holds up his hand as if to stop my forward progress. But I’m already barreling toward an inevitable collision.

“She literally made her name and her reputation in Borealis by pretending to be me. The name she used—Nox? That was my name when I was with the army. She dressed up as me at the ball and fooled everyone. She knew about letters from my mother that even I didn’t know about. She’s better at being me than I am. And if she were thrown overboard, she’d probably just laugh and swim circles around the ship, and you wouldn’t have to jump in to save her. But you would anyway, wouldn’t you? Because you two have this understanding, don’t you?”

I don't know when I lost the battle to my tears, but when I raise my hands to wipe them away, Felix grabs my wrists and pulls me toward him again.

"Emilia." He looks down at me with an intensity that fans a flame inside me. "Are you actually jealous?"

I don't know why it sounds so ridiculous when he says it when just seconds ago it felt so rational.

"She's everything I'm not." I duck my head, but he hooks a finger under my chin and tilts it up until I'm forced to meet his eyes.

"Exactly."

A million unsaid things pass between us in those few moments where we lock eyes. Neither of us wants to look away.

"You are Emilia Aurelius. Daughter of Alector and Alexandra Aurelius and heir to the Borealis throne. You were the chosen of the Crown Prince, a fierce warrior, tamer of wild horses, and a horrible dancer."

I snort and look down for a moment, but when I raise my eyes again, he's looking at me with a renewed intensity. "And you are Mia...daughter of the King of Kings, chosen of God, and bringer of storms. And you are also a horrible swimmer."

The laugh dies on my lips as his eyes dart down to my mouth. My stomach flutters. He's going to kiss me. The anticipation of feeling his skin against mine makes every part of me tingle. He's going to kiss me, and it's not going to be rushed or sad or angry. He's going to kiss me, and I'm going to fall apart in his arms.

"What—why are you—is that blood?"

Felix and I nearly knock heads as we spring apart. Ronan stands in the doorway, frozen and mouth agape.

"Not mine," I inform him as Felix puts space between us. The pleasant numbness his closeness produced evaporates as he stands, leaving the dull ache of pain—physical and emotional—in its wake.

"Someone made an attempt on Emilia's life," Felix says as if he's reciting a report to his commanding officer.

"Again?" Ronan's ice blue eyes widen in disbelief.

"Well, it wasn't your father this time, so that's a nice change of pace." I don't know how I'm certain of that, but I am. This has Cassia and Gloriana's hands all over it. I can't believe with all the significant threats to my life, the one that almost took me out was because of two jealous princesses who want a man I don't even love.

The hurt in his eyes almost makes me regret the comment. Almost.

"I just came to tell you we're to dine with the king and his family in the gardens this evening. But given this development, I'll insist—"

"No." I don't let him finish. "Before you suggest it, I'm not going to hide in my room."

"Emilia, look at you." Ronan gestures to my appearance, and I know I must look like a wreck. Blood still spattered on my nightdress at least, torn fabric, bruised skin…

"Yes, look at her." Felix stands and offers me a hand. I take it and rise as well with as much grace as I can muster. "That's not her blood. She fought off two men who tried to kill her in her sleep. In Aurora, she defended you against would-be assassins. She's not the helpless princess you're used to dealing with. We—both of us—have to stop underestimating her strength and listen to her when she tells us what she needs."

Stunned silence fills the room, but my heart swells with pride. Finally. *Finally.* Acknowledging my strength was exactly what I needed. I don't need a protector. I need a partner. Now he understands.

"Well, Emilia," Ronan says slowly. "What do you need?"

There are so many ways I could answer that, but only one seems appropriate for this moment.

"To go to war."

16

Powerful.

That's how I feel as I survey myself in the mirror hours later.

I'm back in the queen's bedroom, the scene of my attack, but it's free of bodies and blood and is now full of three maids who bustle around to prepare me for dinner.

I assume Felix and Ronan got rid of the bodies of my assailants while I was at the modiste with Verity. She was appalled to learn of the attempt on my life, and I tried to drill into her the importance of having guards you can trust. I still can't believe I was almost taken out over something as simple as jealousy. I relish the idea of seeing the surprise on the princesses' faces when I show up, very much alive, for dinner.

One of the maids tries in vain to cover the bruises forming on my neck with powder, but it's much too light for my skin. I tell her to wash it off. Let them see what I fought through. Let them see I'm not so easily broken.

I've chosen to wear clothing that seems to be much more fitting with the customs in Zephyros than in my home country.

It's a one-piece outfit where the bodice flows seamlessly into loose-legged pants. It's daring for me, and not only because it's pants instead of a dress. Though the legs are wide and flowing enough to appear as a full skirt when I stand still, there is a slit in each leg that stops just above my knees. When I walk, the teal fabric parts and shows my bare leg. Though it's the fashion here, it's far more skin than I'm used to showing, but I find I love it.

The maids and I pass the time, waiting for Ronan to arrive as my escort, trying out various hairstyles for me. It feels strange to have someone other than Hannah fix my hair, but they are quite gentle and talented. When I look at myself in the mirror after they finish, I'm impressed. They've woven my thick, dark tresses into a voluminous braid down the center of my head that is both fierce and sultry. Within the braid are threads of gold ribbon and shimmering beads. When I turn my head and it catches the light, it reminds me of the sun glinting off the sea.

They have just finished lacing the gold sandals up my calf when there's a knock on the bedroom door. Ronan enters dressed in a simple but fine blue top and dark trousers. His eyes widen slightly when he registers my clothing.

"You're certainly embracing the local fashion."

I can't tell if he approves or not, but I'm not sure I care. I feel powerful in these clothes, and courage and confidence are going to be necessary if I have to sit through a dinner with Cassia and Gloriana.

"When in Zephyros..." I reply with a shrug. I shouldn't have to apologize for dressing in a way that makes me feel beautiful.

"I'm not complaining. But I imagine the princesses are going to have lots of thoughts on it."

Let them. It won't be the first time they've had comments on my wardrobe. But I'm not the same person I was back in Aurora, and their opinions mean less than nothing to me.

"We should probably get going," Ronan suggests as he turns toward the door. "Although with you showing up in that get-up, I don't think anyone would have trouble imagining why we were late."

My eyes widen at the implication. But of course, they would assume that. We're supposed to be married. Felix's face flashes before me, and I know I have to tell Ronan now. I owe him that much.

"Ronan." I reach for his hand and pull him back to me. "I need to tell you something." It feels wrong to continue this masquerade as husband and wife without him knowing the full extent of my feelings for Felix.

Blue eyes search my face as he waits for me to continue.

"Felix...he and I..."

He saves me from a stammering explanation by placing a gentle but firm hand on my shoulder. "I know."

I search for despair or anger in his face but find none. More of a resignation than anything.

"I've suspected for a while. Not the details of course, but the way the two of you look at each other... Looking back, I should have known it from the first night I met you. When he came to me before the ball and couldn't stop talking about this amazing girl—woman—he'd escorted into the palace. And maybe that was my mistake. I was just a boy who loved a woman like you were a girl. He saw your strength immediately."

He's more introspective than I've given him credit for.

"I'm sorry I couldn't..."

He plants a chaste kiss on my forehead. "It's okay. Felix is a good man—the best man. Besides, given all that's happened, I'm not in any position to commit to settling down. I have too many unanswered questions."

Don't we all? But I let the conversation end on that note as I take his arm to be escorted to dinner. He fills me in on all he has accomplished today—meetings with the king, procuring food, supplies, and a few basic weapons. Conveniently absent from his list of achievements is disposing of bodies. I can fill in the gaps on my own.

According to Ronan, we are to sail to Solitarius on a ship captained by a personal friend of the queen. He is Insurgo and makes his living mostly by transporting Insurgos from Solitarius to the mainland and back. There's also the illegal trade of a few goods acquired from the island, but nothing like Meridan, Ronan assures me.

Alara and Antioch have been making sure the supplies given to us by the king are loaded onto the ship. They will go ahead and board, meaning there are fewer of us who need to sneak out of the palace. This is for Antioch's benefit, I'm sure. Alara is the queen of stealth, but Antioch struggles to keep up sometimes. If we have to leave in a hurry, then we can't afford for him to slow us down.

Felix, Ronan, and I will exit the palace sometime after midnight and row a boat out to meet the ship, which will have already left the harbor. This is to make it more difficult for anyone tracking us to know which ship, if any, we left in. It sounds like a good plan. Ronan promises this time will be different. I hope he's right.

Ronan leads me to an outdoor terrace composed of the same white columns and marble floor I noted upon our arrival. A table is set up at one end, overlooking the gardens which stretch as far as I can see, but no one is seated there. Instead, several people are gathered at the other end of the terrace where stairs lead down to a courtyard below. As Ronan and I approach, all eyes turn to us.

The reactions are so varied that I almost laugh. The King—Gaius, I've learned his name is—and Verity smile warmly at us, their children ignore us, Cassia and Gloriana glare daggers at me, and Felix... Well, I have to look away from the heat of his gaze. I think if I met his eyes, we might set the whole place on fire.

"So glad you could join us." Gaius welcomes us with outstretched arms. He grasps me by the upper arms and kisses the air on either side of my cheeks. "I was sorry to hear about your mishap earlier. I assure you the guards won't bother you for the rest of your stay."

Mishap? Bother me? Did my assassination attempt just get downgraded to a minor inconvenience? Then I catch Felix's eye and bite my tongue. This is strategic on his part, so I play along.

"Much appreciated, your Majesty."

“Is that a bruise on your neck?” Gloriana arches a perfectly shaped eyebrow at me. “At least the guards didn't inconvenience your honeymoon.”

My mouth drops open at the insinuation that it was Ronan's lips and not a guard's fingers that left the bruises on my throat.

“Gloriana!” Verity gasps. “That's highly inappropriate. A lady doesn't discuss such things.”

The King clears his throat nervously. “Yes, well, I have asked the Lord Commander if he’d be willing to inspect our guard this evening. Given all the unrest, I think we can all agree it’s more important than ever to have a well-trained and disciplined guard.”

I arch an eyebrow at him. Really? As if they haven’t all just acknowledged that it was two members of these same guards who caused me such “inconvenience”? That only further draws my suspicion away from Cyrus and to one or both of the girls in front of me. It’s an oddly comforting thought. As long as I keep my eyes on them, I don’t need to fear them. Cyrus on the other hand…

“Perhaps you’d like to join us, Ronan?” Gaius is saying. “We’ll leave the ladies to their gossip for now.”

Ronan joins Felix, the King, and the little boy I saw yesterday. The child waves goodbye to his sister, who apparently is to remain with the ladies, and bounds down the stairs after the men. I move to follow, but Gloriana steps in front of me.

“Come now, Emilia. You must know that the training ground is no place for a lady.”

With great restraint, I resist rolling my eyes. It seems their jealousy over my prowess with a weapon has not cooled since we last met. They made it perfectly clear then that my ability to defend myself was the mark of a barbarian and not a princess.

"Oh, she just can't bear to let that new husband of hers out of her sight," Cassia chimes in as she comes alongside me and takes my arm. I let her lead me to the edge of the terrace where we can look over and watch the men greeting the small contingent of guards who have gathered below.

"Sisters," Verity warns in a gentle voice. "Be kind to our guest. She is still recovering from her ordeal."

"Yes, very tragic," Cassia agrees solemnly. "I'm so very glad that you're all right."

I'll just bet she is.

"We're so sorry to have missed your wedding," Gloriana says as she joins Cassia and me in watching the maneuvers of the guards. "I'm sure it was so romantic. Did Ronan have much say in it? When we were discussing our wedding, he had such grand ideas."

The not-so-subtle reminder that both of these girls shared a piece of Ronan's affection for a time rankles me. Not because I care for him in that way, but because he's much too good for either of them.

"It was all such a blur," I say, not untruthfully. I can't let them know how much they get to me. It's a battle I won't concede.

"Oh, I would have thought every detail of that night would have been permanently embedded in your mind."

It is, but not for any reason they would ever guess.

"Well, hopefully you'll have a better memory than I do on your wedding night, Cassia. Speaking of which, are there bells on the horizon? Any suitors? I would have thought they would have been lining up to meet you after you were sent home from Aurora. Imagine my surprise to turn up here and find you both with no husbands."

The outrage on their faces is comical, but I know too well what they're capable of to laugh.

"Well," Gloriana huffs as she puts her hands on her slim hips, "at least you brought along a spare."

All eyes turn to the men, down below who chat amicably as the guards break off into sparring partners at their commander's order. Felix's expression belies none of the tension or alertness I know is coursing through him right now. It's not just restraint. He's a better actor than I gave him credit for.

"He is quite handsome." Cassia leans her elbow on the railing and props her chin in her hand with a dreamy sigh. "The Commander is quite the catch."

"It's *Lord* Commander now. Didn't you hear?" Gloriana sneers.

That's on me. By giving Felix a title I have inadvertently made him one of the most desirable men in the entire empire. A man with such military skill who holds high favor with the Queen of Borealis, the prince consort, and—as far as they know—the Emperor himself... He's a prize in any country.

I watch him weave through the sparring soldiers with such confidence that my heart swells with pride. He spots weaknesses and corrects them gently but firmly, reserving his harshest voice for those who refuse to heed his advice. He is likely the empire's best soldier, but you would never know it to look at him. Certainly, he's well-built with lines of muscles that could make any girl blush, but he doesn't flaunt it. He doesn't look for opportunities to showcase his skills. And that makes him all the more impressive.

"His reputation precedes him," Verity cuts in diplomatically. "My husband has heard of his prowess as a commander from many sources. And so young to have achieved such a rank."

I don't disagree. One day, perhaps, I'll hear the story of how Felix ended up with so much responsibility and esteem before the age of twenty-five.

"I'm sure he has other skills as well." Cassia raises her eyebrows at me in question. "He did spend some time sneaking out of your room in Aurora, didn't he, Emilia?"

"Cassia!" Verity admonishes. "That's quite rude."

"It's quite true," Gloriana confirms. "At least if the rumors are to be believed."

"The rumors you started, you mean?" It's work to keep my tone even as I level my eyes at her.

"Well, that's in the past," she says hastily. "Let's hear what married life is like. When are you having children?"

"That's enough." Verity steps forward, but her tone is gentle enough to be ignored, so that's exactly what the girls do.

"Well, we're all curious, aren't we?" Cassia chimes in. "I mean, how does this work? The first heir you produce inherits the Borealis throne? And the spare inherits the Imperial throne?

Maybe you'll be as fertile as our dear sister here and have twins." She nods to the little girl sitting at our feet and then to her brother down below. The little boy has been handed a wooden sword, and Felix is showing him how to hold it.

"Or maybe you're already with child. I did hear some rumors that your illness was related to pains in your abdomen. Covering up your delicate condition?"

"Will the child have blue eyes or brown? Come, Emilia, let's place bets."

I've had enough. I know I should keep it together for the sake of keeping up appearances and maintaining diplomatic relations. After all, we're only here for a few more hours before we make our escape, but if either of them says another word to me about Felix or Ronan, I think I might lose it.

"Emilia." Ronan calls my name and waves up at me from the courtyard. It takes a moment to see through my rage that he's actually motioning me down to join them. I could almost cry with relief.

"Excuse me, ladies." I practically snarl the last word. "My husband requires my attention."

I descend the stairs before I can hear any more remarks from them. The heels of my sandals click on the marble, and I use the cadence to pattern my breathing and calm myself before I join the men. The guards are now milling around the gardens, having been dismissed from their maneuvers. Felix pretends to spar with the little boy while Gaius watches them. Ronan holds out an arm for me to join him.

“If looks could kill those girls would already be six feet under,” he chuckles softly as I take his arm, and he plants a kiss on my temple. “You shouldn’t let them get to you.”

“If you could have heard the things they were saying…”

“It doesn’t matter. We’ll be on our way soon, and hopefully we’ll never have to see them again.”

“I can’t believe you ever considered marrying one of them.”

He gives me a strange look. “They were just a backup plan. You know that. I chose you from the beginning. But since you weren’t willing to commit, I had to keep them around.”

It’s true that I could never give Ronan my reassurance that I loved him. There are several good reasons for that, and one of them is walking my way.

“Finished your inspection, Lord Commander?” I ask Felix as he and the king approach with the boy tagging along behind.

“The guard is in excellent condition. I made a few suggestions, but they are a fine squad.” He directs his comments more to Gaius than me, but I don’t mind. I like seeing him take charge.

“And now we can rest easy.” Gaius smiles and ruffles his son’s hair. “And Pax has learned how to hold a sword. He’ll be ready for training in no time.”

Felix claps the child on the shoulder, and Pax looks up at him with a wide grin.

“Come,” Gaius says, gesturing for us to return to the terrace. “Dinner should be ready now.”

Ronan squeezes my hand and then steps away to walk with Gaius and Pax. Felix lags behind just a bit to walk with me. We don't touch, but he leans in to speak to me so softly that his words are only for me.

"You should wear that into battle," he says as he surveys my wardrobe choice. "All men would lay down arms at first sight."

"Yes, I imagine the Borealis military would look quite terrifying in this."

"*You* look terrifying in this."

My spirits fall. "So, you disapprove?"

"No." He clears his throat and then looks me over again, slower this time. "I think you'll find I wholeheartedly approve."

No one needs to warn me to watch what I eat at dinner. I touch nothing that is handed directly to me except to push it around on my plate with my fork. I'm quite certain the princesses poisoned one of the girls who vied for Ronan's hand. I'm not about to give them the satisfaction of another attempt on my life.

"Your father was quick to abandon the war effort," Gaius observes with a curious look at Ronan as dessert is served. "When he requested our soldiers to help avenge the kings' deaths, I thought it would be a long battle."

"It was an unpopular one," Ronan informs him carefully. "Difficult to fight an enemy with no formal army and no defined territory. And not everyone agreed that the Insurgos were responsible for the assassinations."

Gaius nods. "I will admit it seemed out of character for what we have observed here. They seem to be a largely peaceful group, though I heard you've had some trouble in Borealis."

Trouble doesn't begin to describe it. Perhaps he hasn't heard how Alara and I set fire to and tore down the temple in a single afternoon. I can't imagine my Council back home would want to advertise that shortcoming to our enemies.

"A bit, yes," I answer. Ronan stifles a snort at my downplaying of events, and I kick him under the table. "My chief goal as queen was—is—to negotiate for peace. Our marriage, as I'm sure you must have heard, is symbolic in many ways of the hoped-for union between the empire and the Insurgos. Everyone knows my mother's history, and the hope is that I may have some goodwill with her people."

My people. But I don't want to state it so boldly. I'm sure it's no secret where my allegiances lie, but I don't want to confirm that in a place like this. Especially when it could get Verity in trouble as well.

"At any rate, we are grateful to have our soldiers returning home." Gaius raises a glass to Ronan and I. "Thank you for your peace efforts. I do hope you'll find time to enjoy your honeymoon on this tour and not just barter for peace."

"We hope the worst is behind us," Ronan says. But it's not, and we all know it.

"Here's to peace and happiness for many years to come." Verity raises her glass as well and we all drink. Well, I feign a sip anyway.

"And where will your honeymoon tour take you next?" Gaius asks.

"South," Ronan replies, careful not to lie.

"Will you be meeting up with your father in Austrina then?"

My fork freezes on its way to my mouth, and Ronan swallows hard before answering.

"My father?"

"Yes, word has it he's heading there. They're readying a couple of ships in the Imperial fleet at any rate. A couple of our captains were commissioned to report as soon as possible. One set of soldiers coming home and another setting out."

"Have you heard where he's headed?" Felix asks, though I think we both know the answer. There aren't many reasons Cyrus would need to ready ships if he weren't going to Solitarius. It's possible he could be sailing to Zephyros or even Borealis, but both are far more accessible by ground than sea.

"Nothing official," Gaius shrugs. "Rumors range from a holiday to an expedition of some sort."

"Does my mother accompany him?" Ronan leans forward to make direct eye contact with Gaius. I think back to my limited interactions with the Empress. She was kind if a bit cold, and though there seems to be no love lost between Ronan and his father, I don't think the same can be said for his relationship with his mother.

"I've heard no word of the Empress making the journey."

"So, it's unlikely a holiday then." Ronan slumps back in his seat. He seems surprised by this. Did he not really believe his father would follow us? After all he's seen, was he really holding out hope that Felix and I had exaggerated things?

"So, an expedition then," Gaius agrees. "I wonder what he's looking for?"

Verity meets my eyes then looks away quickly. She's put it together as well. I wonder how much she will share with her husband later when they are alone. Does she feel safe enough to truly share that part of herself with him?

Beneath the table, I reach for Felix's hand. I wish I could tell him how thankful I am that I can be my true self, my whole self, with him. He has seen me as a soldier, a princess, a fugitive, but I think he has always known who I really am. The way he stood up to Ronan on my behalf today is proof of that.

Ronan skillfully changes the subject, but I tune it all out. I'm thinking of Levi instead. When Antioch returned from his outing with Verity, his arms were laden with maps and letters and documents, most of which he carefully stowed away in his pack, which I assume he has taken aboard the ship this evening. He did, however, hand over a single letter to me. It was from Levi.

I haven't been able to bring myself to read it just yet, but there's comfort in knowing it's there. How I wish he were here with me. So much of what I know, what I believe, I owe to him. What I wouldn't give for just a few more minutes with him to ask all the questions that plague me.

A gentle squeeze of my hand brings me back to the present. I'd been unaware my hands were shaking until Felix applied the gentle pressure beneath the table. I chance a glance at him, but he's focused on whatever Gaius is talking about now. I squeeze back to let him know I'm all right, and the small furrow line in his brow relaxes slightly.

Something changed between us earlier today. Everything shifted in that moment he was about to kiss me. I just pray I get the chance to explore it before I'm dead.

17

Given all the excitement we've experienced since we left my city, our escape from Zephyros is entirely uneventful. Thankful doesn't begin to describe my feelings when Felix, Ronan, and I are safely in our rowboat and heading out to sea. I'm too relieved to even focus on the fear that threatens now that I'm back on the water.

I send up a prayer of thanks when Felix sends up a flare to signal the ship in the distance and breathe a sigh of relief when ropes are lowered, and we're hoisted up onto the deck of a ship not quite as large as Meridan's.

When I finally set my feet on the deck of the ship, I fall to my knees and press my hands against the only bit of firm foundation I'll be standing on for a few days. I stop just short of kissing it, but already too many eyes are on me. Instead, I force myself to stand and face the small group that has gathered to welcome us aboard.

Flashbacks to the welcome we received on Meridan's ship almost paralyze me, but I relax a bit when the captain and the group of sailors behind him bow to us. To me.

"I am Captain Lucius, and I am pleased you made it aboard safely." He offers his hand, and Felix steps forward to shake it. "It is an honor to give you passage. The queen has told me who you are, and you will be given every comfort we have at our disposal, though I'm afraid it's not much."

"It will be more than fine," I say as I step up to shake the captain's hand as well. Verity has not steered us wrong so far. I have to trust her in this as well. "We don't need luxury. We just need safe travels to Solitarius."

"And as much as is in my control, you shall have it. I have sailed this route many times over the years. At first, I brought our brethren to the mainland where they might reunite with relatives, but as the persecution continues, I have been returning many back to the island."

Captain Lucius is an older man, old enough to be my grandfather I'd wager, but his eyes are still keen and bright. He searches my face for a moment as if trying to confirm something. "Your friend, Antioch, he says that you are the one who will end that persecution."

A lump forms in my throat, and for a moment I cannot breathe, let alone speak. I look to Felix, and he answers for me.

"She is a servant of our God, and we are simply following His calling. The outcome of that, only God can know."

His answer seems to satisfy the captain for now, and he changes the subject to have two of his men volunteer to take us to the passenger cabins where Alara and Antioch are already resting. I'm beyond grateful to find I have a cabin all to myself. Apparently, Lucius's ship wasn't due to sail for another week, but Verity paid a large amount so that we could have the ship to ourselves and avoid any prying eyes. If I live through this, I will repay her. It seems I'm accruing a lot of debt.

Reluctantly, Felix leaves me alone after instructing me to lock the door behind him. I don't put up a fuss because I'm too tired to fight with anyone tonight—friend or foe. If Lucius and his crew are truly who they say they are, I'm probably safer here than I have been in the last several months.

As I sit alone in my cabin, I try to sort through all I have learned and all that lies ahead. Everything comes back to this prophecy—if that's what it should be called—or belief that God has chosen me to rescue His people. That this chosen one will be marked by signs and wonders and will be a descendant of the great Caspian himself. I don't know exactly where my mother came from so, I can't speak to my lineage, but I can't argue with the signs. Two powerful storms—one arriving in response to my prayers and the other to direct me where God had been leading me to go. But if those things are real, does that mean my dreams are real also?

God, whatever happens, please spare Felix.

The images of the light leaving his eyes as he either burns at a stake or bleeds to death before me pull a strangled sob from deep within me. I love him so much it's become an ache within me. And I haven't even had the opportunity to share that with him yet.

When I prayed for death to come while that man's hands were around my throat, God answered with "not yet." Not a simple no. But Not. Yet.

That I can't wrap my mind around. I'm certainly no stranger to death, and I had even resigned myself to it when Cyrus pronounced his sentence in that Aurora court. I vowed to give my life as an offering. This somehow feels bigger, weightier, and it's not only because I now have Felix to consider.

I know with a surety I feel in my bones that I will do what is necessary. How could I live with myself if I did any less? But there are others' lives to consider now. Every instinct screams at me to wall up any sentiment and protect them all from my destiny. Regardless of the words he's yet to give me, I know this will destroy Felix.

"That's not your burden to bear."

The voice that's been my familiar companion since I left Aurora is a mere whisper now. Still, it calms something inside me.

Denying him my love even for the noblest of reasons isn't something I can bring myself to do. Better to have it for a short time than not at all. And, selfishly, I need his love as well. Right now, I might need it more than I need my next breath.

God, if You have called me to this, equip me. I have no power except what You give.

And scripture that I once held so tightly comes flooding back to me. *Blessed be the Lord, my rock, who trains my hands for war and my fingers for battle.* Levi's final words. I cling to them once again and fall asleep praying.

18

I don't leave my cabin for three days.

Alara, Antioch, Ronan, and Felix all try to visit me, but I turn them away. Food is left outside my door, and I open it only to retrieve the tray and then place it empty back outside.

I eat and I sleep and I pray. All of my energy goes into petitioning God for direction, but He is silent. I pour out my heart and my tears before Him, but I receive no answers. I'm just as clueless as to what happens next as I was when we left Borealis.

On the third day, I wake with an unexplainable peace I haven't felt for much too long. I still have no idea what to do. But what was it Antioch said to me in that prison tower? I must take the journey step by step. And the next step is to stop isolating myself from those who want to help me.

When Felix knocks on my door this morning, I fling it open and hug him tightly. He seems surprised, and it takes him a moment to return my embrace.

"I didn't expect you to answer," he admits as he tucks a strand of my wild hair behind my ear.

"And yet you came knocking anyway." Just as he has multiple times for the last few days. After the first several times I had told him through the door that I just needed space to pray. He respected that, but I could still count on his footsteps outside my door at least three times a day.

"I woke up with a strange feeling this morning. Something is different. I thought maybe that something might be you."

"It might be," I answer with a shrug. Then I look him over carefully. He looks as rested as I've seen him in a while. His eyes are bright, his beard neatly trimmed, and his hair is as tame as it can be. With all this time near the sea, his curls are more pronounced, and I find it difficult to resist reaching up to tousle them. Still, there's something different about him as well. "You're restless."

"You always see right through me." He smiles and fingers the opal on my necklace I have managed to tie around my neck. The clasp is still broken, but I was determined to keep it on me. "I have no mystery left in me."

"On the contrary. I've been realizing just how little I know." It has never seemed like quite the right time to ask the questions I have about Felix, but perhaps we've reached that point now. He seems to agree.

"Come walk with me." He offers his arm but with less formality than usual. I take it and tuck myself against him as we make our way to the main deck and into the bright morning sunshine. I prepare myself for the view of the sea as he leads me toward the railing, and I know he must feel me tense.

"It's all right." Felix directs me in front of him and then encircles me in his arms from behind. It's such an intimate gesture from a man who's usually so reserved. "I don't want you to fear it. Respect it, yes, but not fear."

"It tried to kill me," I remind him.

"Yes, but since when has that ever stopped you from charging ahead?"

A fair point, so I concede it.

"I want to teach you to swim when we get to Solitarius."

"Hmm." I hum a noncommittal response. It doesn't sound like much fun to me, but with the way he's holding me right now, I would probably agree to almost anything.

"You were right."

"What?" That's probably the last thing I expected him to say. I manage to put just enough space between us so I can look over my shoulder into his eyes. The emotion I find there nearly knocks me to my knees. This seems almost too good to be true, and I wait expectedly for his hesitation or for some sort of withdrawal from our closeness in this moment, but it doesn't come.

"Don't make me say it again," he laughs shakily as he loosens his hold on me just slightly and I turn to face him. "You said I couldn't protect you from God's plan, and you were right. If the last few days showed me anything, it's how powerless I am."

I want to disagree, to reassure him that it's not true, except it is. He is powerless, and so I am. I still don't understand how all this works, but I know God's power easily overrides my best laid plans every time. And yet, Felix does hold a sort of power over me, one that I can't quite put into words.

"You asked me a question in Borealis, on your wedding day," he continues, "and I never gave you an answer. I owe you one, and I think I'm brave enough to give it to you now."

My heart pounds so forcefully against my chest, I'm sure he must be able to see it. I know exactly what he's referring to. We stood in the hallway before my wedding with a path laid out clearly before us. I would marry Ronan, and he would return to Solitarius. A path neither of us would have chosen. I'd asked him what he wanted because I just needed a reason not to go through with it, and Felix had deflected the question by asking me what *I* wanted. And I had told him, only to be left desperate to hear him return those words. "Yes?"

"You. I want you if you'll still have me." I know I don't imagine the embers of hope that kindle to life in his eyes.

I open my mouth to respond that yes, of course, I still want him, but no words come out because he's kissing me.

There's something different about this one. I've catalogued each one up to this point, and none of them have been laden with this much confidence, steadiness. Until now our kisses have always been tinged with desperation, urgency, and even a little sadness. An unbalance of power. I taste none of that now. Instead, there's a quiet confidence, a hunger that makes my heart pound and warmth rush through me despite the cool wind off the water.

Even the ending is sweet. There's no rush to pull away, no shame as we both lament our lack of willpower. There is nothing to keep us apart. Instead, he gently pulls away and smiles down at me. He doesn't apologize, and he doesn't run. He's planted his flag as the conquering army, and I mean to let him occupy my heart.

"That's how it should have been," he mutters as he nuzzles my ear. "Our first kiss, I mean. I've thought about it every day since we left Aurora. I shouldn't have rushed it in that tunnel. Because I've spent all these days wishing I could have savored it—kissing you like it was the first time instead of the last."

And that's it. That's exactly why every kiss we've shared has never completely satisfied me. Because it always felt like the last time. It always *should* have been the last time.

"I love you." I give him the words I've withheld for both our sakes. But there's no reason to hold them any longer.

Felix bows his head, and I almost reach out to raise his chin because I desperately want to see any reaction on his face. But I stand still instead. Because this must be a lot to process. I know it is for me. But I have rarely been as certain about anything as I am about the words I just said.

Finally, he lifts his head, and his eyes glisten with what must be unshed tears, though I have a hard time reconciling that with the stoic soldier in front of me.

"I-I didn't realize," he says slowly, "but I think I've been waiting my whole life to hear you say that."

And then I'm in his arms, and he's lifting me up and spinning me around. And we laugh, the first real laugh either of us has had in much too long. Felix loosens his grip on me until I slide down his chest and my lips are level with his. He kisses me, softly, tenderly, as the tips of my toes just brush the ground. He is still holding me up, just as he always has. Just as he always will. I know that with certainty, too.

"I love you, too," he mutters against my lips. I swallow the words and feel hope spring to life within me.

"It's going to be difficult," I remind him because I can't seem to let it go without acknowledging the shadow above us. "Loving 'The Princess Who Was Promised' won't be an easy thing."

"Loving you is the easiest thing in the world," he corrects me. "Letting go will be the difficult part."

But I don't want to think about that, so I kiss him again. Now that there's nothing keeping me from it, I think I might want to spend the rest of my life kissing him.

"Tell me why you love the sea," I say as he spins me in his arms again so my back is pressed to his chest. "You seem so at home on the water."

Felix doesn't reply right away. "I didn't really have much of a choice growing up around the sea and ships."

I resist the urge to roll my eyes even though he can't see my face. So predictable. "Are you going to tell me about it or am I going to have to drag everything out of you?"

He chuckles slightly at this. "As if I could ever resist your questioning. As if I could resist anything from you. I suppose it's time you know." When he puts some space between us and leans on the railing, I let him. Because maybe this story is too big to be confined to our little bubble.

"I grew up in Solitarius with my parents and my brother. We had a happy life. My family was well off by the standards in our city. My father owned several boats and employed fishermen to fish the waters around us. I used to go out with them, and they taught me to sail. I enjoyed all of it."

He seems a million miles away as he stares out across the sea. I wait silently, hoping he'll answer my unasked question.

"I was a curious boy. I liked to explore, and my younger brother always insisted on tagging along. My mother would always make me wait for him when we went out to play with the other children. He was always slowing me down."

I see the subtle shift in his posture, the way his head dips, and know this story is about to take a dark turn. Still, I wait for him to speak.

"I was looking for something for my father one day when I found this old map—a treasure map to me. Right away I wanted to follow it. Maximus begged to come with me, but I told him no. The last thing I needed was him slowing me down. So, I ran off without him…or so I thought. I followed the map as best I could, and it led me to this cave. I was deep into it when I heard Max calling for me. I told him to go home, but he didn't listen. He was trying so hard to keep up."

I'm biting my lip to keep tears at bay. Tears for a little boy I will never know and for the man standing in front of me.

"When he fell, he screamed my name," Felix chokes out. "I tried to make it back to him, but I was too late." With a fist, he rubs his eyes. "He was already gone when I carried him home."

"The grief destroyed my family. My parents grew quiet, and I couldn't bear to see the pity and grief in their eyes. I couldn't live with myself anymore. So, when I saw those Imperial flags on that ship, I decided I needed to get away. I needed a fresh start. I needed to be able to be someone other than who I was."

I step closer and take his hand. He grabs hold of me like I'm a lifeline.

"I stowed away on that ship, and Ronan found me when we were well out to sea. I could have been killed for that, but he begged his father to let me live, to let me stay with them. By the time we reached Aurora, the two of us were inseparable. But I still felt guilty because I had led my brother to his death, and God had seen fit to give me another one."

There are so many things I want to ask, but I can't bring myself to put him through any more of this. The guilt and grief of being responsible for the death of someone you hold dear is something I'm all too familiar with. It's not something that can be assuaged with platitudes.

"And now you're going back." I hadn't realized what a monumental decision it was for him to return to Solitarius.

"I'm going back," he affirms. "Because this is where God has led me. He has forgiven me, and I am learning to forgive myself. I think I need to go home for that forgiveness to be complete."

Felix straightens and faces me, placing a hand on my cheek and letting his thumb lightly trace my lips. "I am so grateful I have you by my side for this. I'm not sure I would be strong enough for it on my own."

I place my hand over his and kiss his thumb. "Then we will be strong together."

19

It's late morning when the call rings out that land has been spotted. I'm about to see Solitarius. As it turns out, that gives me plenty of time to work myself into a nervous mess by the time our ship actually makes port. I absolutely hate walking into a situation I can't prepare for. Since he's been absent for so long, Felix can't tell me much, but Alara fills in a few gaps. She grew up on the island as well, but she left with her family to return to the mainland when she was a child. As such, she's maintained more contact with her home than Felix has. Occasional letters and news reached her in Borealis, and she often sent back updates on the status of the Insurgo persecution to the island.

Solitarius does not have a monarch we'll have to present ourselves to. They've apparently never seen the need for such formality as long as the rest of the empire left them alone. Alara says the people are governed by a group of seven judges called the Synod. She gives Felix a look as she delivers this bit of information, but he ignores her, busying himself preparing our things to go ashore.

"We should probably meet with them first thing," I suggest. "How can we go about requesting an audience?"

"Oh, I don't think that will be a problem," Alara smirks.

Before I can even attempt to puzzle out her meaning, the call comes for us to disembark. The supplies gifted to us by the King of Zephyros are carried down the gangplank ahead of us and stacked into a neat pile on the pier below. Antioch, Alara, and Ronan descend first, and Felix moves to follow them. But I grab his hand and pull him back to me for a quick moment.

"Whatever happens," I begin as I curl my fingers around the back of his neck, "I am with you." I have to stretch up on my toes to press a soft kiss to his mouth.

"And I'm with you. We're in this together." He laces his fingers with mine and leads me down the gangplank to his home.

We join the rest of our group as a young man with a notebook in hand approaches us. "Welcome to Solitarius," he greets warmly. "May I have your names and your purpose here?" His pen is poised over the paper as he looks to each of us, but when his eyes land on Felix, he nearly drops it.

His tanned skin, even darker than my own, blanches and his eyes widen. "Are you… But you can't be?"

Somewhere behind me, Alara chuckles.

"I am Felix Fidelis," Felix replies stiffly, his hand tightening around mine, though his expression remains neutral.

"Yes, forgive me, sir." The man bows then fumbles to record the name in his book. "Y-you look so like your father… God rest his soul."

My jaw drops. This man just *bowed* to Felix. Yes, I know he's imposing and commanding, but he's never provoked that sort of reaction as far as I know. And his father? The muscles of his jaw tick slightly as I know they do when he clenches his teeth. He didn't know. He's barely set foot on the island only to be greeted with news of his father's death.

"May I ask what is the purpose of your visit?"

"We need to see the Synod at once." In complete contrast to my hesitation, Felix's voice is strong and commanding and reminds me of who he is apart from the man who loves me.

Our one-man welcome committee blinks in surprise. "Yes, well of course you would want to. I mean… She is after all… But perhaps you'd like to find lodging first?"

"Now," Felix insists, leaving no room for argument.

The man does a funny bow and then motions us to follow him. We all look to Felix who gives a slight shake of his head.

"Told you," Alara whispers as she saunters past me to take up the lead.

Our odd procession winds up from the docks into the city proper. I suppose it's a city. It's more like what I'd call a town back home. The houses on the outskirts are generously spaced but grow denser the closer we get to what I assume to be the city center. The homes aren't elaborate, but they are simple and sturdy and filled with life. Colorful market stalls line the streets, and children dart in and out, playing games of tag. The people are simply dressed in thin flowing cloth to account for the heat, but most wear a smile or a serene expression. There's a peacefulness here—one we're about to shatter.

As we pass, I notice a curious phenomenon. I'm used to stares and whispers directed at me or Ronan, but no one seems to pay us any mind. Instead, all are directed at Felix. Just like the man who greeted us upon arrival, many look like they've seen a ghost.

Suddenly the narrow market streets open up into a huge plaza, which is more ornate than anything we've seen so far. People mill about the square without a care in the world. Even more merchants have set up here, displaying wares from colorful tapestries to gemstones. These are not warriors. They are tradesmen, and merchants, and artists, and children. Peace is a beautiful thing, but it does not forge soldiers.

A man sits on a bench with a guitar singing a ballad I'm unfamiliar with. For just a moment I forget why we're there, and I begin to drift toward the man until Alara steps in front of me and herds me back into place.

It breaks my heart that my presence might bring destruction on these people. But I don't think Cyrus would hesitate to attack even if I hadn't come here. He's going to either take the Gate or wipe out everyone who might ever threaten his rule. And as I've just seen, he would meet little opposition here.

We stop in front of a basilica comprised of stately marble columns holding a beautifully painted portico. I get the sense the city revolves around this place. This must be where the Synod meets.

Sure enough, our guide leads us up a few stairs and pauses outside the doors before turning to face us. "If you will wait here one moment, I will let them know you're here." He disappears through the doors without waiting for our response.

Felix lets go of my hand and steps a bit forward as if he's considering following the man inside. He pauses, hesitates, and I see his lips moving in silent prayer. Then the door reopens and our guide motions us inside.

"They are most eager to see you, my lord." He directs his words at Felix who walks ahead of our group. How does he know Felix is a lord? We didn't tell him that. "Your mother especially."

Felix stops and I nearly crash into him. Alara mutters something under her breath as I hear the rest of them come to a sudden halt as well.

"My mother?" His voice shakes slightly with the question.

"Yes, my lord. But of course, you do not know. Your mother is now the chief judge of the Synod."

These words seem to reverberate through the spacious nave as we all try to absorb them. I seriously underestimated the emotional toll this was going to take on Felix, but how could any of us predict it?

Without warning, Felix brushes past the man and pushes open the doors directly in front of us. They boom as they hit the walls which open up into the apse. Its semicircular shape pulls all eyes to a focal point where a raised tribunal sits below an ornate dome. The dome is a flash of colors against the sunlight streaming through, and below it, bathed in a rainbow of light, sit seven figures atop the tribunal. Felix's hands tremble as they fall to his sides.

No one moves for a moment. It's unearthly still in here as if no one would even dare breathe. Then a figure stands from her seat and steps into the center of the semi-circle, facing Felix.

Felix's mother is a tall, slender woman. She possesses an enviable grace despite her simple dress and posture. There is something regal about her, though I'm instantly certain she's never been one for jewels or crowns even if she earned them. And she terrifies me. Well, not her exactly, but the thought that she might disapprove of me. I want her to like me, to think I'm a worthy choice for her long-lost son who has just returned home. The son she likely thought dead until this moment.

They stare at each other as everyone around them holds their breath—including me. Even those who know Felix or his mother best seem unable to predict how this reunion will go.

"Felix." Her voice is breathy, soft. As if she has merely exhaled his name from the place where it's been stored within her all these years. It's amazing how much emotion can be contained in just that one word. Maybe it's only because I know some of the story, but I hear longing, pain, disbelief, and love. Overwhelming love. This is a woman who never really gave up on her eldest son and who certainly never stopped loving him. I can imagine her, all these years, whispering his name to herself each night as if issuing a siren call for him to return home.

And now he has. I look to him to find his face transformed with such cautious hope that it makes him look years younger.

This is what I imagine little Felix must have looked like—mussed hair, wide dark eyes, and an almost crooked grin on his face. Gone are the lines from frowns and stern looks. Gone is the hardness in his eyes. He looks like a new man. One who has finally woken up from a long sleep.

His lips part as if to speak, but no sound comes out. Or if it does, it is muffled by his mother who throws herself on his chest.

20

"Mother, I mean, my lady…" Felix struggles with how to address the woman who still clings tightly to him. Gently he takes her by the shoulders and steps back so there is space between them. "I need to introduce you to my companions."

His mother blinks back tears and gives him a wavering smile. Behind her, the other six members of the Synod have yet to move. "Of course you do. Please proceed." She turns to rejoin the others still sitting in the semi-circle. Felix waits for her to take her seat and then turns to us.

"My name is Felix Fidelis, Lord Commander of the Queensguard of Borealis and formerly of the Imperial Guard. Allow me to introduce Alara and Antioch, both of whom have traveled with us from Borealis at great personal risk. Also with me is Imperial Prince Ronan Dominus."

Ronan steps forward until he is even with Felix and nods his head in acknowledgment to the gathering before us. A low murmur greets him in response. I imagine his position is more likely to make him feared than loved in a place like this.

Finally, Felix turns to me. I think for a moment he's going to take my hand, but instead he just holds his out to gesture for me to step in front of him. He will let me stand on my own strength now.

"And this is Emilia Aurelius, rightful Queen of Borealis."

I incline my head slightly as the murmurs that began with Ronan escalate into loud whispers. My mother's name cuts through the din of voices, and my face flushes.

"I am the daughter of Alexandra Aurelius, the martyred queen," I call out loud and clear. "More importantly, I am the daughter of the Most High King and servant of the one true God. We are here to bring you a warning and to ask for information concerning a prophecy and the Gate of Life."

All whispers cease at my words. The room is utterly still, and I suddenly find it hard to breathe. Where do I go from here? Can I really march in here and claim to be the fulfillment of the prophecy that I don't even understand? Will they laugh me out of the room?

I look to Felix for help, but before he can speak, Ronan opens his mouth.

"Emilia is the Princess Who Was Promised."

His voice rings loud and clear into the silence. I can't read the faces of those before us from this distance, but I can tell enough to see that they are not ecstatic that their supposed savior has arrived.

Felix's mother stands again, breaking the spell Ronan cast with his pronouncement.

"That is quite the claim, and this is too important a conversation to have before you are settled and rested."

"It really is quite urgent we speak," I say with increasing desperation. We may have a head start on Cyrus, but I don't want to waste a moment of it.

"I understand," she says with a firm but gentle tone. "But we need a moment to conclude the business we were discussing when you arrived. We can reconvene this evening when we can give the matter our full attention. We have housing we can offer you."

It's a very rational proposal—I can see where Felix gets it from—and one we have no choice but to accept. I'm not sure I'll be able to rest, but it would be nice to have a bath and change clothes before we present our crazy story to our gracious hosts.

"That would be welcome," Alara speaks up. Like Felix, her expression is unreadable to me. What does she think of our reception, and how is she coping with being back in her home country? It remains to be seen. "Perhaps an inn or something, my lady?"

I'm surprised by the deference she offers Felix's mother, and even more surprised when the older woman smiles in return.

"Alara. I have known you since you were a child, running wild around the island with Maximus. There is no need for formality. Call me Miriam, please."

"Perhaps something more private than an inn," Ronan interjects. "We can pay well."

Miriam waves him off. "We don't have an inn as such anyway. Not exactly many visitors to support it. There are some vacant homes near the edge of the city. Their inhabitants have migrated to the mainland. We offer them to anyone in need of a place to stay. Usually, sailors occupy them for a few nights at most, but you are most welcome to stay as long as you like."

"Thank you," I reply, careful to omit any address. I don't know if the invitation to call her by her first name was open to all of us or just Alara. "We sincerely appreciate your kind offer."

"If I may speak." Antioch surprises me by stepping forward and bowing his frail body before Miriam and the others behind her. "I have heard you possess a complete copy of the Aletheia. It is my heart's deepest desire to be able to read from it. Might there be a place, a room near your place of worship perhaps, where I might be permitted to examine the text and pray?"

Thank goodness at least one of us has their priorities straight. That should have been my first request as well. But Antioch is better equipped than any of us to glean what the Aletheia may have to tell us.

"Of course," Miriam agrees. "Daniel," she gestures to a young man who I hadn't even noticed standing against the wall. Upon further inspection, there are a few young men and women at various intervals around the room. Stewards perhaps? "Will you please escort Antioch to the sanctuary?"

Antioch picks up his small pack of belongings and follows the young man through a door adjacent to the large room we stand in now. Just like that, our party is now four. I move closer to Ronan and Felix, and Alara follows suit in uncharacteristic silence. It seems more important than ever that we stay together.

"Now." Miriam clasps her hands in front of her and turns her attention back to us. "Let's get the rest of you settled. As I mentioned, there are several vacant homes. Would you each like your own, or do you prefer to remain together?"

"Together," Felix and I answer in unison. Miriam's eyes dart between us and then focus on her son.

"Felix, will you…would you like to have your things brought home? To my home, I mean?"

Felix's posture stiffens, and I desperately wish I could decipher the flood of emotions in his eyes. "I appreciate the kind offer," he says cooly, "but my place is with my queen."

His eyes meet mine for the briefest of moments, and then he leads the way out of the room without further discussion.

We are given our choice of homes by the stewards who help carry our things to the dwellings. They even retrieve the supplies we left behind at the pier when we were escorted to the Synod. Felix has chosen a house at the edge of the city, closest to the water and—I imagine—furthest from his mother. At the very least, it minimizes the prying eyes that must be dying to know about us.

The house is small but quaint. Whoever once lived here apparently loved color. The walls are painted various shades of blue, and the upholstery on the fabric is faded and dusty but still boasts a variety of shades of greens, gold, and black. It must have been a family because there are two bedrooms, a kitchen, and a common area that houses a fireplace and several comfortable chairs. This is not a home for sailors but rather a place where children's laughter once filled the rooms and cozy nights were shared around the fire.

What happened to this family? Based on Miriam's information, they likely left the island for the mainland. But where did they go? Are they still alive? Or did they burn to death in Cyrus's raids? Are they dead because of me?

Felix and Ronan agree to take the bedroom with two small beds, which leaves the larger bedroom with a giant bed occupying most of the room for me and Alara. I don't like the idea of sharing a bed with her, but beggars can't be choosers. At least we're together.

Once the stewards have helped carry in our luggage and affirmed that they will bring food to stock our kitchen, they leave us to our unpacking. Except I don't really want to unpack my things. I'd like to think I could settle here for a while, but something in my gut suggests otherwise. The restlessness I felt on the ship is still there. As with most things lately, I'm unsure how to interpret it.

Alara opens her pack and places her folded clothes in the top drawer of a dresser against the wall opposite the bed. Then she proceeds to hide various weapons around the room. A dagger goes into the drawer with her clothes. A whip coiled into her extra pair of boots. A small bow and quiver of arrows slide under the bed.

"Where did you get all that?" I'm envious. Nothing makes me feel more in control than having a weapon in my hand.

"Ronan requested some personal defense weapons from the Zephyros king. He and Felix have several things in their packs as well."

"And what about me?"

"You had too many clothes to fit any weapons with your things. But hey, at least you can disarm them with your feminine charms."

I look down at my current outfit—a pair of black pants and an oversized white tunic. In contrast to the outfit I wore to dinner in Zephyros, this shows none of my curves, none of my skin, and none of my royalty. Hardly impressive but certainly functional. But perhaps I should make more of an effort when we meet with the Synod this evening.

I don't feel like arguing with Alara, so I leave her to claim her side of the bed and wander into the common room instead. I'm admiring the fireplace when Felix steps into the room.

Away from public scrutiny, he looks tense rather than calm and collected. His posture is straight, and I can see how he clenches his jaw as he looks me over.

"Is everything acceptable with the accommodations?"

His question takes me aback. Why is he being so formal? What I want is for him to join me, to put his arms around me, and to help me craft a plan for how to present our case to the Synod.

"Of course," I answer as I cautiously approach him. "Are you all right?"

"I'm fine," he lies.

"Felix, it's okay if you're upset. It's a lot for anyone, seeing your mother, learning about your father—"

"I said I'm fine."

I recoil at his coolness. I know it's not aimed at me, but I don't appreciate him pushing me aside.

"You're not, so I'll forgive you for that. Deal with it how you will, and I'll be here when you're ready to talk about it."

"What if I don't want to talk about it?"

"You're not protecting me by keeping your feelings from me. I want to share them all, even the ugly ones."

A flicker of something dances across his face, but it's quickly replaced by the mask I've spent months trying to remove. As much as I want to stand here and beg him to remove it, it would just end in an argument, and there are too many more important uses of my time.

Despite my better judgment, I attempt to recruit Alara to help me carry water to the house so we can bathe. Instead, she suggests a trip to the bathing pool she remembers from her time here as a child. I was looking forward to just sponging myself clean from a basin rather than immersing myself in water, but I'm curious to see more of the island, and it would be glorious to wash my hair.

She explains to Felix and Ronan where we're going, and neither of them object. I think we all have a lot to process, and a couple hours apart would probably do us all good.

I follow Alara out of the city proper and over rocky and rugged terrain. At one point I'm nearly on all fours as I climb up a steep rock formation, and I seriously start to wonder if it's worth all this trouble for a bath.

Then we reach the top and look down upon a gorgeous series of pools formed by hollowed gorges in the black rock. Further out, the rock forms a sort of wall between the pools and the sea. It's terrifying and beautiful in equal measure.

"When the tide is high, waves crest the wall and fill the pools. The sun warms the water so you can bathe in it," Alara explains as she begins the precarious descent to the first pool. "Most people have baths in their homes that they can heat water for, but some still prefer the pools. As children we used to swim here. It's where most of us learned to swim away from the waves."

A crazy thought crosses my mind. "Could you teach me how?"

She stops and nearly slips on a rock. Then she turns back to me with a frown. "You want *me* to teach you to swim?"

"Yes?"

"Aren't you afraid I'll drown you or something?"

I consider it for a moment. "If you wanted to kill me you could have done it already. And I think you like annoying me too much to actually get rid of me."

She purses her lips in thought. "Good point. Although I was hoping to be better than you in at least one thing."

"You're better than me at lots of things," I remind her as we finally reach the edge of the pool. "Ask Felix. I even told him that you're better at being me than I am."

"I could never be you."

I wait for her to follow it with some comment about how I'm too weak or cowardly or indecisive for her to lower herself to that level, but she doesn't say anything more.

After some hesitation on both our parts, we strip our clothes off and lay them on the rocks so we can bathe. Alara produces a bar of lathering soap from her pocket, and we both wade into the water naked as the day we were born.

This water is pleasantly warm and clear and calm. The fear and panic I associate with the sea is diminished here. As long as I focus on the crystal clear water, the way my feet kick sea shells as I walk, then I can tolerate it. More than that, I find I actually like it. After a few careful steps, I sink down into the pool until I'm submerged up to my chin.

I look around for Alara and nearly scream when she pops up from the water an arm's length from me. She shakes her wet head and sends water drops flying that glisten in the sun. It's maybe the first time I've seen her truly smile.

"It's been too long," she says, more to herself than me. Then she laughs and dives back under the water again.

I watch her for several minutes, laughing and diving, and swimming in lazy circles. It's like the water has brought something dead back to life. I want that feeling, too.

So, I hold my breath, steel my nerves, and plunge myself under the water. I can't be under for more than a few seconds, but the change that comes over me when I reemerge is dramatic. I sputter and blink to clear my eyes, but I feel different somehow as if I left something beneath the water.

Alara laughs at me now, but it's a joyful laugh and not a mean-spirited one. Then she passes me the bar of soap so I can begin washing myself. I take my time, inhaling the eucalyptus scent of the soap and closing my eyes to focus on the feel of the water. It's not so scary now. Rather than drowning me, it's cleaning me so I can emerge fresh and new.

After I've washed my hair for a second time and Alara has finished bathing, we turn our attention to swimming. I show her the little I know about staying afloat, which I've only had occasion to practice whenever my military unit was stationed near a pond or something much smaller than the sea. She assesses me and then instructs me to begin kicking my legs while floating on my back. I do and immediately begin to sink. Panic seeps in as I struggle to keep my head above water, but she puts her hands underneath me and gently pushes me back up. I relax marginally and am finally able to flutter my legs in the water while keeping my head afloat.

I lose track of how long we stay at the pool, but when we climb out to dry off in the sun before we dress, my fingers and toes are wrinkled, and I can feel the heat where the sun kissed all the parts of me I usually keep hidden. It's absolutely glorious, and I haven't felt so free in a very long time. Maybe ever. I marvel at the darkness of my skin and appreciate its beauty. It only ever marked me as different, but here I look like everyone else, and I love the golden shade the sun has added to my arms and legs.

The sun is much lower in the sky when we arrive back at the house we've taken over. My stomach is growling, and my feet are cut from walking barefoot over shells and rocks, but the smile on my face is genuine.

When we enter the house, Felix and Ronan both stand from where they were seated at the dining table and look us over. Felix's face flushes and he looks away, but Ronan drinks us both in, though I notice his eyes linger a bit longer over Alara. We must be quite the sight. We are sun-kissed with waves of unbound dark hair falling down our backs, no shoes on our feet, and slightly damp clothes clinging to us. Maybe I should be embarrassed, but I'm not. These are the feminine charms Alara alluded to earlier, and they do seem to have a lot of power.

The spell is broken as Felix removes a cloth covering a basket to reveal fresh rolls. Beside the basket is a large platter of fish covered in some sort of sauce and a bowl of some chunks of yellow stuff that he calls pineapple. I must look skeptical because he picks up a piece with his fingers and touches it to my lips. The sweetness of the fruit is matched only by the heat in his eyes, and I don't break eye contact with him while I'm chewing.

"Ahem," Ronan coughs. I start, blushing as I'm very much aware that Felix and I are not alone in the room. "As much as I hate to interrupt this moment, we were waiting on the two of you to return so we could eat together."

"Where did you get all this?" Alara asks as she claims the chair next to Ronan and immediately helps herself to a roll.

"My mother," Felix answers as he pulls out my chair for me and then takes the one next to it for himself. "She sent her stewards with all this and several more things to last us through the evening. They said it should hold us over until we can shop at the markets in the morning. Most will be closed by the time we go back into the city to meet with the Synod this evening."

"Do we have a time for that?" I ask as I begin filling my plate with the assortment of food before me. I make sure to get extra pineapple. We never had anything like this in Borealis.

"Eight bells," Felix says as he takes a bite of bread. "They have made it an open forum. All the people of the city are invited to attend."

"So, we're not merely convincing seven members of the Synod, but an entire city?" Alara clarifies. "As if we haven't had enough challenges thus far."

I have to agree. "We don't even know what we're really asking for. I had hoped to have a conversation with the Synod, to glean information so we had a better idea what to request. But we can't go before an entire city and seem clueless. We'll lose all credibility."

"We just have to convince them you're the chosen one," Ronan says. "If they believe that of you, they'll give you whatever you need even if it's time to consider your request."

He's not wrong about that, but I don't much like the approach. I don't like walking into a situation uninformed.

"Maybe Antioch will have found something to help," Alara suggests. "He seems to know more about this than anyone."

"I'm not certain about that," Felix mutters. His surliness intrigues me. It's not the first time he's insinuated he might not have a blind faith in Antioch. There's a tension between the two of them that I can't explain. As far as I know, they've rarely spoken just the two of them, but Felix seems a bit wary of him, and Antioch seems too interested in the Commander.

"He's been studying this for years and had access to more information than any of us," I remind gently. "I might not like what he has to say, but I don't have any reason to think he's wrong."

Felix doesn't argue, and we all turn our attention back to the food in front of us. Ronan asks questions about the island and the city, and Alara answers most of them with Felix chiming in with the occasional anecdote. I simply let them carry on as I lose myself in my thoughts.

Everything feels more real, more imminent now that we're here. Part of me never believed we'd make it this far, but we still have so far to travel. I can't even begin to do whatever it is I must until we find the location of this Gate. If the people here knew where it was, all of this would have been resolved long ago. So, what am I hoping to gain by appealing to them?

Maybe I don't need to actually find the Gate. I simply need to stop Cyrus. But he will not stop until he's either wiped out every Insurgo or claimed the Gate's power for himself…which he will then use to wipe out every Insurgo. And if I am to stop him, I need the power of the Gate. It's a circular argument that makes my head spin.

On exactly the eighth toll of the bell, I push open the doors to the meeting hall in the center of the city. Not as forcefully as Felix did upon our first entry, but with enough authority that all eyes turn to look as I stride into the room. I'm afraid if I don't demonstrate some strength, I'll lose my nerve completely.

The theater hall we entered earlier is now full of people. Rows and rows of benches in a semi-circle at staggered levels so that everyone has a clear view of the floor. A clear view of me. A hush falls over the crowd as Felix, Ronan, Alara, and Antioch take their places beside me.

The members of the Synod—all seven of them—sit in chairs on the slightly raised tribunal, which means they are just barely above me. Five men and two women—including Felix's mother—make up their ranks. Most appear to be around the age my parents would have been if they were living. One man is gray and slightly stooped. All are looking me over, appraising me and no doubt evaluating the little they know of me already.

I dressed in one of the gowns gifted to me from Verity in Zephyros. It's simple enough, but the deep blue fabric and subtle adornments set it apart from the clothing that most women here seem to favor. I did, however, leave my hair unbound as I've noted most women do. I want to look authoritative, but not as if I'm a product of the Empire. I need them to believe I am one of them, or this will never work.

Miram rises, and even the few whispers that remain fall silent. Earlier I thought perhaps she took the lead in questioning us simply because of Felix. But I watch the way she commands the room now and think she must truly be in charge. The man who'd escorted us from the docks had called Felix "lord" without knowing anything more than his name. Is this why? Was he born into some sort of Insurgo royalty?

"We welcome our distinguished visitors to the Forum this evening." Miriam's voice rings out strong and true. "The Queen of Borealis and the Crown Prince of Aurora have come to us with grave news from the mainland. I have asked them to address you all this evening so that you may hear whatever petition they put forth."

Unrest ripples through the crowd, and I don't have to guess why. Given what the Empire has done to them and their families, I don't blame them for distrusting two people who claim to have some level of control over that empire.

I look to Ronan only to find him looking back at me with questions in his blue eyes. It seems unfair to ask him to make this speech when he doesn't even believe in it. No, this is my job.

"Greetings to the good people of Solitarius," I begin lamely. Public speaking has never come naturally to me. I don't know how to be diplomatic. So, I just give up and appeal to them as an equal. "I am Emilia Aurelius of Borealis, but I am not its queen. I once thought I could help the Insurgos, help all of you, from that throne, but events of the last few weeks have made it absolutely clear that's not possible. So, I am here not as a queen but as a fellow believer in the one God, the King of Kings.

"I know the persecution our people have suffered at the hands of the empire. When I was a child, I watched my mother burned for simply having the courage to teach her daughter the truth of a God who became His own sacrifice for His people." I take a deep breath and close my eyes before continuing. "I have witnessed the last breaths of those who gave everything to spread the message of hope and peace. I have walked through the ashes of villages and camps where countless lives were lost for no other reason than Emperor Cyrus fears for his throne."

Ronan grabs my hand, and I gladly step back to let him speak.

"Emperor Cyrus—my father—has been informed of a prophecy concerning the Gate of Life. He believes the Insurgos are a threat to his kingdom and the empire as a whole. According to an oracle of Caelus, an Insurgo leader will rise up, receiving power from the Ancient and the Gate of Life, and overthrow all the rulers in the empire."

The older man from the Synod stands, and Ronan pauses. It takes him a moment to cross the floor until he stops just a few paces away from us. There's something in his eyes that reminds me of Levi. Will I never be free of his ghost?

"We have heard a similar prophecy," he says in a surprisingly strong voice. "God has promised to rescue His people and to dwell with them in a promised land."

"Yes, about that." I need to understand this as much for my own sake as for any hope of thwarting Cyrus. "This promised land is a place where God dwells with man. The entrance to this land is through the Gate, right? It is the seat of His power where the veil between Heaven and Earth is thin. This is the place Caspian set out to find, isn't it?"

"Some would say Caspian himself is a myth," one of the younger men from the Synod says.

"Except he's not," interjects Antioch, and all eyes turn to him. There's a fire in his eyes. I can't tell if it comes from indignation or passion. "There are historical texts, secular texts, which support not only his existence but also his rebellion against the empire."

"I agree," says Miriam. "But Caspian and his army disappeared on the excursion and never returned. If they had found such a place, wouldn't they have received the power of God and been able to prevent the persecution that's occurred for several hundred years?"

"Maybe he was not the one." Antioch's voice seems stronger now. "The scriptures indicate there is one who is worthy to approach the throne and be given the power of the Ancient to subdue the nations."

Here we go. There's no turning back from this.

"We believe that person is Emilia," Ronan adds hastily before he can be drowned out by the stirrings of the crowd. They don't bother to hide their unease at this pronouncement as they turn to one another and speak a low dissent. I don't blame them. I don't look like much, and many had already put hope in my mother only to be disappointed.

Antioch clears his throat, and a hush falls over the people. "There are many things that will mark the one chosen to approach the Ancient. The Ruler Who Will Rise Up will appear during the worst persecution when there seems to be no hope. There will be signs and wonders to indicate they have arrived." Antioch pauses and looks at me. "And the chosen ruler will have to make a great sacrifice."

The rumble that drifts through the crowd like a wave has a decidedly more sympathetic tone now. I lift my chin defiantly. I might be the sacrificial lamb, but I want them to know I have the heart of a lion. It's much more difficult to maintain this demeanor when I feel Felix's eyes on me. I don't know how much he knew about the prophecy exactly. We've known from the beginning this mission was dangerous, and it's certainly not the first time my life has been threatened. But this is the first time it's implied that I will willingly give it up. Even with the physical space between us, I can feel the anger and sadness radiating from him.

“And what do you need from us?” Miriam’s eyes are kind, but I see some sadness behind them as well.

“Any information you have. Whatever scriptures that mention the prophecy or the Gate can be filtered through Antioch. He has the most information and may be able to put the puzzle together better than the rest of us.”

“But why do we need to find it?” One of the younger men asks. “Surely God will not deem the Emperor worthy to receive His power. We need only sit back and watch him fail.”

“He won’t stop until he’s dead.” Ronan’s tone is flat, and I know he’s trying hard to keep emotion out of his voice. “If he can’t have the power, he’ll kill anyone who might be worthy to. He’s had no problem putting your people to death on the mainland. He will have no problem bringing his army here if that’s what it takes.”

“Our only hope of defeating him is to find the Gate and utilize the power there to defeat Cyrus.” As if it were that simple. Utilizing that power is the big question mark in all this. How? And at what cost?

“We don’t have an army,” the other woman of the Synod speaks up. “How can you expect to defeat an entire army even with this power with just the five of you?”

She’s being generous. Antioch is no fighter, and I’m not sure I could ask Ronan to kill his father. So, three of us then.

“I have seen God perform miracles at Emilia’s request,” Felix speaks up. He’s been oddly quiet up to this point, but when he speaks, people stop to listen. It’s been this way as long as I’ve known him. "She prayed and a storm destroyed the temple in Borealis. She prayed, and God healed me from a battle wound."

I catch Alara's smirk out of the corner of my eye. She gave Felix that "battle wound", albeit on accident.

"He has done great things before, and He will do them again." It's a confidence that reminds me of the times I've heard him pray. *I ask great things of a great God.*

"And," he continues, "You should also know there are Imperial troops on their way here now."

"Yes," I agree with renewed urgency. "We anticipate Cyrus will come here to begin his ground search for the Gate."

"No, not those troops," Felix interrupts me without making eye contact. "There are soldiers formerly of the Imperial Guard who are loyal to Emilia who are on their way here."

I gape at him. This is news to me. How? And when? And why am I just now finding this out?

"We should prepare accommodations for approximately a hundred soldiers. If there is an area where they can set up camp, they won't require actual housing. I would like to have at least one residence for the officers to stay in."

"You'll have it," the older man agrees.

"Gideon!" the woman cries out. "You can't just unilaterally make that decision. We must vote."

"I have prayed for years for this girl." He gestures to me, and my heart flutters in response. "Even before I knew her name. I have prayed that in my lifetime our brothers and sisters on the mainland would have peace. Are you going to stand there and let the opportunity slip by? I am on God's side, and if He has sent His chosen to us, who are we to argue with her?"

"Is it really wise to welcome Imperial troops into our fold?" Another man speaks up before anyone can argue with Gideon. "It might be seen as a sign of aggression against the Emperor." Several people murmur their agreement.

"My father is already coming for blood," Ronan announces grimly. "He will come with fire and will burn everything to the ground whether you welcome these soldiers or not. You might as well have men who are willing to fight to defend you."

My eyes land on a small girl with wide dark eyes and wild curly hair who stands from the front row. "I will fight," she shouts and raises her fist as if she holds a sword.

Miriam's face blanches, and she motions to someone who grabs the little girl's arm and pulls her back to her seat. Then she turns back to the five of us and nods.

"I can see the necessity of having soldiers here, but I won't force them on the people. The members of the Synod will vote in our private chambers, and our decision will be made public in the morning." To the larger audience of citizens she says, "if you wish to voice an opinion on the matter, you will have one hour to speak to one of us before we vote."

I wonder how many will take her up on the offer?

"In the meantime," she continues, "Antioch, you are most welcome to any information in our archives of scripture. I will have the priests show you where you might find anything you haven't already seen."

She and the other members of the Synod rise and exit the hall in silence. Then the gathered crowd begins to slowly disperse. It seems we are dismissed.

A line of people begins to form at the door the Synod exited through. Poised to give voice to their opinion I suspect. Among the exiting throng, several stop to speak with me or my companions. A few clasp my hand or bend to kiss it. One woman openly weeps as she envelops me in a hug. I'm not sure how to respond, but a man I assume is her husband, pulls her away from me and out into the night. Then, the little girl who stood during the assembly pauses by the door, eyeing me curiously. And I stare right back. I feel a connection with her as if she's who I might have been if I'd grown up here instead of in the palace.

"Emilia, let's go." It's Felix who presses his hand lightly against my back and directs me to a door opposite where the rest of the crowd exits. Though his touch is gentle, I can still feel the anger rolling off him. It reminds me that I'm none too pleased with him either. I guess you can only expect so much to be altered by those three little words.

"We need to go somewhere where we can talk. Just us. We need to get some things straight."

"Agreed," he says tightly.

We cannot afford to be in opposition to each other at this point. Either we're united, or Cyrus will crush us and everyone on this island in his path.

He leads me away from the city center and past the house we've claimed. Now that we're alone, the tension between us has eased, and I lace my fingers with his as if it's the most natural thing in the world. My hand fits so perfectly in his even with all our callouses and scars that they seemed destined to find each other. I don't want to argue with him. We've already wasted so much precious time letting miscommunication and circumstance hold us apart.

We end up on a lonely section of beach that's far from the pier where we came ashore. Things here are serene and unblemished. The moon reflects off the waters, and the stars wink down at us. Felix lowers himself to sit on the sand, and I join him. His arm goes around my shoulders, and I lean into him as we both stare out at the water.

"Felix?" I look up to study his face. The line of his jaw, the fullness of his lips, the rugged scruff of his beard... Next to Ronan, his beauty is understated. Selfishly, I'm glad I saw it first.

"Hmm?" He doesn't look at me, but I don't mind. I can think better when he isn't staring at me with those brown eyes.

"I know you did what you thought best, but I really wish you hadn't sent for soldiers. I'm not the queen any longer, and the soldiers are not under my command."

"Those men never took an oath of fealty to Borealis. They are pledged to me and by extension you. Their number might not be many, but they make up for it in loyalty."

There is no use arguing with him. Truthfully, I appreciate his willingness to act when I was so paralyzed by ignorance and fear. But I do wish he'd told me sooner. "When did you manage to get word to them? How do you know they're coming at all?"

"Before we left Borealis, I spoke with Antony. He begged to come with us, but I asked him to stay behind and gather as many men as he could and meet us on Solitarius."

"With what ships?"

Felix sighs heavily. "I told him to commandeer whatever he needed to in order to get here. Ronan wrote a letter and sealed it with his ring to give him the authority to do so."

So, Ronan knew about this, too.

"I know you're not happy about this..."

"No, I'm not, but I think it was probably the right thing to do. I mean, who are we to stand up to Cyrus and whatever force he brings with him?" Another thought grips me. "And what if we succeed? If Cyrus is killed, who rules Atlas?"

He looks at me long and hard. "I think the crown is yours for the taking."

"I don't want it. I'm not supposed to wear it." Certainly not the Imperial crown, but I find I'm quite content with my decision to leave the Borealis crown to my cousin Titus. "Titus will be a good king once he grows into it."

"I don't imagine he'll thank you much for putting him permanently into that position. He seemed eager to hand it over to you."

"My place is here. I'm not going back to Borealis or Aurora," I say as I watch his face for any hint of a reaction.

"But that's your home, your country," he replies neutrally. But I think I see a spark of something in his dark eyes.

"There's nothing there for me. You are my country now. You are my home."

I know I don't imagine the hope that kindles to life in his eyes. "Y-you can't just say things like that."

"Why not?

"Because if you don't mean it, if you change your mind..."

I silence him with a kiss. Slow and building until we both have to come up for air.

"I mean it." But I think maybe I understand his hesitation. "You're worried about the prophecy. About what Antioch said tonight."

"Of course, I'm worried, but not for the reasons you're imagining. I may not be as well-versed as Antioch in the scriptures and signs, but I don't for one minute believe you're supposed to sacrifice your life to give these people freedom."

"You don't?"

"No, but you do. And that's what scares me. I think the more he feeds you that narrative the more reckless you're going to become. You and I have already clashed about your protection in the past, but how can I argue when it's 'God's plan' for you to die?"

"I know you think I have some death wish, that I'm just going to go charging blindly ahead and risk myself unnecessarily. But I don't want to die, Felix." I touch his face and drag my thumb across his bottom lip. He inhales sharply. "I know you think I do things just to spite you, but even I wouldn't take it that far."

His lips twitch up in a crooked smile.

"I don't want to die," I repeat. "I have so much to live for now. I want to grow old with you. I want us both to have the family we never had as children. So, no, I won't go charging toward my death, but if God requires it of me, I won't run from it."

He takes my hand in his and removes it from his cheek. Then he presses my fingers to his lips and begins to pray.

"God, my Father, it all feels too much right now. I don't understand, but I know You are working. Make us worthy of the work You have called us to. I may not know Your plan, but Your promises are infinitely better than I could possibly imagine. Our hearts are wild, so help us find rest in You."

"Amen," I whisper. My heart is not just wild, it is beating out of my chest. I know now more than ever that the only thing strong enough to pull me away from Felix is God Himself.

21

Sleep comes easily but is anything but restful. My body is exhausted and deep down my spirit knows this is the first safe place I've been in far too long. But my mind is restless, and even when I wake, my dreams are elusive. Not the nightmares that have plagued me for so long. This one has me running through a forest filled with vegetation I don't recognize, climbing up and sliding down rocky edifices, desperate to get to…something. My end goal is never in sight, and in the dream I'm not sure what it is. All I do know is that I must run toward it as if my life depends on it. As if several lives depend on it.

Accepting that no more sleep will come, I slide from the bed, careful not to wake Alara. Her back is facing me, and she doesn't stir when I crack open the bedroom door and slip out. The thought crosses my mind to check in on Felix, but I hope he's had better luck with sleep than I have, so I pass his and Ronan's door without knocking.

The weak light of morning is just visible over the hills and dunes separating the city from the shoreline. I'm sure elsewhere on the island the city is a flurry of activity. Fishermen will probably have been out on the water well before dawn. Others will be setting up their market stalls and preparing to go about their business. But this stretch of beach is quiet, and that's just what I want.

I take my time following the path Felix led me down last night until I'm at the same spot on the beach. At least I think it's the same spot. The water has receded and left behind packed, wet sand covered with shells. My heart quickens when I hear the waves.

It seems it's taken me a very short time to fall in love with the sea despite its attempts to kill me. Or maybe that's precisely why I now love it. My heart has always been drawn to danger and challenge. And while the mountains of Borealis will always hold a special place in my heart, they are too fraught with bad memories.

I watch as the waves climb the shore and then recede to the ocean, pulling with them sand and shells and rocks, leaving behind something new. I crave to feel the same. Here a fresh start feels not only possible but probable. This could be home. With my people. With Felix.

I think deep down that's all I've ever wanted was a home. I had one briefly before my mother was killed, but even then, I think I knew it wasn't what it was meant to be. My mother did the best she could, but I'm sure it was only a shadow of what she'd experienced as a child.

A thought hits me out of nowhere as I curl my bare feet into the damp sand to maintain my balance. My mother grew up here, didn't she? She never spoke of it to me, but I'm sure Levi told me as much, and Antioch has alluded to it as well. At one time, she had been the hope of these people. Could I have family here? Grandparents?

Hope soothes the ache for a family I never knew. It seems too much to ask, but I must. Someone here must remember my mother, know her history.

"I think my son would be displeased to know you are down here alone."

The voice that speaks to me is soft and feminine, and I whirl around to find Felix's mother walking toward me with a blanket in her hands and a gentle smile on her face. The wind whips strands of dark hair from her braid and across her face, but she doesn't seem to notice as her eyes remain focused on me.

"Ma'am." I offer a clumsy curtsy in her direction because I'm not sure what's appropriate here. She's not a queen exactly, but I feel as if she's someone I should show deference to. And, okay if I'm honest, I still really want her to like me.

"There's no need for that." She waves a hand dismissively as she stops beside me and drapes the blanket over my shoulders. I didn't even realize I was chilled until the soft warmth envelopes me like a hug. "If anything, I think I should be bowing to you."

But she doesn't. Instead, she holds the edges of the blanket, clasped together, in front of my chest and looks me directly in the eyes. "Manners and introductions may have been lost in last evening's events, but I could hardly fail to recognize you as your mother's daughter. And then, of course, Felix has hardly stopped talking of you these last few hours."

“Me?” I ask incredulously. Have they been talking through the night? And with all the history and catching up they must have to do, Felix can't shut up about me? Miriam smiles knowingly.

“Even as a child he liked to deflect attention from himself. I expect it will be some time before we can have the conversation about the events that led him away and back again. I am just happy to see his face again, and even happier that you have put a smile on it.”

I resist the urge to tell her I'm not sure how true that is. It's my natural instinct to downplay any reference to the affection Felix and I have toward each other, but the time for that has passed. There is no need for secrecy anymore, especially not with a woman so keenly observant as Miriam.

“This must have all come as such a shock to you. All of us showing up here. Felix returning home...”

“Yes and no,” she hedges. “I certainly never could have predicted the specifics, but I can look back now and see how God was preparing my heart for this. He has been directing me with more insistence toward certain passages in the Aletheia—”

I raise my eyebrows, and my expression must be so startled that she stops speaking.

“Do you have your own copy?” I ask eagerly. “The Aletheia? Besides the one Antioch is studying?”

She blinks at me as if surprised by my enthusiasm. “Well, yes. There are hundreds of copies here. Most households have one. And of course, you would be permitted access to the copy in the archives along with your friend.”

But I don't want to read it with Antioch. I don't want to read it with anyone. The time for letting others interpret things for me has passed. I need to read it for myself.

"There are no copies that I know of on the mainland. All we have is what someone remembered and dared to write down. I have—had—a few verses Felix recalled, but we lost it in...in the shipwreck." I'm not sure what, if anything, Felix has told her about our journey here, but this seems like the wrong time to emphasize that I was thrown overboard by a group of sailors eager to appease a storm. It's not the sort of thing one brags about.

Miriam arches an eyebrow that lets me know she knows, or at least suspects, my story isn't entirely true, but she doesn't press that issue. "Come walk with me. I will lend you my copy."

My heart leaps in response, and I have to take a moment to compose myself as I follow her up the shoreline and back into the city. As we pass our house, I hesitate.

"Perhaps I should let Felix know where I am." If he has just returned from talking with his mother all night and finds I am not in bed, he'll worry. What's more, he might actually want to open up to me about all of this. But Miriam just shakes her head.

"He isn't there. I introduced him to someone this morning, and I expect he'll need some time."

Her response is cryptic, but I don't push for more information. Whatever it is, it seems like something I should hear from Felix when he's ready. So, I just nod my assent and continue to walk with her through the city streets.

"You haven't asked me how the vote turned out," she muses. I inwardly cringe. If I wasn't so distracted, that would have been the first thing I asked her. Felix is probably right—we cannot afford distractions.

"If I can be candid with you, I was unaware there were soldiers coming until Felix announced it to the entire hall. I suppose I haven't been able to completely wrap my mind around it enough to inquire after the logistics."

"Yes, that does sound like my son. I may not know the man he has become, but I knew the boy like the back of my hand. A man of action, just like his father."

A father I will never meet because, just like my own, he's dead. What does Felix's grief for that man feel like? Probably much deeper than that of my own father. Hopefully less complicated.

"He commands loyalty," I say. "I never would have asked those soldiers to come because I would have never thought they would agree to risk their lives for me. And most of them probably wouldn't. But for Felix? They would follow him anywhere."

"The same as he would follow you. Sometimes our place in life is not to be the light but to point others to it."

"You are radiant as the sun, Emilia, but where does that leave me?"

He said those words to me as he was turning in his resignation. As he was preparing to leave me. Before everything changed. Does he still feel any of that resentment?

"But you will be pleased, I hope, to know that we have agreed to welcome your soldiers to our city. We will make the announcement this morning, and I will coordinate with Felix to determine the best area for them to make camp."

"Thank you." It seems too weak a response, but I don't know what else to say.

"There is a caveat," she hedges. "As you will have heard last night, we don't have an army on the island. There are a few guards who help keep the peace regarding minor crimes, but not since the days of Caspian have we been militant. As such, our citizens are uncomfortable with the idea of an army marching through our city. We will ask that when they come into the city, they either conceal their weapons or leave them at their camp. They are, of course, welcome in the city and welcome to socialize and worship with us, but we don't want them marching through the streets on patrol."

How did Felix respond when she, undoubtedly, shared this bit of news with him? Keeping patrols out of the city not only won't help much in the way of protection, it will not encourage vigilance on the part of the citizens either. Hard to get them to take the threat seriously when nothing about their daily lives need change. But if anyone can find a way around this handicap, it will be the Lord Commander.

As I expected, there is plenty of activity as we near the main plaza and the basilica. People shout greetings to Miriam and even to me, and we smile and wave in return. It's a better reception than I could have hoped for. Some of them seem to feel some sort of connection with me. Maybe now is the time to ask about family.

"Did you know my mother?" I ask Miriam.

She sighs as she directs me up the few steps to the basilica's portico. "I did. From what Felix has told me, you inherited not only her beauty but her spirit. She was younger than me so we didn't spend much time together, but you could tell Alexandra was the darling of the village. She lost her father—your grandfather—at a young age. She and her mother never had much money, but she was always running around the city picking up odd jobs and doing so with a smile on her face."

"And how exactly did she end up in Borealis?" It's not a story we discussed before she died. As a child, I just assumed she had always lived in my home country. Not until more recently did I begin to question it.

"You've heard of the great famine?"

"Yes. Felix mentioned that Solitarius provided food to the mainland during that time in exchange for peace."

"We did. But there was another part to that treaty. To ensure peace, approximately every fifty years a woman from the island would be chosen to wed the next crown prince who came of age in one of the mainland countries. It so happened that lot fell to your father."

"Your grandfather journeyed here with the emperor on a voyage to pick out a bride for his son. When your grandfather arrived, he picked me as the daughter of one of the highest judges on our island."

Wait. What?

"He chose you?" But how is she standing here? And why is my mother not?

"I don't think he had any sort of ideations that I would be a good match for your father. It was simply a political move, as I'm sure you understand more than anyone else."

It's a nod to Ronan and his presence there. I'm not sure how she feels about him, but it doesn't seem she has accepted him as openly as Felix has or even as openly as I have. There's some mistrust there, perhaps some blame that he is the one that stole her son from her, although I think deep down she must know that's not true.

"Even though your grandfather chose me," Miriam continues, "I was already in love with someone else and absolutely heartbroken to think I would have to leave my life here behind and to leave him behind. We had already planned to marry. We had a home that we were going to move into shortly, and all that was being ripped from me. So, when the time came to board the ship, your mother disguised herself as me with a veil on her face and boarded the ship to Borealis. I received one letter from her after she left, and no word after that. I didn't know if she was dead or alive. I didn't know what was going to become of her when she met your father, if the match was good for her or not. She never fully explained to me why she did what she did."

I stand there in the middle of the city, mouth agape. One decision and my life could have been completely different. If my mother hadn't left maybe I would have had a home and a father who loved me and even siblings. If my mother hadn't left, she would still be alive.

Miriam takes my hand and leads me through the door to the nave of the forum. "I'm sorry you lost her at such a young age. A girl really needs her mother."

"Some thought she was the fulfillment of this prophecy." I'm not sure what I'm fishing for. Denial? Reassurance?

"Yes." Her reply is slow and measured. "But maybe there are many definitions of this prophecy."

"What do you mean?"

"There have certainly been prophesies fulfilled throughout the ages. The one Antioch refers to—I'm not sure he has it right. The scriptures say one will come to be a sacrifice so that we may approach God. Think about it. This god Caelus that the Emperor believes in. He demands sacrifices, doesn't he?"

"Yes," I agree. "Sacrifices so that prayers will be heard and hopefully answered."

"But our God does not. He *became* the sacrifice according to our scriptures. He conquered death and bridged the chasm between us and His holiness. It is because of that sacrifice that we can freely pray to him."

"But my mother was a sacrifice. I know my father meant it as a sacrifice to Caelus, but if our God is powerful, shouldn't He have prevented that? She's still dead." I have wanted to voice this question for years, but I never truly thought anyone might hold an answer for me until now.

"There was a place where God once walked with man on earth. In our foolishness and greed, we betrayed Him and were cast out. That place is guarded by the Narrow Gate or the Gate of

Life, and we have been trying to get back there ever since. The consequence of our rebellion was not only separation but the pain and suffering we brought on ourselves. We still live with those consequences. Death is a part of life, and if our deaths can count for something more, shouldn't they?"

She pushes open the doors of the apse, and we walk through the large empty room as I ponder her question. Somehow this all must fit together. God's plan to rescue His people from persecution, the suffering of those I loved to further this plan, my position of authority, the displays of God's power in the storms... What does it all mean? Certainly not that I am safe. But maybe not that I am *destined* to die either.

I'm peripherally aware I've left her question hanging, but something more insistent has pulled my attention. As we cross in front of the tribunal and approach the door where the members of the Synod exited the night before, I become aware of a tugging sensation around my middle. In my waking hours, I have only felt it a few times before. The same sensation that pulls me through that unfamiliar forest in my dreams. The same force that warmed my body while I sank beneath the waves and a voice whispered *"You are my plan."*

"You feel it, don't you?" Miriam studies me with a knowing smile. "I thought you would. You have to pay attention, but once you feel it, the sensation never truly leaves you."

She's right. It's both overwhelming and comforting. My feet move forward without conscious thought. I know one thing now, and it's that I must get closer. All else falls by the wayside.

Somewhere behind me, Miriam follows along, but I no longer need her guidance. When I pause in front of two tall wooden doors, I know what I seek lies just beyond them. I look back to her for confirmation.

"What is it?"

"This room is the closest I have ever felt to God's presence. It holds the only true physical representation of His power known to man."

"The Palanquin?" I ask with wide eyes. The existence of such an object is still new to me. I had never heard of it until we began piecing things together just before we left Borealis and Antioch mentioned it. I picture the ones I've seen in the past. It wasn't uncommon for royalty to be carried through the streets on them. Just a fancy box, which held the person of power, mounted on two long poles that porters used to carry the monarch. Somehow, I know this is different.

"Yes. You should see it alone." She squeezes my hand tight. "I can't promise your life will be spared, Emilia, but maybe this will give you some direction. I'll be right out here when you are ready to leave."

Despite the insistence of the pull within me, I'm apprehensive to walk through this door to the unknown by myself. What would Felix say about this? It would be a huge strategic blunder in most battles, but this is war of a different kind.

As I walk through the door, I sense His presence. Not in the ways I've experienced it before in my prayers and my dreams, but something much larger, more awe-inspiring. Every part of me stirs with a slow awakening and everything outside fades away. Part of me knows life goes on just outside of these walls, but awareness of anything outside of this feeling ceases to exist.

My knees bend without my consent, and I find myself lying prostrate on the floor. I don't want to move. I don't want to speak. Only one word plays on repeat in my head.

Holy. Holy. Holy.

It might be hours or only minutes, but when I open the door to tell Miriam I'm ready to go, I'm wrung out. Despite my best efforts, I couldn't even pray. I could only lie there on the floor in awe while time stood still. It felt like light shone into every part of me, even the crevices and shadows I've kept hidden so well. My mind can't begin to process it.

The look on Miriam's face tells me she understands, but we don't discuss it. It's a private thing, I think. Between the visitor and God alone.

She takes me to a much larger room adjacent to the one that holds the Palanquin. Here there is an altar and rows of benches, and I assume this must be where the citizens worship as a congregation. There's something special about this place as well, but everything pales in comparison to what I've just experienced.

Behind the altar is yet another door which opens to a library of sorts. There's an odd hush in the room as a few men sit alone at tables with tomes spread open in front of them. Toward the back of the room, with a table full of books and scrolls, sits Antioch.

"Speak with your friend while I retrieve my copy of the scriptures for you," Miriam instructs.

I wind my way through the tables until I reach the old man. He is bent over and so absorbed in whatever he's reading that he doesn't hear me approach. When I pull out a chair to sit with him, he starts.

"My dear child, I didn't expect to see you here." He pats my hand with his wrinkled one, and I feel guilty about the times I've spoken harshly to him lately. I believe he genuinely cares about me and wants to do right. But I have to remember that he is human just as much as the rest of us.

"How are you? Are they treating you well?" Physically he looks as frail as ever, but there's a new light in his eyes that speaks of vigor and youth.

"They have been most kind," he assures me. "And they have shared with me more than I could have imagined. Between these tomes and the documents the queen gave me, I have so much to sift through."

I try to read upside down to determine what he's currently studying. "That doesn't look like scripture. Just names and genealogies."

"You are correct. There are more layers to this than we realized. The scriptures, the journals, the maps… It is more than I hoped to learn in my entire lifetime."

"What have you learned?" I try to temper my question so it doesn't sound like I think he's been wasting his time. I'm sure there's a good reason he's excited by all this, but what I want is something actionable.

"More than I could possibly speak." He nods solemnly toward a quill and parchment dotted with ink beside him. "When I have finished my notes, I will explain it to you."

That's about the best I could hope for. God knows I couldn't decipher it on my own. It's difficult to rely on others in this way, but also necessary.

While I wait for Miriam to return, I busy myself with studying the maps Antioch has spread out on this table. The ones from Verity, I imagine. Most look familiar to me from my geography lessons as a child, but some are less so. A few appear so ancient that I'm afraid to touch them lest they disintegrate. I settle on a more recent looking map of the island.

To the east of the island is, of course, the sea and then a rough sketch of the mainland's coastline. To the west of the island is more sea and a series of tiny isles that, if the scale is accurate, can't be more than ten miles across for the largest one.

Solitarius isn't large, maybe fifty miles across at the widest point. The capital city we're in now takes up a large portion of the southern land and is surrounded by a natural barrier of rocky mountains and cliffs. From what I've seen, they aren't like my Borealis mountains, which are lush and full of foliage, but instead hard and unforgiving. That must be where they harvest the gemstones I've heard so much about. Between those mountains and on the northern side of the island, the land appears to be much flatter with thicker vegetation. There are no cities marked in this area of the map, but large areas are sectioned off and labeled as farms. Perhaps they supply the fruit and sugarcane I've enjoyed.

By the time Miriam returns for me, I'm beyond ready to leave. I say goodbye to Antioch and allow her to escort me away from the basilica. We walk in mostly silence as my thoughts race with all I have learned and experienced in just a few hours. I am both exhausted and elated. It makes no sense.

Once we're away from the crowded streets, Miriam comes to a halt in front of me to impede my progress.

The fine wrinkles around her eyes are more pronounced as she frowns and looks down from my face to the book she clutches against her body. The calmness she's exuded every time I've been around her is notably absent, and that puts me on heightened alert.

"What is it?" I ask in a whisper, though I'm not sure why. Something in her demeanor warns me not to advertise what she's about to show me.

Miriam stands close and thrusts the book into my hands. It's a small leather journal much like the one Felix used to record what he recalled of the Aletheia.

"This was my husband's," she says in a hushed tone. "It's the second oldest known copy of the Aletheia. Only the one in the sanctuary is older."

"Why is it a secret?" This only leads me to more questions, and I'm not sure my brain can take another layer of this mystery.

"Not a secret exactly, but it was entrusted to my husband's family centuries ago. It contains the scriptures of course, but there are notes tucked inside that I don't think are original. He was very careful that this was never shared outside our family, but he never said why. It would have passed to Felix if he had stayed."

"Then why not give it to him?"

"I thought it might be...painful for him. I want to spare him any pain that I can. If you don't find it useful, then simply return it to me and he needn't be any the wiser."

"Thank you." Both for the information and for sparing her son any hurt. I place my hand over hers and hold her gaze. "Truly. Thank you." I don't even know if the information in this book will be useful for anything, but it's evident that it cost her something to get it to me.

"God has beautiful plans for you, Emilia." Tears form in her brown eyes as she gives me a wavering smile. "I have prayed for you even before I knew your name."

"I'll try to live up to them." Her words about God's plans don't irk me the way they do when they come from others. She just shakes her head.

"Not plans for your destruction or for your sacrifice." She squeezes my hand. "Plans for a hope and a future. He has not abandoned you."

My soul clings to those words as they resonate inside me. When was the last time someone predicted hope rather than destruction? I want to believe it almost more than I want to believe anything. *"You are my plan."* Words whispered beneath the waves come roaring back. Can I dare to hope? I think I have to. It's all I have.

Once I enter the house, I'm relieved to find all my companions are out for the moment, so I'm free to begin reading without interruptions. So, I do just that. I pull a chair near a window in the common room and begin to read. Scripture is supposed to be God's words. And I think I'm finally ready to listen.

22

Nothing could have prepared me for the weight of the words in my hands. Unlike the partial copy Felix gave me, this book is large, heavy, and carefully preserved. It has clearly seen some use over the years, and the ink is fading. The tiny, cramped handwriting is just barely legible on some pages, and I caress them with only the lightest touch. It must have taken ages to copy all this down.

The words are precious. They are organized in sections, some named after the prophets who penned them and others with no name at all. There's no way I could read it all in a day, but I flip through until I find some flowers pressed between the pages. Miriam must have marked these passages for a reason, so I take care in reading them.

A story begins to unfold. About a God who dwelt with mankind until a rebellion separated man from God. About a people who worshipped God but made so many mistakes that it was impossible for them to make it back to Him. About a Son who agreed to be a sacrifice so that it would be possible for man to return to God. About forces of darkness that sought to overthrow God by using people against people.

As unfamiliar as the details are, it's a story I know all too well. I've seen this play out in my own life. I even stumble across some of the passages I've heard Antioch reference. I read them for myself but feel even more confused. Clearly, they refer to prophecies of some sort, but ones that have already been fulfilled or ones yet to come?

God, why don't you have a word that spells it out for me? Tell me what I am to do.

I flip backward several more pages until I come across the only reference I've seen of the Ancient One. A king upon a throne of flames, dressed in white, with rivers of fire flowing out from Him. He is surrounded by an army of thousands attending him, and then someone is brought before Him. The Ruler Who Will Rise Up in glory.

"And to this ruler was given dominion, glory, and a kingdom, that all peoples, nations, and tongues should serve him. His dominion is everlasting and will not pass away. His kingdom will not be destroyed."

I read the words aloud, allowing them to pass my lips and fill my ears. One word jumps out to me, and I cling to it like a lifeline. Him. This scripture seems to indicate this ruler will be a man, not a woman. Antioch told me the translation is vague concerning the gender, but at least someone has seen fit to translate it as a man. Maybe it's just the assumption that a woman couldn't be worthy of this. Maybe it's a mistake on the part of the translator. But I hope not. I keep reading.

"Out of the kingdom a king will arise, and he will be different from the former ones. He will subdue the other kings and speak words against the Most High God. He will persecute the believers and they will be subdued by him for a time. But the Ancient will judge, and his dominion will be taken away, first consumed gradually and then to be destroyed forever. Then the kingdom and the dominion and the greatness of all the kingdoms under them will be given to the people of the believers of the Most High. This kingdom will be an everlasting kingdom, and all the dominions will serve and obey God."

Cyrus's fear makes sense to me now. This passage sounds exactly like what he is afraid will happen to his empire. He thinks I am the instrument of that. No matter how many Insurgo queens married into royalty because of the famine treaty, something about my mother and then me made him believe that the time was at hand. I'd like to argue with it, but I can't.

I flip to the next page and a folded square of parchment falls from where it was tucked against the spine of the journal. I pick it up and carefully unfold the fragile paper. The ink is darker than the lines penned in the book, and from that I surmise that this is a more recent addition, though clearly still quite old.

In the dragon's belly is a consuming fire.

I read the words again. And then again. This doesn't seem to be part of the scripture itself. It's one of the notes Miriam mentioned. Penned by Felix's father? The ink seems too faded to be that recent of an addition, but I suppose it's possible. Regardless, it seems like nonsense. Dragons are the stuff of childish fairytales.

Carefully, I grab the journal by the covers and hold it so the spine is up, and the pages splay open. Another note falls to the ground, and I eagerly snatch it up as well.

Here be dragons to be slain, here be rich rewards to gain . . . If we perish in the seeking, . . . why, how small a thing is death.

A frustrated groan tears out of me. What are these notes doing in here? Given the weightiness of the scriptures, they just seem so childish. A waste of my time. But for some reason, I can't keep from rereading the words. Every time I fold them pack, intending to stuff them back in the pages, only to find my fingers have unwillingly unfolded them once again.

Did Miriam know these were here? I consider asking Felix about them when I see him next, but then I remember how his mother was afraid just the sight of the book would cause him pain. Because he misses his father? Or something else?

Well, probably best not to awaken that particular dragon.

I wake with a sore neck and a stiff back. I've fallen asleep curled in this chair while reading the Aletheia, the cool breeze from the window chilling my skin. A glance out that same window informs me the day is gone. The sun's light is dying, and I can see lamps in the windows of the nearby houses.

"Ahem."

Felix leans against the doorway with a wide, crooked grin on his face. He's clearly just washed because his hair is slightly damp, and his beard is neatly trimmed. It's such a simple yet gorgeous sight. He seems more relaxed than I've seen him in ages.

"What are you smiling at?" I slowly uncurl myself from the position I fell asleep in and stretch my arms over my head. The book falls to the floor, and I quickly pick it up and place it on the arm of the chair. I think it actually feels heavier than before.

"Just you." He walks toward me, and I notice he has a blanket draped over his arm. "The most beautiful thing I've ever seen."

For some reason the warmth of a blush tickles my cheeks and lifts some of the heaviness from me. I'm not used to him being so open in his appreciation of me. As if he's stored it all up for so long, and now that the dam has been demolished it just comes rushing out of him.

He kneels on the floor in front of me and wraps the blanket around my shoulders. I'm not really cold, but I snuggle into it all the same. He carefully studies my hands as he takes them in his own. Neither of us speaks. There is much to say and yet nothing at all.

"Where are Ronan and Alara?" I finally ask. Because it's much too quiet in here for them to be present.

Felix shrugs. "Alara said something about showing him the pools earlier. I haven't seen them since."

"The *bathing* pools?" My eyes widen.

"Well, they're used for swimming, too," he chuckles. "Regardless, I don't think we need to chaperone them. My only real concern is they might drown each other. They've spent more time at each other's throats the last few days than you and Alara have."

Have they? What else have I missed while I've been otherwise occupied?

"At any rate, it keeps them both distracted," he continues. "If Alara asks me one more time to practice with the weapons…"

I perk up at the mention of weapons. "We probably should, you know? It's been a while since I've done any sort of proper sparring or training." I try to play it off, but I can remember exactly the last time I held staff. To get his attention I had goaded him into a sparring match while members of the guard watched. It didn't end well.

"I don't want to see Alara with an actual weapon in her hands. She almost killed me with a bow. I'm not eager to hand her a sword."

Laughter bubbles out of me despite the serious frown on his face. "I imagined she'd be great with weapons."

"She'd like you to think that, but it's not her forte. Stealth and cunning serve her well. The physical part doesn't come as naturally."

It would be a lie to say I'm not pleased by this bit of information.

"Your mother told me they approved the arrival of our soldiers." I'm careful to phrase it as if I've accepted the inevitable.

In truth, I have no idea what I'm supposed to do with an influx of men who are ready to fight but have no opponent.

"Yes. We've decided on a place for their camp, and I've spent the day getting things organized as best as possible. I actually came to tell you that they believe their ship has been spotted off the coast."

I sit up straighter, and the blanket slides off my shoulders. "They're here already?"

"Relax." Felix stands and pulls me to my feet as well. "They're still a good distance off. They won't come ashore until morning at the earliest."

"And how do we know it's not one of Cyrus's ships?"

"This is not an Imperial Navy vessel. It's a larger merchant ship with Borealis colors flying. I suppose it could just be someone hoping to traffic a few loads of sugarcane and gemstones back to the mainland, but I doubt it."

This bit of information does not bring me the comfort it seems to bring him. "And then what happens? Do we just sit around and wait on Antioch to point to a place on a map for us to search? Do we just wait for Cyrus to arrive and set fire to the city?"

Felix studies my face. I stare at the little wrinkle that forms between his brows when he's worried. Then he glances down to the arm of the chair where the Aletheia rests. "Did reading that give you any insight?"

"It was oddly short of details. No treasure map in the back." I shouldn't be so flippant about it. My view of the situation has been altered, but I'm not sure to what end. What I really want is a practical next step to take.

An odd look crosses his face at my comment. "Can I see that?"

He takes it from me and holds his breath as he flips to the back. Staring at the blank last page, he runs his fingers over a jagged edge in the spine I hadn't noticed was there. Something has been ripped from here.

"Felix?" Clearly, this means something to him, but he seems to be wrestling with what, if anything, to say about it.

"There was a map here." His words are barely a whisper, and it takes a moment for me to be sure I hear him correctly. "A treasure map."

I take the book from him and brush my fingers across the torn edge of the paper as well, as if this will somehow make the mission page materialize. "I mean, it could have been anything. You don't know—"

"I know," he insists, "because I was the one who ripped it out."

23

"This was my father's. He kept it hidden in a drawer in his bedroom. He showed it to me once when I was very young. Told me it would be mine one day, and he would explain how important it was when I was older." Felix stares at the book I'm still holding as if it has the power to transport him back in time. "I never gave him the chance."

"I don't understand."

"Do you remember me telling you how I found a treasure map in my father's things and my brother begged to go on the hunt with me?"

How could I forget? Watching Felix relive that story was agonizing. I don't want to interrupt him again, so I just nod.

"I took it from this book. I was curious about what was so special about it. It just looked like a copy of the Aletheia to me, and around here those weren't rare. But when I found a drawing of a map in back, I knew that had to be the reason."

The full implication of his words hit me, and my jaw drops. "Y-you think that map was..."

He chuffs out a sarcastic chuckle. "Ridiculous, right? I mean what are the chances that my father had a map to the Gate, and I lost the one thing that might take us exactly where we need to go? That's crazy."

"Crazy," I repeat. Except it isn't. At least not any crazier than anything else that's happened. And I hate myself for it, but I have to ask the next question. "Do you remember what it looked like?"

With eyes closed, he breathes deep, and his shoulders rise and fall. This is a different side to him than the one he usually shows me, and I don't know how to handle it.

"Parts of it?" But he sounds unsure. I don't want to ask him to relive any part of that memory, but the thought that this might be the information we need wars with my compassion. What if I ask him to do this and it's nothing at all? And even if he attempts it, how accurate are the memories of a child?

"Is there anyone else who would have seen it?"

"No one living. I suppose there's a chance my mother…"

But I'm already shaking my head. Miriam didn't seem to know the details of anything "extra" added to this copy of the scriptures.

"I could find my way back there," he says softly. It seems we've both arrived at the same conclusion. "I can remember where I left the map. Where I was when I heard him scream."

He turns away from me, and I have to bite down on my lips to keep my own tears from falling. My hands shake as I set the book aside and go to him. The muscles of his back tense at my first touch, but he relaxes a bit as I wrap my arms around him from behind and rest my head between his shoulder blades. He laces his hands with mine where they're clasped in front of his chest. There's nothing the least bit romantic about this embrace, yet I feel closer to him now than I ever have.

"You don't need to do this," I tell him. "I will not ask you to do this."

"I know you won't." His heart hammers under my palm, and I ache to take away his pain. "Can I have tonight to think it over?"

"There's nothing to think over. I won't put you through this for something that probably has nothing to do with us."

Instead of answering, he slowly turns in my arms so my face now rests against his chest and my hands join behind his back. Large, warm hands press against my back as if he's the one holding me together. "Do you know what I actually came in here to tell you?"

I assumed he simply wandered in on me sleeping. I didn't realize he'd come with a purpose. "What is it?"

"I have a sister." He chokes out an incredulous laugh that makes his voice break. I don't have to look up to know there are tears in his eyes. And because I know that, I don't hold back my own either.

"You...you have a sister?" Miriam didn't mention anything about another child when I spent the early morning hours with her. But she did say she had introduced Felix to someone, and I guess this must be it. What absolutely horrible timing to find out he has a sister only to have to revisit the death of his brother.

"Her name is Selah. She's six." He pauses, chews on his lip for a moment, then shakes his head. When I look up, I see the swirl of emotions in his eyes. Keeping his emotions in check is one of his strongest traits, but right now they're all on full display for anyone who cares to look. "She's the one who stood up in the assembly and said she would fight."

Of course. The wide-eyed, curly haired child who I'd locked eyes with and who Miriam had quickly silenced. The girl determined to take on a whole army with her imaginary sword.

I like her already. And I'll bet she scares Felix to death.

"She looks like you." My chuckle is watery, but he laughs a little too.

"She looks like Max." His hands brush my hair back from either side of my face and gently cup my jaw. "You would have loved him."

I see a future in his eyes. A happy home where we laugh, and children run and play, and no flames and no army threatens to turn us to ash. But I blink and it's gone. I'm not sure it can ever be.

"I love you," I say emphatically. Because that much I know is true.

24

The imminent arrival of our soldiers nearly shuts the city down. Even while the ship is still a ways off, people line the docks and the shore hoping for a glimpse of the strangers. Unlike my party which rowed ashore in a longboat, this ship comes all the way into the main pier to dock.

Anticipation sends flutters through me as I impatiently wait for the men to disembark. Felix and I stand at the end of the pier, both of us rigid as soldiers in a show of both strength and authority. It only makes sense that we will be the ones to greet them since they are here for us. We'll direct them to the area a few miles down the beach where an area has been designated for their camp.

We haven't spoken any more about the map. I want to give him the space to decide what to do, and there have been plenty of things to occupy our time. I've spent the morning helping ready another house which will be given to Antony and any officers that accompany him as per Felix's request. Felix has spent most of his early morning hours mapping out the camp and purchasing large supplies of food to make sure the men are well-fed.

The gangplank is lowered, and almost before it is stabilized by the dockhands, a tall figure appears at the top. I squint against the sun which silhouettes him, but I think I know that frame.

"Antony!" Felix's exclamation confirms my assumption as the young soldier bounds down the gangplank and directly toward us. I can't contain my smile as he embraces Felix then turns to me with a huge grin.

"Highness." He bows, but I grab his shirt and pull him into a hug.

"None of that," I insist as I release him to look him over. I've always assumed him to be close to my age, but the days of unshaven stubble on his face give him a look of gravitas. He's always been a capable soldier but now he looks the part.

"It's good to see you." Felix claps his protégé on the shoulder. "You made much better time than I anticipated."

"It didn't take me long to round up the men. They took the attack on the city personally. And they were eager to serve you both." Antony looks between us as if confirming a suspicion, then half turns to welcome the next person descending the gangplank.

My jaw drops, and I blink several times to make sure my eyes haven't deceived me. But she's really there, jogging the last few steps into the pier and then running toward me. I open my arms and Hannah, my former lady-in-waiting, runs right into them.

The goodbyes we exchanged in Borealis were hurried and painful, and I have regretted more than once that I didn't say more about how much she meant to me. Especially because I fully believed it would be the last time I ever saw her. Maybe she believed it as well because, unlike Antony, she has forgone any attempt at propriety in favor of clinging to me. I don't mind in the slightest.

"I couldn't leave her behind," Antony chuckles as he and Felix watch us in amusement.

"I wouldn't," she confirms. "Please don't be angry with him."

"Angry? You have no idea how happy I am to see you." Alara has been a poor substitute for the female company I became used to with Hannah. She has been with me nearly as long as Felix.

Hannah steps back to give me some space, and her hand immediately laces with Antony's. Strangely, we have never discussed their blossoming relationship, but it makes my heart swell to see them so happy.

"When everyone is settled, we have something we'd like to discuss with the two of you." Antony sobers a bit as Hannah tucks herself against him.

"Of course," I say, barely able to contain my own excitement. If I'm not mistaken, there will be wedding bells soon.

Hannah and I leave the men to deal with the logistics of unloading the ship and directing our new army to camp. I'll visit them later to express my thanks for their willingness to journey this far, but better to let the chaos die down first.

As we walk back toward the city, we have to wind our way through the crowd that's gathered. Their excitement is palpable as they shout greetings to me and then focus their attention back on the soldiers who have begun to disembark. A few women step forward to introduce themselves and offer their hospitality to Hannah. She seems stunned by this kindness, but I just smile.

"Everyone here is so nice," she marvels as we extricate ourselves from the crowd and head toward the city. I have to remind myself that she's not used to the kindness and generosity these people have shown. Before she became my lady, she was a slave in Aurora to a terrible master who spit in my face when I tried to buy her freedom.

"I can't believe you're really here," I confess. "I have so much to tell you."

She grabs my hand as we walk and leans in conspiratorially. "Can we start with those eyes the Commander was making at you?" She raises her brows as I laugh and fight back a blush.

"There may be some news on that front," I tease. It feels so good to laugh and to have someone to share my excitement with. Hannah has been there every step of the way—from the first moment I realized I felt something for Felix to the torture we endured when my position and his sense of duty kept us apart. She beams in response.

"Tell me everything."

It turns out that Hannah is not the only surprise Antony brought for me. In the early afternoon, Felix steps into the common room where Hannah and I are sitting on the floor taking turns braiding each other's hair. Fatigue dulls his eyes a bit, but his smile is genuine as he beckons us to follow him outside.

In the street in front of the house stands Antony, holding the reins of two horses. One black. One white. I recognize them immediately. My horse Athena and Felix's stallion Ares.

When we were readying to flee Borealis, I had intended to take Athena with me. Felix talked me out of it. She's fast and agile, but she also won't allow most people to ride her. He argued that we'd have to leave her behind when we boarded the ship, and no one was going to take on the care of a horse they couldn't ride. I couldn't bear the thought of abandoning her to strangers, so I'd agreed to leave her behind where she at least had Hannah and Antony to look after her.

Athena comes right to me, and I bury my face in her mane while apologizing for leaving her. It's a trivial bit of comfort in all this uncertainty but comfort all the same.

After making sure the horses are boarded at a nearby stable, the four of us gather at the table for a late lunch. We're just making ourselves comfortable when the door flies open, and Ronan comes barging in. Alara is hot on his heels and appears to have been yelling at him. They both stop abruptly when they see us and take in our two new guests.

Hannah stands and gives a curtsy in Ronan's general direction. Antony also rises but offers the prince nothing more than a deferential nod. Ronan barely seems to notice as he circles the table and takes the empty seat next to Felix, leaving Alara the chair farthest from him. She huffs and then takes it as well. Hannah and Antony exchange looks and then retake their seats.

"Well, since we're all here, we might as well discuss our next steps," Felix suggests as he takes some bread and then passes the basket to me. "I want to begin training with the soldiers first thing tomorrow."

"Training for what?" Alara snipes as she tears into a roll. "If they don't know how to fight by now then we're dead."

Antony visibly bristles at the slight against his men, but Felix barely reacts. "Fighting on sand rather than dirt requires an extra element of balance and leg strength. I have no doubts they're up to the task, but they lack experience on this terrain. I intend to prepare them as well as I can in case it comes down to a fight."

Honestly, I can't see a path where this doesn't end in a fight, and I will be right in the middle of it as well.

"I want to train, too," I announce. "As part of the soldiers."

"Me, too." At the end of the table, Alara's eyes light up, and I know she thinks she's found a way to force Felix to let her swing a weapon. I'd be lying if I said that wasn't a motivating factor for me as well.

"Me, too," Ronan echoes. When I look at him, his eyes are narrowed and focused entirely on Alara as if he's accepting her unspoken challenge.

"Is there even a point in me vetoing this?" Felix asks with a resigned sigh. He looks to the three of us and then to Antony who just shrugs. As the highest ranking of the soldiers, he should get a vote on who trains with them, but he will defer to whatever Felix decides. "At least let me voice my objections before the three of you ignore them. One, the training will not be easy, and I can't afford to make any concessions for you. Two, you will be a distraction to the men—especially you two." He looks from Alara to me. "And three," his eyes search my face as if hoping he can silently persuade me, "there are better uses of your time that can help us."

I consider that last point. I could join Antioch in the archives and hope to stumble upon some bit of information that might point us to our destination. But I feel strongly that if it were as simple as opening the right book, the location of the Gate would have been discovered years ago. What we really need, what might break this wide open, is that map that I know Felix and I are both thinking about.

"I don't care," Alara insists. "I want to train."

"Me, too." Ronan seems determined to prove something either to himself or to Alara, but I don't have the luxury of curiosity at the moment.

"I'll split my time," I finally concede. Felix raises his brows in surprise. I feel the eyes of the others on me, but I stay focused on him. "I want to train. It's been far too long since I've pushed myself like that, and I don't want to get soft."

"You could never," Ronan interjects. It's maybe the first time I realize that he is actually impressed by my skills and reputation and not just feigning so for an audience. I push that aside to contemplate another time.

"But I also know that our only real hope of defeating Cyrus is to find the Gate first. I would be foolish to ignore that. I want to do my own research."

"I can help," Hannah pipes up. I pull my eyes away from Felix long enough to take her in. Her face is open and earnest, and I realize for all her sweetness and gentleness, I have underestimated the fire in her.

"Perfect," I agree. "I will spend the mornings training with the men and then rejoin in the evenings for whatever you have left to teach. The rest of the time, Hannah and I will continue researching and studying every document we can find."

Felix considers this for a moment. I could insist on this if I wanted to, but it's important to me that he supports me. I don't want us to be divided in any way. If the least little crack is formed, it can open into a chasm under all this pressure.

"Agreed," he finally says. "And don't expect any special treatment."

I would never. Either I'll prove myself or I won't, but I don't want to be given the easy way out. Felix's reputation as a commander has not been exaggerated, and I'm eagerly anticipating being under his direction…though that's not a sentiment I'm willing to concede to him yet.

We eat the rest of our meal while making companionable conversation. Hannah and Antony fill us in on the mood in Borealis. Apparently, my cousin Titus has reluctantly resumed his position as sitting monarch, and the court has gone on as if I was never even there. I don't mind. It's probably better this way.

Alara and Ronan remain uncomfortably silent. Even Hannah and Antony, who don't know either of them, glance nervously between them. The tension is thick, and I'm starting to worry that one of them is going to stab the other in the middle of the night.

Felix must sense it, too, because as Hannah and I begin clearing the table after the meal, he announces that the men will sleep at the soldier's camp tonight and leave the house to Hannah, Alara, and me. No one argues, so at least we've avoided that hurdle for now.

"Emilia, Ronan, I'd like to speak to you both in private." Felix's request takes me by surprise as I take a rag to wash the crumbs from the table. The last time the three of us were alone together, Ronan had just walked in on Felix about to kiss me. This is guaranteed to be awkward.

"Give me just a moment to relay instructions to Antony, and then I'll meet you in our room."

He means his and Ronan's bedroom. As if this wasn't going to be awkward enough.

Antony gives Hannah a chaste kiss and steps out the door with Felix. Alara gets one last sneer at Ronan before she turns on her heels and disappears as well. Ronan simply sighs and stalks off to the bedroom to wait on Felix and me. That leaves Hannah and me alone in the aftermath. She looks at me with wide eyes.

"Are they always like that?"

"No," I sigh. "I'm not sure exactly what's going on, and neither of them are likely to be forthcoming about it."

"Are they...together?"

The question stuns me. Alara and Ronan? Granted I've not had much attention to spare for either of them of late, but according to Felix all they do is argue.

"No?" But it's more of a question than I mean it to be.

"It should make training interesting."

"Maybe." But somehow, I don't think Felix will put up with their antics on the training ground.

Felix rejoins us so we end our conversation. Hannah excuses herself to take a nap in the other bedroom as I set my shoulders and prepare for what I'm sure is to be an uncomfortable conversation.

Once we enter the room, Felix directs me to sit on the bed Ronan doesn't already occupy. It's obviously his as it smells of him—leather and the faint spice of the soap he favors. He stands before the two of us, arms behind his back as he begins pacing.

Ronan and I exchange looks as we wait for Felix to speak. Even though I know what this must be about, his hesitation causes anxiety to bubble up from the pit of my stomach. I cross my legs and clutch a pillow to my chest in hopes of containing it.

"What's wrong?" Ronan finally asks. I snort. Better to ask what *isn't* wrong. He cuts his eyes at me and then looks back to Felix. "I haven't seen you like this since—"

"I think I know where the map to the Gate is." Felix efficiently shuts him up with his pronouncement. I hold my breath as I wait to see if Ronan will piece it together. Then again, I don't know how much of Felix's story he knows. But I suspect it's enough to realize this involves the most traumatic event in his friend's life.

"That's crazy," Ronan says, repeating Felix's words from last night. But there's enough hope in his voice to suggest he doesn't believe it's that crazy at all. Are we really so desperate that we're grasping at straws?

"Is it?" Felix stops pacing and arches his eyebrows in question. "I tore it out of my father's book, one that has been passed down through generations. Old enough to contain a map drawn up in Caspian's time."

"So, it's an old map. There must be dozens of those in the archives here. The Zephyros queen gave us some maps as well. Who's to say it isn't one of those? There's no reason to believe the one you found as a child has anything to do with any of this."

"There was a reason my father kept it hidden." His shoulders sag a bit under the weight of realization. As his certainty increases, the color drains from his face.

"Emilia, reason with him." Ronan turns those blue eyes on me. "Tell him this is ridiculous and unnecessary."

"I can't," I whisper. I don't know if either of those things are true.

"You don't understand what it did to him." Ronan leaps to his feet and shoves a hand through his hair as he begins pacing as well. This room is not big enough for all this.

"Ro..." Felix warns.

"No, she needs to hear this." That cool blue gaze levels at Felix and then flashes to me. "He was wrecked."

"She already knows."

The defeat in Felix's voice makes me uncurl from my protective position on the bed. I stand, too, because it seems to be the thing to do when you want to make a point. "If you have to go back, I'm going with you."

The way his face pales at just the thought of revisiting that cave is enough for me to insist on this. Not because I have any sort of desire to descend into the heart of a mountain—quite the opposite actually—but because I think he might actually fall to pieces. Never, not even when one of both of our lives was in danger, have I seen him so rattled.

Without a care that Ronan's watching, I take his face in my hands and direct his gaze down to meet mine. He looks directly at me, but his eyes are a million miles away. "You don't have to do this. We can find another way."

With gentle fingers, he grabs my wrist and pulls my hand down so he can kiss my palm. "I think I have to do it." And I know he doesn't just mean to retrieve a map that may or may not be there. I think he has to do it to make peace with his brother.

"I'm coming, too." Ronan's declaration surprises me with its ferocity. I sometimes forget how close he and Felix are. Practically brothers in their own right. No matter the difficulties life has thrown at them, the love they have for each other is strong. Felix's lack of rejection of the offer speaks volumes.

"I thought you would both insist." He sounds...relieved?

"But are you sure it's absolutely necessary?" Ronan seems unbothered by how close Felix and I are. Instead, he's focused entirely on his friend. As he should be. "Maybe you could just sketch out what you remember of it. Or," he pauses a long moment to consider something, "do you think this cave is it? Did you actually find it as a child?"

I hadn't considered that, but it seems improbable even by our low standards. The feelings that coursed through me as I stood outside the door where the Palanquin sat were powerful. I can only imagine what it would feel like to stand at the actual Gate. It would not be possible to be that close to it and not feel it.

"I don't know," Felix admits. His hand comes to rest lightly on the small of my back, and I straighten my posture as if I can somehow transfer my strength to him.

"If you get me close, I can sense it." It doesn't seem like a secret, but Ronan and Felix both lift their brows at my admission. Maybe it's not the same for everyone, but I'm certain of it for me. "There have been a few times I've been near a holy place. It does something to me, physically I mean."

Ronan's eyes widen, but Felix simply nods his head. He's seen it affect me, and maybe even felt a bit of it himself.

"I need you to promise me something."

I reluctantly drag my eyes up to meet his, because when Felix wants me to promise him something, it usually means it's something I'm going to be opposed to. "Emilia?"

"I hardly think it's fair to ask me to agree without knowing what you want from me."

Something in his eyes shifts, and I swallow hard. For the first time, I get a small inkling of what it would be like if he showed me exactly what he does want from me. Or maybe it's just the magnitude of our situation intensifying everything.

"Don't enter that cave." The request doesn't surprise me. Before I can even respond, he rushes ahead. "I know you're smart, and capable, and strong, but I'm not. Not where you're concerned. I can't lose you."

Those words chill me. Because regardless of the cave, there is the very real possibility that he is going to lose me at some point. Likely soon. I still don't know what to think about the prophecy or the sacrifice, but my hopes for survival are not high. If God Himself doesn't require my life, Cyrus will.

But I won't cause him pain when it's within my power to prevent it. So, I lift myself on my tiptoes and press my lips to his. He kisses me back but with none of the emotion I'm used to from him. He's used it all up on his inner battle. But that's okay. I can be strong enough for both of us now. And I whisper against his mouth, "I promise."

25

Once Felix has set his mind to something, there's no stopping him. We have that in common at least. So even though Ronan and I beg him to wait until morning, he insists on leaving at once. I think maybe he's concerned that if he doesn't go immediately, he'll lose his nerve.

Ronan and I get a few moments alone while Felix retrieves Ares and Athena from the stables. Though he made the walk to the cave easily as a child, we all agree this trip will be much better on horseback. While we wait outside the house for Felix to return, Ronan turns to me with a dark frown.

"Are you actually going to let him do this?" He's tried to hide it from Felix, but he's been agitated from the moment he realized what his best friend was planning.

"You and I both know there's no *letting* Felix do anything." He's not quite as obstinate about it as I am, but he's just as stubborn when he sets his mind to something. Ronan must know that as well. "I think you overestimate how much influence we have over each other." I remember him asking Felix on more than one occasion if he was going to *let* me do something.

"I don't think so." He shakes his head, and I notice how long his hair has grown since we left Borealis. He also wears a few days' worth of stubble that matures him far beyond the pampered prince who barged into my throne room and tried to stake a claim on my heart. "It's obvious that you are each other's weakness."

I blink in response but say nothing. He's not wrong. Something about that unsettles me. But before I can consider it further, Felix arrives leading both horses behind him. Neither wears a saddle, but at least he's managed bridles for them. He thrusts Ares's reins into Ronan's hand.

"I'll ride with Emilia. I'm not sure Athena will let you on her."

It's a transparent excuse. Athena is picky about her riders, but she trusts me. If I'm on her back, she'll allow almost anyone else to ride at the same time. However, Felix is the only other person who's managed to successfully ride her solo. Regardless, I don't argue. I want to feel his closeness as we make this climb.

Neither of them offers to help me up this time. I grab hold of Athena's mane, take a running hop, and swing my leg over her back. I settle right in as if we've had no time apart at all. She snorts and stamps her hooves in approval. Leaning forward, I kiss her neck. "I've missed you," I whisper. By the time I sit back up, Ronan has mounted Ares and Felix stands at Athena's side, looking up at me.

Though I'd love to sit in front and maintain control of my horse, Felix's large frame means he should sit ahead of me to make sure our weight is evenly balanced. Reluctantly, I scoot back until I'm on Athena's rump, and he easily mounts her. Then I slide forward until my chest presses against his back, and I wrap my arms around him.

The steady rock of Athena's gate usually calms me and gives me a sense of security. Not today though. I'm keenly aware of my surroundings as Felix directs her out of the city and toward a narrow path that leads to the mountains. Wet foliage slaps against my legs as we wind our way up the slope, leaving damp patches on my pants. In any other circumstance, I would also enjoy the hard lines of his body against mine, but it makes little impression on me now. My mind is fully occupied with where we're going, what we might find there, and what sort of devastation it's going to wreak on Felix when we do.

After what feels like forever of a steady uphill climb, Felix directs Athena to a seemingly random sharp right into even denser foliage. I have to duck my head against him to keep from being slapped in the face. Branches that merely slapped my legs earlier now tug on them as we pass, threatening to pull me away from him. Behind us, Ronan follows with Ares and curses when a branch hits him across the face.

How can Felix be so sure of where we're going? There's no path here, no broken branches to indicate it's been traveled in forever. And yet, I'm sure he's walked this route a million times in his memories. He pushes us forward with wary confidence.

Still, it's on the tip of my tongue to ask if we're lost when the greenery suddenly gives way to a massive rocky outcropping with a yawning dark hole at the base. With a tug on the reins, Felix pulls Athena up short, and Ronan copies his motion with Ares.

"Wow." I can't help the awe that tumbles from my mouth at the site of the cave entrance. Because it's not simply a large hole in a rock. The shape of it is unmistakable. From the serpentine curve of the rock formation behind it to the jagged edges that line the opening on the top which disturbingly resemble teeth. No, fangs. Because the entrance to this cave looks just like a dragon.

The muscles in Felix's body are taut as a pulled bowstring as he keeps his eyes straight ahead, staring into the mouth of darkness. Then, without warning, he throws his leg over Athena's neck and slides from her back. He doesn't wait with an offer to help me dismount, just retreats a few steps to the closest tree and presses his back firmly against it before sinking to the ground.

I scramble from Athena's back, but Ronan beats me there. He kneels before Felix but doesn't touch him.

"Just give me a minute." Ragged words tear from Felix as he closes his eyes and his breathing increases. The pallor of his skin and the sudden sheen of sweat on him alarms me.

"Emilia," Ronan says in a voice barely above a whisper. I pull my attention from Felix to look at him with wide eyes. "Is it here? Can you feel it?"

In my concern for Felix, I've forgotten I have an actual purpose here. With the concern welling up in me, threatening to strangle me, I have to close my eyes to focus on anything other than what's right in front of me. With more effort than it's ever cost me, I force my thoughts away from Felix and turn them inward.

Here be dragons to be slain, here be rich rewards to gain . . . If we perish in the seeking, . . . why, how small a thing is death.

Words I read—was it only last night?—rush back to me, but I push them aside. I'm not here to slay any dragons, and I certainly don't want to think about the second part of that little verse. Instead, I pray a prayer I read in the actual scriptures.

God, show me Your glory.

Nothing happens. I feel nothing, I hear nothing. And when I open my eyes, I see nothing except two broken men looking to me for answers. I shake my head at them, and Ronan sits back on his heels with a heavy sigh. From disappointment or relief, I'm not sure.

Finally, I can focus on Felix. Though I've never seen him like this, I recognize the manifestations of my own panic attacks. Clammy skin, ragged breathing, rapid heart rate. He could use something to ground himself, but we didn't bring anything with us. Except...

My own hands shake as I reach out for him. His eyes are still closed, but I can tell he registers when I take one of his clenched fists in my hands and begin to work to uncurl his fingers. Over several long seconds, I manage to expose his palm, and I brush my thumb across the center of it. When he doesn't immediately clench his hand back up, I direct it to the center of my chest where my opal necklace rests below the hollow of my throat and between my collarbones.

I can feel Ronan's eyes on me as I work to keep my breathing slow and even. My eyes flutter closed as I focus on every inhale and exhale. Without any instruction, Felix begins to match his breathing to mine. A few minutes more and I feel his hand move against my skin. I open my eyes to find he has taken my opal in between his fingers and rubs his thumb in a circular motion over the top.

Slowly his eyes open, and he takes a long deep breath that raises and lowers his strong shoulders. I say nothing because I know it will have cost him much to let me see him like this. He should get to decide how he emerges from the other side of that.

He holds onto my necklace for a few seconds longer, finally letting it drop against my skin. The stone is warm where he held it. Just when I think he's going to pull away entirely, he presses his palm to my cheek and offers a weak smile.

"You stayed."

Did he really think I would run? That this trauma he's revisiting would be enough to scare me away?

"Of course, I stayed. You can't get rid of me that easy."

Slowly the color comes back to his face, and after a few moments, he has strength enough to stand. Ronan helps him to his feet with a shake of his head.

"You two never cease to amaze me. I really wanted to be angry with either of you, both of you, but things like that make it impossible."

I strangely know exactly what he means.

Felix sets his shoulders and stares down the mouth of the cave once again. He isn't quite himself, but he's certainly in more control than he was moments ago.

"Are you sure?" I reach for his hand as he starts to walk past me. I don't want to think about what happens if he gets in that cave and has another panic attack.

"Yes." His voice is strong, clear, and commanding but his eyes are gentle as they sweep over my face. "This means something. I can feel it."

"Let me go in with you," Ronan insists as he steps forward. I have to admire his courage and devotion because this is not his fight. Not yet at least.

"You stay with her. I need to know she's not going to come rushing in after me." Despite everything, his lips twitch up in a small smile.

"Like he could stop me if I tried," I retort. But I won't because I promised.

"Good point," Felix concedes before his face turns serious again. "There's a pretty steep drop about a hundred yards in. I'll yell back when I get that far to let you know I'm okay. If the map's still there, it's not much past that. I left it under a rock so it wouldn't get lost while I went ahead. I had to keep coming back to check it because there wasn't enough light to see beyond that point."

Nope. I don't like the idea of him climbing down a steep drop in the dark. It's not the way he dies in my dreams, but he still dies. He must see the panic flaring in my face because he envelopes me in a tight embrace and presses his lips to the top of my head. "You better come back to me," I mutter against him. "That's not a request."

"I wouldn't dare disobey a direct order." And then he's gone, leaving me grasping at air as he disappears into the yawning dragon's mouth.

Ronan steps up beside me and wraps an arm around my shoulders. But it doesn't bring me any comfort. So, I turn to the one thing I hope will.

God, please protect him.

With that one request, a warmth I've sorely missed flares inside me. I feed the flame. Words I hadn't realized I'd memorized from the Aletheia spring to mind and rush out of me as a prayer.

I lift my eyes up to the mountains. Where does my help come from? My help comes from God, the Maker of heaven and earth. He will not let your foot slip.

God is my light and my salvation. Whom shall I fear?

Even when I walk through the darkest valley, I fear no danger because You are with me.

"Emilia?"

I don't even realize I've fallen to the ground until Ronan lays a concerned hand on my arm. "What are you...I-I can feel something."

He looks confused, lost even, but I don't have time to explain. This time, I pray aloud.

"My God, my Father, protect Felix. Give him the strength and courage to do what he must. Bring him out safely. Guide his steps and guard his heart."

A shout pierces through my concentration, and Ronan and I both race to the mouth of the cave.

"Felix?" Ronan's call disappears into the darkness of the cave.

"I'm going in." I can't stand by while he's in trouble in there. But Ronan's arms wrap around me as he drags me from the mouth of the cave.

"You promised him, Emilia. We both did. He would never forgive me—I would never forgive myself—if I let you go in there."

He's right. I know he is, but I hate it. Heart pounding, I drop to my knees again.

Please let him be okay. Please. Please.

I repeat the words over and over, barely conscious of Ronan's presence at my side. My heart swells and sweat dots my brow. I pour everything I have into my supplication until a shout shatters my concentration.

Ronan is on his feet in an instant, darting toward the mouth of the cave and calling a response. After a few seconds of silence, I hear the echo of Felix's voice ringing through the cave.

"It's here!"

Tears burst from me in sweet, hot relief, but I don't stop praying. The words flow from me in a torrent, so quickly that even I don't know what I'm praying anymore. It might be minutes or hours or even a lifetime later, but I continue until he's there.

The air shifts around me, but my lips fervently recite my pleas until he nearly tackles me. I keep praying, but not with words. It's a communion of agreement with the words that are now tumbling out of Felix's mouth. A prayer for thanksgiving, for forgiveness, and for a way forward.

When I open my eyes, he's right there. A clay-like mud covers him from head to toe, but his eyes shine. Something is different. Something happened in that cave.

And then Ronan's there with his arms wrapped around us both, and someone is crying—maybe all of us—with relief and emotional exhaustion. And somehow, I just know this has not all been for naught. The crumpled paper in Felix's hand holds the key to all of this.

As if sensing my thoughts, he opens his fist and tries his best to smooth the page out before us. We stare at the crude map that has somehow survived ten years in that cave. No signs of water damage or tears from animals. Barely any mud though Felix is covered in it. Other than being wrinkled, it looks as if it was just torn from the book.

A small bite of disappointment niggles at me. I can't make any sense of it, although I can see why a young Felix thought it led here. Something in the shape of the map as a whole resembles a dragon, but there is no scale to indicate if it's something as small as this cave, or something as large as an entire continent.

"Are you all right?" I try to look him over for injuries before realizing the mud would camouflage them anyway. Besides, the worst scars are internal.

"I…I could feel you praying," he says slowly. "There was a moment I almost lost it, but your prayers held me together." Fresh tears come to his eyes, thinning the mud as they run down his cheeks.

I understand. It's a story he may choose to share with me one day, but I don't need to hear it now. What God chooses to say to a person is a private matter. For now, I'm simply relieved he's okay.

"We have the map." Felix looks down at the innocuous piece of paper like he can scarcely believe it's really there. "This could actually get us there."

I don't have the heart to remind him that we don't have a clue what this is a map of. Though I share his sentiment that it's related to the Gate, there are no context clues to indicate where we should start our search. Although the image of the dragon is too strong to ignore given the notes I also found tucked away in the book.

"We'll give it to Antioch to study. He and the scholars in the archives might remember seeing something that looks like this. When I visited, they had maps everywhere." It's a scrap of hope I'm willing to cling to until proven false.

"So, what now?" Ronan is still in the dirt with us. My admiration for him has grown one hundred-fold today. If only he would open his heart to truly believe.

Felix looks directly into my eyes as he answers his friend.

"I think I'd like to go home."

26

That evening, Ronan returns our horses to the stables as Felix and I enter the house. Alara sits at the table, turning a seashell over in her hands, when she spots us. Her brows raise in alarm, but we don't offer much in the way of explanation. I'm not sure it's explainable to anyone who wasn't there.

The emotional toll today has taken on Felix is dramatic, and by the time we enter his room, I actually have to help hold him up while he strips his muddy shirt off. Growing up in a military camp, half-naked men should make no impression on me, but this is Felix. Heat builds in my cheeks as I leave the room to retrieve a basin of water and a cloth while he changes into clean pants. When I return, he's sitting on the bed, staring into space.

We don't talk as I gently touch the cloth to his face, wiping away the mud that's caked in his beard. I'm gentle when I brush across his lips, but I can't stop staring at them. They seem entirely too decadent to belong to this rugged face. I feel his eyes on me, so I move on.

"No one's ever taken care of me like this."

My heart breaks for him because it's probably true. At least not since he was a boy. Felix is always the one serving, always the one protecting, and everyone just expects him to be his usual steady self. But now that he's let me in, I see the cracks in that facade, and rather than help repair them, I want to shatter them all the way.

"You have me now," I say, making sure his eyes meet mine. "There's nothing of duty between us anymore. That means I take care of you just as much as you take care of me."

With repeated rinses of the cloth, I remove all traces of the cave from his face and neck. But when I press the rag to his chest, he sucks in a breath and stills my hand with one of his own.

"Maybe I should do that." His voice is gruff, and I look up from the lines of his chest to see a swirl of emotions in his eyes. It's ridiculous to feel hurt by this rejection, but it still stings.

"Oh. Okay." I try to turn away so he won't see the disappointment in my eyes, but he holds my hand in place against his skin.

"It's not like that." He clears his throat. When I can muster up the courage to meet his eyes, I see the storm in them. "Something happened in the cave, and I..."

"You don't have to tell me."

"I don't know *how* to tell you," he insists earnestly. There's a note of pleading in his voice for me to understand. "I can't put it into words exactly. But it's like it broke something in me. Or broke something loose. All these things I've kept walled off, they're just there now." His eyes flash down to where he holds my hand against his chest. "And I don't trust myself with you."

He's always been the restrained one, but I sense him testing that now. Still, I'm not about to let him make those kinds of decisions on a day that's left him emotionally raw. It's the sort of thing that could leave us both devastated.

"Can you just be patient with me until I figure this out?"

"Of course." But when he's looking at me like that, it's hard to remember why this would be a bad idea.

"I want to give you what you want." His head dips, and I pull my hand from his so I can hook my finger under his chin and force him to look at me.

"*You* are what I want. I don't know how I can make that any plainer."

He stands slowly as if he's a sail unfurling to catch the wind. Times like this, it still surprises me how large and solid he is when he towers over me. The press of his fingers as they find my waist is hard but welcome. And when he lowers his mouth to mine, I melt in his arms.

Absent is the tenderness usually present in the way he kisses me. Not even a hint of the passion that sometimes tinged our forbidden kisses. No, this is full of need. But I'm not sure what he needs and neither, I think, is he. But I let him continue until he pulls away with a growl that's more frustration than desire.

He wages a silent battle with himself, and I don't step in. This isn't my fight. After a long moment, he picks up the precious map he'd laid beside him on the bed.

"I'm going to take this to Antioch before I go down to camp."

I had almost forgotten he and Ronan were sleeping down there to make room for Hannah to stay with Alara and me until the other house is suitable for lodging. Good. As much as I hate to admit it, he needs some physical distance from me. But he doesn't look like he wants it. He doesn't make a move toward the door. He wants me to ask him to stay. Part of me wants to do just that, but he's already said he doesn't trust himself with me tonight, so I'd only be tempting him if I let him stay.

"Can it wait until morning? You need to rest. Go settle in with your men. Catch up with Antony."

"We both know we don't have the luxury of time. The sooner I get this to him, the faster we may have an answer to all this." He's put out with me. I'm not saying anything he wants to hear tonight. And I think he wants validation that his going into that cave today wasn't for nothing. But again, that's not my battle.

He wasn't exaggerating about all his emotions being close to the surface. When you've held them in for so long, they're bound to come rushing out in a torrent. Both passion and frustration. Love and anger. I know better than to think it's directed at me. Even the passion that threatens to leak through. Maybe I'm selfish, but when he turns the full might of that desire on me, I want it to be because he desires *me* and not just an emotional release.

"Take it to him then." Because he doesn't seem ready to put distance between us, I do. Stepping over to the small wardrobe, I pull it open and toss him a shirt. I'm not sure if it's his or Ronan's, but he doesn't object and shrugs it on.

"But don't be too long. If you don't get enough rest tonight, I'll be running circles around you tomorrow." I try my best to lighten the mood. "And sparring? I'd hate to embarrass you in front of the men."

"But you're going to try, aren't you?" He raises an eyebrow in challenge, but his posture is more relaxed as if he's grateful for the change of subject.

"It's why you love me," I quip.

With brows still raised, his eyes darken, and I swallow hard. "Oh, there are many reasons why I love you. But if we start naming them, I'll never get any sleep."

Wait...is he flirting? I'm still trying to puzzle it out when he has the nerve to wink at me before he walks out the door.

That was unexpected.

When I finally compose myself enough to exit his bedroom, I find Hannah standing in the front room, watching him go from the window. Alara is nowhere to be seen, nor is Ronan. I wonder if they're together. Will Ronan share with her what happened today? Somehow, I don't think so. It's Felix's story, and I think he respects that.

Hannah turns to me when I join her at the window. "I thought he might be staying tonight."

"I think he wanted to." I'm watching Felix disappear into the darkness rather than the expression that crosses Hannah's face.

"But you turned him away? Is everything all right?"

I sigh, and my breath fogs up the glass of the window, obscuring what remains of his silhouette.

"I'm sorry. That was too forward of me."

I take Hannah's hands and smile. "You have never said anything too forward to me. I'm not your queen. I'm your friend, and you have every right to inquire."

She offers me a sad smile and tries again. "You didn't want him to stay?"

"Oh, I very much wanted him to stay, but it would have been for all the wrong reasons." She nods as if she understands this perfectly, and I'm glad. Because I don't know how else to explain it. Except I try to anyway. "It's just that he's always so in control of his emotions. He's the model of propriety and chivalry, and just once, I'd like for him to lose control when it comes to me. I want him to lose control *because* of me."

"I've seen him lose control over you."

"Only when he's angry or scared because he thinks my life is in danger." And it usually *was* in danger.

"So," she says slowly, "you want him to lose control...in other ways. Like those times he kissed you when he shouldn't have?"

Oh.

"I think maybe you want him to be reckless because he makes you feel that way?"

"Well, yes." She's managed to put it quite succinctly. This stems from my own insecurities. I want to see that his feelings for me are as powerful as mine are for him.

"There is no doubt he loves you, Emilia. But you speak different languages. He wants you to be careful because he loves you so much he can't bear to lose you. You want him to lose control because your feelings for him can't be contained. They are the same thing spoken in different ways. If you know how to read him, everything he does screams of how desperately he adores you."

I want him to lose control because I want to know that his feelings for me are so strong that nothing I could do—or have done—could change them. And I'll never know if that's true unless I share with him the one secret I've kept from him. Levi.

"When did you become so wise?"

"I've always been wise." She sniffs with mock haughtiness. "you were just too stubborn to hear it."

Felix features heavily in my dreams that night, but not for the reasons I'd hoped. Over and over again he lies mortally wounded at my feet, eyes pleading with me. But I can't save him. I can't save anyone. And it's a new kind of torture when I wake in a cold sweat, knowing I'm alone only because I sent him away.

My body barely reacts this time. Am I getting used to the nightmares? I don't think so, but I am getting more adept at hiding the effects. But there's no one around except Hannah to notice that I'm nearly jumping out of my skin as I prepare to join the men for training. She attributes it to some lovestruck desire to see Felix, but it's so much more. Thankfully Alara left without me, so I don't have to face her scrutiny.

Already the heat makes my skin clammy as I walk from the basilica where I introduced Hannah to Felix's mother, to the section of beach designated for our soldiers. I'm dressed in my lightest pants and sleeveless shirt, but I can already tell I'm going to sweat with the least movement. Felix was right about needing to acclimate to this terrain and climate.

This section of beach has become its own little village, with scores of tents stretched out across the sands. They are a good distance removed from the sea, out of the reach of high tide I suspect, but I can still hear the waves yawning a peaceful rhythm against the shore. Already several soldiers have emerged from their tents and gathered in a knot near the center of the camp. I spot Ronan and Alara near the edge of this group and head that way.

It's been forever since I've actively trained or stretched my body beyond its comfort levels. There's been the occasional moment when I've used my skills, but some part of me misses the rigor of training. The comradery between soldiers and the delicious ache of muscles at the end of the day.

Chatter falls silent and soldiers pause their stretching to watch me walk through their midst to reach the center of the knot. I should probably stop to speak to some of them, bother to learn their names as they're risking their lives for my cause, but my mission is singular, and the need to lay eyes on him drives me forward.

As I suspect, I find Felix at the center of the group, surveying the men with arms crossed across his chest. His eyes land on me but hold none of the tenderness I've come to expect from him. He has transformed back into the man who met me at my military camp all those months ago. It's equal amounts intimidating and attractive. And it's exactly what I need to shake off the nightmares and fall into formation.

Felix snaps the men's attention back to him with a short bark as I take my place alongside Alara and Ronan, who seem slightly less inclined to murder today.

"He's grumpy today," Alara mutters as we bend forward to touch our toes and stretch the back of our legs.

"He's just in his element," Ronan disagrees. "You've never seen him in this role. You're about to see why my father had no choice but to promote him to the highest rank despite his age."

I think both are true. Felix has put on his role of Commander like a cloak, but I know he's still a little put out with the three of us for insisting we join in. "Whatever. We're still gonna pay for it."

"How do you mean?" Alara asks as we all straighten and stretch our arms overhead.

"Line up!" Felix shouts. "Time for a run."

"That's what I mean," I mumble to Alara as everyone scrambles into lines behind Felix. I'm not exactly sure where this is going, but I haven't run in months, and trying to gain traction on this sand is difficult. And if we're lucky enough to leave the beaches behind, we still have the steep hills to contend with.

Felix starts off at an easy pace down the beach. We do our best to remain in a semblance of formation until he cuts up the shore to a narrower path. Then the soldiers in front of us break rank to make the trail passable for all of us. As I catch my stride, I leave Ronan and Alara behind, weaving my way past the men until I have Felix in my sights. My lungs are already burning, but he doesn't even look like he's broken a sweat.

By the time I catch up to him, a stitch burns in my side, and my calves are on fire from the steady uphill climb. But the reluctant smile on his face when he looks over to see me next to him is worth it. Feeling a bit cocky, I push every bit of energy I have left into my legs and pull ahead of him. Behind me, the soldiers whoop in delight to see their Commander bested. It's short-lived though. Just seconds later he breezes past me, looking as if he's putting forth no effort at all. I give up and fall back among the soldiers, some of whom give me an encouraging smile as they pass me.

I fall to the back with Ronan who has slowed down to stay with a struggling Alara. It seems for all her stealth, she never had the need for endurance training. Besting her at something doesn't make me as happy as it usually does. She's doing this, at least in part, because of me. I take no joy in her struggle.

By the time we circle around and make it back to the beach, my clothes are soaked and sweat drips from the end of my braid. Some of the soldiers are showing signs of fatigue as well, but most simply stretch out their legs and then come to attention, waiting on the next instruction.

Next, Felix leads us through a series of flowing poses which both challenge and stretch our muscles. After the run, my legs shake with exhaustion, but I'm determined to keep up. When I stumble on a particularly difficult move that involves standing on one leg while rotating, I groan in frustration and stamp my lifted foot to the sand. With a deep breath, I try again. This time Felix, who has been walking through the group, correcting forms and giving encouragement stops just behind me.

He's close enough to touch me, but he doesn't. With his hands behind his back, he studies my movements for a while. Finally, when I try and stumble again, he leans in to whisper in my ear.

"You're really bad at this. It's almost as painful as watching you dance."

He's trying to break my concentration, and it's working. I huff out a breath and keep my eyes focused ahead as I try the move once again. "Not as painful as the punch to the gut you're about to get."

"I'd like to see you try."

I fall all the way to the sand, shocked by the mischievousness of his tone. He has the audacity to chuckle as he extends a hand to help me up. I swat it away and stand on my own. Though everyone else is still moving through their forms, I can feel eyes on us.

"You definitely have authority issues. I've seen you move with such grace when you're fighting, but as soon as someone tries to tell you what to do—choreographed dances or forms—you fall all over yourself." He keeps his voice low so only I can hear his criticism, but he doesn't bother to hide his smirk. """Take a break, Emilia. You don't have to be good at everything."

"You promised no special treatment," I remind him.

"Oh, don't worry. I'm going to push you during sparring this evening." There's a glint in his eyes that excites me. He seems so much lighter today. "I have to make up for giving you a pass for swimming."

"You're not going to make me get in the water?"

"I would prefer those lessons to be private." He gives me a once-over, lingering a little longer than necessary on the curve of my hips. I expect him to look away and back off like he usually does any time heat flares between us, but when his eyes slam back into mine, his desires are perfectly clear.

Well, even if he hadn't just given me an out for this section of training, I think I would be useless. Those eyes could melt steel with the heat in them. As I'm usually the one wishing things would go further, I'm unsure what to do now that he reciprocates. It was always a safety net of sorts, knowing that he would not allow his emotions to run away with him, but I don't think that's the case anymore. Something changed when he came out of that cave. Maybe now that I've seen his most vulnerable side and refused to leave, he has finally realized that I'm not going anywhere. Not by choice anyway.

Excitement and trepidation war within me. I have no idea what to do with a man like Felix.

I swallow hard and look away because I can't take the intensity. Now who's the distraction? I can't think straight, let alone focus on training or anything else. "I'll leave you to it then. I'll see if Antioch has made any progress. And I need to check on Hannah. I left her with your mother."

"And maybe get a bit of rest. With those two out of the house, things should be quiet."

We both look over at Ronan and Alara who are moving through the forms while glaring at each other. Alara moves like water, fluid and graceful yet exuding power. Ronan is technically proficient, but he can't match the smoothness of her transitions.

"I'll rest when you do," I challenge.

"Don't tempt me. I'll find you when we take a break this afternoon."

I can tell he wants to kiss me, but this time he does show his restraint and instead walks off with that smirk still on his handsome face.

I bow out of formation and turn to find a place on the beach to sit and watch because I do want to learn these moves. When I do, I see a small figure some ways up the shore effortlessly performing all the moves I'm struggling with.

I have a hunch who this is, and I move toward her until I confirm it. Selah. The little girl from the forum. Felix's sister. Instead of my fellow soldiers, I watch her for a while. Her movements aren't as graceful as Felix's, but she energetically moves from form to form without the least falter of balance. After a while, I decide to approach her.

"Where did you learn to do that?" I ask as I take a seat in the sand near her. She stops, looks at me appraisingly, then plops herself down next to me. No fear in this girl.

"Oh, we do forms all the time," she says matter-of-factly. "I've been doing them with Mama since I could walk."

"You're very good," I tell her.

"You're not."

I laugh at her bluntness. "No, I'm not. That's what your brother told me as well."

"Mama says he's smart. So, if he says so then it's for true." She nods her head gravely as if Felix has just given me a death sentence. But then in the same breath she asks, "are you really a princess? Felix says you had a crown and everything."

"I did." The sparkle in her eyes humbles me. My mother always told me to be grateful for my position because it was every little girl's dream to be a princess. "But I gave it up."

"Why?"

"Well, I decided I wanted to fight instead."

"I want to fight. Mama says some bad people are coming. She says Felix will protect us, but I can do it, too. I know how to hit boys and everything."

"I'll bet you do." I wish I'd had half the courage as this girl when I was her age. "Do you know how to hold a dagger?"

Her dark eyes widen as I pull a dagger from the sheath at my waist. She looks it over carefully as it rests in my hand. Slowly, she stretches out a finger and runs it lightly along the blade. I don't stop her, and she doesn't seem frightened as a bright line of blood wells up on the pad of her index finger. She studies this injury then wipes the blood away on her dress.

"It's dangerous."

"Yes, but much less so if you know how to use it. I could teach you sometime if you'd like."

The smile that lights up her face reminds me so much of her brother that my heart skips a beat.

"Your brother is the one who taught me." Memories of those evenings in Aurora where Felix and I met in secret for him to teach me how to throw the daggers, how to wield them as an extension of my hand, flood back to me. As fraught as it was with danger, those were much simpler times.

"Are you better at daggers than forms?" Her little face screws up as she scrutinizes me.

"Yes," I laugh. "Much better."

She considers this for a moment. Then, out of nowhere, "are you really going to die?"

It's a punch to the gut much like I threatened to give Felix a few moments ago. "Where did you hear that?"

She shrugs. "Mama and Felix talked about it. They said you were special. Sometimes special people have to die. My Papa was special. I had another brother, and he was special. But he died before I was born. His name was Max. Mama says I look like him."

What a heart-wrenching moment it must have been for Felix to meet his sister for the first time and see the shadows of his little brother's face in hers. I wipe furiously at the tears that spring to my eyes, but they just keep coming.

"Don't cry. When I cry my friends call me a crybaby. You have to be brave and strong."

I slide the dagger back into my sheath and reach out my hand to her. I want to tell her what I wish someone had told me as a child when I held back the grief for my mother that threatened to drown me. "You can absolutely be strong and brave and still cry. Sometimes tears are the best way to know you're still alive. Your brother taught me that, too."

Not in so many words, but those times when he held me while I cried tears of grief, anger, or fear... He never once made me question my strength despite my fear that he would see me as weak. Over time I realized I was stronger because of it.

Selah still looks skeptical, but she doesn't challenge me further. I see so much of Felix in her restraint. I wonder what other traits they share.

I leave the little girl on the beach and abandon training to return to the city. It's a mark of the change that's come over me lately. The old me would have insisted on pushing through the forms, would have considered it shameful to admit I couldn't do something well. But I don't see it that way now. Felix is right. I don't have to be the best at everything because I'm not on my own anymore. I don't have to do this alone.

27

I find Hannah in the plaza as I return from camp. She's in the middle of some sort of game with a group of three young girls, and they're all laughing brightly. They're about the same age as Felix's sister, and I can't help but think she should be here rather than studying war and weapons. Or maybe I just see too much of myself in her. A pang of sadness hits me for the girl I might have been.

No one tries to stop me as I wind my way through the basilica. I only take one wrong turn before I finally reach the archives where I found Antioch before. Predictably, he's seated at the same table with books and scrolls spread all around him. This time he sees me coming, and gestures for me to take the chair opposite him.

What I think is going to be a friendly visit quickly sours when I read the dire expression on his lined face.

"Death approaches, my child." Suddenly all the lighthearted banter with Felix, the laughter of Hannah and the children, the sparkle in Selah's eyes are smothered under the weight of his words. As if those dark clouds bringing the thunder and lightning have just rolled in off the sea.

"Death and I have been close acquaintances for some time now," I challenge. I don't want to hear it. I came here for good news, a direction, a heading. But Selah's question haunts me still.

"You should prepare," he continues, ignoring my jibe.

"I'm training with Felix's soldiers." Or I was until I abandoned that for this doom and gloom.

"No, no." He slaps his hand down on the table with more force than I would have thought he could muster. Nearby papers rustle at the motion. He has my attention now. "It is not your strength you should focus on. It's your weakness."

"My weakness?"

"Yes, your weakness. It is necessary."

"Can you please just speak plainly?" Annoyance tingles within me, and I have to fight to remain at this table with him. Why is it when I come to get information, he always has to point out how I'm going to die?

"The scriptures say to take delight in weakness because it is then you are made strong."

I clench my teeth as I try to determine how to answer him. "I am not weak."

"But you are. And you are growing weaker."

How does he know just the thing to say to make indignation flare within me? I've spent most of my life trying to prove to everyone that I'm not weak, that I am worthy. Who is he to tell me I'm weak?

Then I remember he's an augur of Caelus and a converted Insurgo. This man has read more religious texts than almost anyone. He's seen and done things that I can't even fathom. Surely, he can't be wrong. I change the subject to ask about something I've kept off limits from his speculation. But last night has me desperate to know more.

"And what about my dreams?"

"Messages from God to prepare you," he answers as if he expected my question. And he leans forward eagerly. "Tell me what you've seen."

I do. I explain about the dream where two armies clash on a beach while I watch powerlessly from atop a cliff. The one where something deep within me pulls me through a forest with such force that I have no control over my own body. He nods as the words pour from me, taking it all in. But when I mention Felix, his movement stills.

"And what exactly do you see regarding the Lord Commander?" There's something in his eyes that curls a knot of dread in my stomach.

"He's on the ground, dying. Rarely in the same way, but usually bleeding."

"But not actually dead?"

"No." My answer comes out in a ragged whisper as I fight to keep tears at bay.

Antioch closes his eyes for a moment to process everything I've told him. "You remember I told you not to underestimate him?"

"What does that—"

"He is valuable. I did not expect..." he trails off in deep thought.

"What?" I ask desperately. "Tell me, is he going to die? Can I stop it?"

He's silent for a long moment. "I did not expect your stories to be so entangled."

"Please." I hate I'm reduced to begging, but for Felix's life, I would do much more. "Tell me something real."

"Nothing is more real than love and death, and you know more of those than I ever will."

The seed of an idea begins to sprout within me. It brings both fear and a tendril of hope. "Antioch, do you really think I have to die for all this to end?"

"I only said the Ruler will have to make the ultimate sacrifice." His vagueness is infuriating, but I hold my composure because I need an answer to this next question.

"Will my death save Felix?"

"It's not for me to say."

This time *I* slam my hand on the table, and the few men in the quiet room turn to look at us. I don't care. "Give me a straight answer."

He seems unbothered by my outburst. "The greatest love is one who lays down their life for their friends."

My chair screeches then topples over as I shove back from the table and rise to my feet. I want to clamp my hands over my ears so I can't hear any more. But does that make it any less true?

I don't know who I'm angrier at. Antioch or God Himself. Why would He dangle the hope of the life I've always wanted in front of me when His plan is to kill me so the others can live?

You are my plan.

I squeeze my eyes closed as if I can chase away the words that resound in my head. Maybe I never heard them beneath that water. Maybe they aren't real. Even if they are, He never said it was a good plan.

And yet, I think of Selah. If she could grow up in a world where she never has to know the hardship and violence of war, wouldn't it be worth it? There are thousands of children like her who could have a future I never could if I fulfill my destiny.

But my heart breaks for Felix and Hannah and Ronan and even Alara. Their lives will be altered—to varying degrees, of course—by the loss of me…if they live.

Then it hits me. The realization that none of this matters if we don't beat Cyrus to the Gate. It won't just be my death to consider if we don't receive the power from the Ancient.

"Tell me you got something from that map," I plead with him. Bitter tears sting my eyes, but I blink them back. Not here.

Antioch takes a few untenable moments to sift through the papers on the table. Finally, he uncovers a map and smooths it out between us. I recognize it as the one I studied last time I was here. One that came from Verity in Zephyros. He points a shaky finger to the small chain of islands to the west of Solitarius. The ones that are small enough to look like they could be from an accidental inkblot rather than intentional.

"These are the back of the dragon."

"The what?" That word unsettles me like nothing else he's said has. Because what are the chances that a fairytale creature keeps turning up in this narrative?

"The dragon," he repeats calmly. I hate how he's so calm. Doesn't he realize how perilous this all is? "The older maps show it better. Before the Great Wave which buried most of that land beneath the sea. It was one large island. It was discovered centuries ago and named it Draconis. Then a great storm came, and the waves washed so high that most of the island was lost."

That's an understatement. It's just a few small dots on a map. But I have to admit the information sounds promising. We need more information, more evidence. Because how am I going to convince everyone that we need to abandon our post here and travel to this speck of land somewhere west of here? And how would we even get there? If the Synod isn't comfortable with letting the soldiers patrol the city, I can't imagine they're going to volunteer any of their own ships for us to take on a joy ride.

"Can't anything be simple about this?" I say, more to myself than Antioch.

"Narrow is the Gate that leads to life, and few find it," he quotes the Aletheia.

I'm so close to flipping this table, but that won't win me any support either. But the anger that bubbles up in me threatens to spill over. What I wouldn't give to hit something or throw a dagger or two.

The quiet stillness of the room dampens my dramatic exit as I leave Antioch behind with his maps. I don't even register where I am until I find myself blinking into the sun in the plaza outside the basilica. Hannah is still there, but instead of playing a game, the children sit around her now, listening to her tell a story.

This is what I'm going to die for. Not for my own children, which I'll never know, but for these young ones to have a chance to grow up without fear of persecution because they believe the truth. Like Miriam told me, we're all going to die. Shouldn't our deaths count for something? And if there's even a chance that my death will change Felix's outcome, I welcome it.

Once we're hidden behind the walls of our house, Hannah finds the courage to speak to me. She kept her silence on the way back, and I'm sure it's because she could sense the anger rolling off me.

"What's troubling you?" She follows me into the common room and gestures for me to sit on the floor. I do and she sits behind me, taking my braid in her hands without asking.

"Everything," I mutter as she unravels the strands of my hair and combs her fingers through them. "Everyone's looking to me for answers, and I have none. I'm hoping Antioch will come across something useful, but every time I ask, he just points out that I'm going to die."

Hannah gasps, and her hands still in my hair.

Oops. I guess I haven't had that conversation with her yet.

"You're…going to die?" she asks slowly. "Why?"

"Because some prophecy says so."

"A prophecy from the Aletheia?"

Her question gives me pause. "Yes? At least I think so." But I haven't come across this prophecy in any of the passages I've read. No scripture I've read has mentioned this Ruler Who Will Rise Up or a Princess That Was Promised. I've always taken it for granted that my fate was written in scripture, but what if it's not?

"I don't recall that from the bits I've read," she admits. "But Antioch is certainly more studied than I am."

My mind spins as she resumes her combing of my hair. I try to remember exactly what's been told to me and what my mind has filled in. I've read the passages about the Ancient One, about the narrow gate that leads to life, about one who will be exalted by the Ancient One and subdue all kingdoms. But I have never seen them all put together on a page. Is it possible this prophecy is part of the oral tradition perpetuated by the destruction of the Aletheia on the mainland? What was it Verity said to me? She had heard of a promise but that it wasn't necessarily the same thing as a prophecy.

"Do you think it's possible that he got this wrong?" I lay out for her all Antioch's evidence to support my impending death. It rolls off my tongue as well as my own name at this point. I can see how all the pieces fit together, but what if they were never all supposed to belong to the same puzzle?

"I don't pretend to know as much as Antioch," Hannah replies. "And I have never had the privilege to read the entirety of the scriptures. But…I don't believe our God's plan is for your destruction. There are many ways to sacrifice that don't involve giving your life. I do believe He chose you as a conduit for His great power. He hasn't given you power, but He has allowed you to showcase His."

Silence settles between us as she smooths out my hair and braids it back. Confusion muddles my brain as I try desperately to wrap all this up into a neat package. I just can't. So, I settle on the bottom line Antioch gave me in Zephyros. Does it really matter? Either the sacrifice will be required, or it won't. Knowing the outcome won't change the right thing. And that's all I can do—the next right thing.

"It looks like the children took to you quickly," I finally say, eager for a change of subject. What I wouldn't give for just a bit of normalcy. Then I remember that I don't even know what normal is.

Hannah smiles knowingly as she comes to sit on the floor in front of me, signaling that it's my turn to braid her hair. My fingers slide easily through her long, fine hair and then I begin to work it into a plait.

"I told them stories—including the one where a princess rescued me—and then they told me some of theirs," she says with a smile in her voice.

"And what kind of stories do they tell here?" I'm genuinely curious. Most of the fairytales I grew up with were of princesses who needed rescuing or ugly ducklings who grew into unfathomable beauty.

"Mostly stories from the Aletheia. You know, the ones about the lions' den and parting the sea. All the things that are so fantastical that they're hard to believe without faith."

Like the storms that surround me and showed God's glory in ways it hasn't been seen in hundreds of years. Like the way Felix's leg healed after he was shot with that arrow. All things I wouldn't have believed possible if I hadn't seen them for myself.

"They did tell me one that might interest you, though." Her brow furrows as she tries to recall. "I can't remember all of it because all three of them were trying to tell me at once, but I do remember that they said Caspian never died. He just rode away on the back of a dragon and never came back."

My blood turns to ice. No way. There is no way this is a coincidence. The notes in the Aletheia, Felix's map, Antioch's mention of Draconis, and now this?

God, what are you trying to tell me?

The prayer warms me just a little, though I hear no clear answer. Was Antioch right? Are those tiny specks of islands my next destination? But if most of Draconis was submerged, does that mean the Gate is, too? What if it's not accessible at all?

Laughter just outside jolts me from my thoughts. Hannah looks up just as Felix and Antony come through the door, Felix clapping the younger man on the back.

Hannah's face lights up as she stands to greet them. Antony bends his head to kiss her, and her cheeks color with a blush. I can't help but smile at them and how uncomplicated things seem for them. I catch Felix smiling, too.

"He said yes," Antony informs Hannah as he clasps her hands between his and presses a kiss to them as well. I raise a brow in question as Hannah looks nervously over her shoulder to me.

"I hadn't had a chance to ask you yet," she begins as she turns from Antony to me. "We wanted to ask you for your blessing… to marry." She adds when I blink in incomprehension.

For some reason, my eyes go to Felix. But I realize they're waiting on a response from me, so I force myself to address Hannah and Antony. "Of course, you have it. You don't need my permission to be happy."

"It was important to us that you and the Commander both approved," Antony says. "If it weren't for the two of you, we would have never met. And we serve both of you. If you had any objection…"

"We don't," Felix answers for us. Apparently, he's already given his blessing to Antony, but he repeats it again for Hannah's benefit. "I think we would all welcome a reason to celebrate."

I don't have anything else to say as I jump up and wrap Hannah in my arms. No one deserves happiness as much as she does. I don't know the whole story of her life, but I know she's seen more than her share of hardship, and she deserves a man who looks at her the way Antony does.

"We don't want a big fuss," Hannah insists as she wipes a few happy tears from her eyes. "We just want the opportunity to say our vows between God and witnesses."

"I'll have my mother help you with preparations," Felix offers. "She knows everyone. And as much as Emilia would like to, I'm not sure she can take on a task as daunting as planning a wedding."

Maybe he's just being practical. After all, a wedding is hardly high on my priority list. In the grand scheme of things, a wedding would be a trivial use of my time. Or maybe he's afraid after my most recent wedding experience, it would trigger something dark in me to be involved with another one. That's a question to be explored another time.

Hannah fills Antony in on how she spent her time today, and Felix quietly approaches me. His hand finds the small of my back in a simple, comforting gesture. It's been difficult for me to gauge how he's feeling today since all our interactions have been in front of others, but he was definitely toying with me earlier. Now he slides into his familiar spot by my side.

"You're tense," he says in a voice low enough for my ears only. "Everything okay?"

How can I begin to tell him about the revelation that's just rushed through me like a tidal wave? About the sliver of hope Hannah's given me? I need some time to sort this out first. And I need a moment to revel in his presence, the breath that fills his lungs.

"We can talk about it later." I place my hand on his bicep and search his face for some sort of clue as to his feelings. He responds by sliding his arm all the way around me.

“I met your sister today,” I say, changing the subject entirely. He seems content to let it pass as one corner of his mouth quirks up, and his eyes light with mirth.

“She told me she spoke to you. You offered to give her dagger lessons?”

“I did learn from the best.” I lean into him. Hannah’s eyes briefly dart our way, and her grin widens.

“Which means if she’s going to learn, I should teach her. Besides, I think you may be busy with a few wedding things.”

“You just said you didn’t think I should take that on.”

“And I don’t. But I don’t for one minute think you’re going to be able to keep your hands out of it.”

“You do know me well.”

“We won’t be a bother,” Hannah promises as she looks at us in earnest.

“You could never be a bother.” I leave Felix’s side to pull her into a hug. “Anything you want, if it’s in my power, you’ll have it.”

“Well, I guess we better finish readying your house then.” Felix motions Antony to follow him to the door.

“Wait,” I call. “Shouldn’t you rest for a while? Sleep for a bit or at least put your feet up until training this evening?”

His crooked grin melts my heart almost as much as when he comes back long enough to kiss the top of my head. “Don’t worry about me. I’m fine. I’ll see you at six bells for the evening training.”

⁂

Thwack!

I barely register the sound before the impact against the back of my calves sweeps my feet out from under me and upends my world. Sea and sky rush past as I land on my back, exhaling in a soft oomph as I hit the sand. It's not the first time this evening I've been in this position.

Felix looms over me, a grim smile turning the corners of his mouth. "Get up."

True to his word, he has not gone easy on me. For this evening's training, he broke us into pairs for sparring. Predictably, he assigned himself to me. He is the superior fighter of the two of us, but I know I can beat him given the right set of circumstances. But tonight he's taken me to the ground over and over again with apparent ease.

"I need a minute," I mutter as I push myself up. A minute will hardly be enough. There's too much rattling around in my head to think I can compartmentalize it in that short amount of time. Still, I need to train. I need to be prepared. I tuck my legs under me and stand. I've barely gained my balance when he sweeps my legs out from under me again.

"You don't get a minute." He crouches back in a fighting stance as I get to my feet once again. "No one is going to pause a fight because you weren't ready. Now get out of your head and attack me."

I know he's right, and I know he's goading me on purpose, but I react anyway. The staff whirls in my hands as I press toward him with a series of jabs and sweeps. He dodges every single one, and when my momentum carries me too far, he swings his staff around to strike me across the back, sending me sprawling to my knees this time.

"Stop fighting with your emotions," he instructs. "You're better than this. Act like it."

My heart's already pounding with exertion, but his words send anger rushing through me that amplifies every beat. My visit with Antioch earlier soured my mood, and now his words resound in my head. *"You are growing weaker."* I already couldn't keep up with the forms this morning, and now I've let my thoughts distract me from something I normally excel at. But I am not weak.

This time I spring to my feet and drop my bow. Felix is taken off guard by my sudden movement, and he steps back as I rush toward him, discarding his staff as well.

I throw strike after strike, but he blocks them all. I'm a flurry of movement in a rush attack that gives him little time to mount an offense of his own. But I know the exact moment I've made a critical mistake. I lean back to aim a kick toward his head, but he ducks under it and grabs my other leg, twisting until we both crash to the ground, him on top of me and both seething.

Or at least I am. Felix is panting for sure. I've at least made him break a sweat. He pins my arms over my head as he kneels over me, one of his knees resting between mine.

I can't be sure because the sun's light is failing with the evening hours, but his eyes seem darker as he looks me over. I arch my back, trying to push him off me, but it's useless. Antioch is right. I am weak. A frustrated growl tears from me.

Felix arches his brows and leans down. My heart thunders in my chest because I think he's going to kiss me right here in front of all these people. And it would be a welcome distraction from all the thoughts racing through my mind. Instead, he lowers his lips to my ear. His warm breath fanning against my skin sends a shiver through me.

"You're done," he whispers.

"Your restraint is annoyingly epic as always," I grumble as he pushes himself off me.

"What was that?" The flash in his eyes tells me he heard exactly what I said.

"Nothing."

"You're too distracted tonight. I have other things to do besides worry if you're going to get hurt because you're not paying attention. Either get it together or sit it out."

I blink up at him. Something really has shifted in him. He's usually begging me to stay safe, not issuing ultimatums for me to consider.

"Change it up!" he shouts to the rest of the men spread across the sand. After a brief pause, several pick themselves up off the ground and rotate to a new partner. Then Felix looks back down to me. "Find Alara and challenge her. That should give you a chance to take out whatever this is," he makes a sweeping gesture to indicate what a mess I am, "without causing yourself too much harm."

I know he's right, but that only makes me angrier.

He walks off, and I find Alara. But the look in her eyes when she sees me says that sparring with her might not be the best idea. She looks just as angry and frustrated as I feel.

"Truce?" I ask and am relieved when she nods. She joins me in walking up a small hill and where we can still easily watch the action on the beach as we collapse to the sand.

"You first," I say to her, though I keep my eyes forward, searching for Felix or Ronan among all the fighting.

"Everything hurts," she groans. "I think I'm dying."

There's a moment where the only sounds are the clash of metal from the few pairs sparring with swords and the occasional yells of victory or defeat. Then Alara says," your turn."

"Antioch thinks I'm weak, and I'm definitely going to die."

"Well, I can't compete with that," she muses. We turn our heads to look at each other. I crack a smile and then we're both laughing.

"I don't want to, though," I say as we both begin to sober. "Does that make me a horrible person?"

"I'm the wrong person to ask. Although," she directs her attention back to the sparring, "if I had *that* in my future, I'd definitely be a little reluctant to rush to my death."

I follow her line of sight to find Felix sparring with three men. Once again, just how much he was holding back with me is evident. It makes me all the more frustrated that I couldn't get my head together long enough to provide him a challenge. "By the time we get things figured out between us, I'll probably be dead."

"I don't know. He seems different today. A little less...reserved. You should take advantage of that and stop worrying about what anyone else is going to think. Ronan doesn't mind, if that's what you're worried about."

Is she trying to convince herself or me?

My eyes dart back and forth, watching as the soldiers take turns attacking him. I cringe each time he takes a hit, including a particularly brutal one to his shoulder. But I'm taking it well until they all three rush him at once and force him to the ground. One wraps his arm around his neck in a chokehold.

It's just sparring. I know that. But my mind shows me something different. Felix lying at my feet, covered in blood. My heart pounds and red tinges my vision.

"Death approaches."

"Emilia?" Alara's voice sounds distant, and I realize it's because I'm running away from her and toward Felix. Sand flies up behind me as I weave through pairs of men until I reach them.

"Enough!" I pant and futilely try to wipe the sand from my face. The three men who had him pinned have already released him, and one is offering him a hand to help him up. They all turn to look at me with confused frowns. Felix tilts his head to look me over, then addresses his opponents.

"Again." He bends his knees and assumes a defensive position, waiting for them to rush him again.

“Stand down,” I insist as I place myself between him and the soldiers who have the unfortunate luck to be his sparring partners.

“I said again,” Felix commands as he steps forward to stand beside me. The men look between the two of us.

“But she is—” one of them stammers.

“I know who she is,” he barks. “And I am your commander. You answer to me. If you disobey a direct order, you're not going to like the outcome.”

I can see their internal struggle and the fear in their eyes. Part of me can't believe we've made it this far before my orders have come in conflict with Felix's. It's unfair to make them choose because my fears got in the way.

I turn my back on them and face Felix. “Commander, a word?”

His jaw tenses as his posture relaxes from his fighting stance. “Take five,” he addresses the men over my shoulder. The men duck their heads and walk away.

Before I can explain, Felix practically growls at me. “What were you thinking? You can't undermine me like that.”

“I'm thinking that you keep dying in my dreams, and that's all I can see when you're on the ground like that.” My words come rushing out as my hands curl into fists that I rest on my hips. I've never shared that with him. He's witnessed the aftermath of my dreams, of course, but I've never told him that his death is often what wakes me up with a scream.

His face softens. “It hurts to be on that side of it, doesn't it?”

Air whooshes out of me as if I've been punched in the gut. Is this what he feels every time I'm in danger? If I'd known it hurt like this, I never would have taken most of the risks I've taken.

Felix crosses his arms over his chest, and I take note of the grimace he tries to hide.

"You're hurt." It takes all the self-control I possess not to reach for him and assess the damage. Instead, I channel it into indignation and whirl to scan the crowd. "Where are they? They should be punished. They should have known better than to—"

"I asked them to." His words come out through clenched teeth. "They were just obeying my orders. If you have a problem with that, then you punish *me*."

"How can I punish you when you're in charge?" I snap. I am vaguely aware that the sparring around us has come to a halt, and we now have an audience.

He remains just as calm and composed as ever when he says, "You're tying my hands, Emilia."

There's an audible gasp from somewhere among the men. Some may speculate about the relationship between Felix and me, but he has been very careful to address me with reverence and formality in front of the men. For him to use my name as casually—as bitingly—as he has is a breach of protocol.

Unlike last night, I want to provoke him. I want to have it out. I want to vent every bit of this anger and fear I'm feeling on the one person I know can take it.

"You want to be in charge? Fine, you can have it. I never asked for this." And despite my best efforts the tears come. Selah's face flashes through my mind, and I remember how I told her tears weren't a sign of weakness. But I'm a liar. Because that's exactly what I feel as I stare down my commander, my friend, my love and wait for him to react. I'm being unfair and I know it, but I don't know how to stand down without looking like an utter fool. Or maybe it's too late for that.

Something in his face shifts, and I try to anticipate his response. I don't know how much they heard, but we have argued in front of everyone who has pledged their life to fight for us. I am driving a wedge between us. He has every right to yell at me, to send me away, to ban me from training at all. But he does none of those things. With careful even steps, he closes the space between us and takes my hands for all to see. The world shifts, and everything seems right again.

"I know you're angry," he says softly, his words for me alone. "I know you're scared, and you have every right to be. But I'm asking you to trust me. Nobody said you have to do this alone. I want to be your partner in all things."

He's right. Of course, he's almost always right. But in this moment, that is no consolation. Still, I know it's time I let go of that part of me that's desperate to prove myself to everyone. If God has a plan for me, then I'm sure He's already factored in all my flaws and shortcomings. Either I'll live through this, or I won't. Either the sacrifice will be required, or it won't. I think of Hannah's insistence that this is the language of Felix's love, and I decide to listen before I ruin everything.

“I’m sorry.” And I truly mean it. I want Felix to crush me to his chest, to stroke my hair and tell me everything will be fine. But he won’t lie to me, and he doesn’t know the ending of this any more than I do. Somehow, we must figure out a way to manage this together. I can’t do this without him by my side.

But because we still have an audience, Felix does none of those things. Instead, he releases my hands and slowly kneels before me, maintaining eye contact all the way down. My heart lodges in my throat. It takes a strong man to love a queen, and Felix is the strongest. Bowing before me doesn't diminish him in the slightest.

One by one, all our onlookers begin to bow as well. It’s a wave of people dropping to their knees and bowing their heads in deference to me. My eyes sweep across them all until the tears blur my vision. Then I look back down to Felix who deliberately bows his head before me. Once again, he has saved me.

“Rise,” I choke out, loud enough for my voice to carry to the rest of the men. As one they all stand to their feet, coming to attention and awaiting orders. But I only have eyes for Felix who stands before me once again, hands behind his back.

“I could kiss you right now,” I whisper shakily to him, and he blinks in surprise. It's subtle, but I think I see him quickly lick his lips. “But I won’t do anything else to undermine you here. But later...”

He clears his throat and spins away from me to face the men. “Switch partners and resume sparring,” he calls, and an immediate flurry of movement follows. Then he turns back to me. "I might be late tonight."

"I'll wait up," I promise.

28

The moon is high in the sky, and Alara and Hannah have already retired for the night when Felix shows up at the door. He's not alone either. Peeking her head out from behind him is Selah. He shrugs apologetically then reaches for my hand. I take it and let him pull me out into the night. The sky is particularly beautiful with twinkling stars against a black velvet backdrop. The moon is nearly full and bathes us in a soft light. But with all that beauty, I'm only looking at him.

"I helped with the horses," Selah announces as she puffs out her chest. Sure enough, I can just make out Athena where she stands beside Felix's stark white stallion, Ares.

"I thought we might go for a ride," Felix explains, still holding tight to my hand. I hope he never lets go. As long as he's holding on, I can block everything else out, and that's exactly what I do.

"Perfect," I agree. He places Athena's reins in my hands, and a smile curls my mouth as I plant a kiss on her velvet nose. "Hello, pretty one." She nods and prances a bit in approval. Once she stills, I mount her with ease. After I adjust myself on her back, I glance down to find Selah staring at me with wide eyes.

"Can you teach me that?" The awe is evident in her voice, and it makes my heart ache.

"When you're older," I promise and hope I live to fulfill it. It would be so amazing to watch this little girl grow up into a formidable young woman.

"Felix, did you hear? The princess is going to teach me to ride!" She turns to her older brother and punches her fist in the air in celebration. The laugh that booms from him melts something inside me.

"She's an excellent rider. You'll learn from the best." He pats her head, and she beams up at him. "Maybe I'll see about getting you a pony to learn on."

"I'm getting a pony?!" She actually jumps in the air and whoops, and I can't contain a laugh of my own.

"I said, I'll see about it," he corrects. He's so good with her. So generous with his time and affection even though he's known her for such a short time. He was the same with the boy Pax in Zephyros.

"Can I ride with you now?" Her little face holds such hope as she smiles up at him.

"Not tonight, Lala."

He even has a nickname for her already? I'm practically a puddle.

"But why do you have to go? You could stay here, and we could play." As much as I ache to be alone with Felix, I would have a hard time saying no to that child. Good thing she's asking him.

He kneels down so he's on her level and addresses her seriously. "I've been busy lately, so I haven't had a chance to spend time with Emilia. I want to go for a ride with her so she remembers how special she is to me."

It's a good answer, until I remember Selah equates "special" with dead.

"Maybe you can practice with your wooden sword until we get back," I interject, hoping to distract her. But she doesn't even look at me. She's looking at her big brother with a solemn expression.

"Is it because you love her? Is Emilia special because you love her?"

Felix chuckles. "No Lala, I love her, *and* she is special."

But I think Selah had it right the first time. To be the recipient of his love is the most special thing I could imagine.

A thought occurs to her, and she wrinkles her nose. "Are you going to kiss her?"

He clears his throat and rubs the back of his neck before sneaking a glance back at me. "If I'm very, very lucky."

Give this man a four-leaf clover. It's all I can do not to jump down from my horse and kiss him full on the mouth right now. But poor little Selah looks like this might scar her for life.

"Will you come back?" Her lip pokes out in a pout that just shatters my heart. Felix's shoulders slump, and he huffs out a breath as if someone punched him in the gut. He places his hands on her shoulders and looks her straight in the face. I've been the subject of that gaze too many times not to realize that the gravity of it won't be lost on a child.

"I promise." He ducks his head for a moment, seeming to consider something. "Do you know where the tide pools are?" Selah nods with equal solemnity. "We'll be on the beach just before them. If you need me for anything, come find me, and I'll come right back."

This seems to satisfy her. Felix ruffles her hair and stands. I wave to her as Felix mounts Ares, and we trot off in the opposite direction of the soldiers' camp. It's the same path Alara took me on when we visited the bathing pools the first night. After we leave the city behind, Felix nudges Ares into a gallop, and I chase after him.

Athena tosses her head as we sprint along the shoreline. My braid flies out behind me as I lean low against her neck and relish the feel of wind on my face. Felix laughs and looks over his shoulder at me as I spur Athena to sprint ahead. Oh, how I've missed this. Layers and layers of heaviness fly from me as I leave it all behind to live in this moment. There is only the horse beneath me, the waves to my left, and Felix.

I pull ahead of him for just a moment before he and Ares cut us off, and he jumps off the horse before he can even come to a stop. Athena's reins fall from my hands as I perform my own running dismount. Without thought, without reason, we're both sprinting toward the sea as if our lives depend on it. Felix reaches the waves first, but when I catch up to him a half second later, he lifts me mid-run and uses my momentum to swing us around.

I toss my head back and let out the first real laugh in much too long. He's laughing, too as he adjusts his hands on my hips and slowly lowers me down his body. Every hard line of his chest makes an impression as I move against him, my toes finally dipping into the water. Just as my feet rest on the sand, he dips his head to kiss me. It's a gentle brush of lips at first, though not hesitant. I taste the salt on his lips and something else that I want to explore further.

He lets me. His lips part as his hands tighten on my waist, bunching up the wet fabric of my loose shirt. My hands slide into the almost nonexistent space between us to splay across his chest. When I nip at his lower lip, his heart flutters beneath my palm. I sigh, and he ends the kiss with a lingering press of his lips.

"You taste like the wind and the sea." His lips just brush the skin beneath my ear, and a full body chill runs through me. "And the sea has always been home to me." He cups the back of my neck with his large hands and kisses me again.

"I have been waiting for you to do that for far too long," I sigh as I brush my lips over his stubbled jaw, relishing the prickle of his beard against my swollen mouth.

His fingers work the strands of my braid until it unravels and falls in loose waves down my back. A shuddering breath escapes his mouth as he combs his fingers through the tangled strands. There's pure awe in his eyes.

“Stars above, you are so beautiful it hurts.” He tugs gently with his fingers twisted in my hair and groans softly. “And this hair...”

I shatter into a million pieces as he kisses me again. It takes my breath, but I keep on giving. He can have it all. Every kiss, every heartbeat, every breath. And it will still never be enough.

Some indeterminate amount of time later, we both stretch out on the beach, limbs and eyes heavy with the sort of exhaustion that can only come from blissful happiness. I want to stay in this moment forever. And I want a million more of them.

The waves just tickle my toes as I roll slightly on my side to snuggle into Felix. He stretches one arm back over his head causing his shirt to raise and expose just the smallest stretch of skin across his side. His other hand rests on his stomach, palm slightly turned up in an invitation for me to lace my fingers with his. I do just that and sigh at how well our hands fit together—scars, callouses, and all.

“What are you thinking about?” His voice is tinged with sleep though I know he’s not dared to drift off.

“How I don’t want this to end.”

He laughs softly. “I thought this was supposed to be a lighthearted evening. Can you ever just relax?”

“Can you?” I ask as I poke him lightly in the ribs. He winces slightly, and I realize I've pressed against the scar he received from a blade while rescuing me from Cyrus's court. I change my tactic and brush my fingers lightly across the exposed skin. His muscles contract beneath my touch, but he doesn't shy away. "Does it still hurt?"

"Not so much," he answers with an attempt at nonchalance, but I notice he's struggling a bit to control his breathing. I don't think that's from pain, though. "I've had plenty of scars through the years. This is one I wear proudly."

I recall the few times I've seen him without a shirt and remember several scars along his back. I want to know about them all. So, without asking so he doesn't have a chance to refuse, I tug the hem of his shirt upward to expose the tan skin. Felix hesitates for just a moment, then sits up just enough to pull his shirt over his head and toss it to the side. Instead of lying back down, he reclines and props himself on an elbow, facing me. He must register the surprised look on my face because he smiles down at me and says, "I have nothing to hide from you anymore."

It's as if a dam breaks inside me, and a swell of emotion leaves a lump in my throat and a tremble in my voice when I say, "what's this scar from?" as I touch a dark thin line on his shoulder.

"Being thrown from a horse when I was a kid. Ronan and I were riding, and he was showing off. Even though I wasn't very comfortable on a horse at that point, I decided I could do everything he could do. Needless to say, it didn't end well."

"I'm trying to picture you as a follower." I screw my brow up in concentration as I study the shadows on his face in the moonlight. "You're always so decisive and... in charge."

"I learned to be. This scar," he points to one just under his jawline that is usually camouflaged by a thicker beard, "is from one of the few times Ronan bested me in swordplay. I was so awkward and slow in the beginning, but I eventually learned not to copy his movements but invent ones of my own."

"What about those on your back?" I'm cautious in my questioning, because I think I know what the linear lines are from, and they are not an accident. Felix is silent so long that I think he's going to refuse to tell me.

Finally, he says, "Maybe you should ask Ronan. I'm not sure it's my story to tell."

"They are your scars and are therefore part of your story," I remind him gently. I won't force him to tell me, but I hope he will.

"Once, not long after I came to Aurora, I happened upon Cyrus punishing Ronan. I had never seen anything like that. My father never hit us, and all I could think was how I had promised to protect my new friend. So, I put myself between them." He closes his eyes for a moment as if recalling the pain. "The whip had shards of stones and glass in it. I couldn't wear a shirt for days."

Tears prick my eyes for both boys—Felix and Ronan—and for all the pain they endured. It's not a feeling I can completely relate to. There have always been hints of something dark in Ronan's relationship with his father, but I didn't imagine it went this far. "That was very heroic," I tell him.

"It was very stupid. Ronan told me never to stand between him and his father again. So, I haven't until now. Until you came along and gave me the courage to do so."

“We needed each other,” I agree. This isn’t the first time he’s said something like this to me, but it is the first time that it doesn’t come with the weight of expectations.

We spend the next several minutes with him pointing to scars and telling sometimes funny, sometimes poignant stories of how he received them. I touch my fingers to each one until touching him feels as natural as breathing to me. As if by pressing my fingers to his wounds I am claiming them, claiming him, as my own. And he lets me. With each one, he relaxes more and more until he doesn't tense when I touch him.

“And tell me the story of this one,” I insist as we arrive back to the scar we first started with. Felix is such a compelling storyteller that I want to hear this in his own words though I already know the story.

“Well, you see, there was this princess that needed saving.”

I wrinkle my nose at his choice of words, but I don't deny it. He must sense my displeasure because he grins as he leans over me and braces his hand on the other side of my body.

“She had a bad habit of getting herself into all sorts of crazy situations,” he continues as he leans closer to me. His lips just brush my jaw as he kisses along it. “And I just knew I would be the one to get her out of them. Because I could never say no to a damsel in distress. So, I decided to take on an entire squadron of Imperial guards who had been trained by the absolute best commander the Empire had ever seen.”

I snort. Not because it isn't true, but because I know Felix doesn't believe it. He's simply teasing now, but I'm intrigued by where this story is going.

"But, as it turns out, she didn't need saving nearly half as much as I did. And she actually rescued me."

He cups my face in his large hand and lowers his mouth until it's only a breath from mine. My heart hammers against my chest in response.

"Would you still love me if I wasn't...what I am? If I couldn't fight?"

"You have the heart of a warrior. It doesn't matter to me what weapon you choose to wield. I love who you are, not the sword in your hand."

He kisses me long and slow as if we have all the time in the world.

But we don't.

A scream rends the night and sends a bone-deep chill through me. Felix is on his feet before I can even make my body react, but when I do, I see what has caused his face to go as pale as the moon.

Running toward us as fast as her little legs will carry her is Selah. And she's screaming Felix's name.

29

Felix sprints toward his sister with terrifying speed. He reaches her in seconds and scoops her up in his arms. By the time I reach them, I only catch part of what she's trying to tell him through her tears.

"Bad men," she pants, clearly out of breath from the running and screaming. "Bad men with fire."

The blood in my veins turns to ice. Cyrus. It has to be. But I have no time to react before Felix shoves Selah in my arms and whistles for Area. The white stallion lopes over, and Felix mounts him before he even comes to a stop. When he hesitates for just a moment to look at me, my heart breaks at the anguish in his eyes.

"Bring her with you and keep her safe." That's the only instruction I get before he charges up the beach the way we came, Ares kicking up clouds of sand in his wake.

Selah shudders in my arms as tears continue to pour from those dark eyes. I cradle her close to me as I approach Athena, who gives the girl a curious sniff.

"Shhh." I try to soothe Selah by stroking my hand over her mass of curls, and after a moment, she sniffles and looks up at me.

"I ran as fast as I could."

"You did well. You found Felix just like he told you to."

"What if I wasn't fast enough?"

I understand that fear more than she realizes, and I have no answer for her. No consolation at all because I've never found any for myself.

Athena remains perfectly still as I left Selah onto her back and tell her to scoot as far forward as she can. Once she's in position, I mount and then help her turn to face me. I'm going to ride fast and hard, and I can't risk her falling off since she doesn't know how to ride.

"Hug me tight," I tell her. "And keep your eyes closed." I don't want her to see what might be utter devastation by the time we get there. Another chilling thought occurs to me. Antony and his men aren't inside the city. Has anyone alerted their camp? It's entirely possible the entire city could be set alight before they even saw the smoke.

"When I tell you to, I want you to jump down and run to the soldiers' camp, okay? You find Antony and tell him just what you told Felix."

She nods, and I dig my heels into Athena. The horse leaps forward and we're off.

The ride from the city with Felix felt too short, but reversing direction seems to take ages. For a heart-stopping moment, I think I've gotten lost, but then I hear the faint echo of screams. Selah looks up at the sound, but I wrap an arm tighter around her. "Not yet."

We're within sight of the city when I slow Athena and help Selah slide to the ground. "Go directly to Antony and tell him everything. Do not come back to the city until someone comes to get you. Stay at the camp and hide. Do you understand?"

With tears in her eyes, she salutes me and runs off in the direction of the camp. I take a breath to watch her go then dig my heels in again. Athena responds immediately, and we're flying through the mercifully empty city streets. No sign of flames, no sign of chaos, but I can still hear the screams.

When we reach the plaza, I see why. Market stalls blaze, casting the whole scene in a flickering light. But everyone is eerily still. People line the square, eyes focused on something in the center as if they can't look away from the macabre tableau. Where is Felix? Why is no one fighting?

I dismount and push my way through the shocked onlookers. As I get closer to the center, the screams grow louder. Wailing pleas of mercy and sorrow greet me as I stumble forward into empty space and freeze.

Devastation litters the ground in the form of bodies. Probably only a dozen, but all lives snuffed out too soon. With a stab of relief, I find Felix standing over the body of a man dressed in the uniform of Cyrus's Imperial Guard. He looks unharmed, but blood drips from the blade in his hand. His gaze locks with mine for the briefest of moments, then flashes back to the site that has everyone paralyzed.

The blade against Antioch's throat glints in the flickering flames. It's a beautiful silver, and for some reason, that's all I can focus on at the moment. Probably my brain is just trying to protect me from the reality of the situation. But regardless, I admire the detail of the blade, of the hilt, and then my eyes reach the hand that holds it. They trail up the arm to Cyrus's sneering face.

I had forgotten just how much Ronan looks like him, had forgotten the dark hair, the eyes, in the magnitude of his crimes. But it all comes rushing back now. A confusing conflict of emotions that leaves me more bereft than I was mere moments ago. And that's saying something, considering the Emperor is holding a blade to Antioch's throat, and I have no doubt he will not hesitate to kill him.

"Welcome, Princess," Cyrus sneers at me. "How did you like my wedding gift? Where is my coward of a son anyway?"

A hot rage surges through me, tunneling my vision and forcing me closer.

"Emilia," Felix warns, but he doesn't move to stop me.

"Any closer and I'll end him." The Emperor's words are a promise. My focus is entirely on him as I frantically search for any weakness. I'm so distracted from my surroundings that I don't have time to brace myself before someone grabs me in a chokehold, pulling with such strength that my feet lift off the ground.

"Brutus," Felix growls. It takes me a moment to realize he's addressing my captor. Of course, he knows him. He used to be his commander. "Hands off her or you'll pay the price." He wipes blood from his sword on this tunic and twists the blade in his hand. I hope I am never, ever the recipient of the look he's giving Brutus.

"I only came for this." Cyrus gestures over his shoulder to the basilica's portico. There sits the Palanquin with four dead Imperial Guards lying around it. They tried to move it, I realize, and they died for it.

"It's not mine to give." I lift my chin in defiance. "And even if you could possess it, you could not hope to access the power within."

"Bring them!" the Emperor's voice booms over the pounding in my ears as he gestures around the gathered crowd. Four of his guards step forward, each dragging a man with him. Three I don't recognize, but one is Gideon—the Synod judge who was supportive of the army Felix had summoned. The guards drag them up the few steps to the portico and throw them on the ground in front of the Palanquin.

"Pick it up," Cyrus instructs cooly. He doesn't even look to see if his orders are being followed. He just scans the crowd. Looking for a challenger perhaps? Or is he looking for his son?

With some harsh prodding, the four men shoulder the poles of the Palanquin and lift. It seems the whole crowd holds its breath, waiting to see if their fates will be the same as the Imperial guards who tried to lift it first.

Where is Antony? Did Selah make it to him? No one here seems capable of fighting except Felix, and me. I don't even know where Ronan is. And we can hardly take on this many and hope to live. Instead, we're helpless to watch it happen.

"You know nothing of power, but I know you have a weakness for mercy. I know you value these people," he practically spits the last word. "Give the word and no more blood will be on your hands."

The treacherous hope of that promise breaks something loose inside me.

With a quickness I wasn't sure I still possessed, I act in one fluid motion. Fingers curl around the dagger sheathed at my thigh, and I pull it only to stab it into the leg of my captor. Brutus roars in pain and releases me. As soon as my feet hit the ground, I yank my blade from his leg, whirl, and shove my other palm into his face, feeling his nose crunch under the force. Without thinking, I toss the dagger to my other hand and continue spinning until I'm facing Cyrus again. I flip the dagger so I'm pinching it by the blade, and let it fly as soon as my shoulders are square with him again.

Everything up to this point has happened in less than ten seconds, but time slows to a crawl as the dagger flies through the air. Shock and fear register in those icy blue eyes as he ducks to his left, yanking Antioch up with his right arm. He has only just vacated the space when my dagger pierces Antioch's chest.

Then everything explodes. At least it feels like it does in my head.

I'm not aware of telling my body to move as chaos unleashes around me, but I find myself kneeling in the square by Antioch, cradling his head as blood seeps from his wound, and he gasps and sputters his last breaths.

But maybe they don't have to be his last. A thought suddenly occurs to me. If God can heal Felix, if he can rain down fire and destroy a temple, then surely, surely He can save this man who knows so much, who will help the cause so much. And so, as I cradle the old priest, I pray.

"Child." Antioch's voice is so weak I'm not even sure it could be called a whisper. I lean closer just as someone slides to their knees beside us. It's Alara, and she presses her hands to his side then looks up at me with wide, desperate eyes.

"Draconis," Antioch tries again, this time coughing until blood splatters his face. He's not going to make it. "West. Call the bones to life. Breath of fire."

"Shh," I insisted, holding a finger to his cracked lips. I can't pray and listen to him at the same time.

"Alexandra." He calls me by my mother's name as he tries to strain up to reach my ear. Alara is frantically tearing off strips of her clothes to press to the wound where the dagger still protrudes. But it's useless, and I know it. "Felix is the Prince That Was Promised."

The world shifts again, and Alara meets my eyes over Antioch's body. But I can't think about it. Not now. Not when my prayers have to be focused on saving him.

I pray as I have never prayed before for Antioch's healing. I pray God will hear me, that God will heal, but I feel none of the power, none of the emotion that has come with the previous miraculous answers to my prayers.

Instead, there is nothing. There is silence and I hate it. The only sound I hate more is the rattling last breath of the man who dies in my arms.

Alara wrenches the dagger from his chest with a snarl and disappears into the night.

"Alara! Ronan!" Distantly, I hear Felix calling after them, but I can't bring myself to care.

A few moments later, or maybe no time at all—time means little to me at the moment—Felix's arms wrap around me and squeeze me tight to him, pulling me away from Antioch's body. But I fight him as I become aware of a keening sound coming from my throat. It comes from somewhere deep inside me because I'm mourning not only Antioch, but Levi, and my mother, and my father—though that is much more complicated than I care to admit at the moment. But I am mourning all those I have lost before. Those that God has taken from me.

My prayers have done no good after all. I don't know what else I could have prayed. I don't know what else I could have done. Cyrus was always going to kill whoever stood in his way, and it seems he's saving me for last. Perhaps to have me watch the deaths of those I care for—of those who have guided me along the way—before he actually puts me out of my misery. And it is a certain misery, because I feel as if I had not brought Antioch along then he would still be alive. He would be in a cell at the top of the tower, but he would be alive.

Felix holds me so tight that it's almost painful. He yells to Antony—who must have just arrived—to pursue Cyrus. Good.

That means Selah succeeded in her mission. I hope she's hiding somewhere safe and not witnessing any of this.

Felix must be at absolute war with himself, wanting to go after Cyrus but sending Antony instead. But he won't go because I need him. I'm crushed against his chest, and his arms refuse to move from around me no matter how much I press back against him. He is a solid rock that I keep banging my head into, and it makes about as much sense to fight him as it does to bang my head on that rock.

"Emilia. Emilia," he repeats my name over and over, but I don't respond. I have no response other than the raw animalistic sounds coming from me. It's rage and grief in equal measure. Stronger than almost anything I've ever felt. Almost.

And then the rain begins to fall. The soft patter of a few drops breaks through my haze, and then it erupts into a downpour. I cry harder. I don't care that anyone else is around. I don't care that anyone else witnesses this. All I care about is that God has not heard me. He is perhaps the *only* one who has not heard me.

"Let me go," I snarl at him as I resume my shoving. The muscles in his arms tighten around me, and it's no longer an embrace but a submission hold.

"Not a chance," he grunts as I struggle against him. "I may not be able to stop anyone else, but I will not let you run after him. Not like this."

"Stop protecting me!" I yell as I try in vain to make contact with any vulnerable spot on his body. But he knows all my moves and shifts his weight around to avoid all of my escape attempts.

"Not a chance," he repeats with a growl. "Stand down, Emilia."

"Or what?" That's the rage speaking.

"Or I'll make you."

He could, too. Felix knows more ways to render me unconscious than I could begin to fathom. I know he'd never hurt me, but it would kill him to have to use one of those tactics on me. I can't stand the thought of his pain being my fault as well.

With that realization, the fight leaves me. I go limp in Felix's arms, sagging against him as I soak his shirt with my tears. Somewhere in the far reaches of my mind, I'm aware that this looks like weakness. But I can't stop the tears, and I don't want to. Because with the tears comes the emptying of myself. I can feel the heaviness leaking from me, and it leaves me feeling…lighter? Yes, but also numb. And that is a welcome feeling.

"Come with me," Felix whispers against my hair. "I can carry you, but it would really be better if you can walk."

He's right. I need to stand on my own feet and feel the blood-stained earth beneath me. I have to ground myself in something, and prayer and God are apparently a useless option. So, I choose the next best thing.

"I can walk," I mutter against his chest, "if you walk with me."

"Always."

And that is a promise I can rely on.

30

I sit on the edge of the bed in a daze while Felix kneels before me, unlacing my boots. I don't move to help or comment. I just stare down at his bowed head and watch him pull the shoes gently from my feet. I don't feel anything.

"Can you stand?" His tone isn't overly gentle, but rather the one he uses when assessing a situation with his soldiers. The same one he used as he checked me for injuries after I'd been attacked in Zephyros.

I nod and do just that. He reaches for the large blanket that covers the bed Alara and I had shared and holds it up between us. "Undress down to your underclothes. You need to dry off. I won't look."

In this state, it wouldn't matter to me if he did. I seem incapable of feeling anything.

I follow his instructions like a good soldier and strip down until I'm covered in the bare minimum of fabric. Then I tug on the blanket, and he wraps it around me like a cocoon. He holds it closed in front of me but doesn't make any move to close the space between us.

He's still soaking wet from the rain, and his shirt is stained from the blood of the soldier he killed. One he probably trained himself, I realize. Cyrus's Imperial Guard is made of men Felix has trained with and fought beside for years. The chances that he knew the man whose life he took aren't as remote as I would have guessed. After all, he knew the man who grabbed me.

"Are you all right?" I stretch a hand from underneath the blanket and brush my thumb over his lips. A bit of warmth seeps into me as the numbness begins to ebb.

"If you are." He catches my wrist and presses each of my fingers to his mouth in a kiss. The numbness fades a little more as feeling seeps back into me. "Tell me now if there's anything I need to apologize for."

"No," I whisper as I look away. "I'm sorry I—"

"You have nothing to apologize for either." He ghosts his lips along my skin from temple to my jaw, and for a brief moment, I'm reminded of the blissfully happy state we'd been in just before all this happened.

"Selah!" I gasp, suddenly remembering the little girl. "I told her to hide until someone came to get her. She must be terrified."

At the mention of his sister, his expression softens. How selfish am I that I'm just now realizing that he has a family he's probably dying to check on.

"And your mother? Was she in the basilica when they came to take the Palanquin? And Alara and Ronan! Felix, they ran after

Cyrus. They're not thinking straight. He'll kill them both. You need to go, you need to—"

"Slow down." He cups my face in his calloused hands and holds my wild gaze with a steady one of his own. "I am not leaving you alone right now. And before you say something about me protecting you, just know that this time it's for selfish reasons. I need you."

His hands are trembling as he releases my face. "I know there are bigger things than the two of us going on, but you are what matters to me. When I tell you I love you, I mean with every part of me. My heart, my soul. There is no world for me without you. So, when I'm protecting you, I'm really protecting myself. So can you please give me just a minute to assure myself that you're all right?"

"I'm all right," I whisper as awe fills all the places the numbness recently vacated. I knew he loved me, but the depth of his confession swallows me whole.

He walks me backward until my knees hit the bed, and I sink back into it. For a heart-pounding moment, I think he's going to join me, but he kneels in front of me instead. And it's in that posture of deference. My heart stutters as I recall Antioch's last words.

"Felix is the Prince That Was Promised."

⁂

Time passes in a hazy cycle of drifting off to sleep only to be awoken by a fresh set of nightmares. My mother, my father, Levi, and now Antioch parade through my subconscious along with nameless others who died at Cyrus's hands. The grief that poured out of me as I knelt over Antioch's body is but a trickle now. I wait for the guilt to hit me over his death because it was my dagger that killed him, but it doesn't come. Maybe that's because I'm blaming God instead.

Why didn't You answer me?

It's the only prayer I can muster as I try to make sense of everything.

Felix brings me word that Selah is safe at home and sleeping with their mother. He also places an armful of documents and books on the small dresser next to the bed. Antioch's things. I can't bring myself to look at them right now. He checks on me brushes the hair from my face and places a comforting hand on my back, but he doesn't try to make me talk.

When he does finally leave, I can still hear his voice outside the bedroom door. Usually, he's telling people to go away. He and Alara have a particularly loud shouting match where she insists on seeing me and he refuses. There's a whole lot of insults slung between them, and that pulls a smile from me despite everything.

The debriefing with Antony is more telling. He and his men pursued Cyrus across the island but were unable to catch them before they reached the longboats they had brought ashore. They had anchored their navy vessel far out to sea in order to avoid being spotted. They also navigated to the portion of the island where no ships normally approach because of the currents and rocky shores. Everything was meticulously planned while I pranced around like a lovesick princess and allowed my soldiers to be kept from the very place they should have been guarding.

I'm not even worthy to be Your sacrifice. You made a mistake with me.

"I do not make mistakes."

I sit straight up in bed. The words echo so loud that I'm not sure if they are inside my head or not. Hands trembling, I pull the blanket tighter around me.

"But the Palanquin…" I whisper, unsure how to finish that sentence.

"I am not confined to an object. My glory is too great to be contained."

The door flies open without warning, and I look up, expecting to see Felix but finding Alara instead.

"Get up, you useless thing," she snarls at me as she storms across the room. I glance over her shoulder, but no Felix stands outside my door. Hopefully he's resting. That's the only way Alara could have gotten in here.

Hands on her hips, she glares down at me. "You've sulked long enough. There's no time for this now. You can have your little pity party later, but we need to act. We need to be on the move because you can be certain that Cyrus is."

There's that name again. I'm so sick of hearing it. I'm so sick of all of this. I just want to stay in my little cocoon and sleep away any pain that comes.

"What do you expect me to do?" I ask. "What can I possibly do?"

"Tell him." I don't have to ask which "him" she means. Alara has accusation in every syllable she spits at me as if I have purposely kept something from her that she could have used to further the cause. Or to further *her* cause.

"I can't do that to him." In my disjointed moments of wakefulness, Antioch's words have haunted me as surely as my nightmares. I try to recall everything he said to me in our last meeting where I told him of my dream of Felix dying. Something to the effect of our stories were more intertwined than he'd anticipated. But he'd said nothing about Felix being the chosen ruler.

"He deserves to know," Alara insists. "He deserves to know that all this time, he's been the special one, not you."

The words feel like a slap across my cheek. "It's not that simple. I have—"

"You have everything!" Alara snaps. "You always have."

I stare at her in disbelief because I can't believe she truly believes that. Even if she doesn't know me well, she should know enough to know that "everything" has never been within my grasp.

"You don't mean that," I say softly, and somehow my tone seems to temper her anger. Just a touch. "You mean I have everything you've ever wanted."

And it's probably true.

"I lost my sister." Her voice is surprisingly hoarse when she speaks again. "When we were younger. She was taken and I... I lost her. I couldn't let that happen to anyone else. So, I went to Borealis and heard about you and the prophecy. I fought for you before I even knew you because I wanted to be worthy of the Princess Who Was Promised. But then you showed up and you had *both* of them and your ladies...well, I knew I was never going to measure up."

My eyes widen at her confession. She seems like the last person who would struggle with the idea of being good enough for someone.

"You can't be serious. You led a revolution. If it weren't for you, I would be sitting on a throne in Borealis and would have never ventured this far. You pushed me to do more, to be more."

Her laugh is bitter. "All I wanted was a family. I hoped there was a place for me in yours. But you just collect people that adore you and I... well, I don't."

It doesn't come as a surprise, but her words still cut. Before I can protest though, she holds up a hand to stop me.

"I may not adore you, but I do love you. And I would fight for you. What I need, what we all need, is for someone to fight for us. Felix will."

Words fail me, but I would hardly have time to speak them anyway. She's said her peace, and she spins on her heels and exits.

With the blanket still wrapped around me, I stand and shut the door to the bedroom. Then I pull clothes from my pack and dress quickly. It's one of those one-piece outfits like I wore in Zephyros, and I choose it simply because it's most accessible and doesn't require anyone to lace me into anything.

I can't go upending Felix's world on something so insubstantial as a dying man's words. I stare at the pile of documents on the dresser, and anticipation swirls in my stomach. Is this only going to end in more frustration? If my conversations with Antioch left me confused, how much more will his writings?

I carry the books and papers to the bed and spread them out before me. There is so much here, so much that I can't even begin to comprehend. Antioch clearly knew much more than he was able to tell me. I'm not sure if that was on purpose or not. Maybe if we had more time… But it doesn't matter because we didn't. All I have now are what's left of his writings, and what can I possibly do with those? With my knowledge so limited, I'm not even sure I'll be able to understand most of this.

I flip through page after page. There is a rough sketch, a rough copy, of the map Felix retrieved. On this version, Antioch has added notes in his tiny writing. I notice he has written the words "cave" and "army" and "bones" with a question mark. I don't want to think about bones, though he mentioned them as well in his final words. I don't want to think about death. Not mine or anyone else's.

I scan the text of what Antioch has written. Some of it is familiar based on things he has told me since the time I met him in the tower until his death. Things about the prophecy, about the Ruler, and how they would have to make the ultimate sacrifice.

"You cannot have the fire without fuel. The fire of God requires a sacrifice. The ultimate sacrifice."

Below Antioch's summary of the prophecy is a roughly sketched family tree. At least that's what I think it is. There are lines connecting names, some scribbled out, some leading to absolutely nowhere but most connecting in a hierarchy of unfamiliar people.

My eyes drift to the very top where he has written the name Caspian. The one who supposedly never died but flew away on the back of a dragon. The one from whom the Ruler is supposed to rise up.

So, I follow the tree down expecting to see my mother's name show up at some point, maybe even hoping to learn the names of my grandparents, but I don't. I look again and again and again.

But then my eyes fixate on five letters, and my heart stops for a moment because I don't want it to be true.

There it is written right there for me to see in the midst of all those descendants is the name.

Felix.

Felix is the Prince That Was Promised. I let those words sink in, except they don't. Just like when Antioch uttered them, my mind refuses to accept them because I don't want to think about him making the ultimate sacrifice.

Oh, God. My dream? Is this what it means? Felix was always supposed to be the one to die?

I realize with stunning clarity that even if I am somehow still the one chosen to fulfill this prophecy, the ultimate sacrifice for me would not be my life, but the lives of those I love. Of Felix. And I refuse to believe God might require that of either of us.

And I don't want to think that my role in all this has been for naught. As much as I hated the prophecy, at least when I thought it pertained to me, I had purpose. I had something to push for, and I had a sort of rough guideline for how I should be acting. But if it's not me, then what? What was all this for? What am I doing? And more importantly, what is Felix doing?

I know exactly what it means. Felix will have to make the ultimate sacrifice. And he won't bat an eye.

31

I finally emerge from the sanctity of my bedroom with a heavy weight of resignation on my shoulders. Hannah and Ronan turn to look at me from their position at the window with frowns on their faces.

"Where is Alara going?" Ronan asks.

"Is she just now leaving?" I lift a brow as I join them at the window. I would have thought she would have left as soon as she stormed out of my room. Perhaps something held her up.

"Yes," he informs me. "She's angry."

"What else is new?" I mutter as I back away from the window and retreat to the table where Hannah joins me.

"Emilia." There's a warning in his voice that surprises me. I haven't seen him since the attack, but he looks exhausted with deep shadows under his eyes. I don't have the energy to begin to unravel all that he must be thinking or feeling because I think his baggage must be as heavy as mine. "Where is she going?"

"To Felix, I imagine." I sigh in resignation. She's not going to wait on me to tell him. Maybe it's just as well. I'm used to people telling me I'm the chosen one. I have no idea how to deliver the news myself.

"Why?" Ronan sits on my other side. "Is something wrong?"

"What *isn't* wrong?"

Hannah gets up to retrieve a small bowl of pineapple and a cup of water for me. Nausea threatens, so I refuse the food but accept the water. "What's the damage to the city?" I'm eager to change the subject.

"Nothing major as far as loss of property." His answer is succinct as if he almost expected my deflection of his question. "There are a few market stalls that were destroyed, but all the surrounding buildings were fine. The rain extinguished the fire before it could spread."

"Good." I take a sip of water before continuing. "And the casualties?"

Ronan swallows before answering. "The four guards who tried to remove the Palanquin. A couple priests who tried to block their entry into the basilica were killed as well. Then there were a few men who tried to stop the guards from burning the stalls, but they were unarmed and never stood a chance. There would have been a greater loss of life if Felix hadn't arrived when he did."

I wonder how many men he had to kill to subdue the situation. He's a soldier, sure, but I know from experience that you never get used to killing, especially not if they were men he knew.

"And where were you?" I try and fail to keep the accusation out of my tone. He recoils as if I've stabbed him.

"Emilia, I..." His blue eyes flash—Cyrus's eyes. "I was following orders from *your* Lord Commander." He somehow flips the accusation back around on me. "I wanted to be there. I wanted to run my father through with a sword before he could hurt anyone else. But Felix insisted..."

It makes sense to me now. Felix would need to triage the situation immediately when he arrived, and having an emotional and unpredictable Ronan in the midst of things would have only complicated his job. And I don't want to think about what would have happened if Cyrus had laid hands on his son.

"I'm sorry. I'm sorry you had to see any of that."

"I'm not. I know now why it matters so much."

Better late than never, I suppose. But I shouldn't be angry at Ronan. He did not grow up hearing the truth from any source in his life. For all his years, he's been fed the propaganda of the Empire and the justification for every heinous act of those who dared to believe differently than their polytheistic conquerors. He's been privy to more of the secrets of...Wait a minute.

"Ronan, have you heard of Draconis?" It was never mentioned in my geography lessons as a child, but I was also told that Solitarius was an uninhabited island. Ronan knew differently as he visited the island with his father on occasion. What else does he know that I don't?

"You mean that sunken island?" His dark brows knit together in confusion. My heart leaps. "My mother used to tell me stories of what happened there. Not real, of course, but I always wanted to know why it sank."

"Have you ever seen it on any maps?"

"It was there on some of the oldest maps in the library. I always liked the shape of it. It looked like—"

"A dragon," I finish. "And it disappeared under the Great Wave hundreds of years ago, around the time of—"

"Caspian." Hannah, who I had forgotten was even in the room, finishes my thought with a gasp.

Wide eyed, the three of us look at one another.

"Caspian never died. He flew away on the back of a dragon." Hannah's voice is barely a whisper as she recites what she learned from the children's stories.

"Caspian was last seen when he tried to find the Promised Land. The book Felix's father had with the map shaped like a dragon..."

"Draconis," Ronan breathes. "The Gate is on Draconis."

Antioch was right. He wasn't crazy, and he wasn't lying to me. Piece after piece falls into place. Felix is descended from Caspian, so the copy of the Aletheia with the map must have been passed down by his father's family. That's why all the secrecy surrounding it. To protect it from falling into the wrong hands.

"But the island is underwater," Ronan objects. "There's nothing there." I shake my head.

"There were maps in the papers Verity gave us that showed a small chain of islands. Probably only the highest points of the original island remained above water. The entrance to the Gate is there." Certainty grows with each word. Why did I doubt? The answer was right in front of us if we'd only bothered to put all our knowledge together. Hopefully it's not too late to do something about it.

"How are we going to get there?"

Ronan's question is the same one I've been pondering since Antioch mentioned the island to me. "We have to convince the Synod to lend us a ship."

"I don't think it's going to be that easy."

"When has it ever been? But I don't see what choice we have."

"There's been some unrest among the citizens. Some don't feel we did enough to protect them."

Is he serious? "Whose fault is that? They're the ones who made the rules about no patrols in the city. We warned them Cyrus was coming."

"They're just scared." Hannah places a hand on my arm to calm me. "Most of them have never experienced anything like this. And now the Palanquin is gone, they think God has abandoned them."

"That is the one thing they all seem to have in common. They're terrified. Some have decided it's our fault because we brought my father's wrath upon them. Others are desperate for us to act on their behalf. But we must act. We'll lose the little support we have if we don't do something."

"Wait."

The single-word instruction is at odds with everything they're telling me, and yet it resonates with something within me.

We can't. I answer back as though the owner of that single word stands in front of me as sure as Ronan or Hannah does. *If we wait, we lose everything.*

"Where is Felix?" That probably should have been my first question. But I don't want to see him for the first time, armed with this new knowledge, with an audience. There's no predicting how he'll react to the news that Alara is no doubt delivering to him right now. Will he even believe her? Will it change the way he sees me?

"I believe he's meeting with his mother and what remains of the Synod."

"What remains?"

"One of the men died defending the Palanquin and the older man, Gideon, was one of the ones my father took to carry it back to his ship." Ronan hangs his head. "There are five left. Enough for a quorum vote after we present our case this evening."

What case? I'm still processing all the new revelations, including the one that may just shatter the bond I hold most dear. I can't have a plan together in a matter of hours.

"Antony has been working with the Lord Commander to set up perimeter patrols, which will least disturb the citizens," Hannah explains. "They hope to get them approved by the Synod."

Forget patrols. Yes, I wish I argued harder for them in the beginning, but they're no use now. We finally have a heading—sort of—and we need to act on it before Cyrus can.

I consider all that's happened in the last several hours. Our entire world has shifted, and it's not over yet. But my earth-shattering need at the moment is to see Felix and explain to him what I've discovered. More importantly, I need to convince him not to become the sacrificial lamb because I don't think this cause could survive losing us both. That seems the only thing I'm sure of. I will not survive without him.

I find him hours later in the same place we were so blissfully happy before the whole world broke apart. Unlike our passion-filled evening the night before, this stretch of beach is charged with entirely different emotions in the light of day. Ares stands further up the bank, munching on some sort of vegetation there, so I dismount Athena and lead her to him.

Felix doesn't look up as I approach but does lift his arm in invitation for me to press up against him. The protective strength of his arm around me as I lean into his side is a comforting weight.

"I killed a man." I've been thinking and thinking how to approach this conversation, and I keep coming back to the truth. All of it. We're going to emerge from the other side of this as two different people, and I want to make sure he knows everything there is to know about me and my past. Even the parts I'm ashamed of.

"Today?" His head swivels toward me and every muscle in him tenses.

"No." I rest my head on his shoulder and feel him relax. "Months ago. Just before I met you."

"Levi." The name is such a simple response, but it makes my world spin. It's my turn to stare at him.

"You know?"

"Emilia, your name is on everyone's lips these days. It's hardly the secret you think it is."

Should I be relieved he knows? Angry? "Yet you've never said anything."

"You made it quite clear it wasn't something you wanted to discuss. When Alara tried to bate you with it, I saw the pain in your eyes. When we were in Zephyros, Verity told me of her connection with Levi and, by extension, you. I knew not to push it. I wanted you to trust me with it when you were ready."

"And you still..." How do I finish that question?

"Love you? Trust you? Believe in you? Absolutely." He tucks the strands of my hair blowing in the wind behind my ear. "I killed three men last night. Three men that I trained. I ate with them, laughed with them, bled with them. And I killed them. I know what it is to take a life for a greater cause. The righteousness of the act doesn't lessen the guilt."

It's true. "How do you live with it? I've killed men in battle, killed those who attacked us on our way to Aurora even. But when it's someone you know..."

"Either God's forgiveness is enough, or it isn't." He clears his throat and swipes at his eyes. I don't think he's thinking of the three men he killed. He's thinking about his brother. "I spent years punishing myself for something God had already forgiven me for. I missed so much because of it. I never got to say goodbye to my father. I wasn't here when Selah was born. But despite my propensity for self-hatred, God gave me something greater. Something I didn't even know I needed."

My brows arch in question, and he smiles with a shake of his head as if he can't believe I even have to ask. "You. He gave me you."

"I'm not sure that's the prize you think it is." We're getting closer now. Closer to the inevitable truth.

"Can you tell me about him?" Felix removes his arm from my shoulders and leans forward, resting his elbows on his knees. "Levi, I mean."

"You already know," I say heavily. Because it does still feel like an enormous weight on my chest. "You know what I did."

"Yes, but that's not what I asked you. I want to know about him, about how you felt about him. I want to know all of it, to understand."

How can he possibly expect to understand when I still don't? Does he not think I have asked myself and God a million times why it happened? Why it had to happen? There is only so much comfort in knowing it was God's will. Because what does that say about my God? That He would sacrifice a man on the chance that I could fulfill some prophecy seems like a risky plan.

"He...he said I had to do it." The words choke me as I force them out. It's terrifying and comforting in equal measure to consider baring my worst moments to someone whose opinion I value so highly.

"He said I had to kill him. That it was the only way. I had to keep my allegiances secret because all of Atlas would come after us soon, and I couldn't be associated with him if I was to…was to…"

I can't finish the sentence. Because Levi had died because he delivered a message to me that I would be the one to save us all. And he had been wrong. For the first time, that really punches me in the gut. I killed him for a message that wasn't even true. And if Levi could get it wrong, what hope is there for me? I'm not the Princess that was Promised. I'm not even a princess anymore. I gave that up when I left Borealis behind. It all rests on Felix's shoulders now. At least according to Antioch's studies.

"He trusted you with his life," Felix says softly. "That says much about you."

"He trusted me for all the wrong reasons. He thought I was the one. But it's not me and we both know it."

To say it aloud makes it real. There's no going back now. Memories of conversations between us while we were in Aurora where he encouraged me to do more, to be more, flood back to me. Was it encouragement? Or was there something more there? Some disappointment that I wasn't more like Alara even if he couldn't have put those exact words to it at the time. Does that disappointment hold even now? Better to get it over with.

"She told you, didn't she?"

He doesn't have to answer because the shocked look on his face says it all. With his wide dark eyes and slightly opened mouth, he looks like someone just gut punched him and ran away. He'd probably like to run away, too. I know I would. We could board a ship and sail somewhere, anywhere but here.

"She did," he answers with his usual reticence. "I don't want to talk about that right now."

I look over to see that his shoulders are slumped, and he has his head in his hands as if there is a literal weight on his shoulders.

"No, but you want to talk about Levi, and we can't really discuss one without the other." I suppose that's not entirely true, but they're so inexorably linked in my mind that I've accepted it as fact.

"You did what you had to do, Emilia. We've all done things we regret, but Levi knew what he was asking of you. Certainly, it was a huge price to pay, and I'm sorry that you had to be the one to pay it. But that doesn't mean good didn't come from it. You have made his death mean something. You've changed an empire with your actions, and God isn't through with you yet."

"It certainly seems like He is. He has you now. Or I guess He's always had you, but now you know. And let's face it, you're a much better candidate than me."

Felix is exactly the type of person I would choose to ride in and save the day if I were writing the fairytale. He's the one to rescue the princess and slay the dragon. He's the prodigal prince come to reclaim his birthright.

"Stop. Just stop it." Anger tinges his voice as he pushes himself to his feet, leaving me in the sand. "Look, I don't understand any of this. I don't know what it means for the future. But I do know that none of us would be here right now if it wasn't for you. You saw me, Emilia. I was just a soldier hiding away as far as I could get from here, but… You. Saw. Me." He punctuates each of the last three words with a slap of his fist against his chest. "You opened my eyes to possibilities I had never considered. You brought me home. You *are* my home."

He reaches for me, and I let him pull me to my feet and into his arms. He's right. This is home.

"I don't know what happens next," he whispers into my hair as his hands rub circles on my back. "I don't know who is the fulfillment of the prophecy and who isn't. But I do know that my place is with you. Wherever we're going, we're going together."

"Felix." I wait for him to pull back just enough to meet my gaze. "I know where we're going."

32

Walking into the basilica that evening is about as far removed from the first time we entered as it's possible to be. Our party of five has been reduced to three. Antioch is dead, and Alara has avoided me since we learned Felix's identity. I have no doubt she'll be at this assembly meeting, but she doesn't appear to want to ally herself with me so publicly anymore. This time, rather than a single dockworker, Felix, Ronan, and I are now escorted by a squad of soldiers.

The tension is palpable as we stride through the city. Felix has managed to convince them to accept a few small, discreet patrols, but there are murmurs as we pass with our contingent of guards. Ronan was right. It's not going to be easy to convince them of what we need. Support for us is waning.

We are the last to arrive. It appears that every seat in the assembly hall is filled with the exception of two seats on the tribunal. They belong to the judges who were either killed or carried away by Cyrus. But Miriam and the remaining members of the Synod are in their places and waiting for us with unreadable expressions.

Felix and I haven't discussed how his mother feels about any of this. I'm not even sure if he knows. But if she's anything like her son, I have to hope she will hear us out and make the best decision. She stands and calls the meeting to order.

Surprisingly, we aren't invited to speak first. The Synod chooses to give the floor to the assembled citizens, letting them voice their concerns for all to hear. The divide among them becomes apparent quite quickly. People descend from the tiered seats to pace across the floor and make their point. Shouting matches ensue as those who blame us for everything are drowned out by those who still support us so long as we protect them from further harm.

I'm about to disappoint both groups. While they continue to argue amongst themselves, I make my way to the raised tribunal. It's probably a breach of etiquette to approach it without invitation, but I don't have time for protocols.

Silence descends as all eyes slowly turn to me. I breathe a quick prayer and begin.

"What happened here last night was a tragedy. This is what I came to warn you about. Without our help, you can expect more of the same. I have stood in the ashes of villages Cyrus has burned to the ground for nothing more than a hunch that proved false. But even he knows the power here. He's taken the Palanquin, and power like that in the hands of a man that ruthless is a death sentence."

Not exactly the most optimistic beginning of a speech, but I promised myself I would be honest with these people. "But there is a greater power. One we need access to if we're going to defeat his army. If we allow him to cut us off from that, no one and nowhere is safe from his wrath. He's sitting on his ship now with all the information he needs to figure out where this power is located."

Felix was able to sort of confirm this. The watch he set up on the beach where Cyrus and his men landed indicated that the large naval vessel was still anchored out at sea and had not moved since the Emperor returned to it. He's waiting for us to tip him off to the right direction, or biding his time to reconnoiter the island to see if the Gate is actually somewhere on Solitarius.

"What do you propose we do?" Miriam stands only a few feet away from me on the tribunal, but she raises her voice so everyone present can hear.

"We have to get there first." If only it were so simple. "I know where the Gate is. The notes Antioch left paint a clear picture of where we're headed." Clear-ish really. But I'm not arguing semantics.

The hall erupts into another round of shouting matches. Accusations of blasphemy are hurled at me, and my supporters shout insults at my detractors. I step down from the tribunal to meet the loudest among them at their level on the floor.

"This is your best chance," I insist. "We sail to Draconis and find the Gate before Cyrus can."

Pandemonium erupts. It seems everyone here is aware of the ill-fated island on some level. Most think it's a children's story, and those who do believe it's real argue that it's lost beneath the sea. It seems I've managed to unify them after all. They all think I'm crazy.

Over the din of several heated conversations, Alara's voice rings out strong and true. "Felix is the Prince that was Promised!"

Silence falls like an iron gate and rings just as loud. No one even moves except Felix and only then to take my hand.

"It's true," Alara continues as she emerges from the crowd to stand in the empty space at the center of the crowd. She's directly opposite me and looking wretched as if this is tearing her apart. I know better. "The priest, Antioch, he knew it. It was his last words. I heard them. Felix is the direct descendant of Caspian, and he is the rightful leader."

"Alara, stop."

I have to do a double take to realize it's Ronan who's stepped between Alara and me. Of all the people to speak up, he is the last I expected.

"I won't," she insists. "People should know. They should know they have a choice."

"There is no choice." Felix takes a step forward and pulls me with him. We stand shoulder to shoulder, surrounded on all sides by the crowd that's gathered. "There is no taking sides. We all have one goal, one mission. Emilia and I are a team, and I won't let you pit us against one another."

"Felix can make his own choices," I say. "And he's chosen to stand with me. I don't pretend to have all the answers, but I also don't pretend I want to rule you. I just want to find a resolution that keeps us all safe and allows us to worship the one, true God."

"She's right. Forget the prophecy. It doesn't matter."

A low murmur rises up from the crowd, and I can feel their unease. What Felix has just said borders on blasphemy, but I realize I don't disagree with him. Of course, it matters to the two of us, but that's our own private battle. But I can almost guarantee that no one here is thinking about the prophesied leader having to make the ultimate sacrifice.

Except, perhaps, Miriam.

She steps from the onlookers into the center of the room, and everyone falls silent again. With her quiet elegance, she looks much more like a queen than I've ever felt. Miriam looks from me to Felix. She must have thought about the prophecy and what it would mean for Felix. To have just been reunited with her son only to have this looming cloud of sacrifice hanging over him must be a great weight to carry. It's a good thing she doesn't know my dreams or that my greatest sacrifice—if I am the prophesied one—would not be my own life but Felix's. And I can't change that. To do so would be to diminish my love for him, and even if I was capable of that, I wouldn't do it. He deserves all the love I can give him for as long as I can give it.

"That's enough for tonight." Her words ring out with authority and leave no room for argument. But I want to call out in protest. We can't just table this discussion. There's no time. We need to act.

The crowd around us begins to jostle forward, but Antony and the other guards step between us and the rest. Felix presses me forward with a hand on the side of my back as we follow Ronan and Alara from the basilica before things can get too out of hand. Angry shouts follow us as we stumble out into the still night of the plaza.

Felix barks an order at Antony and the patrol guards stationed outside then charges ahead. He seethes beside me as we follow Alara and Ronan at a distance in the direction of our house. I'm not so sure it's such a good idea to have Felix and Alara within the same four walls at the moment, but he's hyper-focused on her. I can only imagine what he means to say to her in private.

This new dynamic between us shakes me. Usually I'm the restless, hotheaded one, but now that Felix is on the prowl like a panther, I try hard to remain calm. Truthfully, I'd like to tear my claws into Alara for the drama she's just caused and the anxiety she's raised in Felix. All for her own selfish motives. But I don't think Felix needs my help defending himself. I've never seen him like this. Not even when he's been upset with me or Ronan for our recklessness.

Ronan and Alara enter the house ahead of us, and I try to grab Felix's arm to delay him, but he's set on his target. I'm relieved to see that Alara is nowhere in sight when we walk through the front door, but Felix doesn't seem deterred by this either.

"Where is she?" His voice is that rough, gravelly tone he reserves for barking orders or scolding a wayward soldier.

"Felix, calm down," Ronan says with raised palms. He's standing between Felix and the closed door to one of the bedrooms as if that will actually stop him. "Both of you just need a minute to breathe and then you can talk about it."

"She's already done plenty of talking." Felix takes a step forward, and I step between him and Ronan, putting my hands on his chest to stop him. He pauses and looks down as if he's just realized I'm here. His face softens a bit, and I know we've just avoided the volatile confrontation...at least for now.

"Come with me," I say softly. I reach for his hand, but he pulls it away before I can grab it and spins on his heels with a growl. Ronan and I watch as he disappears into the common room.

After a moment of heavy silence, Ronan sighs and takes a step toward the room. I stop him with a raised hand. "No, let me," I insist. "You deal with her." I nod toward the closed door behind which I'm sure Alara is seething. I can't imagine she took it well when Ronan sent her to her room. He frowns, and for a moment I think he might argue with me. But then he sets his shoulders and nods.

"Good luck."

"You too," I reply with a solemn nod. Then I watch him disappear behind the door. I wait for just a few seconds to make sure I don't hear screaming from the other side of the door then turn my attention to the common room.

There's no door on the room, so I hear the steady cadence of Felix's boots as he paces the floor before I even see him. He's wearing a path in the rug in front of the fireplace, hands locked behind his back and head bowed.

"Felix?"

He looks up and stops pacing, but the tension remains in his shoulders.

"I don't know what to do," he admits.

I want to walk toward him, to comfort him, but the energy radiating from him is like that of a caged animal. So, I wait warily just inside the room and let him talk.

"I wasn't planning on telling anyone. There's no point. What does it even matter what the prophecy says? The end goal is the same. And who would believe I'm sort of royalty anyway?"

"But you are," I remind him as I take a few steps closer until I'm only a couple arms' length away. "You are descended from Caspian. Your mother is chief judge of the Synod. And more importantly, you are a son of the Most High King."

He shakes his head as if he refuses to believe it. "This whole journey has been about serving you, protecting you. I never wanted a crown for myself. I only wanted to support you and your destiny. It was God's will."

Felix drags a hand through his hair and turns to face away from me. "But now she's opened this door that can't be closed. Everyone knows and they'll be expecting... something. Even I don't know what they want me to do. More importantly, they're going to take sides. Instead of uniting us, Alara has divided everyone."

"It doesn't have to be that way. As long as you and I are agreed, then they can't split us apart. No one needs to choose." At least not the people of Solitarius. I suspect there will be a point where a choice must be made, but I can't afford to think of that right now.

"I'm sorry," he says, his back still to me. "You've dealt with this sort of pressure for months now and handled it beautifully. I have no right to be upset when you're so calm."

"I like seeing you upset," I admit. "At least I know you're human. For a long time, I wasn't sure anything could penetrate that calm exterior you had."

When Felix turns to look at me his eyes catch the light of the fire and seem to burn. A heat licks up my spine as if I've been set alight as well.

With a few long strides, he pins me against the wall with a force that knocks the breath from me. Or maybe it's not the impact at all, but the ferocity of the kiss that siphons all the air from my lungs. It's a hard kiss tinged with passion and urgency that reminds me of the kiss that started all of this in the escape tunnel in Aurora. My lips part to breathe, but he's right there—finally taking and taking instead of giving.

"Felix," I gasp when he moves his mouth from my lips to my jaw. If he hears me, he ignores me. One of his hands is braced on the wall next to my head, and the other has a firm grasp on my hip. His fingers press into my skin as I reach to tangle my hands in his curls. I've waited forever to really touch them, and they're every bit as soft as I imagined. I tug gently until he groans, and a shiver dances through me.

I throw my head back and bang it against the wall. I see stars but I don't know if it's from that or the pleasure of his lips on the newly bared skin at my neck. But I need his mouth on mine more than I need my next breath. So, I pull on his hair again, guiding him back to my lips. Yes...yes...*yes.*

My hands find the bare skin beneath the open collar of his shirt. I can feel his heart pounding against my palm as I run my hands down his chest, tearing open his shirt and sending buttons clattering across the room.

"Hey, I liked that shirt," Felix mumbles as he continues to kiss every part of my face.

"I'll sew the buttons on later," I promise as I take the two tattered sides of his shirt and try to pull him even closer to me.

"Do you know how to sew?"

The question gives me pause. My reaction causes him to stop long enough to take a look at the frown on my face.

"I'll have your mother teach me."

"Do you really want to tell my mother why this shirt is now buttonless?"

"A problem for another time," I insist as I kiss him again, smiling against his lips.

I could live forever in this moment. A few minutes where nothing exists except the two of us and no space between us. Forget the epic quests and prophecies. This is what I was put on earth to do.

But of course, it can't last forever. I'm not conscious of who ends the kiss, but we both let out ragged gasps as our lungs swell, hungry for the air we've deprived them. With our chests heaving, Felix rests his forehead against mine and closes his eyes. His pants of hot breath accentuate the heat in my cheeks. I close my eyes, too, and try to slow my heartbeat. When he chuckles softly, I open my eyes to find him looking at me with undeniable adoration and desire.

"What's so funny?"

"I never knew it was possible to feel this way. It wasn't even a dream of mine. I couldn't even fathom what loving someone like this would feel like. But it's just...sometimes how much I love you just swells up in me like a wave, and I can't contain it. And I've never really had an emotion that I couldn't control, but for this I don't want to. I want to love you wildly, recklessly. And I want to do it for the rest of my life."

Oh.

The implication of his confession hits me like a tidal wave. My cheeks ache from the smile that stretches across my face. "Okay. I'll allow it."

The laugh that erupts from him is big and full and quite possibly the most beautiful sound I've ever heard. His body shakes against mine, and I know for certain I want this, too. As if it were ever really in doubt.

"I just told you that you make me reckless, and you gave me the most calm, controlled response that's probably ever come out of your beautiful mouth."

"Well, one of us has to be rational."

He opens his mouth to protest—because we both know I'm not the level-headed one of this duo—but I cut him off with a firm kiss. And soon we're both laughing uncontrollably, and gratitude swells up in me. How lucky am I that I get to listen to him laugh for as long as we both live?

But just as quickly, a dark thought sobers me. The prophecy. The sacrifice. No matter which way this goes, I'm not sure we both make it through this alive.

And so, I kiss him again, this time softly, tenderly, and try to put a whole lot of unsaid things into it. He kisses me back just as softly, and his hands gently cradle my face.

I'm not aware of crying until his thumbs wipe away the wetness on my cheeks. I open my eyes and look up to see his eyes glistening too. That's when I know we are on the same page. Felix is equally aware of how short this might be. And he loves me anyway. He's opening his heart to a pain I'm not sure either of us has ever known—to love someone so completely and then have it cut brutally short. And that can only mean one thing. He intends to be the one to make the sacrifice.

"I love you," I say in a voice that barely reaches a whisper.

"I love you," he repeats with such sincerity. "For right now and for always and come what may."

"Amen," I agree, and I kiss him again.

He is a strong, fierce, unstoppable force. All things that I am not. And yet…there's a vulnerability in the way his fingers brush across my spine, in the shaky expanding and contracting of his chest. A weakness that makes me feel strong. Is this what Ronan meant when he said I made him want to be a better man, a good king? Because I think I understand that now. Felix, though clearly the better choice of this promised ruler, makes me want to be better as well. As if it's really not out of the realm of possibility for me to become this person so many people think I am. That he thinks this of me is nothing new, but him making me believe it of myself is.

"Now is not the time to be brave… or stupid." He whispers the words between kisses and then buries his face in my hair as if he already knows I'm scheming to keep him out of harm's way.

But I know he's wrong. "It's precisely the time. It's the right thing to do."

Felix pulls back from me, holding me at arm's length. I don't have to say what "it" is. We've known this possibility existed since we learned of the prophecy. He searches my face as if he will find some sort of acquiescence there. But we both know he won't. I've made up my mind on this because there is no other way. He towers above me, his dark waves of hair framing a countenance that wavers between the stoicism of a soldier and the vulnerability of a man grappling with the unbearable.

"Mia." His voice is raw with the gravity of our situation. "We can't ignore this. It's going to happen, and we need to talk about it. Decisions will have to be made, maybe spur of the moment, and..."

I place my hand on his chest, and the gesture makes him pause. I know there is no universe where we will agree on this.

We will both do what's necessary, but if there is a choice, it's one we will literally fight to the death over.

“My fear isn't dying,” I say as I hold his gaze. My voice is steady though I feel anything but. “It's losing you.”

I see the subtle shift in his expression, the clench of his jaw that speaks of a silent vow he's made with someone. God perhaps? He has always been my shield, my unwavering guardian, and in the depths of his deep brown eyes, I read the unspoken truth: Felix would lay down his life for me without hesitation. And that is a reality I can't survive.

His hand reaches out and brushes a lock of my long dark hair behind my ear—an intimate gesture laden with a heartbreaking tenderness. “Mia,” Felix's voice is almost a confession, “I've always known the risks, and yes, I would sacrifice myself if it meant you could fulfill your destiny. Maybe that's my destiny, too.”

There it is. An admission that both shatters and fortifies my resolve. “But that's just it, Felix. Your life is not yours to give—not for me.” The words strain in my throat, heavy with the weight of a thousand unsaid thoughts.

“If that's what I'm called to do, I wouldn't be laying it down for you. You can protect me from a lot of things, but you can't protect me from God's plan.”

My words tossed back at me sting. I hate feeling so helpless. “Then I’ll think of something else,” I say with just a tinge of desperation. “I just need time.”

“We don’t have time. You know we don’t. If we have even the slightest hope of catching up to Cyrus, we have to go now.

We have to unite the people and go. We'll figure out the rest on the way."

Or we won't. Because I'm not sure it's possible to make any sort of plan when everything is so uncertain including our destination and what we might find there. I'm just going to have to trust God will lead me, and right now that feels like the most monumental task I've ever undertaken.

"Let me lead, Emilia." He strokes my hair. It's the conclusion I knew he would come to if given enough time. He doesn't resent the role, just the way Alara forced him into it. "I was born for this, and it's time I step into this role. I can't keep running from it."

I consider his words. It's true. He was quite literally born for a moment like this. The Prince that was Promised. And I don't want to take that away from him because it's necessary. Both of us are necessary.

"You *were* born for this," I say as I caress his bearded cheek. "And I would never dream of stopping you from leading your people—our people. But you have to know I would follow you anywhere."

He looks resigned. I know my words have hit home. Felix would give his life for me, and we both know it. But more than that, more than he loves me even, he believes in his God and the cause, and he won't do something to stand in the way of that. So, though I don't say the words, my eyes plead with him: if you love me, let me go. And I see something shining in those dark eyes that tells me he is now resigned to do exactly that.

"Whatever happens, we are a team. All I'll ask is that we don't try to hide things from each other. No secrets. If you have some crazy plan, then tell me about it first. I won't try to stop you, but I can help you. Trust me to help you."

A bit of shame warms my cheeks as he places rough hands on either side of my face. He's right. Thinking I had to do it all on my own has been my way of operating for too long. It's a lonely, bitter path, and I need look no further than Alara to see the evidence of that. What could be accomplished if I honestly believed that Felix supported me and my decisions? What could we do if we worked together? I think it's time we find out.

"Together," I say with a mix of determination and dread. We seal the promise with a slow kiss.

"Is everything ok in here?"

I reluctantly pull away from Felix to look over his shoulder and see Ronan in the doorway. Embarrassment heats my cheeks until I realize Ronan is a little disheveled himself. I raise an eyebrow in question, and he has the good graces to duck his head and rub the back of his neck. What exactly have he and Alara been up to?

"We're fine," I answer because Felix seems incapable. His hand that's braced against the wall next to my head clenches into a fist, causing the muscles in his forearm to go taut. He's still angry with Alara. "How are things in there?"

"It's taken care of."

I don't care how vague Ronan's trying to be, I see his swollen lips and the flush on his face. I've been the cause of that before, so I certainly recognize the signs. But with Alara? It just screams disaster.

Felix seems to agree. He looks his best friend over then shakes his head. "Really? That's not exactly the tongue-lashing I had in mind."

"I said, it's taken care of," Ronan insists as he crosses his arms over his chest.

What is happening? They stare each other down in a silent argument I can't begin to wrap my mind around. I expect Ronan to stand down any minute now, as he usually does in the rare times I've seen Felix challenge him. But he doesn't. He's as resolute, as steadfast as... As a man in love.

No way. I gave it a passing thought when Hannah mentioned it before but never any serious consideration. They can't possibly...

But the flush on Ronan's face, the challenge in those blue eyes, the mussed hair all suggest that they are. Or at least entangled in some way. Something snaps into place within me.

"You," I jab a finger at Ronan, "walk with me."

"Emilia—"

"And you," I whirl on Felix and pin him with a glare. "Go to bed."

His brows raise, and he tilts his head in question, but I leave no room for argument.

"You need to cool off, and you," I turn back to Ronan, "have some explaining to do."

Both of them look a little stunned, but neither dares to argue with me. Felix moves toward the front door, and I narrow my eyes at him.

"Where do you think you're going?"

He frowns in confusion. "To bed? Back to camp?"

"You're not sleeping at the camp tonight." I point toward my bedroom door. "You better be sound asleep in there when I get back."

Heat flares in his eyes and just reaffirms my assessment that we both need to cool off. But I can't possibly imagine sleeping apart from him now that we're both aware of just how little time we likely have together. We'll just have to exercise a little self-control, and with any hope, he'll already be asleep when I return.

Instead of heading to the bedroom, he comes back to stand in front of me. His hands tangle in my hair as he cups the back of my neck and presses his mouth to mine. I sigh into his mouth as my lips part for him.

Somewhere behind Felix, Ronan clears his throat. "I get the point, Felix. Hands off."

I laugh as we break off the kiss. As if Ronan would try anything with me after all we've been through the last several weeks. Still, I don't object to Felix claiming his territory.

"Don't be gone too long," he instructs in a low voice. Then he claps Ronan on the back and heads into the bedroom, already pulling his shirt over his head.

33

"You can tell Felix that display back there was entirely unnecessary. I think you know that, or we wouldn't be here."

I can feel Ronan's icy stare cut through the balmy wind as we walk along the beach. I've been indecisive on what exactly I want to say to him, but he seems to know my intentions anyway.

"I don't think it was for your benefit. But yes, he's been a little preoccupied to notice the clues. Honestly, until tonight, I didn't think much of it."

"Are you angry?"

My head snaps to him. "Angry? How could I possibly begrudge you any happiness when I put you through so much to find my own? I might not understand it…"

"That makes two of us." He rubs the back of his neck ruefully. "I didn't plan to fall for her. It just happened."

"You know what this means if we win?" Alara as Empress. I can't begin to wrap my mind around that thought. It's everything she's wanted. No wonder she was so eager to dismiss me when she thought Felix gave us the better shot at winning. She wants the crown. I just hope she wants Ronan, too.

"I'm not thinking that far ahead," he admits. "There are...complications."

I don't ask. I can only imagine that Alara is a whole ball of complications.

"How are you coping with everything else?"

"What? Like my father calling me a coward while he steals the most powerful weapon we have against him, kills the man who might have actually understood any of this, and then having to run after Alara who thought she could single-handedly end this?" He laughs. "I'm still upright, so I'd say I'm faring very well."

"It's not fair you got dragged into this."

"No one drags me anywhere. I may have been shocked, devastated even, at what I saw in Borealis, but I chose to come along. I spent years sticking my head in the sand where my father and his ambitions were concerned, and it's time to get some answers of my own."

"And have you?" I know he spoke a great deal with Antioch, maybe even some of Felix and Alara, but he's yet to really ask me a question about any of this.

"Some," he admits with a shrug. "But I still have many more unanswered questions."

"Then ask," I encourage. "I will answer anything I can."

He considers my offer for a moment then stops walking. I mirror him. "Why do you call God your Father? I would think, given both our circumstances, you would understand better than most that fathers are not the exemplary creatures most people laud them as."

"That's true," I concede. "But I never really had a father growing up. I never knew what it was to be loved unconditionally, to have someone make me feel safe, to feel loved."

"But Felix does all those things, doesn't he? Surely the most noble man on the continent can give you that."

I smile. "Felix does give me that, but that's because he also believes in God. We would not be capable of loving each other the way we do without being shown such an example. And we do it imperfectly, but God does not."

"Even if it means one of you will have to sacrifice your life for this?"

"Even if."

"How can you be so blasé about it?"

"I'm not. I take the responsibility very seriously, and I would be lying to you if I said I welcome it. I don't. I want years and years with Felix. I want a lifetime. But I have known enough love and joy in the moments we've had to fill my heart. And if my death—" I clear my throat because I still can't bring myself to really consider *his* death. "If my death means more people have the opportunity to know the God who is the author of all this, then it's a worthy cause. He is the only thing that matters. Felix and I work because we both agree on that. It's the thing that brought us together."

"Can I hear you pray?" he asks quietly, almost as if he's embarrassed by the request. Admittedly, it takes me off guard.

"You've heard me pray. At the cave, remember?"

"Yes, and it moved something in me. I can't explain it, but I've been chasing that feeling since then."

Perhaps that's why he sought out Alara? It's not a fair assumption for me to make.

"My prayers are nothing compared to Felix's."

"I've never heard him pray. I know he must, given everything I've learned about him, but he's felt he had to hide that part of himself from me until now."

That must have cut deep. That Felix didn't trust him with the most important part of his life has to hurt. So, I take his hand and turn toward the water. We look up at the sky dotted with stars, and I inhale deeply.

"God, I am utterly lost. Honestly, this feels a lot like defeat. I'm hurt and wounded, and I don't see a clear path through this. But I know You can make a way."

"Can you talk to Him like that? You just—you were so honest." I imagine it is a shock to him when every prayer to Caelus is a formal recitation.

"He prefers honesty over formality." I close my eyes and continue. "Narrow is the gate that leads to life and few who find it. But we're not seeking power. We are seeking You." It's a distinction I hadn't realized I needed to make until just now. "Show us Your glory. Make believers of all nations."

A wave barely grazes my toes before receding, and power that feels like lightning jolts through me. My eyes fly open, and I drop Ronan's hand.

"Emilia? What is it? Are you all right?"

But I can't answer him right away because someone else is speaking to me.

"Step into the water."

I can't. Suddenly all the fears of drowning I've so successfully bottled up come rushing back in a torrent. My breath quickens and a cold sweat breaks out on the back of my neck. Why now? I've run headlong into the water with Felix, swam with Alara. So, why is the fear manifesting now?

"You must."

As if I have no control over them at all, my feet shuffle forward, burying in the sand as I inch closer to the water.

"Emilia?"

"Shh," I insist without looking back at him.

"My grace abounds in deepest waters."

I've reached the point on the shore where the next wave should soak my legs. But it doesn't. I watch with wide eyes as the wave breaks and then rushes all around me to kiss the shore.

My feet are dry. Something hums in my blood as I shuffle another step forward. Holy. This place is holy.

But I don't understand. I've been on this beach before and never felt this. The Palanquin is gone from the island. There's no reason this stretch of shore should manifest God's presence like this.

"I am alive in you. It is My breath in your lungs. My rhythm your heart beats to. Will you trust Me?"

Will I?

"Ronan," I whisper as I watch the water swirl around me but not touch me. "We have to get Felix. Now."

I sprint back to the house with a speed I didn't know I possessed. Every part of me is on fire, but not from exertion. This is awe, assurance, and a little bit of crazy. Somehow, I force my feet to slow as I push through the front door and head for my bedroom.

The sight that greets me makes me pause entirely. Felix is sound asleep on his stomach, arms folded under a pillow with miles of tanned skin showing across his scarred back. His breathing is deep and even, and I'm fairly certain this is the first good sleep he's had in too long. And I'm about to interrupt it.

The bed sinks slightly under my weight as I sit next to him. He doesn't move. I stretch out a hand and brush my fingers between his shoulder blades and down the length of one of the scars. I hope against hope there is a day in the future when I can explore all these lines of his body. I hope we live to see it.

"Felix," I whisper as I lean closer and place my palm flat on his back.

"Come to bed, Mia," he groans sleepily, his voice rough as sandpaper.

"I wish I could."

He rolls over and wraps his arms around me, pulling me across his body until I'm halfway draped across him.

"You can." Half hooded eyes, heavy with sleep stare me down as he kisses me gently. I don't return it, and he stops. When he pulls back, he looks wide awake.

"What's wrong?"

"About those swimming lessons..."

"Emilia?" He adjusts himself so we're both in a sitting position and studies me. This is the test of how much he loves me. If he doesn't think I'm crazy for this, then nothing will faze him.

"I know how we're going to Draconis."

34

No pressure. At least that's what I tell myself. Just pretend like there aren't hundreds of people standing behind you, waiting for you to fail spectacularly.

It was a restless night of explaining over and over to those closest to me what my plan was. Felix was the easiest to convince, of course, and Ronan was a close second. He witnessed what happened on the beach, and though I expected him to scoff or give me some logical reason why this was insane, he didn't.

He managed to convince Alara, I suppose, because she showed up this morning along with most of Felix's soldiers. To their credit, all were willing to follow Felix and Antony's command, but Felix suggested a few stay behind to protect the city as best they could. We have no way of knowing if Cyrus will return. Even now, he could be searching more remote parts of the island. Hopefully, if he sees I have left, he'll follow me rather than terrorize these people.

"Emilia?"

The question in my name barely registers as I take those first tentative steps into the water. Or at least I try to. The closer I get, the more the water recedes. To my left and right, the tide line remains unaltered, but in front of me, for two or three feet, the water avoids me. As if something in me repels it.

"Just take the next step."

Veins thrumming in anticipation, I take a cautious step forward. This time the waves don't merely go around me, they actually rise up on either side, reaching my calves as if some barrier holds them back.

"Do you see this?" Excitement pitches my voice high as I turn over my shoulder to make sure Felix sees it as well. Despite the repeated assurances in my prayers and witnessing this on a much smaller scale last night, it's difficult to believe it's actually happening.

Water splashes as he jogs to join me, and then the sound stops. The waves have receded for him as well. Side by side we stand, a space of nearly ten feet covered by sand only as the water rises up on either side. His mouth drops open, eyes wide in what I know must mirror my own expression.

"This isn't normal, right?" I have to check because I know nothing about the sea, but this shouldn't even be possible.

"Not even close," he agrees in a whisper. "You were right. This is it."

Awe tinges every part of my being, flaring up inside me like it's looking for an escape. Tears fall down my cheeks, though I don't feel like crying. It's the only way it can leak out, I suppose.

Because it's too big to contain. Bigger than this whole ocean, in fact.

Reaching for his hand, I take another step forward. Then another. We move in small increments like that until the waves reach just above his head on either side. Other than my cheeks, I am completely dry. Not even a droplet of water has reached me. I stretch out my hand that isn't holding onto Felix and barely manage to brush my fingertips along the wall of water. My hand comes away wet, but the wall remains intact.

I touch my fingers to my lips and taste salt. Beside me, Felix has begun a low prayer that I lean in to hear.

"Do not fear, for I have redeemed you; I have summoned you by name; you are mine. When you pass through the waters, I will be with you, and when you pass through the rivers, they will not overflow you."

Not a prayer exactly. He's reciting from the Aletheia. He repeats the words over and over until I join him, and the waves on either side of us flare up seemingly in response to our voices.

As much as I have come to love the sea, I don't relish the idea of walking for miles across it while waves threaten to pour down and drown us at any moment. The lump in my throat makes it hard to swallow. The last time it tried to kill me, it was nearly successful. I'm not eager to give it another chance. But this is the path laid out for me.

Water spills from the top of the wave wall into our dry cocoon, sending me stumbling backward. It moved in response to my fear. Felix looks from the swirling puddle in front of us to me with wide eyes.

I can't do this.

"You *aren't doing this."*

I swallow a gasp at the response. *God, please, let there be some other way. We can appeal to the Synod again. We'll get a ship...*

"Am I not the God who created the sea? I have placed the boundary it cannot cross. The waves toss and roar, but they cannot cross what I have established. I have made a way for you and all who follow."

But are all these people behind me going to be crazy enough to follow me into the sea?

"Emilia!" Ronan shouts my name from the shore, and Felix and I turn to see the crowd behind us has more than doubled. Among the soldiers stand several of the citizens—men, women, and children. Miriam and Selah stand at the front of the group.

"What are they doing here?" I hiss to Felix. If they've come to stop us…

"They're here to pray." A smile lights his face as he keeps his eyes on his mother. "I told her about your plan last night. I thought the more people we had praying as we crossed, the better it would be. One people, one petition. I didn't know if they would come."

But come they have. Almost in unison, they move forward. Antony calls the soldiers into formation, and Alara and Ronan take their place at the front. Felix and I remain in our position, fingers intertwined while we survey the people before us. Those who believe—not in either of us—but in the God who holds all the power.

Felix lifts his chin, and for a moment I think he's going to address the crowd. Instead, he closes his eyes and begins to pray.

"God our Father, creator and sustainer of all. Nothing exceeds Your power. Nothing is too great for You to do. Your might is infinite, Your love boundless, Your grace limitless, and Your name...Your name is glorious. So, I humbly come to ask great things of a great God."

A roar rends the heavens as waves soar toward the sky. I whip around and gasp. There is a narrow path as straight as can be, parting the way through the sea. The water rises so high I can't see where it ends, but it has bared the depths of the sea.

Gasps and exclamations ring out from the shoreline as people drop to the sand and begin to pray in earnest. My heart thrums with an awareness of holiness. Of glory. How many times have I asked God to show me His glory? The storms in Borealis, those in the sea, they are nothing compared to what's before me now.

Oh God, forgive me for the times I doubted, for the times I questioned You. Keep my eyes on You instead of the waves. Your plan is all that matters.

Felix turns to face the path as well, his hand finding mine again. Everything is amplified by our connection. I know he feels what I feel. With a deep breath, his eyes find mine as well.

"We maybe don't come back from this," he says quietly. No fear in his tone, no judgment, not even any pleading with me to stay behind and stay safe. We go forward together.

"Maybe not," I agree.

"I meant it when I said I wanted to love you wildly, recklessly, for the rest of my life."

"Can't get much more reckless than this." The corner of my mouth ticks up in a half smile.

"No," he says. "No, you really can't."

We step forward into the sea.

We march for more than a day. It's eerily quiet except for the rhythmic cadence of our steps. No one has much to say. I hope it's because they're all praying.

As the sun dips lower into the sky, I look to Felix for direction. We can't set up camp in the middle of the ocean, but no one has any idea how much further we have to go. The maps indicate Draconis is west of Solitarius, but the distance remains a mystery, especially since so much of it was swallowed by the Great Wave.

I pray for strength and endurance as we march through the night. No one complains, but I know we all feel the weariness in our bones. The light of the moon and stars is barely enough to illuminate our next step, but I take it anyway, just like Antioch instructed me to do.

Guide my steps, God. Make a way in the darkness.

Every bone in my body aches, and I'm wrung out from the constant state of alertness, of prayers. I pour myself out with each breath and yet somehow, I refill enough for the next one. I glance to my left and behind me and find that Ronan is carrying Alara on his back as she rests her head, eyes closed, between his shoulder blades.

"Do you want me to carry you?" Felix catches me looking at them.

It's so very tempting. His arms are possibly the only place I could marginally relax right now. But he already carries so much, and not just our packs.

"No, love," I answer softly. "I need to take these steps for myself."

He nods in understanding. No further explanation needed.

We continue through the night with monstrous walls of sea on either side of us. If I look too long, the darkness of the water terrifies me, takes me right back to that storm that nearly killed me. But I keep my eyes forward on the path God has laid out for me.

The first pink light of morning is just tinging the sky when I notice our path slopes upward. I shake the exhaustion from my head and lift my eyes. And gasp.

Before us lies a mountain. There's no other way to describe it. The sand blends into rock that slopes upward and appears to reach a plateau. Felix grabs my hand and squeezes. He knows it, too. This is it.

We've reached Draconis.

Climbing the slope with our packs and gear takes longer than I'd anticipated, but there's a renewed sense of urgency now that we've reached our destination. The path through the water is narrow enough that only three people can walk side by side, and

Felix and I fall back with Alara and Ronan to let all the soldiers pass in front of us. I know Felix wants them on shore before me so they can sus out any potential danger. I'm just concerned that the waves will crash down around us the moment I step out of the water.

When the last group of soldiers has reached the plateau, Felix, Ronan, Alara, and I exchange looks. An unspoken oath passes between us. Forgotten is all animosity, jealousy, or grudges. There's no room for that here. Only trust. Trust in our God and that we will stand by each other as long as we breathe.

Ronan and Alara take the lead with Felix and I bringing up the rear. We walk side by side the last few steps up the slope, the walls of water growing shorter with each step. We're almost there. A humming begins in my veins, making my head swim. Though I'm exhausted, it doesn't explain the sudden pounding of my heart. There's only one thing that causes it to beat this way.

I set foot on the plateau and stumble. The world spins, and I mentally brace myself to collapse on the sand, though my arms seem incapable of bracing me for a fall. But calloused hands grab my forearms and steady me as I fall back against Felix's chest. Behind us, I hear the roaring crash of the waves returning to their boundaries. We made it.

"What is it?" he asks in a whisper. I can tell by the slight tremble in his voice that he feels it, too, though it doesn't seem to have affected him physically. Even Alara and Ronan have stopped in their tracks and stare at me warily. As if my response might be some sort of alarm bell preceding whatever awaits us.

“I don't know exactly,” I confess as he relaxes his hold on me slightly. I take the opportunity to reach for his hand, and he twines his fingers with mine without hesitation. “But you feel it?”

“Yes,” Alara answers for everyone. “It's here, isn't it? The Gate?”

I can think of no other explanation. It’s similar to the way I felt when I knelt before the Palanquin. The dreams I've had where I'm pulled toward something I can't see felt a lot like this. But I have no explanation for those either. And I don't want to dwell on them because along with those dreams came the dream of Felix dying on the ground before me, and that's not a thought I can afford to entertain now. Not ever.

35

Felix gives the order to make camp at the edge of the tree line on the beach. Things look entirely different now that the waters have returned to their rightful place. I stand with my back to the trees, looking out across the water. You would never know there was a mountain beneath there. The plateau at the summit where we now stand looks like any other beach I saw on Solitarius. Behind me, in the distance, are even more mountains, and I feel certain I will be climbing them before all this is over.

We don't bother erecting tents at the camp. Honestly, everyone is just so tired that it seems foolish to waste effort on that when we could spend the time eating then sleeping. It took nearly the entire day to summit that mountain, and now the light is dipping low in the sky again. No one has slept in nearly two days.

The soldiers claim their spots with their individual squads and stretch out their bedrolls. Most who are not assigned to the first watch fall asleep immediately, but a few gather around to share food from their packs.

I roll out my bed slightly away from the others but still well within the parameters of the watch Felix and Antony set up. Both of them are still walking through the crowd of soldiers, speaking to some, clapping them on the back, thanking them for their loyalty. It's something I should be doing, but that isn't enough to make me join them.

Instead, I open my pack in search of some dried meat. While I was busy convincing everyone to walk across a sea with me, Hannah took care of packing my bag. I hate that she didn't get her wedding with Anthony before we left. But if I survive this, I will make sure it happens.

Finding the meat, I shove a piece in my mouth then rifle around to see what else she has packed. My hand closes around something leather, and I know what it is before I even pull it from my pack. The Aletheia.

I stare at the cover for a while, undecided if I should open it. Then I notice two ribbons, like the ones Hannah sometimes uses to braid my hair, sticking out of the pages. I open to the first one and read.

The sacrifices of God are a broken spirit—a broken and contrite heart God will not reject.

Hope leaps in my chest. Then I flip to the other ribbon just a few pages after.

He heals up the brokenhearted and binds up their wounds.

Also on this page is a folded note stuck into the spine of the book. I unfold it with trembling hands and see Hannah's loopy handwriting I've only seen a handful of other times.

Emilia,

There is more to sacrifice than death. What God breaks, He also heals. There is another part of scripture (I don't have time to find it before you leave) that says 'God is within her. She will not fail.' These are the words I will pray while you are gone. Make sure you come back. You have to dance at my wedding.

Felix rolls out his bed next to mine with a confidence that dares anyone to comment. No one does, of course. Then he sits next to me and slides an arm around my back. Silently, I hand him Hannah's note and watch him while he reads it.

"Dancing, huh?" He hands it back to me with a smile. "She shouldn't have mentioned that if she actually wanted you to come back."

"I know," I sigh with exasperation. "There will be no dancing at our wedding."

He tilts his head and studies me. "Our wedding? Does that mean you agree?"

"What?"

Flecks of gold light up those deep brown eyes that look at me in earnest. "Emilia, I meant it when I said I wanted to love you for the rest of my life."

"So did I." I place my hands on either side of his face. The hair on his face is beyond stubble now and has grown into a full beard.

"So, if I made my vows before you and God, that would be enough?" He looks hopeful, almost childlike with the wide innocence in his eyes. I know what he's asking, and I know why he's asking it now.

"Yes. But not now."

I hate the disappointment that flashes in his eyes. "Why not now?"

"Because I don't want to rush this just because we're both aware that one or both of us might die tomorrow. I love you. And I will still love you when we return to Solitarius. I am already yours in all the ways that matter."

And to make sure he understands, I kiss him slow and deep. We're right out in the open for any and all of the soldiers to see, but I don't care. I want him to understand that there has never been nor will there ever be anyone for me but him. But I selfishly want those moments where we make those vows to each other before God to be ours alone and not shared with a crowd.

"And I am yours," he exhales shakily as he rests his forehead against mine.

"Felix." Ronan marches up to us, apparently oblivious to our cossetted position. The conflicted look on his face is enough to pull Felix away from me.

"What is it?" Felix is on his feet, placing a hand on Ronan's shoulder.

"I can't—I don't know…Whatever you and Emilia felt when we walked on shore…I want to feel it, too. I mean, I think maybe I feel something."

Light and warmth flare inside of me. This is God at work in the prince. This is the culmination of all he has seen and heard on this journey. And it's not going to end in a loud declaration for all to hear, but in a quiet moment with his best friend.

"Go," I mouth to Felix as he chances a look down at me.

He leads Ronan several feet away from me to a secluded area along the tree line. I can still see them, and I can catch snatches of their conversation, but I try not to listen to give them some privacy. Instead, I stretch out on my bedroll and tuck the Aletheia and Hannah's note back in my pack.

I'm in that blissful haze between sleeping and waking when Felix brushes some hair from my face and presses a kiss to my temple. I smile with my eyes closed as I hear him climb into his bed next to me. The sand shifts slightly, and I roll over to my other side to face him. I open my eyes to find him grinning back at me. He looks exhausted but happy as he stretches out on his bedroll.

"Did you finally convince Ronan to rest?"

He nods as he stifles a yawn with his fist. "He's so excited, so hungry. He wanted to know everything I could tell him."

"I liked listening to you tell the stories," I admit. As much as I tried not to listen, I am so attuned to Felix's voice that I couldn't block it out when he began telling Ronan stories from the scriptures.

"Yes, you enjoyed it so much that it put you to sleep."

"Because it's soothing. Your voice, God's promises... It's like when I hear you pray. There's power in it, but also peace and confidence. When I hear it, I feel safe and assured. When you speak, God listens."

“Do I need to remind you that you're the one that prayed down a storm in Borealis, and whose prayers held back the sea?”

“Hmmm,” I muse. “That did happen, didn't it?”

“It did,” he confirms with mock solemnity. “I was there.”

I can feel exhaustion tugging me back under, but I reach my hand into the space between us, and he takes it in his much larger one. “Promise me you'll always be there.”

Felix pauses then raises our joined hands to his mouth to kiss them. “For as long as I live.”

And sleep takes me before I can respond.

36

"Lord Commander!"

The shout stirs me from my sleep well before the sun makes an appearance. Felix is on his feet next to me before I can even open my eyes. I lie still as two soldiers from the watch approach him. He glances down at me and catches me staring right back.

"Rest," he insists with a weary expression.

"I need to hear—"

"I will tell you everything. Sleep every moment you can."

He greets the soldiers and directs them several yards away where they engage in a hushed conversation. Of course, I can't go back to sleep. It's not that I don't trust Felix to relay the information, but the urgency in the soldier's tone suggests this is not merely a routine report. They've found something, and it's not good.

Felix dismisses them with a nod, and they run off to execute whatever orders he gave them. When he turns his attention back to me, he frowns to catch me watching him.

“Sleep,” he mouths with a stern look as he clasps his hands behind his back and walks calmly into the midst of his sleeping soldiers.

Instead, I sit up and watch him strategically approach a single man in each group—squad leaders, I assume—and wake them to impart whatever information he’s just received. One by one, the men rise and follow him to the next squad. He has gathered eight in total, every squad and section leader, when they all head down to the water to speak.

It's much too far away for me to hear what they’re saying, but I watch them closely. Felix speaks first, no doubt disseminating the new information to the group as a whole. Then he looks at each of them in turn as they respond to him. It’s evident by the way he focuses on each one that he trusts them and values their opinion. That’s why he’s such a remarkable leader. That’s why he was born for this.

Their meeting lasts only a few minutes and then they all salute as Felix walks away. I don’t bother to pretend to be asleep as he returns to me with a shake of his head. I expect him to begin readying his pack, to wake Ronan, to do something, but he just lowers himself to his bedroll. He grabs my hand and guides me back so I’m lying next to him once again.

He doesn’t speak for a long moment, instead studying my face and brushing the hair that keeps falling forward to obscure my vision.

“No nightmares?” he asks as he finally tucks the wayward strands behind my ear and lets his hand come to rest on my side.

"No nightmares," I affirm. Of course there weren't. I don't need to dream them when I'm living them. From the moment the power on this island nearly knocked me to the ground, I've known this is the place I've seen in my dreams.

"The scouts have been out all night getting the lay of the land. It's much like this stretch of beach. Wide shores that back up to a forest. Further in, there are mountains, and the far side of those mountains end in cliffs overlooking the shore on that side."

I take it all in, analyzing each piece of information. If the scouts can report all that in the short time we've been here, then the island itself must be quite small. Which means there's not much point in trying to hide if we were followed. Cyrus's crew could have hardly failed to notice the entire sea parted for us. Hopefully it was enough to draw him away from Solitarius, but I'm not eager to meet him here, either.

Felix watches me process the information and must realize when I reach this inevitable conclusion.

"There is a ship anchored off that cliffside beach. The scouts reported dozens of boats rowing for shore."

Dozens? Given the number of men those boats can hold, Cyrus must have hundreds of soldiers with him. Our entire force is barely a hundred. What chance can we possibly stand against that might?

"I've given the orders for each squad to ready," he continues. "We either meet him in battle, or we brace ourselves to defend."

"Defend what? We have no idea where the Gate might be. What's the point in defending this section of beach?"

"My thoughts exactly," he agrees with a grim nod.

"So, we engage." The decision makes my stomach roll. But isn't that what we came here to do? We cannot let them get to the Gate first, and if we attack before they are settled, maybe we have a shot at driving them back to buy some time.

"That was my order."

Order. So, he wasn't exactly asking for my opinion. I find I don't mind. I might be an excellent soldier, but I trust Felix's mind on matters of strategy. Come to think of it, Alara might even be useful in that regard. Regardless, it's the only reasonable course of action.

"What I need to know from you, is do you want to accompany the army to Cyrus's camp? Or would you like us to buy you some time while you search for the Gate?"

"I'll be wherever you are." There's no question about it. I'm not sending him into battle—a battle we have little chance of winning—while I run all over the island. If we go down, we go down together.

"I knew you would say that." He kisses my forehead with gentle pressure. "But the truth of it is, I'll be wherever you are. If you choose to search for the Gate, I'll accompany you and leave command of the army to Antony."

I consider it. Felix and I could probably cover a large portion of the island while Antony distracts Cyrus. Especially if Ronan accompanies the army.

My heart sinks at the thought. Though I know every soldier here would fight valiantly, I would be depriving them of their best weapon if I removed Felix from the battle. I would effectively be sentencing them to death.

"We go with the army," I say with more bravado than I feel. "If we go down, we go down together."

"Then I'll give the orders. It's not far to their landing point, but in the dark and with as much stealth as we can muster, it will take a few hours to get there. I'd like to have the element of surprise."

"Agreed. Give the orders, and I'll pack up our things."

"Don't bother. If we survive, we'll return here. Absolute necessities will be carried by each squad. We don't need anything extra to slow us down."

The candor with which he says it sobers me in a way nothing else has. *If we survive.* He's being practical and rational and all the things that both frustrate me and endear him to me. He's exactly who we need right now.

"Felix," I call as he rises to leave. "Give Ronan and Alara the choice."

"You know they won't stay out of a fight."

I know. But is it too much to hope that one of us survives?

"Still, give them the choice."

He nods and walks away. I immediately bow my head and begin to pray.

Blessed be the Lord my rock who trains my hands for war and my fingers for battle. Make a way for us like only You can. Deliver us from the hands of the Empire so that Your kingdom may reign.

All that's left to do is hope I made the right decision.

⁂

We stumble through the forest with as much stealth as we can muster in near total darkness. Though the moon and stars were bright on the beach, the cover of trees prevents most light from illuminating our steps. It's slow going as we traverse tree roots, rocks, and even small animals that would halt our progress.

I can't see the forest around us, but I can feel it. If I close my eyes, I can picture it from my dreams. It's lush and full and more of a jungle than an actual forest. It feels alive as if it hums with a heartbeat all its own. The air is hot and sticky as wet leaves continually slap us in the face. The only thing missing is the tug in my gut I experienced in the dream. For now, all I have to lead me are the scouts and soldiers in front of me.

With too little rest, it doesn't take long before exhaustion settles on me. I know the others must feel the same. But Felix keeps pressing forward, and we all follow. Even Ronan and Alara, who have been noticeably quiet since we left the relative safety of our camp. Seems we're all contemplating our mortality at the moment.

The nonexistent path before us finally begins to lighten as the trees thin. Felix slows our progress as we approach the edge of the vegetation. I step up beside him so I can take it all in. To our left in the clearing is a steep rocky cliff overlooking the beach below.

The beach itself is covered in tents and fire rings. Hundreds of men mill about on the shore as they continue to set up their camp. No urgency, no worries. And my eyes finally find the reason why.

In the center of their camp, surrounded by at least ten men, is the Palanquin. Within the circle of guards sit four men who I assume to be the men Cyrus took from Solitarius to carry the Palanquin for him.

Anger licks through me at the audacity of the emperor. How dare he parade God's presence as if it's something he could tame?

"I want that back," I whisper to Felix. "We can't allow him to defile it like that."

"One thing at a time, love," he whispers in return. "Are you ready?"

Am I? Not at all. But I don't think I ever will be.

"What's the plan exactly?" Ronan asks, coming up beside us.

"Making it up as I go along," Felix mutters then motions everyone behind him forward.

Ronan and I wait a beat, exchanging glances, then follow.

"I don't find that as reassuring as he wanted it to be," the prince whispers to me.

"Me neither," I admit. "But I trust him with my life. With all our lives."

So, we march forward. By some miracle, we're almost upon them when Cyrus's army seems to realize we're there. They are so arrogant, so relaxed, they hadn't even bothered to set up a watch or send out scouts yet. Otherwise, they would have sensed us long before now. We have well and truly caught them off guard.

Imperial soldiers scramble to sheath their weapons and stumble into formation as orders are screamed above the chaos. All the while, we march calmly toward them. We don't waver, we don't panic. We simply follow Felix.

He raises a hand to halt us about fifty yards from the line of troops the Imperial army has managed to cobble together. I take my place at his side, just behind him, and Ronan takes the same position on the opposite side. He holds Alara behind him with an outstretched arm.

"Cyrus!" Felix's voice booms out, and all the troops fall silent. How can he possibly command not one army but two? They should charge us, attack us, because they easily outnumber us four to one. But they're waiting on orders from their emperor, and Felix is summoning him with the authority of a man born to rule.

There's some shuffling in their ranks, then Cyrus pushes forward to stand in front of them, long sword at his waist and murder in his eyes. I can feel it even at this distance.

"How dare you address me?" His voice projects with equal authority and an added layer of malice. "You are nothing. Just a mistake that I allowed to live. I should have killed you when my son discovered you on our ship. And just where is my wayward son? Cowering in some corner while you fight his battles for him as usual?"

Ronan steps forward to stand even with Felix, and I follow.

"He is my brother," Ronan shouts, "and the best of us. And we owe you no deference. Not when you have slaughtered thousands of innocents because of your insecurity."

"Insecurity? I was protecting my throne, your throne."

"My throne?" Ronan scoffs. "You tried to have me killed. You would have succeeded if Emilia hadn't intervened. And before that, when I was young, you would have killed me if Felix hadn't stepped in. But I'm done letting people fight for me. This time you face me."

What is he doing? The last thing we need is to goad Cyrus into action.

"Ronan." Alara's voice pleads in a tone I've never heard from her. But she doesn't move. She holds her place right where Ronan left her.

"Well, I'll admit this is unexpected. My coward of a son issuing me a challenge." I can feel his eyes shift from Ronan to me. "And the princess. Do you still love him? Will you fight to save him?"

He doesn't know. He still thinks me in love with Ronan, thinks he's my weakness. And he will kill him if he thinks it will devastate me.

"I can fight for myself." Ronan draws his sword and soldiers on both sides shift into battle positions.

Cyrus laughs. "I can be reasonable. There's no need for so many to die. If you return my wayward son to me, then I'll let the rest of you live out your days on this god-forsaken island."

God-forsaken? How ironic.

"Why does he want you?" I ask in a low voice. Every muscle in Ronan's body is taut, ready to spring into action. I have to talk him down before he does just that.

"He thinks I'm a weakness to you—to both of you." His blue eyes have darkened to almost navy as he looks between me and Felix.

"And he wants the pleasure of exacting your punishment himself," Felix adds with a grim nod. "I will not let that happen."

"Nor will I," I insist. I still remember the way Cyrus grabbed my arm hard enough to leave a bruise my first night in Aurora. Ronan endured years of much worse.

"He thinks now that he has the Palanquin..." Ronan's head falls as he trails off. Something in his reaction, in his defeat, chills me.

"Ronan, what is it?"

"He thinks if he makes the sacrifice then he'll be able to access the power in it. He's read the same things Antioch did. He needs me to be his sacrifice."

"Can't one of you make a decision?" Cyrus's cold laugh booms across the distance. "That's what happens when you divide power. But I can be reasonable. Let's settle this in the old way. Your best man... or woman... against mine. If you win, we'll sail home and leave Solitarius in peace so long as you agree to never return to the mainland. If I win, I'll spare your lives so long as you swear fealty to me in front of the entire empire."

He doesn't mean it. No way I can trust him. But he's dangling that little bit of hope in front of me hoping I'll take the bait. The least loss of life. The men Felix took with him from the Imperial Guard are some of the most formidable warriors in the empire, but we are hopelessly outnumbered. Our force is one hundred strong at the most, and Cyrus has hundreds of men behind him. I imagine he's collected the best soldiers the other countries supplied for the brief war with the Insurgos.

One on one I could defeat most men. I'm not as strong, but I'm quick and agile, and I can swing a sword to rival almost anyone in the empire. Almost anyone.

"Let me fight." Ronan addresses Felix, hand still gripping his sword. His longing is tempered only by the rage in his eyes.

"You can't possibly think we'd let you do that after you've just admitted he'd like nothing more than to slit your throat over that altar."

"It can't be you." Even if I thought Ronan had a chance to beat Cyrus's best soldier, I can't risk something happening to him. If we somehow miraculously win this, he inherits Aurora's throne. Without him, the country plunges into chaos.

"I wouldn't ask that of you." He flinches under my touch as I rest a hand on his chest. Cyrus doesn't know that my heart doesn't belong to Ronan. He thinks that by taking Ronan out of the equation I will be undone. He also knows Ronan is Felix's weakness as well, having given the Commander the scars across his back that were meant for Ronan. If Ronan dies, Cyrus takes out Felix and me with one blow.

"He wants to take advantage of our emotion. We have to be rational, controlled," Felix predictably insists.

Though I'm giving it a valiant effort, I feel neither of those things.

"Why not take me?" I shout across the divide. I feel Ronan's stare and the tension radiating from Felix. "You want a sacrifice? Kill two birds with one stone."

"Besides the fact that we already tried that with your mother, it would be no sacrifice at all for me to kill you. It would be a pleasure." The ice in his tone lets me know he means it. This is personal now.

"Will you please stop trying to rush to your death?" Felix keeps his voice low so only Ronan and I can hear. "I understand it's your decision who to send forward, but we both know if you go, I'm going to follow."

Of course he is. He said we needed to be rational and controlled, and I know he's right. He is the definition of both. He's also the love of my life and the commander of my army. I don't want to risk him, but I know he's the best choice.

"You only have to ask me once."

It's the same thing he said to me when I wanted to beg him to save my father but didn't know how. Just like then, I know he's my best chance. Unlike then, I'm fully aware of what I stand to lose if he doesn't succeed. Unlike then, I'm not asking him to save a life but to take one. I don't think Cyrus will yield. This is meant to be a fight to the death.

I wish there weren't so many eyes on us. The need to touch his face, to convey everything I feel for him rises up like a tidal wave, but I push it down. The depth of our connection is one of our greatest strengths, and I don't want to show that to Cyrus. Besides, this is his calling. He asked me to let him lead.

"Yield if you must, but make sure you come back."

"I'm not going to yield. But I'm not afraid. I know who I believe in."

So do I, but that hasn't saved so many I love from death. "I love you," I say, though I don't dare fling myself into his arms like I'm desperate to do. But I can't let him go forward without the reminder.

He turns his back on Cyrus, something I know goes against every instinct he has, and locks his eyes with mine. He reaches for my hands, shielding me from the emperor's view.

"Every pain, every wound, every moment of loneliness has been worth even a second of your love. I have no regrets when it comes to you."

Tears sting my eyes, and I don't even try to blink them away. My heart shatters. This can't be the last time I speak to him. I still have so much to say. I don't want a moment. I want forever.

"Come back to me. That's not a request."

"I love you, too." He squeezes my hands then drops them. Antony steps forward, and Felix gives him a few hurried instructions. What needs to happen if he dies, I suppose. I don't bother listening. If he dies, I'm done. I just hope my death will be quick.

Ronan embraces Felix then releases him. With a deep breath and a firm set to his shoulders, Felix steps forward into the space between our army and theirs.

Cyrus laughs in triumph. He turns and shouts something to the men behind him. Seconds later, the ranks part, and four men appear carrying the Palanquin. My heart thunders in my chest as they set it down about a quarter of the way between their front line and ours. They can't call on that power, can they? Surely God will not allow it. But if they can…

Behind the Palanquin is the biggest man I have ever seen. He's a head taller than anyone near him, well-muscled, and lethal looking. I swallow hard. Felix is faster, no doubt, but I'm not sure his strength can match this man. I had higher hopes when I assumed it was Cyrus he would be facing.

"Ludo," Felix greets with a nod of his head. He knows the man. An ember of hope kindles in me.

"Commander," the giant responds with a nod of his head. A good sign. Whether conscious or not, he has just acknowledged Felix as his commanding officer. Perhaps the loyalty is still buried in him as well.

God, please…

The man—Ludo—turns back to exchange words with the emperor. Cyrus's face reddens, and he charges forward to shove Ludo in Felix's direction.

"He doesn't want to fight him," Ronan whispers beside me. I hear the hope in his voice, too. His father might not intend to honor the deal should they lose, but there's every chance his soldiers will. They have more honor than their leader. There's a chance we make it out of this alive, though a very slim one.

Ludo stumbles forward and reluctantly draws his sword. Felix follows suit. They approach and circle each other around the Palanquin. I can picture the expression on Felix's face. I've been the recipient of it as he studies me in the sparring ring and observed it when he watches his men face down their opponents. He's looking for a weakness, a point to strike.

Ludo raises his sword and swings it in a blow Felix easily defends. Still, he doesn't deliver a strike himself. He circles back around until he's on our side of the Palanquin again. I catch a glimpse of his face and see his lips moving. Praying. He's praying.

"Pray!" I shout at our army. "Pray where you stand, but keep your eyes open."

I don't look to see if they obey, but I feel the result of their collective prayers surge through me as though I'm some sort of conduit. Wave after wave washes over me, and I push it forward, toward Felix, toward the Palanquin.

Felix blocks blow after blow, but even from here I can see they are halfhearted. Finally, he takes his chance to attack. He comes at Ludo, his blade merely a flash of metal against the rising sun. The clash of steel on steel rings out as Ludo does everything he can to block the blows. But Felix has him on his heels, and he stumbles backward to the ground. Felix plants a foot on his chest and holds the blade to his neck.

Both armies hold their collective breaths as we wait to see how he will react. After a tense moment, Ludo throws aside his sword and lets his head fall back to the sand.

"I yield," he yells. Felix steps back, not daring to sheath his sword despite his apparent victory. And it's a good thing. Because as soon as he turns to face us, Cyrus charges forward toward him.

“Felix!” I scream a warning, but he turns just in time to see Cyrus drag Ludo to the Palanquin, pull a dagger, and slit his throat.

37

Blood sprays out, staining the gold of the Palanquin with dark red splatters. Felix crouches in a defensive position, sword at the ready, but Cyrus isn't coming for him.

He's holding the dead soldier's head so he continues to bleed out on the symbol of God's presence.

"Caelus!" he screams with a mad glint in his eyes I can see from here. "Pour out your wrath on these infidels. Rain fire!"

Sure enough, a rumble of thunder sounds, and clouds roll in from nowhere, darkening the light of the morning sun. Behind him, Cyrus's soldiers break rank and begin to run into each other as they try to retreat from whatever plague their leader has called down.

Alara steps forward and grabs my hand as we await the devastation as well. She's murmuring the same words over and over again as her eyes remain locked on the scene playing out before us. "Our God is a consuming fire." The same words written on the message she attached to the flaming arrow she shot at the temple in Borealis.

I take up her prayer as the sky darkens to a blackness that prevents me from seeing even a few feet in front of me. Felix is still out there somewhere, but I can't put eyes on him. All I can do is pray.

Lightning rends the sky, nearly blinding me with its brightness. Thunder roars, and the seas seem to recede. Then the clouds begin to glow an ominous orange and red around their black forms. Alara squeezes my hand harder, and I return the gesture. Ronan takes her other hand, and we all shout out prayers as the sky explodes with fire.

What must be thousands of flames rain down from the blackness overhead with the precision of an expert marksman. In rapid succession, they crash to the ground at the Palanquin, setting it ablaze. Then they continue to fall behind the boundary the first fall established. Torrents of fire pour out on Cyrus's camp setting tents, supplies, and men on fire. Screams are muffled only by the thunderous roar of fire pummeling the beach.

Heat flares, singeing my lungs even from this distance as I watch in horror as fire encircles Cyrus, the dead soldier he's still holding, and about a third of his army. They are spared for the moment, but well and truly trapped within the flames.

"Felix!" I scream his name, eyes frantically searching for him in the light of the fire. But it's absolute chaos. He's too close, too close! No, no, no, no, no!

A scream tears from my throat, shredding everything inside me on its way out. Even our soldiers have broken ranks. Antony grabs me by the arm and tries to pull me back, but I shake him loose and sprint into the darkness. I don't need a light to direct me toward him. I am the flame, and if he is harmed, I'll consume everyone in my path.

I collide hard with a figure running in the opposite direction and fall to the ground.

"Emilia!"

The relief I feel at the sound of his voice takes the wind out of me, but there's no time to revel in his safety. Felix pulls me to my feet none too gently and drags me back toward the safety of our ranks.

"Fall back!" he yells as he runs forward. "Back to camp!"

The soldiers don't need to be told twice. We sprint, my hand in his, until I can't pull in a breath. My lungs seize, my side aches, and I don't even stop moving when I dry heave and nothing comes out. Felix slows, tugging me behind a tree and pressing my back against it. His chest heaves, and his eyes are wild as they search my face. Neither of us can speak, but we hold an entire conversation with our eyes.

It's lighter here than it was on the beach, but I can't get a good enough look at him to tell if he's injured. So, my hands seek out what my eyes can't tell me. I run them over his chest, his arms, his sides and come away with no blood or hisses of pain from him.

"Can you move?" he asks as my hands reach his face, searching for any wounds there. But it's just as perfect as I remember as my fingers take a familiar path over his temples, his cheeks, his neck. "Emilia, we have to go. Can you move or should I carry you?"

"No, I can run. Let's go." I suck in a deep breath and resolve to ignore the pain in my side. I don't know where Ronan and Alara are. Antony would have led the charge of our forces to fall back. I pray all my friends are safe. It's the only thought I can spare about what just happened if I want to stay functional and upright. I can consider the rest when we're relatively safe.

Felix takes off but soon slows his stride to match pace with me. I want to reach for his hand, but we both need to remain untethered for balance over this uneven terrain.

By the time our camp is in sight, my pace could barely be called a run. Felix slows to a walk beside me, then scoops me up in his arms. I don't protest. I press my face into his chest and inhale smoke and leather and sweat.

"I was scared it burned you," I admit in a soft voice that I'm not sure he can even hear.

"I'm okay," he assures me with a press of his lips on the top of my head. "Lungs burn a bit, but it's nothing really."

"Did it get Cyrus?" The last I saw of the emperor, he was cut off from his army by a wall of flames on both sides.

"Not that I could see," he answers grimly. "I had hoped that would end it all, but I think he still lives."

"And the Palanquin?" I so wanted it back. Not because I believe it could save us, but because I can't stand the thought of it in Cyrus's hands.

"Ablaze when I saw it. It didn't exactly seem to be burning up, though. It was on fire, but it wasn't burning."

"So, he still has it then."

"I don't think he'll go near it any time soon," Felix says as we reach the place where we laid out our bedrolls just a few hours ago. The site is undisturbed, even peaceful looking, as if fire didn't just rain from the sky a few miles from here.

"Why not?" I ask as he sets me down beside my things.

"You should have seen his face." His expression turns dark. "That was the look of a man who has called on gods he didn't believe in. And he paid the price dearly."

"But he wants Ronan. We didn't plan on that."

"No," he agrees, "we didn't. I didn't count on him knowing anything about the sacrifice, but I suppose his efforts to gain intelligence from the Insurgos before he annihilated them was effective."

"And it's never once crossed his own mind that his life might be the sacrifice required and not the son he claims to care for."

"I'm sure it hasn't." His face softens as he brushes the back of his hand down my cheek. "Not everyone is as selfless as you, nor as reckless."

"I'd do it all again," I raise my chin at him, knowing he's still upset with the way I offered myself to Cyrus.

"Well aware," he grumbles then kisses me. It ends far too soon for my liking, but we hardly have the luxury of time.

"I'll need to send men to keep an eye on Cyrus's camp so we can know the extent of the casualties. I also want to extend our perimeter guard so we can have the earliest warning possible if what's left of them decide to attack."

"I agree," I say, though it's not necessary. Felix is more than capable of making these decisions without me. Still, I appreciate him letting me know his plans ahead of time. "I don't suppose you'll let me take a watch?"

"You suppose correctly. If you feel you need to make yourself useful—which you don't—study that map. I asked Hannah to pack it with your things. I know it's vague, but see if there's anything you can get from it or Antioch's notes."

It is probably the best use of my time, but I'm not sure what I could glean from Antioch's writing that I haven't already seen. A bunch of genealogies that point to Felix as the heir of Caspian, a few sketches of the map Felix retrieved with his notes about bones and caves and the breath of life. I have no idea what any of it means, but it sounds too much like whoever is chosen is supposed to give their breath of life as a sacrifice as they rot to bones in a cave. There's nothing in that I want to share with Felix if I can help it. Not with his history.

Felix excuses himself to hand out orders to the various squads and to confer with Antony on how to execute his plans. I lower myself to my bedroll and begin to read.

Night has fallen, and I'm still pouring over the pages by the light of a torch I've wedged in the sand with a few rocks. It isn't much help, and I have to lower my nose almost to the page to make out any of the writing. I can't say that I know much more than I did when we returned to camp early this morning. I have practically memorized the map, which I now assume to be of a cave probably located somewhere on this island. That will be helpful assuming I can ever find this cave and work up the courage to go in it. So far on this journey, I've added a fear of heights and a fear of drowning to my repertoire. Why not add claustrophobia and fear of the dark as well?

I barely notice when Felix stretches out on his bed with a groan. Not until he pulls the paper from my hands and lays it on the ground behind me do I look at him.

"Any news?" I ask. He's been busy all day with coordinating spies and patrols as well as rations. While I've been reading notes, he's been seeing that we are fed, have a latrine dug, and have a source of water other than what we brought with us.

"Early reports indicate that as much as a third of his army was incinerated."

I suck in a breath. All that death. It should feel like justice, retribution for all the Insurgo villages Cyrus burned, but it just tastes like ash in my mouth. No one else should have to die for this. No one except maybe me. Hannah's notes still give me just a bit of hope though. Her words ring through my head.

There are many ways to sacrifice that don't involve giving your life.

"Emilia?" Felix brushes a tear from my face with his thumb. I hadn't even realized I'd let it fall. "What are you thinking?"

"I don't know," I answer honestly. Because the thoughts are racing through my head too quickly for me to pin one down.

"We could attack them now while their defenses are down and their numbers reduced," he offers. "We're still outnumbered, but there's a chance we could pull it out."

He doesn't need to tell me it would be a bloodbath. No matter the odds, Cyrus will not yield, and he will take no prisoners…except maybe Ronan. I shudder to think what his father would do to him.

I look past Felix to where Ronan and Alara sit together a few yards away. They look to be deep in a heated conversation. Alara jabs a finger into Ronan's chest as I've seen her do before, and he throws up his hands in exasperation. I can detect the intensity in their hushed tones but not the exact words. Probably better that way. I have enough problems of my own to worry about.

"I'd like to avoid a battle if at all possible," I finally say. "I know that's probably unrealistic, but there's still hope that we find the Gate. I know it's here somewhere. I can feel it."

It's true. The hum of holiness hasn't left me even in the chaos of the day. It's not as startling as when I first set foot on the island, but it's there all the same. I just need it to give me some direction.

"I could send out a scouting party," Felix offers halfheartedly. Because he already knows what I'm going to say to that.

"We both know it has to be me. No one else is going to be able to sense it. And while I think your map may give us direction once we get close, it's not going to narrow down the area we need to search."

"So, you think the map will help? It was worth it?" Those brown eyes I love are so full of hope that I can't stop myself from cupping the back of his neck and pulling his face toward mine for a kiss.

"It will help," I assure him. "But only you can decide if it was worth it."

"If it means all those innocent lives will be saved... If it means Selah gets to grow up in a world with no threat of war and the freedom to worship the God she chooses, then it will absolutely have been worth it."

I couldn't agree more.

38

By the time the sun rises, I'm more exhausted than when I laid down the night before. At least twice I woke up with the recurring nightmares, and the second time Felix pulled me hard against him until I drifted back to sleep.

Between the moments of sleep I do get, I toss and turn with a restless energy I can't explain. Felix readjusts himself around me every time I move, but I know I'm keeping him from resting, and he desperately needs it.

Finally, as the first pale light of the sun creeps over the horizon, I sit up and look out at the sea.

"Mia?" Felix mumbles, his voice thick with sleep as he reaches out for me. His eyes open when his hands don't find me.

"I need to walk," I say. It just feels like the right thing to do.

"It's not safe."

"Just down by the water," I assure him. "I'll stay in camp."

"I'll come with you."

I lean back and run my fingers through his mussed curls with a smile. He groans sleepily. "Rest. I've kept you up all night."

"Make sure you come back."

I look into those brown eyes, so full of love and concern, and my heart swells. I don't deserve him, but I pray to God I can keep him.

There are a few soldiers stirring as I make my way down the shore to the water's edge. I wave to Antony who is sitting around a fire with a few other men. He gives me a deferential nod and a tired smile. Suddenly I'm overcome with gratitude for all the people this journey has brought into my life.

It's been less than a year since Felix rode into my military camp and changed my life. Less than a year since Levi first hinted at the prophecy that would shape all this. In that short time, I've had my life endangered more times than I can count, worn more crowns than I care to think about, and fallen in love…almost twice. What I felt for Ronan was never really love. I can see that clearly now. But the affection I felt for him was real. It just couldn't compete with Felix.

God, You have a plan for my life. I can see now all the ways You've orchestrated the people I needed at just the right time. From Hannah, Antioch, Verity, and even Alara… They have each held a piece of this puzzle. Give me strength when the time comes to do what must be done for their sakes. For every life that has been lost in this war. Don't let their deaths be in vain. Grant me the courage to fulfill Your plan.

I don't receive any sort of clear answer like I sometimes do when I pray. But the peace that comes over me is very clear. God has guided each of my steps as Antioch said He would. He has led me through fire and storms and across a sea. And I have to believe if He set this plan in motion, He will see it completed. I am terrified and honored to be part of it.

The sun continues to rise, bringing fiery orange color to the edge of the ocean and sky. Waves beat a steady rhythm against the shore, just close enough to touch my toes where I sit in the sand. I simply sit for a long while, watching the sun inch closer and closer to the clouds above. It spills pale golden light where the clouds break, then fades to the palest blue of the sky.

Felix joins me without a word. He sits with his knees bent and elbows resting on them. The sea breeze blows his hair, and he tilts his head back to breathe it all in.

"I can see why you love it," I say after a long silence. "The sea, I mean."

He doesn't answer right away, and I don't push. It's the sort of silence I don't feel compelled to break. But finally he does.

"Did you know, the scriptures say that God once spoke to the waves, and they instantly calmed?"

"I didn't." I haven't had a chance to read everything in that book yet. Hopefully one day I will. "What did he say to the waves?"

"Be still."

"Be still," I repeat. It's the same thing His voice said to me when I was drowning. It made no sense to me then, and it still doesn't. How can I sit still when the restlessness I felt last night has only increased the longer I've sat here? There's peace, sure, but much stronger is the need to act.

"Any more news from the patrols?" I ask him.

"It appears Cyrus is still wading through the burned bodies and completely assessing the damage. He had a few more men killed over the Palanquin."

"It's still there?" I perk up. Logically, it feels as though we should go after it. After all, we know where it's located, and I feel confident we could carry it out without being struck dead. But the constant hum inside me seems to douse that idea. That's not the next step.

"Yes," Felix answers gravely. "Still sitting exactly where it was yesterday. I'm not sure what he hoped to accomplish with additional sacrifices since his first one was so disastrous…"

"Perhaps he's trying to call on a different god." Caelus might be the king of the gods in the empire, but he's only one of six.

"Perhaps." But Felix doesn't elaborate. "When do you want to go scouting?"

I give him a sidelong look. Honestly, I was prepared for more of a fight over this idea, but there's only understanding in his eyes.

"As soon as possible," I say quickly before he can change his mind. "You aren't going to give me a list of reasons why it's a bad idea?"

"It's the right thing. I can feel it, too, now." He places his hand over his chest. "There's a pulling sensation there. I think we need to take advantage of it while one or both of us can feel something."

"Do you know how irrational this is?" I smirk at him. "There's no logic, no practicality to following a feeling."

"There is when that feeling has yet to steer me wrong. After all, it led me to you."

"You know Ronan and Alara are going to want to come along," I say with a sigh. And as much as I'd like it to just be me and Felix, I won't deny them this when they've come this far with us.

"Ronan's already caught me this morning to ask what the plan was."

"Are he and Alara speaking? I heard them fighting last night." I really don't want to take a grumpy Alara with us.

"They looked cozy when I saw them earlier," he answers with a shrug. "I never would have put those two down for a happily ever after."

"I don't think it's that simple." But that's a matter for another time. Because if we don't make some progress, no one is going to be alive for a happily ever after.

It's midday before Felix, Ronan, Alara, and I set out with our packs into the forest. The deeper we go, the more alive our surroundings become. In the daylight, my eyes confirm what my head knew in the dark—these are not the evergreen trees of my mountains in Borealis. The verdant hues are varied, bright, and lush. Moisture clings to the leaves in what I assume to be a perpetual state. As humid as the air is, I don't think this forest is ever dry.

Few words are exchanged as we make the steady climb up the mountain I could see in the distance from the beach. There's no lack of sound though. More bird calls than I've ever heard, chirping of insects, and the occasional growl of some sort of animal fill our ears as we push on. I lead, but Felix is only a step behind me, keeping his eyes and ears open for any ambushes that might be waiting for us.

Antony and the army are in a holding pattern at camp. Felix instructed them not to attack Cyrus unless provoked but to maintain the patrols and scouting efforts. With any luck, they will have an uneventful time of it until we return with news of the Gate's location.

The pull in my chest grows stronger as we make the ascent. My feet grow heavy under the weight of it, but I do as the voice in my heart tells me and just take the next step. As I do, I recite one of the notes I first found tucked inside the Aletheia.

In the dragon's belly is a consuming fire.

Our God is a consuming fire.

Just thinking the words ignites the flame within me, and I redouble my efforts and push harder. It's not lost on me that I don't know exactly what I'm looking for, but I'll know it when I see it.

When we begin to lose light, my optimism falters. We've been walking for hours with nothing to show for it. As small as the island is, I had hoped we would have at least discovered the location of the cave I believe we're looking for by now, if not the Gate itself.

"We should find a place to camp for tonight," Felix suggests while reaching for my hand to slow my pace. He looks over his shoulder to Alara and Ronan who look dead on their feet. "We're not familiar with his terrain, and I don't trust it in the dark. Better to pause now and resume in the morning."

It's a mark of how exhausted I am that I don't argue with him. Alara and I find a rock to sit on as Felix and Ronan go about pitching two tents. It's no easy feat with this sloping terrain, but they manage to level out a small area with some branches and leaves before pitching the tents on top of it.

"Do you think we're close?" Alara asks as we watch the men.

"It feels closer than it did on the beach, but nothing like my dreams yet."

"We've never actually discussed your dreams." She sounds…hurt? "I mean, I get why I would be the last person you would want to share that sort of thing with, but…"

"Felix is the only one who knows," I tell her before she can go too far down that road. "Well, Antioch knew a bit, too."

She hangs her head at the mention of his name, and I realize I never checked on her after his death. I don't know what happened when she and Ronan ran after Cyrus that night. I'm not the only one who's been keeping things close.

"You were so quick to believe him about Felix." I broach the subject carefully. We also haven't discussed how she outed him in front of all of Solitarius.

"It wasn't really that difficult to believe if you've been paying attention." There's no malice in her voice. "Felix is a born leader.

Even as children, he was one of the eldest of our play group, but he commanded so much respect. And I know how he values the cause…how he values you."

"And you wanted it to be him."

"Yes," she hedges, "but not for the reasons you probably think."

"So, not because you think he's superior to me in every way and that my indecision and hot-headedness is going to get everyone killed? Because I don't disagree with you on any of those points."

Alara huffs a laugh. "Okay, maybe for *some* of the reasons you think. But it's more. I told you I lost a sister to this war. I don't know if I can bear to lose another."

She reaches for my hand and squeezes, refusing to look at me as she does so.

I'm stunned. A sister? This has been her way of showing me she thinks of me like a sister? I'm honored? Shocked? Confused? Definitely confused.

I'm saved a response as Felix and Ronan finish the tents and approach us. Alara jumps to her feet as if she's afraid she might catch feelings. She pats the daggers at her waist and addresses Felix.

"I'll take the first watch."

"I don't think—"

I cut off Ronan's objection with a shake of my head. "That's a good idea," I tell Alara. "Wake one of us when you get tired."

She nods, and I walk with Felix toward our tent, leaving Ronan and Alara to work out their own issues. He holds the flap open for me, and I duck inside, smiling when I see he has spread out our beds so that they overlap. Wordlessly, he pulls his shirt over his head and tosses it to the side.

I don't blame him. Every part of me is sticky with sweat, but I don't have the luxury of stripping to sleep. Not if either of us wants to stay focused on what we came here for. He toys with the hem of my tunic, then seems to reach this conclusion as well. There's so much promise in his eyes as he drops the fabric and lays down. I follow and tuck myself against him despite the heat. I don't know how many more of these moments we have left, but I intend to savor every one.

"I think it will be tomorrow," he says as he runs his fingers over the length of my braid. "Whatever is going to happen, will happen tomorrow."

I just nod. Because I feel the inevitability as well. "We're getting closer," I agree.

He shifts his weight to position himself so he can look directly at me. "Whatever happens—"

"No, we're not doing that." I press a finger to his lips to silence him. "We're not saying goodbyes." Then I kiss him so he can't speak anymore.

His mouth immediately parts for me. I tease for just a moment then deepen the kiss. I take his bottom lip gently between my teeth and pull a groan from him. I shift my weight forward until he's on his back and my upper body is pressed against his. He's mine for the taking if I want to. It's not a loss of control on his part exactly, more like surrender. I could have every part of him. His hands remain firmly on my sides, never venturing up or down to explore, but I do feel them quake a little. It's a heady rush to know I can make him tremble like this.

Then he's gently pushing me away and rolling back to his side. To lessen the sting of the rejection, he gives me a slow, sweet kiss very at odds with the ones I just bestowed upon him.

"You can't tell me not to say goodbye and then kiss me like that." His smile is a bit sad as he trails his fingers along my cheek. "I love you too much to let you make this decision when you aren't thinking clearly. You wanted to wait until we return to Solitarius to marry me. I think this is worth waiting for as well."

I duck my head as the warmth of embarrassment heats my cheeks. But he doesn't shy away from me. Instead, he pulls me against him, and I roll so my back is pressed against his chest. Then he leans in to ghost the shell of my ear with his breath.

"I am already yours completely. When we get home, I'll let you claim every piece of me."

I fall asleep with that promise ringing in my ears.

39

Once again, my sleep is fractured and plagued with hazy dreams. They're not enough to wake me, but Felix's tossing and turning is.

"You need to sleep," I tell him after the fifth time he's woken me with his movements.

He looks me over with an apology in his brown eyes. "I'm just restless. There's too much on my mind to sleep."

I know that feeling all too well.

"Are you scared?" I ask in a small voice. Because I'm terrified. The closer it comes to daylight, the surer I am that today will be the culmination of our journey.

"I'm not afraid to die," he whispers as he nuzzles his face in the crook of my neck. "But I need you to promise me that you will live."

"Felix, it's not—"

"Emilia." There it is again. The tone that conveys so many nuances into a single utterance of my name. Pleading with me to make a promise I have no control over keeping.

"You will fight to live," he clarifies as if he can read my thoughts. "You are a warrior, and I know your strength. At least promise me you'll use every weapon at your disposal to stay alive no matter what happens to me."

It's a crushing blow to my heart. I'd rather die than lose him. I trust our God, but I cannot fathom a situation where I can go on without Felix.

"I promise," I whisper. I hope I can keep it.

Those two words relax him marginally, but he doesn't roll over to go back to sleep. Instead, he sits up and reaches for the shirt he tossed aside a few hours ago. He pulls it over his head and drags his fingers through his hair. I recognize his posture. He's leaving.

"Where are you going?" A bit of panic flares inside of me. Is he going off on his own to finish this? He has to know I won't allow it.

He leans down to kiss my temple and brush a few loose strands of hair from my face. "Relax. I'm going to relieve Ronan from watch. I heard Alara pass it to him a while ago, and if I can't sleep, I might as well make myself useful. I'll wake you when it's time to pack up and move on."

This time he gives me a long, slow kiss that makes me melt into the hard ground we're sleeping on. "Sleep, love. You need it."

I watch him duck out of the tent with a sleepy smile on my face. Then I close my eyes, hoping to dream about a future with many more moments like that.

It might be seconds or maybe minutes later, when I'm just on the hazy edge of sleeping and waking, that yelling from outside the tent jolts me upright. Ice shoots through my veins as I jump to my feet, reaching for the first weapon I can find. I take two daggers in my hand.

There's no time to think as I charge from the tent, adrenaline sharpening my reflexes despite the exhaustion. It's later than I thought because there's just enough light in the sky for me to make out five figures before me. Two are Felix and Ronan. The other three are not our allies. Cyrus's men.

My instincts kick in, and I don't hesitate as I charge toward them. Alarms ring in my head that there could be more of them nearby, but adrenaline propels me forward without caution.

"Leave the others!" one of the men shouts. "He only wants the prince!"

My heart stutters at the implication. They've come to take Ronan. Despite the catastrophe on the beach, Cyrus still intends to try to use him as a sacrifice. I will not let that happen.

Two of the men come for Ronan. He wields his sword, deftly blocking their every blow but unable to get in any of his own either. They aren't going for a killing blow, I realize. They intend to take him alive and leave the rest to Cyrus. With a cry, one of the men disarms Ronan, sending his sword flying feet away from them.

I glance to my left and see the third man facing down Felix. I hesitate. My gut insists I help Felix, but Ronan is weaponless with two attackers. One clubs Ronan in the head with the pommel of his sword, and the prince staggers forward to the ground, still conscious. Each of the men grabs one of his arms and begins to drag him away. My hesitation costs me the chance to take one of them off guard.

I make my decision just as Felix dispatches the soldier he's facing. The man slumps to the ground with a gurgling cry, and Felix pushes him aside as he rushes toward Ronan. I'm on my way, too.

He gets there first. His sword flies in a frenzy as he attacks the man on Ronan's right. Steel clashes on steel as the man tries desperately to defend himself against the flurry of blows while still maintaining his hold on Ronan. But the man on the left takes advantage of being ignored and reaches for his dagger. I know I can't get there fast enough, and I don't have a good angle on him. I flip one of my daggers in my hand, pinch the tip, and let it fly. It lands in the neck of the man Felix is battling. He releases both Ronan and his sword as he falls to the ground clutching his throat. He makes the mistake of grabbing the handle and wrenching it from the wound with a gurgling cry. He's as good as dead.

Two down.

With rage in his eyes, Felix raises his sword to end the man on the ground as Ronan fights against his remaining captor. Time slows to a series of sluggish heartbeats as I watch the only remaining opponent tighten his grip on the dagger he's unsheathed and shove it forward, plunging it right into Felix's side.

He screams, I think. At least his mouth opens wide as he throws his head back. I can't hear anything except the pounding of my pulse in my ears. It seems to take the remaining attacker forever to reel backward in shock, release his grip on Ronan, and turn to run. It takes significantly less time for me to flip my other dagger and throw. It flies straight and true, landing between the man's shoulder blades and sending him crashing to the ground.

All of that can't have taken more than a few seconds, but an entire unlived lifetime flashes before me as I watch Ronan scramble across the ground to cradle Felix. My heart seizes, a primal fear clawing at my insides.

My brain can't process it. It refuses to. I see Felix clutching his side, blood pouring out between his fingers as he curls in on himself. I see Ronan holding Felix's head up and searching for the wound so he can apply pressure. I see Alara emerge from her tent with a sword in hand. But it's too late. It's all too late.

Then all that compresses into a single instant, and I'm down on my knees in the dirt, pulling Felix to me as he gasps for air.

His face is already gray underneath his bronzed skin. Ashen even. Of course, it is. My fire, which has burned so hot within me since we left the mainland, has turned him to ash. And there is no way to rebuild from ash. All those who love me eventually burn.

"Please," I choke out as I press a trembling, bloodied hand to his cheek. "You have to stay awake."

His eyes, so full of determination, find me, and a sad smile tugs at his mouth.

"Keep going." His words are so soft and raspy that I have to lean in until my cheek nearly presses against his to hear them. "You must."

"I won't leave you." My breath hitches as I push down a sob. "I can't."

"What should we do?" The panic in Ronan's voice tells me I'm not exaggerating the graveness of the situation.

"Keep pressure on that," I insist, placing my hand over his and feeling the slow, shallow rise and fall of Felix's chest. He's breathing but it's labored, and the pain in his eyes shatters me. "Can you carry him?" I ask Ronan.

"No," Felix insists, grabbing for my hand. I take his and press it to my mouth. I taste the metallic tang of blood.

"I told you that we're not leaving you," I snap. "Stop trying to be noble and keep breathing." I try to adopt his authoritative tone and demand obedience, but the sob in my voice and the tears rolling down my face speak more of panic than control.

"Alara." She's at my side instantly, awaiting instructions. "Run as fast as you can back to the camp. Tell them what has happened. Bring men and a stretcher back here so we can get him out. And tell Antony to ready the soldiers for attack."

"Mia," Felix whispers.

"No. I'm done holding back. Cyrus made this personal, and I'm going to make him regret it."

"Don't we need the Gate for that?" Ronan asks.

"Alara, go!" I shout and hear her crash through the trees, back down the mountain.

"Emilia," Felix tries again. This time I give him my full attention.

“You shouldn’t speak.” I stroke his face as my eyes frantically search him. Looking for what?

“Listen,” he chokes out. He laces trembling fingers with mine and presses them to his chest, right over his heart. It shudders a rapid rhythm under my palm. It’s not good, but it’s still there. Then he directs our hands toward my chest to rest over my heart. My pulse is steadier, but it gallops as if it might just leap out of my chest. “Listen here.”

Warm brown eyes stare me down, willing me to understand what he doesn’t have the words for. What is…

Then I feel it. The tug, the pull, the undeniable urge to move. He feels it, too. My eyes widen at the implication, but I try to shove the feeling down, to bury it under my worry for Felix, for all of us. This isn’t the time for this to happen. It can wait just a little longer.

But it can’t. A quick glance over my shoulder tells me the man I hit in the back with my dagger has regained his feet enough to disappear. Perhaps he’ll die on his way back to tell Cyrus of our location, but I wouldn’t bet on it. The odds are against us all today.

“You have to go.” Felix pats the place over my heart then fingers the opal dangling from the necklace at the hollow of my throat. “It’s not about you and me anymore. Not when we’re this close.”

“You have to promise to hang on.” I can no longer contain the sob that has been building within me. I feel the gentle pressure of Ronan’s hand on my shoulder, but I only collapse further onto Felix, burying my face in the crook of his neck. Then it’s his touch

I feel. The light presses of callused fingers on my cheek, wiping away my tears.

"Alara's getting help," Ronan reminds me. "I think it's a punctured lung. If we can get him back to camp..."

But I know the odds are slim. It took us hours to get here yesterday. Even if she sprints the entire way, precious minutes tick by.

God, please, please, please don't take him from me.

"Ronan, grab a bedroll and place it under him. Start dragging him toward the camp. It will hurt, but it's the best chance he has." I can't imagine the agony it's going to cause him, but there's nothing else for it. Better to have him alive and in pain than dead.

Fortunately, Ronan doesn't ask questions. I press my hand to Felix's side as Ronan removes his and sprints toward the tents. Blood oozes out between my fingers, but it's not gushing. That's a good sign, I think.

"You have to go," he insists again. The quiet urgency in his voice gets my attention like nothing else. Despite the labored breathing, the blood dripping from him, the pain he must be in, he manages a ferocity in his tone that captures me. "I could not live with myself if I was the cause of our failure. If Cyrus came for Ronan or you... Emilia, I could not live with myself. Please don't ask me to. I need you to finish this for us."

My heart is in so many pieces I'm not sure I'll ever be able to repair it. Because he's right. I know he's right. But I simply cannot fathom that this could be the last time I see him.

"God is within her," he quotes, "she will not fall."

"Listen to me," I whisper as I press my forehead against Felix's. My eyes flutter closed at the feel of his breath fanning my face. "You will live. It's not a suggestion, it's not a hope, it's an order. You will live, and we'll go home, and I'll marry you. And when I'm making you mine, I'll kiss this scar and remember how close I came to losing you. But I will *not* lose you. Do you understand?"

He huffs a laugh. "I would not dare disobey my queen."

"I am not your queen."

"You've ruled over my heart from the moment you recognized me at that ball. From that day forward, you were my queen." He tilts his head just slightly, angling to press his lips to mine.

"Don't you dare kiss me goodbye," I warn, my voice shaky with tears. "Save your breath."

"I can't breathe without you." He kisses me anyway. It's just the barest press of lips, but it pierces my heart. Instead of dulling the tug in my chest, it only intensifies it.

Here we are, with both my nightmares coming true. Felix bloodied on the ground, and this incessant pull inside me that will not relent no matter how I try to ignore it.

And so, I do maybe the most difficult thing that I've ever done.

I run.

I run away from Felix and towards something I can't see. My feet slip and slide over terrain I'm unfamiliar with and everything inside me screams to run back to him, to the familiar, to the safe, but something that is other than me, still deep inside me, pulls me forward as if I have little choice of my own.

"Fear not, for I am with you. Be not dismayed for I am your God. I will strengthen you, help you, and uphold you with my righteous right hand."

I don't know if those words are inside my head or out, but they propel my every step. Easier said than done. My fear is overwhelming, but I've seen my God perform miracles and wonders. He calmed a storm, parted the sea, and poured fire on our enemies. If He can do all that, certainly He can handle my fear.

40

I know it as soon as I lay eyes on it.

As if the pull inside me, strong enough now to nearly make me sick, wasn't enough, the mouth of this enormous cave looks exactly like the open mouth of a dragon. Similar to the one Felix took me to on Solitarius. It's a great big yawning opening, probably four times as tall as me. Light peaks through in intermittent rays through the cracks of the rocks overhead.

Here be dragons to be slain, here be rich rewards to gain . . . If we perish in the seeking, . . . why, how small a thing is death.

No small thing, indeed, but something much greater lies before me.

"Lead me," I whisper the prayer. Then I step forward with more confidence than I feel. It's drawing me in. Further up and further in.

I stumble over the uneven rocks forming the floor of the cave. Some pebbles, some boulders, and some jagged formations that snag the sleeves of my tunic. When the fabric tears, I rip it from my arm and fashion it into a makeshift torch with a branch lying near the entrance to the cave. It takes a bit longer to find rocks that will produce a spark, but eventually the fabric catches fire, illuminating the expanse of rock before me.

I think I liked it better when I couldn't see. Though the light doesn't reach far, it still shows me a cavernous opening before me, and I hear flowing water below.

Slowly, carefully, I climb down the rocks. I nearly drop the torch twice but manage to hang on. When I reach the bottom, my feet slide into the cool water of a gently flowing river. One step. Two. Testing the depth as I wade it.

Water rises to my waist as I push my legs through the weak current. I hold the torch aloft and keep my eyes in front of me where another rocky formation waits for me to climb.

Pain is my companion now, overwhelming even the fear and grief I feel for leaving Felix behind. My palms and knees bleed from where I drag myself up the rock faces and through narrow passages so tight, I barely dare to breathe. But I always take the next step.

As I emerge from one such passage, I have to blink from a light shining down ahead. How can there be light? I'm in a cave. It shouldn't be possible.

Mist curls around my feet as I move toward the light. Then my eyes travel up and up and up. Hundreds of feet above me is a large circular opening in the cave. Through it, sunlight pours in, illuminating a valley just below me. In the center of the circle of sunlight is a tight grouping of tall, narrow trees. They stretch toward the opening as if hoping to escape.

I take another step, eager to see this marvel up close. But when I half slide down the rocks to reach the valley floor, I freeze. What I assumed to be rocks bleached by the sun scattered across the valley floor are in fact something much darker.

Bones.

Just outside the copse of trees is a literal valley of bones.

I gasp as Antioch's notes come back to me. Bones, human skeletons, lie on the rocky ground as far as I can see. I don't know what occurred here, but it seems to possibly be some sort of massacre. What else would cause several people to die in a single place in this number? But though the fear whispers, a much louder voice roars inside of me. There is no other way to describe it, but a roar. It fills my ears, my lungs, my every breath, and it screams safety and power and something else that I have never been able to define, but that I always associate with my God.

He is here. I know it. The Ancient One. I have finally arrived at the Gate.

I tremble as I walk forward, trying not to step on the bones. And then suddenly, from nowhere, from an inexplicable place, a wind rushes through this dark cavern and ignites a fire in the center of the cavern. A fire so bright that it lights the entire place. The trees are still several hundred yards away, so it's not their wood that burns. This is something else entirely.

It burns orange and blue and white and gold and seems otherworldly. This is not a manmade fire. This is a sign. This is a wonder. This is my God. Though the wind still roars around me, there's an utter stillness in the cavern and in my heart. I can't explain what I'm seeing, hearing, and feeling, but I know it's something I'll never forget.

I can see now from wall to wall of the giant cavern, that the bones littering the rock floor are mostly clad in some sort of armor. Swords lay to the side of several of the soldiers. So, this was an army of some sort… but an army slaughtered in this remote place? It doesn't make any sense. I don't understand. There is so, so much that I don't understand. And I don't even know where to begin asking for answers. But I'm saved the necessity of asking when a voice—can it really be called a voice when it's both in and out of me—speaks directly out of the fire.

"Welcome my daughter," it says, and I hear it. And I feel it. And I taste the eucalyptus and sea salt on the air that now whirls around me, pulling my hair up in dark tendrils until it nearly stands straight up from my head.

Hair rises on my arms and a shiver runs down my spine, though I am neither cold nor afraid. Well, that might not be entirely true, but it's a different sort of fear than any I've encountered before. Not fear for my safety or fear for my life but fear more like awe. I somehow know that the voice from the fire could destroy me with a single word. And yet He has welcomed me and called me daughter.

And I know He is what I have come here for. Nothing else matters. Not Felix, not Ronan, not Cyrus's army. Nothing matters but this flame, this fire, and this voice.

I fall to my knees, somehow finding a bare spot on the ground, and bend forward until my forehead touches the cool surface of the rock.

"My King," I say in a quivering voice. I hardly recognize it as my own. "My God," I correct.

"Well done, my daughter," the voice says. "You have traveled far and fought a good fight, but your war is over."

At this, I lift my head despite the awe I still feel. The war is over?

No, He doesn't understand. I thought He could see everything, that He knew everything, but He must not know. Must not know that Felix is dying. That Cyrus threatens to overrun us all. That Cyrus will use the power I feel coursing through me right now to rule the empire and to wipe out the rest of the Insurgos and install a false god permanently into the pantheon of beliefs within the great empire.

God must not know, because if He knew He would never say the war was over. No, it still wages.

"My King," I say with more courage than I feel, "the Emperor has landed on the shore. He is coming. He will be here soon. He will follow my trail here and take the power and—"

"The power is not his for the taking," the voice says. "Neither is it yours. The power is mine alone. I am the King of Kings. I am the Ancient. I am the Heir of all. No one can take my power from me no matter how mighty they think themselves. The war is over because I say it is over. I will fight for you. You need only be still."

"Be still?" I ask slowly because I'm not comprehending the words. Be still. Surely, He doesn't mean that. We must act. We must have a plan. We must ride into battle with braveness and ferocity. With His signs and wonders leading the way. We must show our strength. 'Be still' does not tally with the situation. "But Cyrus—"

"I will handle Cyrus," the voice interrupts. "He is not yours to deal with. He has called on gods he does not believe in and yet refuses to acknowledge me. I will deal with him as I see fit. I have called *you* to be still. Have I not shown you my signs and my wonders? Have I not stood in the fire with you? Have I not parted the seas and given you hope when you had none? You think I am finished while I'm not. I will give you an army—this army, this army of bones—to show you that the fight is not yours. The fight is mine. You are merely a conduit for my power. As you have been all along."

An army of bones? Maybe I did hit my head because I do not understand this. What am I supposed to do? Carry a sack full of dried bones back to Cyrus on the beach as some sort of show of aggression? It makes no sense. What am I gonna do with a bag of bones? I came for power. I came for understanding. I came for help.

"Who do you say that I am, Emilia?" the voice asks as if it can read my mind, but then again, I'm very sure He can. He knows exactly what I'm thinking. I don't even need to speak it, but I do anyway.

"You are my God. You are the true king. The only one worth fighting for, which is why I want you to help me. To let me fight. To let me win this battle—this war—for you, for the Insurgos. So, we can worship you freely and show the world you are the true God."

"I do not need you to fight my battles for me. I am the one who breathed the world into existence. I sprinkled the stars into the night sky. I raise the sun in the palm of my hand every morning and lower it below the horizon every evening. I raised mountains and carved canyons. I sent rushing waters over the earth. I parted the sea. It does what I wish. And you think that I cannot fight my own battles? This army that lies before you did not perish at the hand of another army. This army was destroyed when they turned their backs on me, and now they will have their moment of redemption. And you will learn the power I possess, that I will fight my own battles, and that your purpose is solely to point others to me.

"When the time comes, when the heat of the battle is upon you, when the moment seems most dire, you will not pick up a sword. You will lift your hands toward the heavens, and you will pray to me. You will ask for protection and guidance, and I will grant you what you ask. But you must not pick up a weapon. The war you wage is against principalities and powers that are far beyond anything physical. Therefore, your weapon must not be physical. You will pray. You will call out to me, and I will save you and your people. And I will do miraculous things that will show everyone who I am. The people will know this day, who the true king is, who the heir to this world truly is. I am the Ancient Heir, and those who find their way through this narrow gate have truly found me. I will be their king, and they will be my people. I will prosper them and give them their promised land."

"And what of the sacrifice?"

Another gust of wind rushes over me, nearly knocking me backward despite my kneeling position.

"Stand, my daughter."

I can do nothing but obey.

"Now step into the flames."

Surely, He doesn't mean that. He can't mean that. He must know what fire does to me, given my history with Cyrus, with my mother, with everything that's happened.

I don't know. I just don't think I can do it. But there's this insistence that won't leave me alone, that almost pushes me forward. And though I'm terrified and shaking, my foot steps out almost without my consent. And I'm moving forward slowly, carefully avoiding the bones all around me, until I'm right up next to the fire.

It is neither warm nor cool, but it brings some sort of comfort that fills me. And yet there are chill bumps on my arms because there's an other-worldly sense to it. I suppose that's accurate given the source.

"Come closer, my daughter. Into the flames."

But I stand still, ironically, as He has instructed me to do. My feet are just on the edge of the flames, but I can't bring myself to take that last step. Even though His voice comforts me, there's a fear that lives inside me too.

I close my eyes, remembering my mother and how the flames engulfed her. She was bound and went to her death willingly for this same God that now beckons me to step into the flames. I don't miss the irony there, and I'm sure He doesn't either. So how can He ask this of me? How can He ask me to take this next step while knowing my history, my past and, in all likelihood, my future? Yet I remember what Antioch said to me about taking the next step, even though the whole path is not illuminated. I also remember the feeling of taking a step and not knowing the ground was going to fall out beneath me. I don't know which will be true of the step I'm about to take, yet I feel I must take it if I am to ever move forward. If I am to save the Insurgos, if I am to ever be able to live with myself, if I am ever to leave this cavern, I must step forward.

Ashes.

I have always feared the flame, but now I know what I must do. I must become it.

Ashes.

I've been afraid of burning—of burning those I love to ashes. But that's not what's happening here. But I know now that passion, that burning, was placed inside me for a purpose and burns just like this flame. It's time I do something about it.

Ashes.

So, I take that last step, and I become the fire.

And I burn.

41

I expect the pain, but it doesn't come. The flames lick around me, and everything else disappears. I can see nothing but blue and white and orange tinged with red. I am conscious of nothing except this moment, the here and now. And I am not alone. There is someone else in the fire.

The Ancient. The Heir. The King of Kings.

I can't see Him exactly. There are no features to make out, but the shape of a man stands before me, beside me. Without thinking, I bow before Him and press my forehead to the ground. Who am I to even stand in His presence? All my bravado melts with the flames and morphs into a weighty peace. I am not alone.

His hand cups my chin and lifts my head. Again, my eyes see nothing but flames, but I feel His presence all around me, hotter and more brilliant than the fire.

"Emilia, my daughter." The Ancient's voice feels like it's coming from inside me rather than without. As if it's been buried in my heart all along. "This is the moment I created you for. You have been my plan since before you were born."

"But I am not the Ruler Who was Promised. That's Felix."

"I am the one who made the promise, and I decide what the fulfillment of the promise will be. Felix will have his own role in it."

"But how? He's dying." Tears spring to my eyes as I remember his ashen face, the weak press of his hand against mine.

"I am telling your story. I will tell Felix his own story. It has not come to an end. I am the Ancient of ages past and the hope and heir of ages to come. I am the fire and the sea. I rule over all and in all. Do you think anything is too hard for me? Do you think any situation is too small or too large to be under my control? It is not. I hold the power of life and destruction in my hands—the same hands that hold you. I know you, Emilia. You are my precious child. I know your heart—your doubts, your fears, and your love and devotion. You are my daughter and the heir to all good things I would give you. When you passed through deep waters, I was with you. You now stand in the flames and are not burned. I will consume the armies before you and turn them to ash. I will give you beauty for your ashes if you will but exchange your heaviness for praise of me. Of your king, your true father."

All around me, the cavern begins to rattle. Distantly, my mind contemplates all the things it could be—an avalanche, a floor, a fall of trees—but nothing pulls my attention from the being in front of me. He is causing this. I feel certain of it.

"Look, my daughter. Examine the bones you stepped over on your way to me."

Every hair on my body stands as I turn to take in the scattered bones that littered the path here. But there are no bones. In their place are the bodies of nearly two hundred men. Actual men. With hair and skin and the remnants of their armor. Not just men, an army. I fall back to my knees, mouth agape.

"When your hope is dried up like these bones, I will give life again."

"Please, God," I whisper. "Let them live again."

"Call to the winds, and I will breathe my life into them. They will march forward as your army."

The words come to me as if I've always known them.

"Come, breath, from the four winds and breathe into these slain, that they may live."

A swirl of wind whips through the cavern, so fierce that I clamp my eyes shut and curl up into the smallest position possible. All around me there are gasps and shouts, and when I dare to open my eyes, an entire army stands before me. The breath of life in their lungs, and the power of God in their eyes.

I stare. They're really there. Where there was nothing but dry bones and hopelessness now stand mighty warriors, ready to answer my call to the cause.

The front line of men part, and I gasp. Striding toward me with even, confident steps is a man that looks so like Felix it makes my heart ache.

Caspian. It can be none other than the high lord himself. This was his army. This cave was the dragon he rode away on, never to be seen again. Except I am seeing him, and he is bowing to me.

I wait for instruction from the Ancient, but nothing more comes. I look behind me, and the fire has vanished, leaving not a single ash or ember behind.

"My Queen." Even Caspian's voice reminds me of Felix. He holds out a hand to me. I offer a shaking hand to him, and he takes it. His skin is just as warm, maybe warmer, than mine. Though he was bones just moments ago, there is nothing about his appearance that suggests it. He kisses the back of my fingers and releases my hand. "There is a battle to fight, is there not?"

Am I really about to lead this army down a mountain, march into Cyrus's camp, and end this once and for all?

Yes. Yes, I am.

It occurs to me, as Caspian gathers his soldiers into ranks and files, that I have no idea how this many men ended up in this cave. Or maybe it wasn't a cave at that point. The Ancient told me this army was destroyed for turning against Him, for their betrayal. What if it was their betrayal that brought out the Great Wave that sank most of this island? Perhaps that's how they died.

Now their hearts beat for redemption. As does mine.

Rather than marching back the way I came, which would take ages to crawl through those narrow passageways, Caspian orders them to march forward. I follow without question. Much like Felix, he commands respect and obedience without harshness.

We exit the cave on a beach I don't recognize. Caspian seems to know exactly where he's going though. Something pulls him forward just as it pulled me toward the cave. There's no tug in me now. Just a consistent hum of power that's not my own.

As we march on, cliffs rise high on my left as the waves surge up the shore on my right. It looks much more like the portion of beach where Cyrus made his camp than the one we set up on. A few more minutes confirms this.

We round a corner, and the sounds the cliffs and waves had blocked roar over us. Battle cries and the cacophony of steel on steel accompany the melee before us. A true melee. This is no organized battle. This is chaos.

Caspian shouts something to the men behind us, but I don't listen. I can't take my eyes off the sight before me. How long was I in that cave? Long enough for Alara to reach camp with my orders and for Antony to march on Cyrus. I search the mass of soldiers and the bodies on the ground, looking for anyone I recognize, but this far away, I can't make out faces.

"You have your orders?" Caspian's voice finally breaks through my shock, and I start to look at him.

"My orders?" I'm weaponless. My daggers and the sword I briefly wielded were left behind with Felix and Ronan. I have nothing to attack with.

I can't pick up a sword. No weapons. That's what the Ancient told me. My weapon is prayer, and just now, facing down the violence in front of me, it feels hopelessly weak. But I know better. I may be weak, but He is strong. It's what Antioch had tried to tell me. Now I understand.

"Yes," I choke out. "I have my orders."

"Up there." Caspian points to the clifftop nearest us, which overlooks the beach below. It's not as tall as some of the others around it, but it's still a significant climb. "Your position is up there. Our God will fight for you. You need only be still."

He doesn't wait for my response as he swings his sword to the battle in front of him, and yells for his men to charge.

42

I don't know how I make it to the summit of this cliff. My palms, already raw from scraping across the rocks of the cave, now pour blood from the deeper cuts the cliff tore into them. My entire body quakes with exhaustion, but giving up is not an option. I am a soldier, and these are my orders. I will fulfill them with my very life if that's what's required. I only hope my courage holds up if the moment comes.

The battle below me is absolute chaos. Hundreds of men clash, sword against sword. It sets my teeth on edge and sends a chill down my spine. Fear wraps icy fingers around my heart. Those are my men down there, my friends even. And they are dying.

If anything, the arrival of Caspian's troops has produced more chaos, and I realize my army will not immediately know they're here to help.

Show them the truth. Unite them against the common enemy.

Prayer is all I can do. Even a shout from this distance wouldn't reach them. For his part, Caspian and his men seem to know exactly who the enemy is, and I watch them strike down soldier after soldier from Cyrus's army as they charge into the melee. Antony will see Caspian, I tell myself. He'll see him and see the resemblance to Felix. He'll know somehow.

God, I hope so.

I reign my thoughts in before they can drift too far afield. If I think of Felix, of Ronan, even Alara, I'm useless. My fear and worry will paralyze me.

Somehow a scuffle of rocks breaks through the silence in my head, and I open my eyes to see the very last thing I expected.

Cyrus stands before me in his finest armor and a truly impressive sword held loosely at his side. He's panting a bit from having just climbed up this cliff, but there's an evil leer on his face that leaves little doubt what he's come here to do. Does that mean Ronan's already dead? Has he abandoned his son in order to kill me instead?

No. God, please, no.

My eyes squeeze shut, and tears roll down my face. I can feel the heat, the wetness of them on my cheeks, and I focus on that rather than my fear. Rather than on my lack of a weapon. My nails dig into the palms of my hands as I try to restrain from reaching for any sort of makeshift weapon—a rock or anything I could defend myself with. But I'm not supposed to.

"Be still."

My blood runs cold, and my heart pounds as if it's trying to pound out a lifetime of beats in the few moments I clearly have left. Though I think I could take the sword from Cyrus if I tried, I've been instructed not to fight. Everything in me balks at this. Self-preservation screams out that it would be stupid not to disarm the man and cut off the head of this snake. Wouldn't that solve everything?

"This foe has already been vanquished."

The words ring loudly inside my head until the sounds of the storm and battle below are drowned out. All I hear is the voice of the Ancient. Then it's as if I'm right back in that fire. Warmth swells up inside of me, and I'm gripped with both awe and determination. And then a certainty that could not have come from within me overwhelms me, and I know just what to pray.

God, the outcome of this battle is not uncertain. You have already won the victory. Declare it now over these armies. Declare it over me. Show them your glory as you showed it to me. Announce your coronation as King of Kings. Show them that you yourself are the Ruler that was promised.

"Where is your God now?" Cyrus yells over the wind and the roar of battle and crashing sea. All the noises I'd blocked out come roaring back. "Who will save you now?"

"My God is able to save and deliver anyone He wants to. He will do so at your expense, Cyrus. You and your army will not live to see another sunrise." The words that spill out of me are not my own. Sure, my mouth moves, and the voice is mine, but the certainty of this promise is from something much higher than me.

Cyrus throws back his head and laughs. "There is no one to save you. My son has run like the coward he is. Your Commander is dead or dying. And you—you have no weapon. You have no power. You have no hope."

He's right on almost all accounts. Almost.

I close my eyes again, determined to stay the course no matter how much everything inside me screams to run or to fight. To do anything except be still. But my God has not failed me yet. Even when He has wounded me, His healing has made me stronger in the broken places. I will not turn my back on His faithfulness now.

I remember the words I heard Felix praying on a balcony in Borealis what feels like a lifetime ago. *"Nothing exceeds Your power. Nothing is too hard for You to do or too good for You to give. I know I ask much, but I ask great things of a great God."*

And with my eyes closed, awaiting what is sure to be a death blow, I add my own words. *You make the darkness tremble. The deeper the darkness, the brighter Your glory shines. Light up the skies and show them all Your glory.*

I hear the whistle of steel as I imagine Cyrus drawing his sword, but I keep my eyes closed, and I keep praying. I don't want him to have the satisfaction of seeing any residual fear in my eyes. Because I *am* afraid. But I pray anyway.

God, be the all-consuming flame, the fire that lights the way and burns away all things unworthy of You.

The clang of steel on steel makes my eyes fly open despite my determination to keep them closed. And there, just a few feet in front of me, is Felix.

On his knees, chin lifted in defiance as he holds back Cyrus's sword from me with his own sword. He is the only thing between me and the death blow. Where did he come from? How did he make that climb up here?

It's impossible that he's here, that he's even alive. My heart lurches into my throat as I reach out and place my hand on his back to assure myself this isn't some sort of delusion. Heat radiates from him as the muscles of his back quiver with strain against my touch. He's holding on but barely.

My lips move in prayer, and I feel power rush through me like the wind in the cave. I don't dare look away from Felix and Cyrus, but I keep my mind focused on begging God for our salvation. He has not brought us this far to let us fall. He has promised victory, and there is no victory for me if Felix loses this match.

Felix's breath comes in ragged gasps as he holds his position between me and Cyrus. I know there's a dagger somewhere on him, and all it would take is a quick movement for me to unsheathe it and plunge it into the emperor. But I can't. I won't. My weapon is prayer, and I wield it with more power now than ever before.

Cyrus is straining, too. His ice blue eyes are wide as he bares his teeth at Felix and pushes their crossed swords further toward him. Then his eyes flash away from Felix and to me. A cruel smile curls his mouth, and I know he can taste victory. He twists his wrist slightly, causing Felix to lose more ground to him. The Emperor's blade reflects a dark gleam, just like his soul.

"This is the best you have?" he taunts. "The brave Commander and the helpless princess. What a pathetic end to a futile rebellion."

This is it. At least if we're going to die, it will be together. I wrap my arms around Felix, shoring up his biceps as they tremble against the weight of Cyrus's sword. But I'm not at full strength either, and I'll only be able to hold him up for a few minutes at most.

Suddenly, Felix and I both fall forward, me on top of him, as Cyrus raises his arm and releases Felix's sword. For a brief unexplainable moment, I think we've been given a reprieve. Then I see Cyrus is only drawing back for the death blow.

Movement from just behind him catches my attention for the briefest of moments before the bloodied blade of a sword pushes through Cyrus's chest, and he crashes to his knees.

Ronan stands behind him, chest heaving, eyes blazing. He looks every bit an avenging angel.

The next moment is an eternity. Cyrus's eyes widen in disbelief. He looks down at where the blade protrudes from the near center of his chest. The strike was as precise as it was lethal—a lifetime of familial discord culminating in a single, decisive strike. He slides forward, slipping off the blade still held in Ronan's hand. He twitches once, twice, then goes still.

Ronan's face is a mask of anguish and resolve as he stands over his fallen father. The magnitude of what he's just done washes over him, taking all the color from his face. His sacrifice—because I know from his reaction that it was a sacrifice—has just paved the way for our freedom.

But the future still feels uncertain. Felix shudders beneath me as he tries to get to his feet. Fresh blood seeps from the wound in his side, and his breaths are ragged and uneven. It cost him everything to reach me in time.

He's trying to get to Ronan, to comfort his friend. The prince drops to his knees behind his father's body. His shoulders slump and begin to shake with what I can only assume are sobs.

Before Felix can make it to his feet, something darts in front of Ronan, nearly knocking him to the ground. I'm on alert, ready to spring into action, but the sight of long, dark hair stops me.

It's Alara. She's also appeared from nowhere and thrown herself into Ronan's arms without a care of who's watching or that he's still gripping a sword.

I turn away because this feels like a private moment I shouldn't intrude on. The enormity of what he's just done likely won't hit Ronan full force until later, but this initial shock is more than enough to process. And it's a grief that belongs to him but not to me. I am not sorry Cyrus is dead, though I am sorry it was Ronan who slew him. I know what it means to take a life, what it costs. It is a high price that leaves a debtor's mark even when the price has been paid. Because even though God offers forgiveness, forgiving yourself is more difficult. This I know well.

Felix falls back against me, chest heaving, as his weight pushes us both back until my back presses against a rock. I follow his gaze as he stares past Cyrus's still form to Alara and Ronan. They are utterly still but so entwined around each other that I can't tell where one ends and the other begins. Part of me feels I should say something, do something, but my body refuses to respond. I'm keenly aware of Felix's deep inhales and exhales as he pants from exhaustion, but he doesn't speak either. There are no words for this. No shouts of joy, no celebratory cheers. It is a victory, but right now it feels like no win at all.

Far below us on the beach, the sounds of metal on metal and shouts of men still ring loud and true. The battle still rages, both armies unaware of what has transpired up here.

Something tugs at my hand, and I look down to see Felix lacing his fingers with mine. A heady warmth surges through me as he begins to pray. I don't think. I just squeeze his hand, close my eyes, and join his whispered words with a prayer of my own. The din of the fighting fades away until it's replaced with a ringing silence.

The silence is so loud that it pulls me from my prayer. I open my eyes and notice Felix has stopped praying as well. He still holds tightly to my hand, but his gaze is towards the cliff's edge now.

"Do you hear that?" His voice is a gruff whisper. It's the first thing he's said to me since arriving on this cliff.

"No," I reply with a shake of my head. I don't hear anything, and for some reason that terrifies me.

"Me neither." Felix lets go of my hand and starts to push himself to a standing position before collapsing to his knees with exhaustion. I try to go to him but find my limbs are shaking and will in no way support my weight either. Instead, I drag myself over to him, rocks pressing into my bleeding palms but with a pain I no longer register. It seems so inconsequential right now.

He looks me over as if seeing me for the first time since I left him in the forest. Dark eyes search my face before his mouth sets in a grim line, and he nods. As if I know exactly what he means by this, my body instinctively follows as he crawls over the rocks to the cliff's edge. I join him there, our sides pressed together as we lie on our bellies and look down at the beach below.

My jaw drops.

Every soldier still standing is utterly still. No fighting, no running. Maybe not even breathing. Every eye is focused on the sky over the sea where dark clouds have formed with an unnatural uniformity. The black mass begins to swirl, the edges fanning out slightly against the deep blue sky. Then, from the center of the tornado, bursts bright white-orange flames.

Just as they did last time, they seem to target Cyrus's camp, or what's left of it. Tents burn as do the men who run from the flames. Charred remains litter the beach as the fire consumes the material and bodies scattered about.

Then, as a wave, every other soldier—mine, Caspian's, and what remains of Cyrus's—fall to their knees. The flames sweep over their heads, turning anyone still standing to ash.

Thunder booms, but I know it's not the natural kind. It's the voice of the Ancient, but He isn't speaking to me this time. I watch as Caspian slowly rises, his head still bowed.

"Who is that?" Felix gasps in a whisper.

"Caspian." My voice is just a breath as I whisper his name. "He brought his army."

I feel Felix's eyes on me, but I can't look away from the scene on the beach. I don't know what's happening in the exchange between the high lord and the Ancient, but a moment later, Caspian turns to his men, and four of them rise.

With quick, purposeful strides, the men make their way through the bodies and kneeling men and surround the Palanquin. I know with an eerie certainty they've done this before. They kneel as one, then rise, each bearing a pole of the holy relic on their shoulder.

Caspian's soldiers—bones just hours ago—rise and let out a victorious shout. Their joy, their triumph is so overwhelming, the warmth of it seeps into my bones even at this distance. At their lord's command, they assemble into formation around the Palanquin.

I watch as Caspian lifts his hands toward the swirling clouds in the sky. His mouth moves, but there's no way I can hear his words. But seemingly in response to them, another spout of flames pours from the cloud. This movement isn't aggressive like the first wave. Rather, it's a fluid flow of fire that swirls in the air and takes shape.

A chariot of flames drawn by two white-flamed horses glides down from the heavens and sweeps across the beach, parting all the men still kneeling on the ground. It rests in front of Caspian, and without hesitation, he steps forward into the chariot. Into the fire.

At his movement, the black clouds above begin to spin faster, sending gusts of tunneling wind through my hair that would surely knock me down if I wasn't already on my belly. It blasts against my face, and I slam my eyes shut against the force of it.

Seconds later, it stills. Cautiously, I count to three then open my eyes.

Caspian is gone. And so are his men and the Palanquin. So are the black clouds that brought such destruction but also victory. For every soldier in Cyrus's army has laid down their arms. Some are openly sobbing while others remained bowed.

Tears run down my face, too. Maybe from the stinging wind, but probably from the awe of it all. I reach for Felix, needing something firm and stable to hold on to, but my hands find only the rocks beside me. My head whips in his direction, and my heart leaps into my throat.

Felix lies on his back, hand pressed to his newly opened wound, eyes squeezed shut in obvious pain. A gasp chokes me as I crawl to him and pull his upper body into my lap. He groans, and his eyes flutter. My fingers find his on the place against his side, and my other pats his cheek lightly.

"Open your eyes," I plead. "You have to stay awake."

His eyes blink open slowly. "I don't think I can make it back down," he admits. "It hurts so much."

And it must. I've never heard Felix complain. Not when he took an arrow to the leg or another, less serious, stab wound to the side.

“I can carry him.” Ronan appears in front of us, eyes dull but hands outstretched. Alara stands just behind him, warily studying Felix.

I hesitate because it already looks like he’s carrying too much. But what other choice do we have? The army is too far away for me to yell for help. One of the three of us could go for reinforcements, but it would take so long for them to arrive. With reluctance, I nod to Ronan.

“Wait,” Alara says, placing a hand on Ronan’s arm to still him. “All three of us can do it. Ronan, grab him under his arms, and Emilia and I will take his legs.”

We’re just about to roll Felix to his side and begin the painful process of lifting him when I hear a familiar voice calling my name in the distance. I pause and listen.

“Emilia! Princess?!”

Antony. A swell of relief washes over me.

“Here!” I yell as loud as I can and gesture for Alara to run toward the voice.

Seconds later, Antony tops the cliff with ten men following him. He slides to a stop when he sees Felix, his face paling.

“I thought I saw you standing up here in the battle,” he pants as his eyes dart from me to Felix. “Then I saw the prince head in this direction. I didn’t know… The Commander? Is he…”

“Still alive,” Felix mutters with his eyes closed.

“He can’t walk down,” I explain, though I’m sure it’s obvious. “I don’t know how he made it up here in the first place.” He has a lot of explaining to do when we get home. Because we are going to make it home.

"Nothing could keep me from you," Felix whispers as his eyes flutter open again. One side of his mouth ticks up in a crooked smile. "Not even death itself."

"Stop being dramatic. You're not going to die," I insist and hope I sound more confident than I feel.

"No, I'm not. Because you made me promises." He removes his hand from his side and brushes his bloody thumb over my ring finger. "I intend to make good on them." His eyes drift up to meet mine, and the emotion there makes it hard for me to breathe as well. "*All* of them."

43

It takes some time to sort out the aftermath of the battle. I have never been more thankful for Antony who oversees the majority of tasks while I watch over Felix. He is stable but still in considerable pain. So, when Alara disappears and then returns with some mashed berries she offers for the pain, I don't question her. I've had enough experience with her concoctions that I'm well aware she knows exactly what she's doing.

The remaining men in Cyrus's army—the former Imperial Guard—have officially surrendered. The four Insurgo men they abducted from Solitarius were not among them. I don't know if they died in one of the attacks or were executed by Cyrus on his quest to find a sacrifice to access the power in the Palanquin.

Antony calls for Ronan who presides over the remaining hundred or so men and receives their oaths of fealty. He is the heir to the Aurora throne and the Atlas Empire. He accepts their words with a gracious nod, then retreats to Alara. It's too much to ask of him now, but there isn't a choice. There never has been for us.

Royals don't have the luxury of choice when it comes to responsibilities. And, for whatever doubts I had about the prince when we undertook this journey, he has proved himself worthy in my eyes to wear the crown.

After much coordination between armies and consolidation of remaining supplies, we board the Imperial naval vessel and sail for Solitarius. The decision of who stays and who goes will be dealt with when we are all fed and rested. I cringe to think what the citizens of Solitarius are going to think about my bringing not one, but two armies to their shores.

As it turns out, I needn't have worried.

When our ship docks the next morning at the same pier I arrived at just a few days ago, a crowd gathers to greet us. Though I'm reluctant to leave his side, I leave Felix with Antony and the others who will carry him from the ship while I descend the gangplank to break the news to his mother.

I don't have to look far. Miriam stands at the front of the crowd, her grim expression in stark contrast to the cheering and singing going on all around us. It must be a mother's intuition, but she knows something is wrong. By her side is Selah, who looks just as serious. Her eyes scan the disembarking soldiers behind me, no doubt looking for her brother.

"Felix?" Miriam asks in a tone low enough to be for my ears only as I reach her.

"Alive," I say with a sigh. Her shoulders slump with relief. "He's in some pain, but Alara was able to give him something to dull some of it. He needs to see a healer as soon as he's off the ship, though."

"We'll bring him to my house," she insists, leaving no room for argument. "There is plenty of room, and he'll have every comfort I can provide. Selah, run and fetch Galen and have him come to the house."

The little girl hesitates for a moment, then throws her arms around me in a quick hug before disappearing into the crowd.

"I'm sorry I couldn't keep him safe." The apology feels necessary even though Felix is a grown man who can make his own choices. But I feel like Miriam had entrusted me with her only son, and I brought him back broken.

"Emilia." She presses her hand against my cheek with a knowing smile. Just like her son, she conveys so much in just speaking my name. "Felix was never destined for 'safe'. But if he's anything like the little boy who left home, he loves fiercely, and that requires risk."

If she only knew how much. But that's between Felix and me. Maybe Ronan and Alara, too. Though we haven't spoken about what happened on that cliffside, nor of the attack in the forest before we all parted ways, the bond forged between us is stronger. None of us could have survived it without the others. We are stronger together.

"I assume the Synod will want a full debriefing." I change the subject because the emotions she's dredging up threaten to overwhelm me.

"Later," Miriam answers as she clasps my hand. "There's much to say, but it can wait until everyone is settled. Look, there's Felix now."

I look over my shoulder and see he's shuffling down the gangplank rather than being carried. A rueful smile tugs at my lips. One of his arms is draped around Antony and the other around Ronan. Of course, he had to walk.

As soon as they reach the pier, Antony turns to say something to Ronan, then abandons his position to run straight for the crowd. I'm confused until I see him lift Hannah high in the air and then pull her down for a kiss. My heart flips with happiness for them. They'll get their wedding after all.

Felix scans the crowd, and I see the exact moment he finds me. His face lights up as if she hasn't seen me for days, and he points in my direction so Ronan knows which way to help him. I don't wait for him to reach me. I approach the men and slip under Felix's arm, taking Antony's place as his crutch. His hand drapes over my shoulder, and his fingers stroke the end of my braid.

"We made it," I say softly as I look up into his handsome face which has begun to regain some of its color. "We're home."

It takes a week for Felix to heal enough to be up and about for more than a few minutes at a time. Though he's begged to join me, Ronan, and Alara at the house we share at the edge of the city, I've insisted he remain at his mother's house and close to the healer Galen until he's been cleared. Galen insists Felix was very lucky, and the blade only pierced a small portion of his lung, which should heal on its own. I know it wasn't luck.

Ronan and I gave a briefing to the Synod on what transpired on Draconis. At the conclusion, Ronan announced his intent to return to Aurora as the king. To my surprise, his first decree was that the people of Solitarius should choose a figurehead to represent them and their interests in the Atlas empire. His instruction sends the Synod scrambling until he tells them he'll allow them six months to make the decision before he will require the presence of the one chosen in Aurora so he can make a proclamation to the rest of the empire that Solitarius is a real and legitimate part of the political landscape.

I'm proud of him for thinking so clearly. The complicated grief that must war within him has not prevented him from taking charge as he must, but I wonder the toll it will take on him as he returns home.

Two weeks after we return from Draconis, Ronan and his army are ready to set sail for the mainland. They'll be returning home in the Imperial vessel his father brought over. Felix gave all the soldiers who arrived with Antony the option to return as well. A few took it, but most of them have decided to stay, including Antony and Hannah. If Solitarius is to be a contributing member of the empire, they will need an army, and this is a good start.

Felix and I stand shoulder to shoulder at the entrance to the pier as Ronan and Alara approach hand in hand. Despite what I witnessed on that cliff, the sight is still strange to me. And yet somehow perfect. They stop in front of us, and we all look each other over. Then Ronan breaks the stillness as he drops Alara's hand and steps forward to wrap Felix in an embrace.

Felix hesitates for just the breadth of a second then returns the hug with a fierce one of his own. I feel as if I'm intruding on something special between the two of them, so I look away and find Alara staring at me strangely, almost wistfully.

I pause because I'm not sure what to do. But it seems clear to me what Ronan's intentions are and what Alara's destiny is to be. So, I do what I have been taught since I was a child. I bow my head and curtsy deeply.

"Highness," I say with all sincerity as I bend my knees. She is queen in all but the crown, which will surely be waiting for her when she arrives in Aurora. And she deserves it.

For just a moment nothing stirs between us, and then I'm pulled to my feet and wrapped in a hug that stuns me. Alara pulls me tight to her and whispers in my ear. "Thank you...for everything.

"You were born for this," I say, hugging her back just as tightly.

She holds me back at arm's length and searches my face. "I have no idea what I'm doing. I don't know how to be a queen."

My heart aches for her because I know that feeling well. "Just be you. That's the person Ronan fell in love with. That's the girl he chose to stand by his side while he undertakes this enormous task. And more importantly, that's the woman God chose for this role. He chose you, and He doesn't make mistakes."

"You don't think He could have gotten us confused?" She offers me a wobbly smile.

"Not a chance. I'm clearly the better looking one. No way He could confuse us."

She laughs and hugs me tight.

44

We stand on the beach at sunset. Warm sand slides between my toes as I shift my weight in anticipation. It's the first time I've been alone with Felix for more than a few minutes since we returned from Draconis.

He has healed almost miraculously. The occasional pain still plagues him, but like my nightmares, it has faded. He has added another scar to his body and lived to tell about it.

His hands trail up my sides until his fingers tangle in the blowing strands of my hair. A smile tugs at his lips, and he cradles the back of my head to tilt my mouth up to his for a kiss.

There's something different. The hunger and heat that flooded our last few kisses are still there, but there's a deeper current. Something much more permanent and binding. His lips slide from my mouth to my jaw, and I tilt my head back to give him better access.

"I met with the Synod today," he tells me as his lips ghost over my skin.

I smile with my eyes closed. I knew this was coming. No one has disclosed it to me, but I knew given time, the Synod would come to the obvious conclusion.

"They want to make me their ruler…their king." His mouth pauses at the sensitive skin just below my ear.

"What did you tell them?" I ask, my voice heavy with bliss.

"That I needed to talk to you."

I lean back so I can look at him fully. It's not unexpected, but I had hoped I wouldn't have to talk him into accepting the role he was born for.

"You know I will support you in whatever way I can. You deserve the chance to lead."

"I won't do it without you," he says firmly, hands drifting down to my waist.

"You don't have to," I frown in confusion. "I'll be behind you every step of the way."

"I want you beside me." A small worry line forms between his brows as he purses his lips slightly. "I want you as my queen—as my coregent. Either we both wear the crown or neither."

I consider the terms. I left my crown in Borealis and had no intention of ever picking it up again. For my whole life, it brought me pain, death, and obstacles. But it also brought me Felix.

"You are Caspian's heir." I press a hand to his cheek, and he leans into it. "You were born to be king."

"And you are the only one who made me believe that could be true. I spent more than half of my life believing I was not good enough to come home. I didn't deserve forgiveness; I didn't deserve grace. I needed to earn it. But at that ball, you saw my hands, my hard-earned callouses, and knew who I was despite the mask. All the years spent training, pushing, and punishing my body for my transgressions culminated in that moment. Later you saw every scar. Right here on this beach, you touched every one, claimed it, redeemed it. And I felt invincible."

He kneels before me and reaches into a pocket. With trembling fingers, he produces a ring. It's unlike the ring I was supposed to wear upon my marriage to Ronan. It's not dainty or flashy. This is strong and lovely. The metal is some sort of rich, dark gold, and an opalescent white stone shimmers in the center of the band. It reminds me of my necklace in the way the colors shift, but there is no darkness in this stone.

"I am asking you to be my queen. More than that, I'm asking you to be my partner."

It's not nervousness, because I've never been more sure of anything in my life. Rather it's like a spring of joy that threatens to bubble over. Even he can't contain it. Tears make his brown eyes glisten in the dying sun as he takes my hands in his much larger ones.

"Yes," I whisper. He is worth it. Worth the price of a crown, the hardship of ruling, the sacrifices of service. But we are both living proof that God heals the brokenhearted and wounded.

Felix slides the ring onto my finger, and I immediately pull him to his feet. He leans in to kiss me, but I stop him with a hand on his chest. I made him a promise, and I intend to keep it.

When I was a girl and dreamed of my wedding day, I never imagined it like this. It's nothing like I prayed for. It's infinitely better. Just the two of us before God. I will make my vows to the ones who matter most and them alone. I don't need a dress or cake or any sort of fanfare. With my words, I will claim Felix as God's gift to me. My husband.

"I was never sure of who I was, who I was supposed to be, but you were. Even when I didn't believe in myself, you believed enough for both of us. You saw my strength and encouraged it even when it broke your heart." I can't help but wipe away a tear that rolls down his cheek. "I promise to love you with all that strength and much more. In every mundane task and every adventure. In every argument and in every moment of joy. I choose you. I vow before God to honor and cherish you in every moment, through His strength and not my own. To love you as wildly and recklessly as I always have, but with a commitment that is solid and lasting."

I can't keep up with the tears sliding down his face now. He's so different from the soldier who rode in my military camp to whisk me away to Aurora. He was closed off to me then, but now I see him for exactly who he is.

"I spent so many years running from my past. What I didn't know was that I was running straight to you. You brought me home." He takes a shuddering breath and cups the back of my neck, letting his thumbs rest just on the corners of my jaw. "I vow before God to make a home with you, to love you on the good days and bad. To cherish your strength and support you in weakness. I promise to be your partner in all things. And I promise to love you without abandon, without limits, and—occasionally—without control."

There's nothing left to say. Nothing that can be put into words anyway.

We fall into each other that night, claiming the grief and hurt and scars of the other as our own. But we also devote hours of adoration to every line and curve until I know him better than I know myself. As I promised, I kiss his most recent scar on his side and whisper a prayer of thanks that I'm able to do so. We have both been broken, but we are stronger in those broken places.

It turns out the pleasure of Felix losing control is nothing compared to his slow, deliberate attention focused only on me. Each touch, each kiss, is filled with adoration as I twine my soul with his. He's done waiting, and so am I. Each press of his lips sets my soul ablaze.

I give into the fire.

And we burn.

THE NARROW GATE SERIES

THE TRILOGY:

The Broken Crown

The Desolate Reign

The Ancient Heir

COMPANION NOVELS

The Resurrected Vow- APRIL 2025

The Silent War- 2025

SCRIPTURE REFERENCES

The quote beginning "Here be dragons to be slain…" is from *Catholic Tales* by Dorothy Sayers and can be read in its entirety at https://digital.library.upenn.edu/women/sayers/cathtales/dls-cathtales.html

The scripture referenced in the Aletheia has been sourced from various translations of the Holy Bible. While I intend to stay true to the spirit and meaning of any scriptures quoted, some license was taken for the sake of the narrative. This is in no way intended to undermine the sanctity of the scriptures, and instead is a demonstration of the importance of using God's guidance rather than man's as a means to interpretation. This is by no means an exhaustive list, but please see the following scriptures for their true and accurate translations.

Psalm 144:1

Psalm 46:5

Daniel 7

Isaiah 61

Zechariah 2:5

Psalm 51:17

Psalm 147:3

Exodus 14:14

Jeremiah 29:11

Esther 4:14

Psalm 23

ABOUT THE AUTHOR

Amory Cannon is an author of Young Adult and Romantic Suspense novels. Her favorite things include autumn (anything pumpkin spice), Harry Potter (proud Ravenclaw), and Sherlock Holmes. She published her first book under the name Amryn Cross while working as a forensic scientist. Her non-writing time is filled with running, crafting, and snuggling her two dogs—Luna and Argo. She currently resides in Tennessee.

Visit her at her website amory-cannon.com or on Instagram @amory.cannon

www.ingramcontent.com/pod-product-compliance
Lightning Source LLC
Chambersburg PA
CBHW020242030826
48979CB00030B/2487/J
* 9 7 8 0 9 9 7 3 9 0 3 8 4 *